the face of God

By Bill Myers

Soultracker

The Wager

The Face of God

Blood of Heaven

Threshold

Fire of Heaven

Eli

When the Last Leaf Falls

The Bloodstone Chronicles (children's fantasy series)

McGee and Me (children's book/video series)

The Incredible Worlds of Wally McDoogle
(children's comedy series)

Blood Hounds Inc. (children's mystery series)

Secret Agent Dingledorf and his trusty dog, SPLAT
(children's comedy series)

Faith Encounter (teen devotional)

Forbidden Doors (teen series)

BILL MYERS

BESTSELLING AUTHOR OF *ELI* AND FIRE OF HEAVEN TRILOGY

the face of God

ZONDERVAN™

GRAND RAPIDS, MICHIGAN 49530 USA

ZONDERVAN™

The Face of God
Copyright © 2002 by Bill Myers

This title is also available as a Zondervan ebook product.
Visit www.zondervan.com/ebooks for more information.

This title is also available as a Zondervan audio product.
Visit www.zondervan.com/audiopages for more information.

Requests for information should be addressed to:

Zondervan, *Grand Rapids, Michigan 49530*

Library of Congress Cataloging-in-Publication Data

Myers, Bill, 1953-
    The face of God / Bill Myers.
      p. cm.
    ISBN 0-310-22755-0
    1. Clergy — Fiction. 2. Americans — Arab countries — Fiction. 3. Terrorism —
Prevention — Fiction. 4. Arab countries — Fiction. I. Title.
PS3563.Y36 F33 2002
813'.54 — dc21

                         2002004150

Published in association with the literary agency of Alive Communications, Inc., 7680 Goddard Street, Suite 200, Colorado Springs, CO 80920.

Interior design by Beth Shagene

Printed in the United States of America

05 06 07 08 09 10 /❖ DC/ 15 14 13 12 11 10 9 8 7 6 5

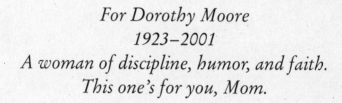

For Dorothy Moore
1923–2001
A woman of discipline, humor, and faith.
This one's for you, Mom.

preface

Today is September 11, 2001 — the day the skyline of New York will forever be changed, and, no doubt, the hearts of Americans as well. Ironically enough, as I keep half an eye to the TV for ongoing developments, it is also the day I finish writing the first draft of this novel.

As I watch the smoking remains, I feel a certain fear stirring within me regarding this story. I fear that there may be those who will pick this up in the hopes of finding an excuse to exercise more hate and bigotry toward our Islamic friends and neighbors — even toward terrorists. That is anything but my intent. Disagreeing with a person's theology or even their actions, no matter how hostile, is not an excuse to hate. On the contrary, Christ commands us to do the opposite. The evil in this story is something far darker and more sinister than a disagreement in politics or theology. It is something that lurks in every seeker's heart — Christian, Jew, Muslim, Eastern mystic, and, I suspect, even atheist and agnostic. And as it was exposed and hopefully expunged from my own soul during the writing, my prayer is that this same effect will be had upon others during the reading.

There is also some violence in this book. There was no way of getting around it and remaining true to the story that needed to be told. However, as my guideline, I tried to follow the way Scripture uses it — never gratuitously, always based upon actual events, and whenever possible depicting the very worst of it "offscreen." That said, this book is still inappropriate for younger readers, and if you are, say, under seventeen, I would ask that you please hold off until you are older.

And now for the appreciations. Thanks to my intercessor friend who has again prayed and fasted me through this journey; also to Louis and Janey DeMeo; Brad Phillips; Larry Murphy (www.iealfm@aol.com) for his expertise in Islam; Tom Morrisey; the guys from I.S.I. — Keith, Tyler One, Tyler Two, Joey, Cole, Smiles, Greg, Evan, and Mike; my research assistant, Doug McIntosh; Lynn Marzulli; Lissa Halls Johnson; Ed Penney, Joe Musser; Greg Johnson; Clark and Gail Whitney; Dave Lambert for the coffee in Santa Monica; Sue Brower for the coffee in Atlanta; Pastor Larry DeWitt for the free lunch and insight into the epilogue on the very day I needed to write it; and, first and always, to Brenda, Nicole, and Mackenzie.

Blessings,
Bill Myers
www.Billmyers.com

You have persevered and have endured hardships for my name, and have not grown weary. Yet I hold this against you: You have forsaken your first love. Remember the height from which you have fallen! Repent and do the things you did at first. If you do not repent, I will come to you and remove your lampstand from its place.

Revelation 2:3–5

the face of God

chapter one

"Jill..."

She gave him a brief nod, indicating that she'd heard.

"Come on," he urged, "the rest of the group is waiting."

Her brief nod was followed by a brief smile, indicating that she'd heard but was in no particular rush to do anything about it.

"Jill..."

Another nod, another smile.

He shook his head, frustrated and amused. After twenty-three years of marriage he knew the futility of trying to hurry his wife when she wasn't interested in being hurried. He sighed and glanced around the tiny shop, one of a hundred stalls squeezed next to each other inside Istanbul's Spice Bazaar. Every inch of floor space was covered and every shelf was filled with spilling bags and open barrels of nuts, candies, fruit, seeds, pods, stems, leaves—some fresh, some dried; some ground, some whole—more spices and herbs than he'd ever seen or smelled in his life.

The aromas were dizzying, as were the bazaar's sounds and colors. A menagerie of vendors beckoning the passing crowd to "come, see my jewelry... perfume for your lady friend... a souvenir for your children... beautiful key chain to ward off evil eye ... finest gold in all Turkey... natural *pirinc,* good for much romance... Visa, Mastercard accepted... come, just to talk, we have some tea, my friend, just to talk."

It was that last phrase that did them in yesterday. They'd barely left the hotel lobby before a merchant was escorting them into one of the city's thousands of oriental rug shops. They'd made it clear they were not buying. The rugs were beautiful but there was no room in their house nor their budget. The owner nodded in sympathetic understanding. But after two hours of chitchat, pictures of a brother who lived in America, and more than one glass of hot tea, they found themselves viewing his wares and feeling obligated to at least purchase something — which they did.

Seven hundred and fifty dollars' worth of something!

But today was another day — he hoped.

"Jill . . ."

She nodded. She smiled. And she continued talking to the leather-faced shopkeeper. The bartering was good-natured. Jill had purchased a quarter kilo of *halvah* — a deadly rich concoction of ground sesame seed and honey. She'd already paid for it, but before passing the bag to her, the old-timer tried to persuade her to buy more.

"I'm afraid it will make me even fatter," she said, pretending to pat an imaginary belly.

"A woman of your beauty, she could eat a hundred kilo and it would make no difference."

Jill laughed and the man threw Daniel a wink with his good eye, making it clear the flirting was all in fun.

Daniel smiled back. It was obvious the fellow liked Jill. Then again, everyone liked Jill. The reason was simple. Everyone liked Jill because she liked everyone. From the crankiest congregation member to the most obnoxious telemarketer, his wife always found something to like. And it wasn't a put-on. The sparkle in her eyes and delight in her voice was always genuine. Unlike Daniel, who had to work harder at his smiles and often thought his social skills were clunky, Jill was blessed with a spontaneous joy. And that joy was the light of his life. A day didn't go by that he didn't thank God for it — even as high school sweethearts, she a cheerleader, he a tall, gangly second-stringer for the basketball team. He could never figure out what she saw in him, then . . . or now. But he never stopped being grateful that she did.

As the years of marriage deepened their love, she had moved from someone who always touched his heart to someone who had become his heart. In many ways she had become his center, a constant point around which much of his life revolved. He cherished this woman. And though he seldom said it, her heart and love for others was a quiet challenge and model that he never ceased striving to emulate.

Yes, her love for people was a great gift — except when they were on a tight schedule, as they were now, as they always seemed to be. Because no matter how friendly you are, it takes more than a sincere smile to keep a forty-five-hundred-member church afloat.

"Jill ..." He motioned to his watch, a Rolex. It had been presented to him by the elders for twenty years of faithful service. Twenty hard-fought years of sweating and building the church out of nothing. Originally he'd hated the watch. Felt it was too flashy for a pastor. But because of the politics involved, he'd forced himself to wear it. You don't keep a forty-five-hundred-member church afloat without understanding politics.

"This I do for you," the shopkeeper was saying. His good eye briefly darted to someone or something behind them. "I sell you one-quarter kilo and give you an extra quarter for free."

"No, no, no ..." Jill laughed, suspecting another ploy. "Just one-quarter kilogram, that's all we need."

"No." The man's voice grew firm. "I have made up my mind."

"But we only have enough to buy one-quarter."

"This I have heard." The shopkeeper spoke faster. He turned his back to them, momentarily blocking their view. "But for you, I give a most special gift." When he turned to them, he was already wrapping it in the same slick, brown paper he had used before.

"Please," Jill said, laughing, "you don't understand."

Again the man's eye flickered to somewhere behind them. "I understand everything," he said, forcing a chuckle. "It is free. I make no joke." He dropped the item into the bag and handed it to her.

"But I can't. I mean, that is very generous, but I can't accept — "

"You must," he said, smiling. "It is the Turkish way." He glanced behind them and spoke even faster. "It is an old Islamic custom."

Jill frowned. "An old Islamic cust — "

He cut her off with growing impatience. "It is good for your soul. It will help you hear the voice of God. Go now." He waved his hands at her. "Leave my shop now. Go."

Jill glanced at Daniel, unsure what to do.

He hadn't a clue.

She turned back to the shopkeeper, making one last attempt. "Listen, I don't think you understand. We are only paying for — "

"Leave my shop now!" His impatience had turned to anger. "Do you not hear? Leave! Leave or I shall call the authorities!"

Jill frowned. Had she inadvertently offended him? Had she—

"Leave! *Allah Issalmak.* God keep you safe!" He turned his back on them and set to work organizing a nearby barrel of pistachios.

Again the couple exchanged glances, when suddenly two uniformed men jostled past them. In one swift move they grabbed the shopkeeper by the arms. He looked up, startled. He shouted at them but they gave no answer. He squirmed to get free but it did no good.

"Excuse me!" Jill reached toward them. "Excuse—"

Daniel grabbed her arm. "No ..."

She turned to him. "What?"

Although he wanted to help, he shook his head.

"Dan—"

"We don't know him. We don't know what he's done."

The shopkeeper shouted louder. He pleaded to the crowd but no one moved to help. The two men dragged him from the stall and out into the cobblestone street, where his shouts turned to panicked screams as he kicked and squirmed, trying desperately to escape.

Again Jill started toward him, and Daniel squeezed her arm more firmly. She came to a stop, not liking it but understanding. Off to the side someone caught Daniel's attention. He was a tall man dressed in a dark suit and a brown sweater vest. But it wasn't the clothing that attracted Daniel's attention. It was the man's focus. Instead of watching the shopkeeper, like the rest of the crowd, he was scrutinizing the two of them.

The look unnerved Daniel but he held the gaze—not challenging it but not backing down, either. The man gave a slight nod of greeting. Daniel hesitated, then returned it until his line of sight was broken by more uniformed men rushing in. They shouted at the crowd, forcing the people to step back as they began scouring the premises, rifling through the bags and barrels, tipping them over, spilling them to the ground.

When Daniel glanced back to the man in the suit, he was gone. But Daniel had an uncanny sense that they were still being watched. He leaned toward Jill and half whispered, "We need to go."

"What are they doing?" she demanded.

"I don't know but we shouldn't be here." He wrapped a protective arm about her shoulder, easing her forward.

"What are they doing?" she repeated. "What's going on?"

"I don't know." He guided her through the crowd.

"Where are they taking him?"

Daniel did not answer. Instead he continued moving them forward. He didn't look back for the man in the suit. He didn't have to. He knew he was still there. And he knew he was still watching.

"But, Ibrahim, with the greatest respect, the Qur'an calls for only 2.5 percent of our profit to go to the poor."

"That is correct. And now I wish for us to double that."

A palpable silence stole over the *Shura*, the council of ten men, most of whom were under the age of thirty-five. They came from various countries — Egypt, Iraq, Libya, Afghanistan, Syria, Jordan, Lebanon, Azerbaijan, and of course right there in Sudan. Each was well trained; many held degrees from universities in the West. Each was responsible for a specific operation within the organization. And now as Ibrahim el-Magd spoke, he knew each was quietly calculating the financial impact his imposed charity would have upon each of their divisions.

Abdullah Muhammad Fadi, in charge of the organization's European and American businesses, continued speaking as he reached for his laptop computer. "So by doubling it, we are changing it to . . ."

Ibrahim el-Magd already knew the figure. "Five percent of 1.8 billion increases our *zakat*, our charitable gifts, to ninety million dollars."

The silence grew heavier. Only the rhythmic beating of the overhead fan could be heard. With quiet resolve Ibrahim surveyed the *mujihadeen* sitting about the table, his dark, penetrating eyes peering into each of their souls. They were good men, devoted to Allah with all of their hearts and minds. Despite their devotion to family, they had left behind wives and children for this greatest and most holy of wars. They had given up all for this, the most final *jihad* that Muhammad himself, may his name be praised, spoke of.

Across the table, young Mustafa Muhammad Dahab cleared his throat. "May I ask ... may I ask why this sudden increase in charity?"

Ibrahim turned to the youngest member of the group. Mustafa was a handsome fellow who had not yet taken a wife and who, according to sources, was still a virgin, Allah be praised. He would make a great father, a great husband. More importantly, he was becoming a mighty man of God. At the moment he was in charge of managing and laundering drug money for the Russian Mafia — a one-billion-dollar operation for which their organization received twelve percent. Ibrahim did not begrudge the boy his question. He knew he merely asked what the others were thinking.

For the briefest moment he thought of sharing his vision of the night — the dream that had returned to him on three separate occasions. The dream of a face. A terrifying, blood-covered face. A face twisted with rage and fury. A face so covered in its opponent's blood that it was nearly unrecognizable. Nearly, but not quite. Because Ibrahim knew whose face it represented; he sensed it, felt it to the depth of his soul. It represented the face of God — the face of Allah as he poured out his great and final wrath upon all humankind.

Ibrahim stole a glance at Sheikh Salad Habib, his chief holy adviser. Although every man in the room had memorized the Qur'an as a boy, it was Sheikh Habib who helped interpret it in terms of the jihad. Knowing Ibrahim's thoughts, the old man closed his eyes and shook his head almost imperceptibly. Such truth as the dream was too holy to share; it would be considered blasphemy, at least for now.

Ibrahim understood and quietly raised his hand toward the table. "It is no small honor to be chosen as Allah's great and final winnowing fork. And for such honor we must all increase our devotion and our commitment. Time and time again the Western infidels have proved how power and money corrupt." He leaned forward, growing more intense. "This shall not, it *must not,* happen to us." He looked about the table. "This small gesture — what is it but merely a reminder that it is Allah and Allah alone whom we serve. Not ourselves. And if necessary, if we need another reminder, I shall raise the percentage again, to ten percent or forty percent or, if Allah wills, to one hundred percent." He lowered his voice until it was barely above a whisper. "This is the time, my friends, above all other in history. This is the time to purify ourselves. For our families. Our world. This is the time to take charge of every thought and deed, to remove every unclean desire — ensuring that all we say and think and do is of the absolute and highest holiness."

Ibrahim looked back to Mustafa. The young man nodded slowly in agreement. So did the others. He knew they would understand.

After a suitable pause Yussuf Fazil, his brother-in-law, coughed slightly. Ibrahim turned to him. They had been best friends since childhood. They had grown up together in a tiny village on the Nile. Together they had studied the Qur'an, attended Al-Azhar University in Cairo. And though Yussuf had chosen Ibrahim's sister for his younger, second wife, it did little to bring them closer — for they were already family, brothers in the deepest sense of the word.

"What about the remaining stones?" Yussuf asked. "What progress is being made?"

Ibrahim was careful to hide his irritation. His insistence that they wait until the stones were retrieved had created a schism within the council, an ever widening impatience lead by Yussuf Fazil himself. Yet despite the group's frustration, Ibrahim remained adamant. They already had four stones. They would not begin the Day of Wrath until the remaining eight were found and consulted. He turned to the group and gave his answer. "Another has been sighted in Turkey."

"Only one?" Yussuf asked.

Refusing to be dragged into yet another discussion on the issue, Ibrahim glanced at Sheikh Habib. The old man took his cue. His voice was thin and reedy from lack of use, from his many days of silent study and prayer. "It is our belief — " He cleared his throat. "It is our belief that the remaining stones will surface very, very quickly."

Ibrahim watched the group. He knew many considered this action superstitious, even silly. And because of Yussuf, he knew that number was increasing. But he also knew the absolute importance of consulting with Allah before unleashing his greatest and most final fury. Still, how long could he hold them off? Plans for the Day of Wrath had been under way for nearly four years. And now as the day finally approached, they were supposed to stop and wait? How long could he hold them at bay? A few weeks? A month? Every aspect of the plan was on schedule. They were nearly ready to begin ...

Except for the stones.

Sensing the unrest, Sheikh Habib resumed. "There have been several rumored sightings, all of which we are pursuing. Europe, Palestine, here in Africa. It should not be long."

Mustafa Muhammad Dahab asked respectfully, "And we are certain they will enable us to hear his voice?"

The sheikh nodded. "According to the Holy Scriptures, just as they had for Moses, the twelve stones, with the two, will enable the inquirer to hear and understand Allah's most holy commands."

"And yet the additional two stones you speak of, are they not —"

The rising wail of an air-raid siren began. Tension swept across the table. Some of the Shura leaped to their feet, collecting papers; others moved less urgently. But all had the same goal — to reach the underground shelter as quickly as possible.

The compound, like many others of Ibrahim el-Magd's, was well protected by armored vehicles, tanks, antiaircraft guns. At this particular base in northern Sudan there were even Stinger missiles. Since the vowed retaliation for the World Trade Center, such precautions were necessary for any organization such as theirs.

Ibrahim rose to his feet and gathered his robes. Although he was anxious to join his wife, Sarah, and his little Muhammad in the shelter, he was careful to watch each of the Shura as they exited. He owned a half dozen camps scattered throughout the Middle East. Less than twenty people knew this was the compound where they would be meeting. In fact, to increase security, the location had been changed twenty-four hours earlier. The odds of the enemy choosing this particular time and this particular location to launch a strike were improbably high — unless there was an informant. And by watching each of the men's behavior, Ibrahim hoped to discover if any was the betrayer.

The first explosion rocked the ground, knocking out power and causing the white plaster ceiling to crack and give way. Pieces fell, shattering onto the table before him.

"Ibrahim!" Yussuf Fazil stood at the doorway, motioning in the darkness. "Hur — "

The second explosion knocked them to the ground. Dust belched and poured into the room.

"Hurry!" Yussuf staggered to his feet, coughing. He raced to Ibrahim, then used his own body as a shield to cover him as they rose. Supporting one another, they picked their way across the cluttered floor. The explosions came more rapidly as they stumbled into the dark hallway, as they joined office personnel racing toward the tunnel with its open steel door ten meters ahead. Ibrahim could see the people's mouths opening in shouts and screams, but he could not hear them over the thundering explosions.

He arrived at the tunnel and started down the steep concrete steps. The reinforced shelter lay twenty-five meters below — a shelter that security assured him could never be penetrated, even by the West's powerful Daisy Cutter bomb. The earthshaking explosions grew closer, throwing Ibrahim against one side of the tunnel, then the other. They continued mercilessly, lasting nearly a minute before they finally stopped.

Now there was only silence — and the cries of people down in the shelter. Ibrahim emerged from the stairway and joined them just as the emergency generator kicked on. Nearly forty faces stared at him, their fear and concern illuminated by the flickering blue-green fluorescents. Two tunnels entered the shelter — one from the living quarters, one from the office area. His wife and little boy had no doubt entered through the living quarters.

"Sarah!" he shouted. "Muhammad!"

He scanned the group but did not see them.

"Sarah!"

Still no answer. People started to stir, looking about.

"They were outside," a voice coughed.

Ibrahim turned to see a secretary. Her veil had fallen, revealing black hair covered in plaster dust, and a face streaked with tears. "They were outside playing when the . . ." She swallowed. "They were outside playing."

Ibrahim shoved past her. He began searching the group, holding his panic in check. "Sarah!" The people parted for him to pass. "Muhammad!"

There was still no answer. He turned and started toward the office tunnel.

"Ibrahim!" It was Yussuf's voice. "Don't go up! Not yet! It is not safe!"

He paid no attention as he arrived at the tunnel and started up the steps two at a time. Bare lightbulbs in wire cages lit his way.

"Ibrahim!"

His heart began pounding. Up above he could see the dull, hazy glow of daylight.

"Ibrahim!" The shouting persisted but he did not answer.

The higher he climbed, the thicker the dust grew. But it was not the dust of his beloved desert. No. This dust tasted of plaster and concrete and destruction. He arrived at the top of the steps and saw the steel door half twisted off its hinges. He stepped through the opening, crawling over a jagged piece of concrete as he entered the hallway. It was illuminated by dust-choked shafts of sunlight. He looked up and saw that much of the roof was missing.

"Sarah!" The dust burned his throat. He coughed violently and staggered forward. To his left was the collapsed wall of the communication center. And beyond that more daylight. He choked and gagged as he climbed over another concrete slab, slipping in the debris, splitting his shin on the broken cement. "Muhammad!" He entered the room, side-stepping fallen desks and shattered computers until he reached the gaping hole where a wall had been. "Sarah!" More coughing. He could barely breathe.

He climbed through the opening and jumped to the ground, hitting so hard that he heard his ankle snap. But he barely noticed as he continued forward, coughing, choking, limping. "Muhammad!"

Everything was eerily still except for the desert wind and ... He strained to listen. Was that a voice? "Sarah?" he called.

There it was again. A woman. Crying.

He started toward it. "Sarah ..." Limping, squinting through the dust, he continued forward until ... There! Thirty meters ahead. The color of dirt. The form of a woman kneeling with her back to him.

"Sarah?" He limped toward her.

She was weeping.

"Sarah?"

At last she raised her head and looked over her shoulder. His heart sank. It was just as he feared. Though the face was coated in blood and dust, he instantly recognized her. "Sarah!"

He hobbled toward her.

She held something in her arms. A form — much smaller, covered with the same blood, coated in the same dust. Then he saw the face. It was not crying. And though its eyes were open, it did not move.

The anguish leaped from Ibrahim's heart before he could stop it. "*Muhammad . . .*"

∗

"These caves, were they not excavated first in . . . what was it?" The stooped old man from the Israeli Department of Antiquities and Museums turned to his two colleagues — one a heavyset middle-ager, the other a frail thirtysomethinger.

Before either man could answer, Helen Zimmerman spoke up. She didn't mean to interrupt, but it had always been difficult for her to remain silent amid ineptness and ignorance — both apparent strong suits among these three. "It was in 1885," she answered. "And later, in the 1970s, the area was surveyed by Barkay and Kloner for Tel Aviv University's Institute of Archaeology."

The old man eyed her suspiciously. "No . . . I believe the later date was 1968."

Of course he was wrong, dead wrong; it couldn't have possibly been 1968. But Helen knew she had to play the game. Though it killed her, she managed to choke out the words, "Yes, 1968 . . . I believe you are right."

The old duffer nodded, pleased with his superiority.

Helen led the officials behind the altar of the Church of St. Etienne, just a stone's throw from Jerusalem's Garden Tomb and only two blocks from Damascus Gate. As she moved down the worn limestone steps into the cave's musty, cooler temperatures, she could feel their eyes watching her. At least that's what she'd anticipated. That's why she'd worn the tailor-fitted slacks and snug-fitting shirt — neither immodest enough to offend their Orthodox sensibilities but definitely enough to hold their interest. All part of the game.

They arrived at the cave's entrance hall, a fifteen-by-twenty-foot room surrounded by six burial chambers — two in the north wall, two in the east, and two in the west. She removed her baseball

25

cap and shook back her hair, allowing the thick auburn curls to fall suggestively to her shoulders.

"And you think ..." The middle-ager coughed. It could have been from the sudden change in temperature or out of self-consciousness. Helen hoped the latter. "And you think your group can find more artifacts here?"

"I know we can," she said with a smile, holding his eyes a moment — not long enough to be flirtatious but long enough to fluster and cause him to look away.

Good, she had him. One down and two to go.

"And why exactly is that, Dr. Zimmerman?"

She turned to the old-timer. "Our resistivity meters, as well as ground-penetrating radar, indicate there are at least three more hollow spaces underneath this floor, perhaps four."

"Burial vaults?" Thirtysomethinger asked.

"Perhaps ..." She reached to the scented handkerchief about her throat, slowly working it loose. At least that was her intention. Unfortunately, she'd tied the knot just a little too tight. She pulled harder. Still nothing. *Great,* she thought. *Just great.* But that's okay, she'd improvise. She'd simply dab the perspiration at the nape of her bare neck with her long, slender fingers.

Thirtysomethinger swallowed, causing his Adam's apple to bob up and down.

She continued, pretending not to notice. "But regardless of what it may or may not be, the chances of it belonging to the First Temple Era are high — and each of us knows the rarity of such finds." She lowered her fingers to the top of her open blouse, gently wiping away the dampness. "Do we not?"

Again Thirtysomethinger swallowed.

The old-timer cleared his throat. "We can appreciate your interest in this area, Dr. Zimmerman, and your expertise. But the committee's decision to grant permission to dig here — well, it would be much easier if you ... that is to say ..."

"If I were to embrace your literal interpretations of the Scriptures?"

The old man shrugged. "There are many groups interested in the First Temple Era, and if word of your theory were to spread ..."

Helen had been expecting this move and knew it was time for the speech. The one she'd given a dozen times in a dozen such situations. "Gentlemen, as a child of Orthodox parents, I can appreciate your devotion to the Holy Word. But as I have proved in my research of Mizpah as well as my assistance at Megiddo as well as numerous other locations, there is no archaeologist more qualified, none more committed to finding truth, than myself. I am a woman of science, gentlemen, of cold, hard facts."

She gave a dramatic pause before driving in the stake.

"I have no bias. I have no agenda to prove or disprove. I am only interested in truth. That is why my work is so frequently published and why you have agreed to meet with me today. If the Scriptures are truth, then you having nothing to fear. My care and exactness will only validate their authenticity."

That was it, short and sweet. She had finished — well, except for holding the eyes of Thirtysomethinger a bit longer than necessary to make her point. Well, a bit longer than necessary to make *that* particular point. He swallowed again, giving his Adam's apple the workout of its life, then glanced away.

Two down.

Again she reached to her handkerchief, giving the knot another tug. And then another, somewhat harder — until it finally gave way, but with such force that her elbow shot out and nailed Thirtysomethinger directly below the left eye.

"Augh!" he yelled, doubling over and grabbing his face.

"I'm sorry!" she cried. "Are you all right? I'm terribly sorry. Here, let me see."

He shook his head.

"No, please. I'm so sorry. That's ... Really, I'm so sorry." And she was. More than they could imagine. Because it always happened. Whenever the stakes were raised, whenever she got nervous, she'd inevitably come down with a severe case of ... well, there was no other word to describe it but clumsiness. Severe, incredible clumsiness.

Of course Thirtysomethinger assured her that everything was fine. But when he was finally persuaded to remove his hand, she saw the large red mark on his cheek. She could only imagine what stories would be flying around the office about how he had acquired his shiner. It was an unfortunate setback but not the end of the world. She'd just have to work doubly hard to reestablish the mood. She had to. Because once she mended fences with Thirtysomethinger, there was still the old-timer to work on.

She stole a look over at him. The old codger would take a bit longer but that was okay. She had been playing the game for nearly a decade, ever since grad school. She knew the rules. She knew what men were like. And she knew the disadvantages of being a woman in their world. But she also knew how to use those disadvantages to her favor — even if it meant utilizing these somewhat demeaning tactics.

Now they would move deeper into the cave. In its intimacy she would share with the old-timer her deep respect for the Scriptures — and eventually confess how she looked forward to someday embracing their inerrancy as he did. Yet for now, as a scientist, she must force herself to simply look at the facts. It was all true. She never lied ... unless she had to. But it would take time. Still, the old guy would eventually join his colleagues in supporting her proposal. That's how it worked. Dr. Helen Zimmerman, University of Washington professor of archaeology, sighed wearily, almost audibly. Like it or not, that's how it always worked.

Daniel Lawson sat in the tour bus parked outside their hotel and endured another verbal barrage from Linda Grossman. Boy, could that gal talk. Nine times out of ten it involved issues she thought the church needed to address. And what made it even worse was that nine times out of ten she was usually right. She was definitely a woman on a mission, which explained her going back to college for her master's degree in education. It would also explain why on two separate occasions she had applied to be their director of Christian education. Unfortunately, she was a woman, and though the position didn't involve the actual teaching of men, as the Scriptures prohibit — well, she was still a woman.

At the moment she had attached herself to one of the elderly ladies, Darlene Matthews, and was sitting with her behind him, doing her best to increase the old woman's self-esteem.

"You should see the lovely scarf she purchased, Pastor. And at such a low price. She's become quite the bargain hunter on this trip. Haven't you, Darlene?"

Darlene shrugged, the crinkled skin of her face glowing from the attention.

"Don't be so modest. Tell Pastor what the shopkeeper started off asking."

"Really, Linda," the old lady murmured, too embarrassed to speak.

But not Linda. "One and a half million lira. Can you imagine that, Pastor? They wanted one and a half million lira for one little scarf."

Daniel shook his head. "That seems a little steep." As he spoke, he noticed movement through the bus window behind them. One, then two, blue-and-white cars with *"Polis"* written across their doors slid to a stop in front of the hotel.

Linda rattled on. "That's what she thought. So she — well, go ahead, Darlene, tell Pastor what you did."

Darlene looked up nervously.

He smiled. "Please, tell me what happened."

She took a timid breath, then finally began sharing the trials and triumphs of buying a scarf in downtown Istanbul. Daniel continued to smile and tried his best to stay interested, particularly after Jill's criticism of him earlier that morning. *Not loving his congregation?* What was she talking about? After all he'd done? After all he'd sacrificed?

Still, even now as he listened to Linda and Darlene, he caught himself dropping into autopilot, uh-huhing and you-don't-saying whenever appropriate. Of course he rebuked himself. After all, he was their pastor; these details should be interesting to him. They certainly were to Darlene. And as a pastor, wasn't it his responsibility to "rejoice with those who rejoice" and "mourn with those who mourn"? Even if it was over a scarf? So why during the past few years had it become so difficult? When the congregation was one or two hundred members, his interest and compassion had come easily. But now — now that they were up to forty-five hundred, now that he had in essence moved from senior pastor to CEO — it had become next to impossible. Yet impossible or not, it was still a requirement, a command. And despite the difficulty, despite his failure, he would strive to obey it. That was Daniel Lawson's trademark. Regardless of the cost, he always obeyed.

"So I told him that the scarf was far too expensive and then I turned and I started walking away, and then he called back to me

29

and said he would make an exception and sell it to me for only one million lira, and I said ..."

Daniel glanced at his watch, then out the window. What was taking Jill so long? Again he tried to focus.

"... it was still too expensive and that I really meant it. Then he said ..."

And again he failed.

Initially Jill had been opposed to going back into the hotel. This morning the group was only going to visit the palace museum, Topkapi Sarayi. Why did she need to cover her shoulders for a museum? But Daniel was gently insistent and explained, as he often had to, that a pastor's wife needed to go out of her way to appear modest. As usual, Jill didn't see his logic and had dug in—good-naturedly, but dug in nonetheless. And it wasn't until he offered to go back to the room himself that she told him to stay put and headed off the bus to the hotel.

But that had been—he glanced at his watch—twelve minutes ago.

"... and then he dropped the price once again to eight hundred thousand lira. Can you believe that, Pastor—eight hundred thousand lira?"

Daniel gave another nod of interest and glanced about the bus. There were forty-two of them on this year's tour. The same tour he and Jill led church members on every year—six days in Israel, one in Ephesus, yesterday and today in Istanbul, tomorrow Athens, then Rome. It was always the same, and though he knew he should be enthusiastic, though he tried to be enthusiastic, he had grown bone weary of the routine. But not Jill. No sir, she thrived on mixing with the people and getting to know them as they traveled together. She always had a great time on these things. Until last night ...

Until the incident with the shopkeeper. Until they arrived in their hotel room, unwrapped the halvah, and discovered it wasn't exactly an extra piece of candy that he'd slipped into their bag. Instead it was a strange, rectangular-shaped stone. It was about the size of one of those complimentary bars of soap they give you in hotels. Yet it was anything but soap. By its green color, Daniel guessed that it was some type of emerald. It appeared very old and was worn smooth—so smooth that the written inscription on the front, which looked Arabic or Hebrew, had nearly disappeared.

"... and so I told him it was still too expensive and that I really didn't want to waste any more of his time, and then he said to me ..."

Daniel nodded as he reached for the stone in his pocket. Silently he ran his fingers over its smooth edges. It was obviously stolen. The cagey old merchant had simply passed it on to them to get rid of the evidence. Both he and Jill had agreed to turn it over to the authorities first thing that morning, once they got the group up and going through the museum. But the fact that it was illegal didn't bother them as much as did the dream. Jill's dream. The one that had led to her criticism about his lack of love for the congregation. The one that had caused her to cry out in her sleep, waking both of them earlier that morning ...

"It's nothing," she had said somewhat sheepishly as they lay together in the small hotel bed.

But her voice betrayed her and he persisted. "Please, tell me ..."

"It's just the excitement from that stone and the old man's arrest, that's all."

There it was again, the uneasiness. He reached over and snapped on the bedside lamp. "What was it, Hon? Tell me, what's wrong?"

She shook her head.

"Tell me," he softly persisted. "What is it?" He waited. Finally she turned to face him. That's when he saw the tears. And that's when he reached out and took her hand. Was it his imagination or was she trembling? Gently he repeated, "What's wrong ..."

She took an uneven breath. He said nothing but waited until she was ready, until she finally spoke. "It was about you."

"Me?"

She tried to smile but didn't quite succeed. "You were all decked out in some sort of holy man's garb — you know, with the robes and everything."

"Like a priest, a Catholic priest?"

"No ... fancier than that. Like one of those paintings from the Old Testament. You know, the high priest with all those robes and a turban and that vest thing in the front. And there was the stone, our stone, right near the center of the vest."

"And that was scary?"

She shook her head.

"What, then?"

31

She took another breath. "You were weeping. It was the weirdest thing. You couldn't stop crying. And when I asked you why, you tried to answer but couldn't. You were too overcome."

"With what?"

She wiped her face and looked at him. "With love. God's love. You were overwhelmed with his love for your congregation. It was incredible. I've never seen anything like it ... especially from you."

The last phrase surprised him. "Especially from me?"

She said nothing but glanced away. He could see that he'd stumbled upon something, and tried again. "I'm not sure what you mean. Are you saying I don't love the congregation?"

She looked down at his hand.

"What is it?" he asked.

She shook her head.

"No ... please, tell me."

She sighed, then with quiet resolve answered. "You used to love them like that, Danny ... but that was a long time ago."

"What?" He tried to hide his incredulity. "What does that mean?"

"I think ..." She paused, constructing her thoughts. "I think you love *serving* God ... and I think you love serving his people. But I don't think you really love either of them, sweetheart ... not like you used to."

The words were a shock. If he didn't love God and his people, why was he killing himself serving them all these years?

"But it's okay," she said, reaching up to his face and gently pushing the hair out of his eyes. "Because you'll get that love back, Danny Boy. He told me."

"Who?"

She smiled.

"Who, Jill?"

"The face."

"Face?"

"Of God."

Daniel blinked. "I thought you were dreaming about me as a high priest."

"I was. You were a high priest and you were wearing that stone and then it started to glow. And the brighter it glowed, the more your face ..." — she swallowed — "the more your face started to

32

twist up and contort, like you were being tortured or something. And then suddenly ..." — she took another breath — "suddenly it was covered in blood ... so much blood that I couldn't even recognize you, until at that instant I somehow knew. I was no longer looking at your face, but at ... at the face of ..."

"God?" Daniel asked.

She nodded, then answered hoarsely, "Yes. I've never seen such pain and passion. But it had also become yours — your pain and your passion. And then he spoke. And then you spoke. It was you but it wasn't you. It was like the two of you were the same ... sharing the same face ... the same passion. And then you spoke ..."

Daniel hesitated, almost afraid to ask. "What did I say?"

"You said ... you said, 'I hear his voice, Jill. I finally hear his voice.'"

"And then?"

She swallowed again. "And then I woke up."

The conversation had been nearly six hours ago, yet it continued to haunt him. The images were so strange and eerie. And the accusation. Of all she had said, it was the accusation that ate at him the most. Not love God? Not love his congregation? How could she possibly mean that?

He ran his fingers over the stone again. *"It will help you hear the voice of God,"* the old man had said. Yeah, right. More likely to give you spooky dreams and send you to a Turkish prison for possession of stolen goods. He sighed. Yes sir, the sooner they got it into the hands of the authorities —

"Pastor Lawson!"

Daniel glanced up to the front of the bus. The hotel's young desk clerk stood at the door. "Pastor Lawson ..."

Darlene stopped her story.

"You must come!" the desk clerk shouted. "Come at once!"

Daniel rose to his feet. "What is it? What's wrong?"

"Your wife."

A cold knot gripped his stomach. "Jill?"

"Come!"

Daniel raced up the aisle to the bus door, then down the steps. "What's wrong?" he demanded. They started running along the sidewalk to the hotel. "Tell me what's wrong!"

33

The young man did not answer. He didn't have to — it was written all over his face. They entered the hotel and rushed through the carpeted lobby, jostling more than one patron, until they reached the brass doors of the elevator. But Daniel didn't stop. He headed straight for the stairway, throwing the door open so hard that he nearly shattered its glass window. Trim and still athletic, he took the worn marble steps two at a time. He flew around the second-floor landing, grabbing the iron railing to make the turn, and sailed up to the third floor. He burst through the door, barely winded — until he saw the other door, the open one at the end of the hall. *Their* door. Her clothes were strewn across the carpeted floor inside the room. Two or three police stood about. Suddenly it felt as if someone had punched him in the gut.

He sprinted down the hall. As he arrived, a roly-poly official with a mustache turned to block his entrance, but Daniel easily pushed past him and into the room. That's when he saw her — sprawled on the carpet between the doorway and the bed, her chest heaving, her white blouse soaked in blood.

"Jill!"

He shoved through two more officials and dropped to his knees at her side. He wanted desperately to pick her up, to hold her, but knew better.

She heard his voice and opened her eyes. They twinkled slightly in recognition.

"Get a doctor!" Daniel turned to the police. "Someone get a doctor!"

"He is on his way," the mustached man answered.

"Danny Boy ..." Her voice was a faint whisper.

"Shh. Don't move. They'll be here. They're getting some help. Don't move. You'll be okay."

She tried to shake her head but broke out coughing, wincing in pain.

"Don't move, don't move." He reached down to her belly, to the soaked, slashed shirt. A wave of nausea swept over him when he saw her stomach. He looked back to her face and forced out the words. "You'll be ..." His voice constricted. "Hang on, you'll be okay." Turning, he shouted over his shoulder, "Where's the doctor? How long's she been this way? Get a doctor!"

The men shuffled, trading glances, examining the tops of their shoes.

"I see him," she whispered.

Daniel looked back to her. "What?"

"His face." She was looking directly at him. "That awful, passion-filled face."

"Shh," he croaked. "Don't talk. Will someone get a doctor!"

"I'm going to leave now, Danny Boy." Her voice grew fainter.

He lowered his face closer. Hot tears sprang to his eyes. "No," he fiercely whispered. "You can't ..."

"It's going to be okay."

"You can't!"

"I have to." Her voice was mostly breath now. "It's the only way."

"No. We're supposed to grow old together, remember? We're supposed to laugh at each other's wrinkles. That's the deal, remember?" He angrily swiped at his tears. "You can't leave ... not now, not like this."

"He loves you, Danny." The words were nothing but air.

"No!" Tears splattered from his face onto hers. He tried wiping them away but only smeared the blood from his hands across her cheek.

"And you'll love him ..."

"Stop ... be quiet. You need your strength. Be quiet now."

"He promised. You'll hear his voice and you'll love him."

"No ... You can't go. You're all ... You're all I have."

"You'll have him ..." — the words were barely audible — "soon ..."

"No, you can't ... You can't go ..."

She gave him the faintest trace of a smile, part sad, part understanding.

"Listen to me ... Listen!"

She did not respond.

"No, you can't ... Listen to me. Listen to me!"

But she no longer looked at him. She no longer looked at anything.

"No! No ..."

He felt hands taking his shoulders. They tried pulling him away.

35

He fought them. "She'll be okay. She's just ... She'll be all right ..."

The hands continued to pull.

"She's okay." He looked up at them, images blurred by tears. "She's just ... Where's the doctor! Somebody get a doctor!" He turned back to her. "Jill!" And still they pulled, beginning to drag him away. *"Jill ..."*

chapter two

They said it was one of the largest funerals ever held in Rockford, Illinois. The mayor, dignitaries, leading businesspeople, kids from the local college — everyone was there. Well, everyone but Daniel. For him it was only a dream — one he watched from the outside like a detached observer. But that wasn't the case with the congregation. For them it was the event of the year. Everybody pitched in, making it more memorable, more elaborate, than anything he'd ever officiated. And he did officiate it. Jill meant too much for him not to. Then of course there was his position in the community. If he really believed what he taught about God and faith and eternal life, then he must not be overcome by grief. He could be deeply touched by it, saddened, even tearful. But never overcome. That was his job. He hated it but he knew the rules. So with the help of Bill White, his associate pastor, and other respected clergy in the community, he somehow pulled it off — both at the church and later at the graveside service.

But he'd been so busy being in front of people and being "on" that he'd had no time for himself. Or for her. That's why he'd slipped out of the potluck in the church gymnasium and returned here to the cemetery, to be alone with her — to try to make it real. Except for the occasional tear blurring his vision, he had not cried, neither in public nor in private, not since the hotel room in Istanbul. There were just too many details to take care of, too many loose ends to be tied up, and yes, too many people to impress. Ah yes, life in the fishbowl. There were few things he hated as much about his job.

The sun hung low in a steel gray sky as he pulled up the Taurus and shifted into park. The grave site was to the right and up a small knoll. The tent had already been dismantled. Now there was only the trampled grass and freshly packed dirt. They wasted little time.

He turned off the ignition and sat in the silence — the hollow, empty silence. He took a deep breath and exhaled. He did this a hundred times a day now, and a hundred times a night. But it never worked. Nothing relieved the impossible weight on his chest. She'd been gone seven days now, and every hour as the initial shock and numbness faded, he felt more and more of himself missing. He knew all about the stages of grief, had helped hundreds through losing their loved ones. But this. This wasn't the loss of a loved one. This was a loss of himself. His life. So why couldn't he cry? He hadn't eaten in he didn't know how long. Had given up on getting any sleep. So why couldn't he cry? Even here, even by himself?

He reached for the door and opened it. This time he heard the alarm chiming and removed the keys from the ignition — proof he was getting better (he'd locked himself out of the car twice since they'd been back).

He was still thinking in terms of *they*. Maybe he always would. And why not? They'd been married to each other longer than they'd been single. They'd been *they* longer than they'd been Jill or Daniel.

He stepped out of the car into a sharp breeze that cut from the north. He could smell its coolness mixed with traces of spring. He closed the door and turned toward the grave. But for some reason he could not walk toward it. How odd. It was as if he'd suddenly lost his strength. This was the first time they'd been alone since Istanbul, and for some reason he couldn't move. He leaned against the car, felt its coldness seep through his slacks. He took another breath, mustered all his will . . . and failed again.

This was ridiculous. Here he was, a middle-aged jock, still in semi-good shape, and he couldn't find the strength to walk up a hill? No. This was unacceptable. He would walk up there and he would be with her; it was as simple as that. If he had to wait until midnight for his body to cooperate, he would wait until midnight, but he would be with her. He took another breath, turned his coat up to the cold, and stuffed his hands into his slacks — the same ones he'd worn when she'd been killed. The same ones that still held the stone.

He knew it was there. Had discovered it during the service that morning. But not in Istanbul. In Istanbul it had completely slipped his mind. With the hotel room burglary (that's what they'd concluded) and the murder (because she'd stumbled upon the burglar) plus all the red tape of a death inside a foreign country, not to mention the preparations to fly her home and now the funeral, he had completely forgotten about it.

He pulled the stone from his pocket. The sun was dull, making it nearly impossible to see its dark green color. He turned it over in his hands. Then over again.

"It will help you hear God's voice," the old merchant had said. Daniel pushed the scene from his mind, but another replaced it.

"It was glowing near the center of that vest thing ... and then I saw your face, God's face, and then you spoke."

"What did I say?"

"'I hear his voice, Jill. I hear the voice of God.'"

His fingers traced the worn inscription. What could it be? He thought of Bill White. He was friends with some museum department head over in Chicago; maybe they'd know. Or know of someone who knew.

"You'll hear his voice, Danny."

He closed his eyes. What he wouldn't give to hear a voice now, to know that God was still there, somewhere, anywhere. The thought surprised him but it was true. Along with Jill's departure there was also God's. And for that matter, his own ... at least according to Jill ... at least when it came to loving God and his congregation.

"You used to love them, Danny ... but that was a long time ago."

The accusation rang in his ears as clearly as the first time he'd heard it. And regardless of what he did, it remained ... amid the 3:00 a.m. vigils, the standing at her closet pressing her clothes to his face and breathing in deeply, or the staring into her bathroom drawer with its lipstick, eyeliner, and hairbrush — items too sacred to disturb. Or yesterday when he caught himself picking up the receiver to call her from the office. Amid it all, the criticism remained, wafting through his mind like a gentle, persistent breeze. And with it, the accusation that somehow he may have brought all of this upon them himself.

"I have to leave," she had said. *"It's the only way."*

The only way for what?

"You used to love them, Danny ... but that was a long time ago."

He took another gulp of the cold air and stuffed the stone back into his pocket.

To hear the voice of God, he mused, silently shaking his head. If it were only possible. Because now, more than ever —

A movement caught his eye. He looked up to see a young man traipsing up the knoll toward the grave. Tall, disheveled, with a shaved head, he held a video camera to his face, apparently taping. This time Daniel found the strength to push himself from the car and start up the hill. The youth spotted him and immediately turned the camera in his direction.

"You're late," Daniel called.

"I told you the flight wouldn't be till 5:30."

"And I told you we don't have funerals in the middle of the night. You could have come yesterday or the day before."

"And you could have held off until tomorrow. I had some things I had to take care of."

Daniel struggled to keep his voice even. "There are other schedules we have to work around, Tyler. Other programs at the church."

"There always are, aren't there, Dad?"

The comment stung. Daniel had a dozen retorts — all involving the world not revolving around the convenience of some nineteen-year-old. But it had been five months since they'd seen each other, and this was not the time to fight. Besides, he didn't have the strength. "Listen, would you mind turning that thing off?" he asked.

The red light on the camera kept glowing. "Just chronicling my life," he said. "A little father-son reunion."

"Come on, Tyler. Not now."

The young man continued to tape.

Daniel tried again, softer. "Please."

Finally the light went out and the camera lowered. Now Daniel could clearly see the face of his son — the scraggly goatee, the ears with their multiple piercings, and those deep green eyes, eyes identical to his mother's.

✳

Daniel had barely turned onto Calvin Park, one of Rockford's older, tree-lined streets, when he spotted the white-and-blue police car parked in front of the house. He turned up the blacktop driveway and pulled far enough ahead for Tyler to park his beater Toyota behind him. Up on the porch an officer stood next to the open front door. He barely glanced up as Daniel climbed out of his car before he returned to his notes.

Daniel strode behind the Taurus toward the house as Tyler bounced up the driveway, slamming on his brakes, almost hitting him. But he barely noticed. "Excuse me?" Daniel called out. "Excuse me?"

The officer glanced up.

Daniel arrived at the bottom of the porch steps and started up them. "What's going on?"

"You the owner?" the officer asked. He was a good-looking kid in his early twenties.

"Yes, I'm Daniel Lawson — what's going on?"

"Dad?" His son slammed the Toyota's door and moved toward them. "What's up?"

"You had a break-in," the officer said.

What little strength Daniel had mustered since the cemetery quickly drained. "What?"

"This afternoon, a couple hours ago, according to the neighbors." He nodded across the street. Daniel looked just in time to see Mrs. Austin's curtains fall back into place. "You Daniel Lawson, the pastor?"

Daniel felt himself growing numb, once again starting to see things from that faraway place.

The officer repeated, "Sir, are you the pastor Daniel Lawson?"

Daniel may have nodded; he didn't know. He turned and stepped through the doorway into the entry hall, the very hall whose ceramic tile the two of them had laid three months earlier.

"Are you the Daniel Lawson who just lost his wife?"

"Yeah, that's him," Tyler's voice answered.

"You have my condolences, sir. My sister, she attends your church."

Tyler may have responded; Daniel didn't hear. The officer may have answered; he couldn't be certain. He had just entered the living room . . .

Both walnut end tables were overturned, and the brass lamps, anniversary presents they'd given each other eight years earlier, were flung to the floor, their beige shades bent and broken. The sofa lay on its back—every cushion ripped open, with yellow white stuffing hanging from their gashes.

He felt himself growing more detached, starting to float. *Stop it!* he scolded himself. *Get ahold of yourself!*

He arrived at the china cabinet, the one whose price they'd argued over two Christmases ago. It lay on its side, its glass shelves and doors shattered. Inside, the white porcelain angels, the ones he'd bought for the last several gift occasions, lay in broken lumps. *Well, not all of them are broken. Maybe if I'm careful, I can salvage some. And the others, maybe I can glue them back together again. Yes, I can do that. It will take time, but I certainly can—*

"Dad ..." His son's voice was far away, from another world. "Are you okay?"

Stop it! They're watching!

He drifted down the lit hallway toward the bedroom, his feet shuffling, sometimes tripping over the dozens of pictures and frames ripped from the wall. Family pictures. *She loves pictures. Every place we go, everything we do, she takes pictures. It makes Tyler and me crazy.*

"Pastor Lawson ... Sir?"

He was in the bedroom. The mattress had been slashed and overturned, bedding stripped away, pillows ripped, drawers thrown open, their contents dumped on the floor. Clothes had been yanked from their closets. Her clothes. Blouses. Dresses. Coats. He turned away. He could not bear seeing them on the floor.

"Dad ..."

He drifted to the adjacent study, where bookshelves which he made himself had been pushed over. Books covered the floor. Their books. The ones they read together, sometimes out loud to each other.

"Sir ..."

Answer him! His sister goes to your church! He waded into the books, looking down, unable to see the titles for the water in his eyes. He recognized the red and black cover of one of her journals, the ones she wrote in, as far back as he could remember.

"You need to sit ..."

Answer him! What will he think?

"Pastor ..."

Weakling! Answer him. Answer him!

He couldn't tell if his knees were buckling or if he was kneeling. It made no difference. Now he was sitting in the books. Clutching a journal. Her journal. It smelled of worn leather and paper and dust.

"Pastor Lawson ..."

He tried answering but no words came.

"Are you okay?"

He knew he should rise. For what? He'd forgotten. For them. He was a pastor. He was supposed to be strong.

"Dad ..."

He looked up, saw their wavering shapes in his tears. He looked down to his hands. He was holding something. The red and black cover of her journal, the one she always wrote in, as far back as he could remember. Where did he get this? Would she be angry that he was reading it? He would put it away. Soon. Yes, soon. But for now he'd just sit. Just sit and hold her. Yes, just for a while. Just for a while ...

✳

Danny and Tyler were at it again tonight. Funny, Tyler won't be sixteen for weeks, but he's already trying so hard to be his own man on his own terms. Even if it means being wrong, which he usually is. Tonight it was over youth group. Once again he found some excuse not to go (he said it was homework, which is a stretch, since he's not concerned about it any other night of the week). Of course Danny saw through it and didn't cut him any slack, threatening to drag him to the church if he didn't go. It almost got physical, and I'm afraid for the day when Tyler decides to call Danny's bluff. The boy is so angry, so full of frustration and rage. Of course I don't agree with him, but to be honest, I understand. How difficult it must be to have a father who is always right. And Danny always is. Sometimes too right. How can you be your own man if you're lost in the shadow of someone's perfection? I've tried pointing this out to Danny, but he insists

there is no excuse for compromising godliness and holiness.
He says it is our duty to "train Tyler up in the way he should
go." Of course he's right. In these matters he's always right.
Still, I just wish I could make him see what he's doing to him.
Please, Lord, speak to him, do whatever is necessary to make
him see.

Daniel slowly closed Jill's journal. He glanced at the guest room's radio alarm. It glowed a crimson 5:48 a.m. Once again he thought of last night's meltdown, and once again he winced. How could he have been so stupid? And in front of Tyler and the officer. If you don't eat, if you don't sleep, that sort of thing is bound to happen. He'd made a mental note to pick up some food over at Hilander's Market. Some bananas, maybe some soda crackers, anything to keep fuel in the machine so he could keep it running. The good news was, he was feeling better. He'd even managed to doze for a couple hours here in the guest room. Not their room, of course. He'd never be able to sleep there. He glanced at the clock. It still read 5:48. But that was okay; he had a lot to do. There was still plenty to clean up from yesterday's break-in, and —

"I just wish I could make him see what he's doing to him."

The phrase jarred him from his thoughts. What had she meant? That he was the cause of Tyler's failures? He'd made his fair share of mistakes, sure, but no more than any other father. He reached over and set the journal on the nightstand.

"Please, Lord, speak to him, do whatever is necessary to make him see."

See what? That to strive for holy living is wrong? That he should just wink at his son's laziness and immorality? Feeling his anger start to rise, Daniel tossed back the heavy quilt and swung his feet to the floor. He sighed heavily as he ran his hand through his short salt-and-pepper hair. He wouldn't bother to throw on a robe. Why should he? It was just Tyler and him now. He rose and padded out to the hallway in his boxers and T-shirt.

The beige Berber carpet felt coarse to his bare feet. For the most part the broken glass had been picked up and the pictures stacked haphazardly on the dining room table. The police weren't sure of a motive, though they suspected robbery. After all, her jewelry was missing. But they had not touched the computers, TV, CD player, or anything else. "Actually," the officer had confided, "it's more like they were looking for something. Why else would they rip up your mattress and sofa cushions?"

Well, whatever their motive, they left their victim with the same sense of violation, the same outrage and fear, as did any other burglary. Yes sir, the emotions were piling up, there was no doubt about it. But he could handle them. If he prayed a little longer, worked a little harder, he could handle them. After all, he was a pastor. He may have lost his wife, even his son, but he still had his church, he still had God.

And yet ... and yet ...

He tried to push the thought from his mind, but like the other emotions, it kept finding a way to sneak in. The truth was, in comparison to his love for Jill, the church meant nothing to him.

And God? The thought slowed him to a stop. He tried to block it but it rushed around his barriers. He still revered God, yes. He still honored him, absolutely. But in comparison to Jill's love ... He stopped, ashamed. Embarrassed. What was he thinking? Had Jill become an idol in his life, something he placed ahead of God? No, he'd not put her before God; he knew that. He'd not put anything before God. He would give up his life for God. And yet, and yet ... the love he felt for her, in comparison to the love he felt for —

No. He would not go there. It was a lie. He was overwrought, that's all.

"You used to love them ... but that was a long time ago."

No. He was a pastor, a servant of God. That had always been his dream. Since childhood. It's all he ever wanted to be. A servant of —

"I think you love serving God and his people. But I don't think you really love either of them, sweetheart.... Not like you used to."

"No!" The word came from his lips and startled him. He took a breath, then wiped his face and resumed walking. Up ahead the light from Tyler's room spilled into the hallway. He called out, "Tyler ..." His voice was thick. "Ty, you awake?"

There was no answer.

He continued toward the room. It would be good to have him home ... at least for a while. At least until the arguments began. Neither had mentioned how long he would stay or when he would leave. Daniel doubted that Ty himself knew. And such prying would only lead to another fight.

"I wish I could make him see what he's doing to him."

Again he pushed the words from his mind. When he arrived at his son's doorway, he wasn't surprised at what he saw. The boy was sprawled on his bed, faceup, arms flung out, sound asleep. He had not bothered to take off his clothes. An empty Dominos pizza carton lay on the floor along with a handful of empty Coke cans. One had been knocked over, spilling its caramel stain across the carpet — the very carpet they had replaced after his departure last year. There were the half dozen CD cases, the months' worth of accumulated mail (he'd never filed a change of address), and a dozen magazines, some with covers and content that had been clearly banned from the house.

Daniel's attention came back to the stain on the carpet. It was just a little thing but so typical. New carpet and a new mess that would stay until somebody else cleaned it up. And since they'd been having quite the battle with ants lately, and since the creatures were such experts at sniffing out anything with sugar ...

Daniel sighed and turned to get a wet rag from the kitchen. Then he caught himself. No. The boy was nineteen. It was time for him to exhibit a little responsibility. He couldn't be picked up after his whole life. And if he didn't want to pick up after himself, then let him experience the consequences ... ants and all.

The resolve gave Daniel little pleasure. He snapped off the light and turned to leave. But he couldn't move. Instead he slowly turned back and watched his son sleep. At one time this child had been the hope of his life. Incredibly bright, disciplined, self-assured. He'd had everything going for him. What possibilities, what dreams ...

Then came the teen years and the tearing and shredding of those dreams. Now he was just a slacker, like so many others in his generation. No purpose, no ambition, and as far as Daniel could tell, not even a belief in God. Slowly Daniel shook his head, feeling the all-too-familiar knot in his gut. How he loved this child. But what a sad breaking of the heart he had become.

By now his eyes had adjusted to the room's dimness. He could see moonlight spilling onto the bed, illuminating the boy's face, his arms, his hands. Moonlight that glistened off the shiny white scar tissue running along the inside of each wrist. Daniel tried not to stare, but of course he couldn't help himself. Those scars — every time he saw them, thought of them — they never ceased to broadcast his failure as a parent.

Failed parent. *"I wish I could make him see what he's doing to him."*

Failed pastor. *"You used to love them . . . but that was a long time ago."*

He slumped against the doorway, leaning on it for support. "God," he whispered hoarsely. "Where are you? What's going on?"

"You used to love them . . ."

"I don't — "

"I wish I could make him see . . ."

"I don't know . . ."

"I have to leave; it's the only way . . ."

"What am I supposed to do?" he croaked. He felt the resentment growing. "Answer me! *Answer me!*"

But of course there was no answer. Not from Jill. Not from his son. And certainly not from his God.

He remained leaning against the doorway, angry tears burning his eyes. How long he stayed there, he wasn't sure. But finally he righted himself. Reaching out to his son's door, he slowly closed it. If Tyler wanted to sleep all day, he could sleep all day — ants and all. But not Daniel. The house was a mess and he had much to do. As always, he had much to do.

✳

"How long will he remain like this?"

"It is hard to tell. With this type of head trauma, he may remain comatose for days, a week, or perhaps . . ." The doctor let the phrase hang. He was too frightened of Ibrahim el-Magd to continue.

Sensing the fear, Ibrahim turned to him. "I want only the truth, Doctor."

The doctor took a breath. "The truth is . . . no one can be certain."

Ibrahim nodded before turning back to his son. It was difficult to look at the little boy with the tangle of tubes and wires protruding

47

from his arms, his chest, his head. But he looked nonetheless. This was his child. "When may I take him home?"

There was another pause. Ibrahim waited patiently. He glanced about the room with its peeling white ceiling and blue walls. It was not yet nine o'clock in the morning, and the heat had already reached one hundred degrees. From the open window came the faintest stirring of air — a questionable trade-off for the smell of diesel exhaust, overripe fruit, and raw sewage that accompanied it. But this was downtown Khartoum, capital of Sudan. Such things were expected.

Finally the doctor answered. "Taking him from the hospital is not something I would recommend. He needs twenty-four-hour supervision."

"He will have it. When may we move him?"

The doctor shifted nervously. "Of course we will do whatever you wish. But for his welfare it is best he remain under our supervision ... until his condition improves."

"And that will be ..."

"That is up to your son ... and to Allah."

Ibrahim remained looking at his little boy. "I understand."

Once again silence settled over the room. There was only the hiss-click, hiss-click of the respirator along with the angry traffic down on the streets and a leper begging, *"Floos ... Floos ... Floos ..."*

At last the doctor cleared his throat. "I shall be outside at the nurses' station when you reach your decision."

Ibrahim nodded but continued staring at his son. The doctor turned and exited. When he was gone, Ibrahim motioned to his bodyguard, a young man in a flowing white *galabiya* and turban. The youth nodded, slung down his AK 47 to pass through the door, and disappeared.

Now Ibrahim was alone with his decision.

How deeply he loved this child, his only son. How he longed to stay at his side, constantly uttering prayers to Allah for his recovery. Yet there was the face, the face of Allah twisted in rage, covered with the blood of his enemies. Time was so short. Final preparations were being made. Just yesterday the last of the pharmaceutical labs had completed manufacturing its portion of Allah's Agent. Now they would begin placing the canisters and prepare to send out the seven briefcases with their seven heroes. Of course, this was all predicated upon finding the last of the stones, upon hearing the fearful and all-powerful voice of Allah.

The voice of Allah ... Ibrahim marveled at the coincidence of timing. Silence for so many centuries and now his voice about to be heard. But it was no coincidence. Merely confirmation. As the Day of Wrath approached, as Allah prepared to perform this, his greatest act of purification, it only stood to reason that he would speak. And what a privilege to be the one chosen to hear. Yet even that was not arbitrary. The many years of faithful service had been difficult, nearly impossible. But Ibrahim el-Magd had been tested and proved worthy. He looked down at his son. Just as he was being tested once again and once again must prove worthy.

"Ibrahim?"

He turned to the door. It was Dalal, one of his secretaries, a recent graduate from the International Islamic University in Islamabad. Her beauty was great, even behind the veil. Coal black eyes, thick, dark lashes. But that was not why Yussuf had chosen her. Instead it was for her organizational skills, her efficiency, and her insight. In just the few short months since she had joined jihad, her gifts had proved invaluable.

"Yes?" he asked.

"If you wish to stay, I will make arrangements for the entourage to spend another night."

Ibrahim looked back at his son a moment, then slowly, almost imperceptibly, shook his head.

"Are you certain?" she asked.

He looked back at her. How clearheaded she had been throughout the ordeal. As Sarah and the other women collapsed into their own self-centered grief, Dalal arose to shine in both wisdom and sensitivity. "Yes," he answered, "I am certain."

With that she nodded and stepped out.

Once again he was alone. A fly had entered the room. It buzzed and tapped against the screen, unable to escape. Soon it would join its dead brothers scattered across the dirty sill.

Ibrahim bent low and kissed the child's shaved head. It smelled of soap and alcohol. Taking the boy's hand, dirt still under the tiny white crescents of his nails, he raised it to his lips and gently kissed it. "You are more than a son," he whispered. "You are the hope of my life." His breathing grew heavy, labored. He took the little hand into both of his own and slowly lowered himself to his knees. Now he was level with the boy's face. Tears welled up and filled his eyes. "But I have much to do, little one. Allah has called me to a great and fearful task and I must obey." He swallowed at the ache in his throat. "Your mother will stay here with you and I will visit. Whenever it is possible, I will visit."

Resting his forehead against his boy's hand, he waited until he was sure he had enough strength to rise. Then slowly he stood to his feet. "I will pray for you often and I will think of you always. But I have much to do, little one. So much to do."

Ibrahim el-Magd turned and walked out of the room.

chapter three

The office lab was cramped and overflowing. Pale yellow light filtered its way in through a single, wire-meshed window at the far wall. The rest of the walls were covered either in shelves sagging with brown, dusty books or in glass cupboards bulging with ancient artifacts — pieces of pottery, baskets, bones, baskets of pottery, baskets of bones. Under one set of cupboards sat an old wooden desk buried in papers, one stack rising an easy eighteen inches high. Across from it, under more cupboards, was a black bench where the huge man sat, with Daniel and Tyler standing on either side.

"It's not authentic; I'm certain of that. Still, with such things one can never be entirely certain until one runs all the appropriate tests."

"Authentic?" Daniel asked. "Authentic what?"

Dr. Benjamin Hermann, an immense man with thin, oily hair and multiple chins, director of archaeology at Chicago's Field Museum of Natural History, cleared the phlegm from his throat. He adjusted his jeweler's eyepiece and hunched over the bench to take a closer look at the stone's worn inscription. "You say you bought it in Turkey?"

"Istanbul," Daniel answered. "It was a gift to my wife."

Tyler, less patient than his father, repeated the question. "What do you mean by 'authentic'?"

Hermann gave no answer as he continued peering at the stone. He shifted his weight on the metal stool, which creaked in protest. Every breath he took sounded as if it took tremendous effort. It probably did. "About this inscription — and by the way, you're right; it is Hebrew — "

Daniel nodded.

"It's a name. The biblical name Levi."

"Levi?" Daniel said.

"As in one of the twelve tribes of Israel."

Daniel nodded. "The tribe God selected to be priests to his people."

"That is correct." The man turned his head and coughed, his entire body rippling from the effect.

"You said it wasn't authentic," Tyler persisted. "Authentic what?"

Daniel threw a cautionary look to his son. Bringing him along was another attempt to reach out, as much for himself as for Tyler. After all, it had been five months since they'd talked—longer than that, if you count the months of arguing and shouting before he stormed out. Now, however, they had something to share. Their sorrow. On two occasions he had caught his son crying. Both times he had wanted to sit down and talk with him, to connect with the one person who understood and shared his grief. But try as he might, he just didn't know how. He'd hoped the eighty-minute drive to the museum would provide the opportunity for sharing. But Tyler had quickly found a techno-rave station on the radio, which he'd cranked up to ear-bleeding capacity. So much for sharing.

Dr. Hermann dislodged the eyepiece from the fleshy folds of his socket and looked at Daniel. "You're a pastor, correct?"

"Yes, Bethel Community, over in Rockford."

"Are you familiar with the breastplate of the high priest?"

"From the Old Testament?"

"Yes."

"It was an article of clothing he wore over his chest."

"His heart, to be more precise," Hermann corrected.

Daniel nodded, not appreciating the difference. "It was to remind him of the twelve tribes of Israel that he represented before God. But what does that have to—"

"What part of the breastplate represented those twelve tribes?" Once again the man turned his head and coughed, and once again the stool groaned.

Daniel frowned. "Pardon me?"

"What part of the breastplate was used to represent the twelve tribes of Israel?"

"It had stones set into it . . . twelve different stones."

"Correct."

"Each stone representing one of the twelve tribes." Daniel's interest rose as he spoke. "Are you saying that this stone . . . are you saying that this could have been one of the stones set in the — "

"I am saying nothing. It is no doubt a fake, a facsimile — "

"Of one of the twelve stones?" Tyler interrupted. "Levi's stone?"

The stool creaked as Hermann reached over and set the rock on the lab bench. "Yes. It is the correct size and seems to be the proper gem."

"An emerald," Tyler interjected.

"Yes," Hermann patiently answered, "an emerald. Then of course there is this inscription, which upon initial viewing appears to be accurate, though it's doubtful that . . ."

Hermann droned on but Daniel barely heard. His mind was already racing with memories of Jill's dream, memories of breastplates and high priests and a stone and —

"Dad?" He heard Tyler's voice in the distance. He was not sure when Hermann had finished talking, but now his son was speaking. "Hey, you with us?"

Daniel blinked, trying to refocus. "Sorry."

"Is there a problem?" Hermann asked.

Daniel shook his head. "It's just . . . my wife had a dream. The evening she was given the stone, the night before she was, uh — "

"A dream?" Hermann asked.

Daniel nodded. "In it I was wearing the breastplate of the high priest."

"Really?" Tyler asked.

Again Daniel nodded.

"That's quite a coincidence," Hermann said.

"I was wearing the breastplate and that rock . . . it was attached to it, and it had started to glow."

Neither Tyler nor Hermann moved, obviously waiting for Daniel to continue. "She said that my heart . . . my heart became like God's heart . . . my face too. And then she . . ." Daniel swallowed, noticing his mouth had grown strangely dry.

"Go on," Hermann said.

"She said that I told her I had finally heard the voice of God." Daniel hesitated, unsure whether he should go on. But they continued waiting, so he took the plunge. "And the merchant, the one who gave the stone to her in the first place, he said the same thing: 'This will help you hear the voice of God.' That's what he said. 'This will help you hear his voice.'"

Silence stole over the lab. For a moment there was only the sound of the heating ducts and Hermann's labored breathing. Daniel looked to him. "Is it possible?" He glanced down to the rock on the counter. "Could that stone ... could it actually allow a person to hear God's voice?"

"No." Hermann's abruptness startled him. "It could not." The big man turned his head and coughed.

"But the dream, the merchant —"

"The breastplate and its stones, they had nothing to do with hearing Yahweh's voice. This type of stone was not the stone used for that."

Tyler frowned. "*This* type of stone?"

"Even if it was genuine. No, as you said, this type of stone was kept over the high priest's heart, along with the others, to remind him who he was ministering to."

"*This type of stone?*" Tyler repeated. "Was there another type?"

"Of course."

"What other type are we talking about?"

"They were called the Urim and Thummim," Hermann said.

"The two stones the high priest used to find God's will," Daniel added.

"Precisely."

"But Scripture only mentions them a few times," Daniel said.

"More than a few," Hermann corrected. "They are mentioned by name at least seven times and are inferred more than that."

"What did they do?" Tyler asked.

Hermann answered, "Whenever the king or high priest had a question to ask Yahweh, they would turn to the two stones for an answer."

"They were like dice," Daniel explained, "used in casting lots to find his will."

"That is one interpretation," Hermann said. "One that leaves the religious and scientific community a bit more, how shall we say, relaxed. But there is nothing in the Bible to indicate that is correct. In fact, there are portions that actually refute such an interpretation. There are, however, other theories."

"Such as?" Tyler asked.

"Some believe that the Urim and Thummim glowed in various ways to indicate various answers. Others believe that when used in conjunction with the gold thread of the high priest's breastplate and possibly one or more of its stones, they acted as some sort of receiver, enabling the wearer to actually hear the audible voice of God."

Tyler softly whistled.

Daniel sat speechless. There was that phrase again, *the voice of God* ...

Hermann gave a husky chuckle. "Now, if you could find *those* two stones, you'd have yourself a real discovery."

Daniel nodded, but he was once again lost in Jill's dream, her words, the promise of the shopkeeper ... Looking back to Hermann, he asked, "Have people ever looked for those two stones? I mean, there are all sorts of crackpots looking for the lost ark and the Holy Grail and the like ... but have people ever searched for the Urim and Thummim?"

The big man shrugged. "A few. Interestingly enough, in the past several months more and more rumors have been circulating, one charlatan or another claiming to have found them. Or as in your case" — he nodded toward the emerald — "one of the twelve. But as far as any reputable scientist ..." He shook his head. Pausing for a moment, he cleared his throat and said, "No, I take that back. There is one person. In Jerusalem. An archaeologist. It is by no means her primary focus, but she does specialize in the First Temple Era."

"First Temple Era?" Tyler asked.

"Yes, that was the last time they were officially seen ... until the Babylonians came in and ransacked the city in 587 B.C. Since she specializes in that time period, I imagine she has dabbled some with the Urim and Thummim as well as other temple artifacts."

"She ever find anything?" Tyler asked.

Again Hermann shrugged. "Nothing of significance, though from time to time she does get published."

Daniel remained silent, his mind still racing.

Again Hermann cleared the phlegm from his throat and reached for the stone. "Listen, let me run those tests . . . just to make certain it is not authentic, and then — "

Tyler interrupted. "How long will that take?"

"Forty-eight, seventy-two hours. You can pick it back up Sunday afternoon, Monday morning."

"Shouldn't we have some sort of receipt or something?" Tyler asked. "I mean, if we left it with you without any proof that it's ours, you could — "

"Tyler," Daniel admonished.

"No, that's quite all right," the big man said. "It's not a bad idea."

Still feeling a need to apologize, Daniel added, "I'm sorry. It's just that, well, this was my wife's, and — "

"Not to worry; I fully understand." With more than a little effort, the man rose from his stool. "I'll make you out a receipt, we'll run a few tests, and by Sunday we'll have put an end to all your suspicions."

"Thank you," Daniel said.

"No problem." The man wheezed as he waddled across the lab toward the old wooden desk. "My pleasure."

✳

"To hear God's voice. Can you imagine how cool that would be?"

"I thought you didn't believe in God," Daniel said.

The two of them had barely entered the car before Tyler had started talking . . . and talking. It reminded Daniel of the boy's younger days when he was all questions and enthusiasm — before everything became cool and jaded with irony.

"I never said I didn't believe in God," Tyler argued. "I just don't buy all your neatly wrapped, preshrunk versions of him, that's all."

"My what?"

"Never mind."

"What?"

"I don't want to get into it."

A half year ago Daniel would have been happy to leave it at that — one less conversation meant one less argument. But now . . . "No, please," he said, slowing at the northwest tollbooth and tossing the coins into the basket. "Tell me what you mean."

Tyler gave him a look to see if he was serious. Apparently, he passed the test. "Just think of it," he said with returning enthusiasm. "What would it be like to actually know what God says? I mean, I'd give my right arm to hear him speak, wouldn't you?"

"You would?" Daniel asked in surprise.

"Of course; why wouldn't I?"

"I don't know; I just thought — "

"To really hear what he wants."

"But . . . you can hear that now," Daniel said.

"How?"

"Through the Bible. Through church."

Tyler snorted in disgust.

"What does that mean?"

"I'm not talking about your interpretation of the Bible, Dad. I'm not interested in what you boys at Club Christ come up with."

"Club Christ?"

"Your little cookie-cutter God machines."

Daniel frowned. "I'm afraid you lost me."

"I'm not talking about all your dos and don'ts. I'm talking about actually hearing God. I mean, wouldn't that be awesome?"

Daniel coughed slightly. "Actually, the dos and don'ts you're talking about, the instructions that are in the Bible, that *is* how we hear from him."

"No." Tyler shook his head. "The Bible, maybe, I'll give you that. But not your particular interpretation of the Bible, or your rules or your — "

"*My* interpretation?" Daniel interrupted.

"Yeah, you know, your King James's everybody's-gotta-look-and-act-and-dress-the-same-and-never-question-my-leadership-cause-I'm-Pope-Pastor. You know, that version."

Daniel felt his confusion turning to anger. Tyler was back to pushing all the old buttons again. It was as if he'd never left.

"You know what I mean," Tyler continued, "where you're always looking over your shoulder, worrying if the other guy thinks you're holy enough?"

Striving to keep his voice even, Daniel replied, "You don't think there's a place for holiness?"

"Whose holiness? Yours or God's? Whose standards are we talking about?"

"Is that what you think I do? Make up my own standards?"

"I told you I didn't want to get into it."

"I know, but — "

"It's all religion, Dad," Tyler said, sighing in exasperation. "And religion is what killed God."

Daniel's frown deepened. "For you?" he said, trying to understand. "It's what killed God for you?"

"For everyone. Religion is what killed God."

"I'm sorry, I don't — "

"It's what nailed Jesus to the cross. Not the Romans. Not the Jews. Religion. Good, old-fashioned, God-never-does-it-that-way-he-only-does-it-our-way religion."

For a moment Daniel's anger gave way to being impressed with the depth of his son's thinking. Unfortunately, Tyler didn't leave it there.

"I mean, what would happen if we all suddenly had access to God? If nobody had to jump through your particular hoops to get to him?"

"I make people jump through hoops?" Daniel heard his voice rising. "You don't think I'm trying to help, that I'm serving them out of love?"

"You love being God's man; that's pretty obvious. You love the idea of serving him, but I don't think you know the first thing about actually loving — "

The rest of Tyler's comment was drowned out by memories of Jill's admonition: *I think you love serving God . . . and his people. But I don't think you really love either of them.* The similarity left him stunned. It took several seconds before he found his voice. When he did, he tried backpedaling to safer waters. "So you think religion is what killed Jesus Christ?"

"Not just Christ," Tyler said. "Look at the Crusades, the Inquisition, Northern Ireland, all the slaughter and inhumanity done to man. All in the name of religion. Not for God but for religion. I mean, just look at Mom."

Daniel's eyes shot to him. "What?"

Tyler looked away.

But Daniel persisted. "What did you say?"

Tyler shook his head.

"No, please, tell me what you mean."

There was another pause. Only when Daniel's silence made it clear he would not back down, he got an answer. "You said Mom went up to that hotel room by herself."

"Right. I offered to go, but she — "

"To get a sweater, right?"

"Right."

"Why?"

"Why?" Daniel frowned. "Well, to wear. Why else?"

"To cover her shoulders, right? You said she went up there to get a sweater to cover her shoulders."

"Right."

"So she'd look modest."

"Well, yes, in part, but — "

"For who, Dad?" Tyler's voice suddenly cracked with emotion. "For God? You don't think he's ever seen bare shoulders before? Who was she having to look modest for, Dad?"

Daniel opened his mouth but no words would come. "You think..." He cleared his throat. "You think *I* killed her? You think that *I'm* responsible for her death?" He'd run the scenario a thousand times in his head, blamed himself a thousand times for not being the one to get the sweater. But this...

"No, Dad." Tyler turned to him in frustration, his eyes glistening. "That's not what I'm saying."

Daniel barely held his anger in check. "Well, it sure sounds like — "

"No, that's not what I'm saying! You're not listening!"

"I'm right here; I'm listening!"

"No, you're not!"

"You're saying I killed your mother!"

"No! You didn't kill her! Don't worry, you're still all innocent and perfect. You're *not* the one that killed her!" Tyler's shouting brought silence to the car. Then quietly, his voice still unsteady, he continued. "Your religion did it. Just like it killed Jesus, just like it's killed millions — your religion, that's what killed Mom."

For a moment Daniel couldn't see the road. If he could have reached over and slapped his son, he would have. How dare he make such accusations! Who did he think he was! Who did he think he was talking to!

But when he looked over to Tyler, he saw that the boy already knew he'd gone too far. Now he stared out the side window, careful not to let their eyes meet as he quietly sniffed. Was he crying? Daniel watched as his son discretely wiped his eyes and continued looking out the window. Why was he crying? He wasn't the one who had just been called a killer.

Daniel turned back to the road, his chest a knot of conflicting emotion—anger, anguish, pity, guilt. How was he supposed to respond? How could he ease this boy's pain? Why should he try? The accusation had been made, the unspeakable spoken. Yet there he was, his only child, motherless, crying, all alone . . .

How long they rode like that, Daniel wasn't certain. It took Tyler to finally break the silence. Even at that, he did not turn to his father but continued looking out the window. "I'm sorry," he mumbled, then sniffed again. "I had no right to say that." Another sniff, his voice clogged with emotion. "Sorry."

Daniel wanted to answer but still did not trust his voice. Then there was the matter of his own tears.

So the two traveled home in silence—except for the techno-rave which Tyler reached over and turned back on. The blessed, pounding, techno-rave . . . drowning out the silence and the terrible, aching emptiness.

✳

Dr. Helen Zimmerman rested her forehead against the mildewing tiles. She watched as the water ran off her body and swirled into the rusty drain. It wouldn't last long; the room's water heater was pathetically small. But she'd enjoy the lukewarmness for as long as possible. After all, this was a time to celebrate. The Israeli Department of Antiquities and Museums had finally granted her permission to begin excavating the caves at St. Etienne's.

What a joy, what a privilege. It had been tough but once again she'd won. The only problem was that over the years, each victory seemed just a little more hollow.

She reached for the coffee mug of Chianti sitting on the ledge below the cracked window of the shower stall. She filled her mouth, held it until it burned, then swallowed. More would follow.

What had her father said? *"Give your life to your work, and your work will take your life."* But he had no idea what it was like to be a woman struggling in a man's world. And it was a man's world, make no mistake about it. She'd learned that at the tender age of eight, the summer Uncle Eddie had moved in with them and began paying nightly visits to her room. Despite his threats and pleas and cajoling, she eventually broke the silence and sobbed the truth into her mother's arms. But instead of compassion she was met with discipline. Severe discipline. After all, she was just a girl and Uncle Eddie was a man, a respected man. There was no question as to who was really telling the truth. Granted, the visits stopped and were never mentioned again, but Helen had already learned of the power of men. It was their world and, as a woman, you had to work twice as hard just to be even; you had to be twice as good just to succeed.

And she was succeeding. First her bachelor of science at the University of Washington, then later her Ph.D. And now, at the seasoned age of thirty-six, she was tops in her field. Well, almost. Another five, maybe six years and she would be there. Just as she had planned.

And then what?

That was the problem. Because the harder she worked, the closer she came to reaching her goal, the more empty it became. Nobody had warned her. The rules were to win the race, to cross the finish line and collect the prizes. Nobody had warned her that once she got there, the prizes would mean nothing.

She inhaled, then blew out, spewing the excess water off her lips. *"Give your life to your work, and your work will take your life."*

Then there was Mom. *"You should find your joy in being a good wife, a good mother."* Good old Mom.

Not that she hadn't tried. Between degrees she'd found herself engaged to a nice Jewish boy from a nice Jewish family. The only problem was, the nice Jewish boy was as self-centered as every other boy she'd met. Oh, he paid the proper lip service, at least in the beginning. But it soon became apparent that he expected her life to revolve around his — *his* hopes, *his* dreams, *his* aspirations. Still, if that's what it took to be happy, she was willing to go through with it — until she caught him in bed with her best friend five days before the wedding.

Then there was Dr. Richard Nectil, a renowned archaeologist ten years her senior. Together they would work side by side, husband and wife, the perfect team, making their discoveries and changing the world. Unfortunately, the only thing that changed was his behavior. She knew he liked to drink; she just didn't expect it to be a problem. Nor did she expect the beatings she received for nearly three years. She wasn't sure if it was her broken jaw or his extramarital affairs with the interns that forced her out. In either case it had become apparent that men were not to be trusted. Regardless of what they said or how they pretended to behave, they were liars and users. It's not that a good man was hard to find; it's that they didn't exist.

After the marriage she had her fair share, more than she cared to remember. They were good teachers, though, and soon she learned the importance of never getting involved. More importantly, she acquired the ability to use them just as they used her. It was all part of the game, all part of surviving. And tonight Brent Appleton would be no exception.

He'd called earlier that morning. Asked if they could have dinner. He wanted to discuss the possibility of her working for them again. Something regarding a stone that an associate in Chicago had contacted her about. Dinner would be fine. Brent was funny, had great stories, and most importantly, was deeply connected to the Israeli government. Of course he would want to go to bed with her. But it seemed a small price to pay. After all, he did have the connections, and in this world connections meant everything. Besides, it gave her something to dress up for, an opportunity to drag herself out of the doldrums of victory and be charming — even if it only lasted a few hours, even if it did have its price.

The water was colder now. She brought the cup back to her mouth and was surprised to see that it was already empty. But that was okay; there was more in the bottle on the toilet. And why not? This was her day to celebrate. Just her, the Chianti, and later that evening Brent Appleton. It didn't get any better than this. She took a weary breath and stared down at the water as it flowed off her body and disappeared forever down the drain.

Yes sir, it didn't get any better than this ...

Daniel stared at the words in his Bible. He'd read them, preached from them, dozens of times over the years. But now for the first time he finally understood. And with that understanding came the gut-wrenching realization.

"What have I done?" he whispered. "Dear God, what have I done?"

Much of what Tyler had said in the car had been wrong. Brutally wrong. And every time Daniel thought of the words, that religion had somehow killed Jill, he got angry. So why did he keep thinking of them?

"Just like it killed Jesus, just like it's killed millions — your religion killed Mom."

Now that accusation had joined the arsenal of others. *"I think you love serving God and I think you love serving his people. But I don't think you really love either of them, sweetheart . . . not like you used to."* And from her journal: *"I wish I could make him see what he's doing to him. I'd give anything to make him see."* And let's not forget those wrists. Those shiny white scars reflecting in the moonlight that were forever etched in his mind.

He had known they were related — the wrists, the words, the memories — but he wasn't sure how. Like beads from a broken necklace, they lay randomly scattered across a table, begging for him to find the connecting strand.

And now at last he had . . .

It was right there in Revelation, the last book of the Bible. Just four verses. He had read and reread them a half dozen times. Had meditated upon them. Had prayed over them. Had dropped to his knees, begging God to remove the accusation filling his soul, to lighten the weight that had begun crushing his heart.

But God did not. And though the words were not audible, Daniel Lawson knew his Lord had finally spoken. He had started the vigil before midnight Saturday. And now as dawn broke Sunday morning, he reached for the phone to call Bill White, his associate pastor. It was an impossibly difficult decision but he knew it had to be made.

＊

"Now, I know many of you feel I'm acting too hastily, this close to Jill's passing. And perhaps I am, at least in part. But in another sense I should have taken this step much, much sooner . . ."

Daniel took a breath and swallowed. This was harder than he'd thought. He looked across the twenty-one-hundred-seat auditorium — the oak, the sparkling brass, the burgundy carpet, the theater seats, TV cameras with big-screen projectors on either side of the stage . . . and the faces, so many faces. All looking at him, all expecting him to have the answer. Well, he had the answer all right, but not the one he or they wanted to hear.

Bill White had asked him to hold off on the decision for a few more weeks, to wait until he was more rested. The fact that Bill was one of only a handful of African Americans in the church and was terrified at becoming the interim senior pastor had no doubt influenced his thinking. But Daniel was confident of him, had handpicked him, had carefully trained and nurtured him through the ranks. Whether he felt it or not, Pastor White was ready for the challenge. And even if he wasn't, Daniel still had no choice in the matter. Although much of his faith had been shaken and shattered, he still knew enough, trusted enough, to obey what he'd heard.

"As your pastor, my job has been to lead you into a deeper walk of holiness. That's been my goal ever since we started Bethel Community some twenty years ago, way back in that side room at the Denny's restaurant. But now . . ." — he took another breath — "now I'm not so sure anymore. To be quite frank, I'm not so sure what direction I've been leading you."

It had been a long time since he'd heard the sanctuary so silent. He looked down at his notes, noticed how tightly his hands gripped the podium. But he could do this. He had to do this.

"For me to pretend to be your leader, when I'm not even sure where God is leading . . . well, I'm afraid that's incredibly unfair to you and me. After all, you can't be a leader if you don't know where you're leading." He forced a smile. No one smiled back. Particularly Oscar Matar, a permanent front-row fixture. He wasn't sure why his eyes landed on the man. Although he was on the board of elders, he was far too intense for Daniel's tastes. With Oscar it was all or nothing — all of the time. Maybe it was his passionate Arab heritage; Daniel wasn't sure. But whatever the reason, the man was always gung ho and absolutely inflexible when it came to his interpretation of God's Word. And the Lord protect anyone, layman or pastor — particularly pastor — who got in his way. The two of them had been at it more times than Daniel cared to remember. And as difficult as leaving would be, Oscar Matar was definitely one member he would not miss. In fact, life would be a lot more—

"You used to love them ... but that was a long time ago."

The memory surprised him. Particularly in connection with Oscar. After all, he'd bent over backward to work with the man, striving to be cordial, doing his best to be there for him. Wasn't it just last year that he'd spent the night praying with him over his dying daughter? What more was to be expected of him? What more could he do? Apparently, plenty. With some effort he managed to look away from the man and continue.

"A good friend recently told me ..." He stopped and cleared this throat. "A good friend recently told me that I had fallen out of love with God and his people. She said that I loved the idea of *serving* you ... but that I no longer ..." — he took another breath — "that I no longer *love* you ... or love God. Of course this made me angry. I'm a Christian, the head of a large, successful church. I've devoted my entire life to serving God and his people. How could I not love them?

"But her words ... and others ... they continued ringing in my mind and in my heart. Louder and louder. I pleaded with God; I begged him to show me the answer. And now he has. It's in chapter two of the book of Revelation." He reached down to his Bible and noticed his hands shaking. Quickly he flipped to the section and continued. "In it Jesus is talking to another leader, another head of another church. And this is what he says: 'I know your deeds, your hard work and your perseverance. I know that you cannot tolerate wicked men, that you have tested those who claim to be apostles but are not, and have found them false. You have persevered and have endured hardships for my name, and have not grown weary.'" Daniel hesitated, took a breath, and continued. "'Yet I hold this against you: You have forsaken your first love.'"

He looked up at the congregation. His mouth was strangely dry. "And that, my dear friends, as embarrassing as it may be, as humiliating as it is to admit ... is the current state of your pastor. I don't know how it happened. I don't know why it happened. But I know it has happened. I have forsaken my first love. And as difficult as it is, I know I have to respond. So ..." — he forced another smile — "as of this morning I am taking an indeterminate leave of absence from this pulpit."

Glances were traded; people started to murmur. He immediately spoke over them. "And I am leaving you in Pastor White's most capable hands." The murmurs increased. He continued a bit louder. "For how long I am not certain. That will be up to God. And lest any of you think I'm making some grand, heroic gesture by stepping aside, let me finish God's admonition in the Scriptures to this leader ... and to me."

He looked back to the Bible and read: "'Remember the height from which you have fallen! Repent and do the things you did at first. If you do not repent, I will come to you and remove your lampstand from its place.'"

Daniel closed the book. His hands were trembling even more but he pushed on. "And that, my friends, is what I must do. Repent. Not for you, not even for this great church to which I've devoted my life. No, I am not stepping aside for you. I am stepping aside for *me*. For my very soul."

He spotted Charlie Rue, the church's oldest hippie. Once a top sound technician for professional rock groups, the man had become a zealous Christian. Unfortunately, the zealousness had never quite worn off. Like some sort of spiritual gypsy, he wandered from one revelation to another, always getting worked up about his latest discovery, regardless of its theological soundness, and always wanting to share it with as many people as possible. Then of course there was his worship — nothing but raw emotionalism, giving little thought to the embarrassment he caused those around him. Unstable, immature, overemotional — yes sir, Charlie Rue was everything Daniel tried to avoid, in life and in people. That was probably why, even though he was an excellent sound technician, they always found an excuse to use somebody else.

"You used to love them ..."

Again the phrase surprised him. Certainly it wasn't in reference to Charlie.

Daniel turned to the final page of his notes. His hands gripped the pulpit so hard, his knuckles were turning white. But he was nearly finished. "Like Martha in the Bible, I've been so busy serving that I've forgotten to love. I've forgotten to love God as a son." He glanced about, hoping to see Tyler, but knew his efforts would be in vain. "I've forgotten to love as a father ..." He heard his voice grow thinner. "And I've forgotten to love you as a pastor."

He blinked away the moisture filling his eyes. There would be no self-pity. He had a job to do and he would do it. He reached for the glass of water he kept inside the pulpit, but his hands shook so violently that he quickly returned it.

He looked back up and his gaze landed upon Linda Grossman. He had not seen her since the tour bus in Istanbul. Never afraid to speak her mind, always the warrior, Linda challenged everything — including his pastoral decisions. And although he did his best to appear fair and respectful, he realized this was another member of the congregation he would definitely not miss.

He tried to swallow, then continued. "I no longer hear God's voice, my friends. I no longer know what he is saying. Oh, I can read his words in Scripture. But those words have become dead, as lifeless as stone. They have no heart, no flesh. I can read his Word but I can't hear his voice. And if I can't hear his voice . . ." — again he tried to swallow but it was hopeless — "and if I can't hear his voice, I am no longer qualified to speak his Word."

There, he had said it. It had been spoken. Now it was just a matter of bringing the sermon to a graceful end, of assuring everyone that Bill White would be more than capable to take the helm, of promising them that the church would continue ministering and spreading the gospel, and of encouraging them that with their prayers he would eventually return to them stronger and more committed to God than ever before.

But even as he closed the service, even as Bill called the elders forward to pray over him, even as he clung to the pulpit, ordering himself not to crumble, Pastor Daniel Lawson sensed another truth emerging . . .

He knew he would never again return.

"So now what?" Tyler asked.

Daniel shrugged. "I'm not sure. They want to keep me on salary, but — "

"As what, a charity case?"

Daniel let the comment go. He was too tired to fight. They stood together in the cemetery in the sharp afternoon light. Daniel had been alone there for nearly two hours — standing, kneeling, pacing. And of course praying. You don't lose a wife, your job, your whole purpose for living, without a little praying. Tyler had joined him a few minutes earlier, having just arrived from the museum in Chicago.

The silence between them grew, interrupted only by the faintest drone of traffic on the distant interstate and the irritating croak of a blue jay. In the air was the sweet smell of freshly cut grass, the first mowing of the season. When Tyler resumed speaking, his voice was softer, almost earnest. "She'd be proud of you, Dad."

Daniel nearly thought it was a compliment, but he knew better. "You weren't even there to hear me," he said. "How would you know?" He regretted the words before he finished. What was wrong with him? Why couldn't he carry on a civil conversation with his own son? "I'm sorry," he mumbled. "It's been a hard day."

Tyler barely seemed to notice. "No, I'm serious," he said. "To have the guts to stand up in front of all those people and admit you're wrong. To up and quit your job, just like that — I mean, that church was your life." Then quietly he repeated, "She would have been proud."

Daniel turned to look at him. The boy was actually sincere. He dropped his eyes to Tyler's hand and to the stone in it. "What did Dr. Hermann say?" he asked.

"He wanted to keep it and run a bunch more tests, just to be sure, but now he thinks ..." Tyler raised the emerald, casually holding it between his fingers. "Now he thinks he might have been wrong. He thinks this might actually be the real deal."

Daniel stared dully at the stone. He knew he should feel something — excitement, incredulity — but he felt nothing. Instead he simply nodded. After a moment he looked back at the grave. "They said it would be four more weeks before the headstone comes in."

"Dad, did you hear what I said? This is the real thing. Right out of the Bible. Right from that high priest guy's vest." He grew more excited. "Not only from his vest, but this was *his* stone. The high priest's stone. From the tribe of Levi. Think of it: this puppy, along with those other two, those Urim and Thummim thingies, may have actually helped people hear God's voice!"

Daniel searched for something to say but he could find nothing.

"So what do you think?"

"I think ..." — he took a deep breath — "I think for one little rock, it's sure caused us a lot of trouble."

It was Tyler's turn to grow pensive. "You think this was what they were after when they killed her, don't you?"

The thought had lingered in Daniel's mind every day since they'd left Turkey. That and the crushing guilt for not being the one to get her sweater.

"And the break-in at our house?" Tyler asked. "The same thing?"

Daniel took another breath. There was no way of telling but it seemed plausible.

Tyler stared back at the stone. "You may be right. It sure seems like somebody wants to get their hands on this thing."

Daniel gave a half nod. "So . . . what did Dr. Hermann suggest?"

"That we turn it over to him. Remember those rumors about the Urim and Thummim? About their resurfacing?"

Daniel nodded.

"I guess talk is really heating up. Anyway, he offered to send this thing straight to his archaeologist friend in Jerusalem to get her to verify its authenticity . . . and to get her input."

"And you said . . ."

"Once I got her name, I said we weren't interested."

"Because . . ."

"Think of it, Dad. Look what we've got here. Something right out of the Bible. The high priest's stone. Something they used to talk to God with. And we've got it right here in our hands."

Daniel scowled. "If it's authentic, which we're still not completely certain of. And even if it is, without the other two, the Urim and Thummim, it's entirely — "

"Exactly. Without the other two it's nothing but some fancy paperweight. But . . . what would happen if those rumors were true? What would happen if those other two stones have been found?"

Daniel turned to him. "Your point being?"

"We've got a major piece of the puzzle right here, right in our hands. A piece that people are willing to kill for. A piece that Mom . . ." — Tyler swallowed — "that she died for."

Again Daniel saw his son's grief and again he wished he could help relieve it. "What are you saying, Ty?"

"I'm saying, let's find those other two stones, those Urim and Thummim things."

Daniel snorted in amusement.

"What?" Tyler asked.

"You're being ridiculous."

"Am I?"

"Of course." Daniel buttoned up his coat, more for something to do than for any chill, and prepared to leave.

"Dad, this isn't being ridiculous."

Daniel gave a tight grin of indulgence and turned for the car.

But Tyler stayed at his side. "This is not ridiculous."

Daniel sighed heavily. "We would have no idea where to start, how to even begin."

"We've got that archaeologist in Jerusalem. We've got —"

"Jerusalem?"

"Yes."

"So what are we going to do, hop on the next jet to Jerusalem?"

"Why not?"

"Why not?" Daniel's laugh was more scornful than he intended.

But Tyler held his ground. "Why not?"

Daniel mentally riffled through the reasons — his job, his responsibilities as a pastor, as a husband, as a . . . — but as quickly as each one surfaced, it fell, until he was left with only one response. "It's crazy, that's why not." He continued toward the car, Tyler glued to his side.

"'I can read his Word but I can't hear his voice.'" You said that this morning. 'And if I can't hear his voice, I am no longer qualified to teach his Word.'"

Daniel turned to him. "You *were* there."

"Think of it, Dad. We've got a piece of the puzzle right here in our hands." He held it up. "Do you think this was just an accident? Of all the billions of people in the world, for you and me to get it? What about this God who knows the number of hairs on our head, who's supposed to care for every detail of every life? Do you think this just accidentally slipped past him?"

Daniel opened his mouth but did not speak.

"And what about Mom's dream? And the promise she got — that you'd hear God's voice? Isn't that what she said to you? Weren't those, like, her very last words?"

Daniel lowered his eyes, then glanced at the stone.

"'You'll hear his voice.' Isn't that what God promised her? Isn't that what she said you'd do — hear his voice?"

"She was speaking metaphorically." It was a lame argument but the only one he could think of.

"Was she? And what about that merchant, Dad? And Dr. Hermann? Were they all just speaking metaphorically? Is that what you're saying, that it's all just coincidence, that none of it matters?"

Daniel continued staring at the stone. Against his will, memories of Jill's dream flooded in . . . and of course those words, those final haunting words. *You'll hear his voice, Danny . . . You'll hear his voice and you'll love him again.*

Tyler continued presenting his case but Daniel barely heard. Because the more he stared at the stone, the more his common sense began slipping away, the more his argument started to fade. And by the time they arrived home, had another dinner of macaroni and cheese, and for the first time in years talked halfway into the night, Daniel Lawson knew he would be returning to the Middle East. This time with his son.

✷

"Come now, my friend." He nuzzled into Helen's neck, playing with a strand of her hair. "It is not like you haven't worked with us before."

She pulled back from him and took another sip of champagne. "And the last time I did that, I promised myself never again."

"Helen . . ." Brent Appleton sat up on the leather sofa, pushing aside his thick blond hair, revealing those killer blue eyes. "We have made a good team before, have we not?"

"I am an archaeologist, not a spy."

"Of course, of course. But sometimes it is necessary for one hand to wash the other."

She turned to him, trying to keep her eyes focused through the alcohol. "What are you saying?"

"Nothing that you don't already know." He rose from the sofa and crossed to the bottle of champagne on the counter — their second of the night. "You don't seriously believe you were able to secure the St. Etienne dig all on your own, do you?"

Helen's jaw dropped slightly. "You arranged that?"

"Not entirely." He refilled his glass and lifted the nearly empty bottle to her. She shook her head. "However, as you can imagine, there were other teams also interested in the site. Many other teams. And if word spread that you chose not to help us ... well, in some circles that might be mistaken as anti-Semitic." He returned the bottle to the counter. "Not a good perception, given the fact that so many Orthodox are now involved in the permission process."

"Meaning?"

He shrugged. "Permits may be given; permits may be revoked."

"You'd pull the permit?"

"Not me." He headed back to the sofa. "Others perhaps but never me." He sat beside her. "I will always be your biggest fan; you know that."

"What do you want me to do this time?"

"It is very simple."

"What?"

"Look at the stone, verify its authenticity."

"That's it?"

"You will need to stay with him for a while. Find out his motives. His plans for the future. And of course what he intends to do with the contraband."

"Contraband?"

"Such artifacts were once the property of Israel, were they not?"

Helen gave no answer.

He leaned toward her, once again brushing his lips against her neck.

"And that's all I have to do?" she asked. "Just stay by his side?"

"Mm-hm ..."

"How long?"

"A week. Perhaps two. However long he and his son are in Israel."

"And you can assure me that the dig will remain mine?"

"Absolutely," he murmured.

He reached for the glass in her hands and she let him take it. It seemed a fair exchange: check on some rock that would prove fake, and find out the man's intentions ... for an archaeological site that others would kill for. Of course she felt resentment over the obvious blackmail, but ...

He rose to his feet and took her hands.

... if that's what it took to survive, then that's what she'd do. After all ...

She stood to meet him and they kissed.

... that's how you operated in a man's world. Give 'em what you've got for what you want. It was a fair trade ...

They separated and he took her hand, leading her toward the bedroom.

... and if what you've got no longer means anything to you, then it makes the deal all the sweeter.

part
two

chapter four

"Have you no respect as to where you are standing?" The young woman stared into Tyler's video camera, unflinching. Her liquid black eyes flashed in irritation. "Must you always be filming?"

"What am I disrespecting?" Tyler answered, grateful for another excuse to zoom in to a close-up of those deep, engaging pools of darkness. If they were back home, he'd swear she wore colored contacts. But not here. Out here everything about this Egyptian beauty was for real ... her long black lashes, her thick hair falling to her shoulders, and a face and lips to stop your heart. "Besides," Tyler said, continuing his defense, "what difference does it make to you? What do you care about this place?"

"It is one of the most holy mountains in the world. It is where Moses himself received the Law for his people."

"I thought you said you were Muslim."

"We still believe much in your Bible. And the Scriptures say these very rocks upon which we are climbing were so sacred that anyone who touched them died."

"She's right," Daniel said, finding a rock and sitting nearby.

"You're kidding," Tyler argued.

Daniel shook his head.

"Really?"

"Sure. In fact ..." — Tyler glanced from his viewfinder to see his dad reach into his pack and start rummaging for his pocket Bible — "let's just take a peek and see what it says for ourselves."

Oh brother, Tyler thought. *The guy can't stop preaching even out here in the wilderness.* He stole an embarrassed look at the beauty, hoping to build some sort of "fellow sufferer" bond with her. But she sat in the shaded nook of a rock, knees pulled to her chin, and waited with interest to hear. Although she wore a modest, ankle-length dress, it was easy for him to imagine a figure as captivating as those eyes.

They'd met yesterday evening on the final leg of their flight from Rome to Tel Aviv. Nayra Fazil was a third-year student on holiday from Al-Azhar University in Cairo. She was going to visit family in Bethlehem. Her major area of study was Middle East history, so she and Tyler's father had immediately hit it off. But by the look of things, it was taking Tyler a bit longer to get into the race. Actually, by the look of things, he wasn't even inside the stadium.

When Dr. Helen Zimmerman, the archaeologist who had agreed to meet Daniel and Tyler at the airport, left word that she would be detained for forty-eight hours, the three had agreed to share a *sherut* from Tel Aviv and ride to Jerusalem. And since Nayra had hiked Mount Sinai with her cousins as a child, and since it was one area Daniel had never visited, and since they were talking about places where God's voice had been heard ... well, here they were.

It was no easy trick, but she had convinced another cousin to let her borrow his Toyota Land Cruiser and subject it (not to mention their kidneys) to several brutal hours of bouncing and banging — first to Port Taufiq on the Suez Gulf, then down and across the Sinai with even more body-punishing ruts and potholes, until finally they arrived at St. Catherine's, a Greek Orthodox monastery built in A.D. 342 at the foot of *Djebel Mousa,* the Mountain of Moses.

But that had been a vacation compared with the climb they were now making straight up the side of the mountain. Granted, there were steps carved into the stone that had taken some monk twenty years to complete, but some of those steps were as high as two feet apiece. This was their third stop to catch their breath, more for Tyler's sake than Daniel's or Nayra's.

"Ah, here we go," Daniel said, finally finding the section in the Bible. He cleared his throat and began to read: "'On the morning of the third day there was thunder and lightning, with a thick cloud over the mountain, and a very loud trumpet blast. Everyone in the camp trembled. Then Moses led the people out of the camp to meet with God, and they stood at the foot of the mountain. Mount Sinai was covered with smoke, because the LORD descended on it in fire. The smoke billowed up from it like smoke from a furnace, the whole mountain trembled violently, and the sound of the trumpet grew louder and louder. Then Moses spoke and the voice of God answered him.'"

As his dad read, Tyler panned the scenery with his camera. "The voice of God," he mused. Here in the most desolate, godforsaken place he had seen in his life, God was to have supposedly spoken. Here in this lifeless wilderness of rock and wind, upon this dead mountain of red granite. That's all there was here, nothing but red granite. Everywhere he looked, granite. Everything he touched, granite. Mountains of it, soaring, plunging, spewing. No vegetation, not a trace of moisture. Just granite — pebbles, rocks, boulders, towering cliffs, cascading faces. Nothing but red granite.

His father continued. "'The LORD descended to the top of Mount Sinai and called Moses to the top of the mountain. So Moses went up and the LORD said to him, "Go down and warn the people so they do not force their way through to see the LORD and many of them perish. Even the priests, who approach the LORD, must consecrate themselves, or the LORD will break out against them."'"

Daniel came to a stop. Now there was only silence and wind. He closed the Bible and reached down to a small rock at his feet. "Think of it," he said. "If we had touched this rock four thousand years ago, we'd have been killed."

Tyler zoomed in for a close-up as his dad silently turned the stone over in his hands.

"Not because there's anything mystical or magical about it," Daniel added, "but because it touched another rock, that touched a rock, that touched another, that touched another, that eventually touched the foot of God."

"Sounds pretty intense," Tyler said.

Daniel nodded. "The awesome holiness of God."

Just as reverently, Nayra quoted, "'Praise belongs to God, the Lord of all Being, the All-merciful, the All-compassionate, the Master of the Day of Doom.'"

"What's that?" Tyler asked as he turned off the camera and replaced the lens cap.

"Part of the Al-Fatiha, the first chapter of the Qur'an. Every child has it memorized."

"That's intense, too," Tyler admitted as he returned the camera to his backpack.

Daniel nodded, seeming to think about it a moment. Returning the Bible to his own pack, he rose to his feet and slung it over his shoulder. "Well, we'd better get going if we're to reach the top by sunset."

Reluctantly Tyler followed suit. "You really sure you want to do this?" he asked. "Spend the night up there praying and all? Sounds kinda spooky, if you ask me."

Daniel adjusted his pack. "You guys can head back down to the monastery if you want; they've got plenty of rooms. But as for me . . ." He looked up the steep slope in front of them. "Think of it, Ty. The actual place where God stood. The very place he spoke." He took a deep breath. "It just seems that if we're serious about hearing his voice . . . well, I can't think of a better place to start than here."

Nayra quietly repeated, "'Even the priests, who approach the LORD, must consecrate themselves . . . or the LORD will break out against them.'" She adjusted her pack. "Indeed, this is a most holy place."

Daniel nodded silently. Then he turned and started up the rocky trail. Nayra stepped in behind him. And Tyler, giving a reluctant sigh — "Whatever . . ." — brought up the rear.

They called it the Farm. At one time that's exactly what it had been for the family of Ibrahim el-Magd. But that was a long time ago, before his parents made their millions in oil and later real estate. Located seventy-five kilometers north of Khartoum in Sudan, it was now used for something very different.

"What of the Turkish merchant?"

"He is no longer a concern."

Ibrahim el-Magd gave his brother-in-law Yussuf Fazil a look. The man explained, "His information was too valuable. We felt it should go no further."

"Meaning?"

"Meaning he is no longer of concern."

Ibrahim grew silent as they walked through the concrete hallway. He knew full well what had just been said, and it did not please him. Still, the merchant from Istanbul was not the first casualty. Six men at last count. Six men had died in search of the stones. Seven, counting the merchant. And Ibrahim suspected they would not be the last. "What of your daughter?" he asked. "What progress is our Little Bird making?"

Yussuf Fazil gave a smile. The two of them loved his daughter equally. Bright, articulate, brave, and as dedicated to Allah as any woman could be, nineteen-year-old Nayra Fazil was Ibrahim's favorite niece. Technically they were not related, as she was the daughter of Yussuf's first wife, his older one in Cairo. But it made little difference in Ibrahim's appreciation of her. In fact, when they'd received word of the American pastor's find and heard that he was coming back to resume his search, it was Ibrahim who suggested assigning her to keep an eye on his progress. She would be told nothing of Allah's Day of Wrath, but watching the pastor she could do. And although Yussuf was still opposed to waiting for the stones, he had agreed.

"She has already made contact with the man and his son," Yussuf answered. "She will inform us if he meets with further success."

Ibrahim nodded. For the pastor's sake, he hoped he would not meet with success. It would give him little joy to order the man's death. Unlike his colleagues, Ibrahim took the more moderate interpretation of the Qur'an, believing that the sincere people of the Book should be respected. Though they were misinformed, though they embraced a corrupted revelation, if they were sincere, they deserved respect. Still, sacrifices had to be made. For the greater good, sacrifices by all had to be made. He thought of their pigeons, his and Yussuf's, when they were children in the village. And he remembered their favorite, a great black male by the name of Samson . . .

"Can we not take care of it until it gets well?" eight-year-old Ibrahim begged. *"Can we not—"*

"No," Yussuf said.

"But he is our favorite."

The two of them stood alone in the pigeon coop, the afternoon sun hot and white, beating down upon them through the wire mesh.

Yussuf answered with the somber wisdom of a boy nearly two year's Ibrahim's senior. "He is sick."

Ibrahim looked down at the pigeon before them. It lay on the unpainted wood that was splattered with white droppings of a dozen birds. Birds the two of them had raised for nearly a year. Birds of which Samson had been the first.

"But we can make him well." Ibrahim's voice quivered.

Sadly Yussuf shook his head. "He will contaminate the others. If we do not kill him, he will make his brothers and sisters sick. We do not want that, do we, Ibrahim? We do not want them to catch his sickness?"

Tears fell from Ibrahim's eyes. One splattered onto the gasping bird's breast.

"We do not want that, do we?" Yussuf repeated.

Ibrahim shook his head. He did not look up to his friend. He knew what must be done.

"You do not have to stay," Yussuf said. "You may go to the house."

Ibrahim shook his head, wiping the tears. No, he would stay. He would stay right there in the pigeon coop until the deed was done.

Gently, carefully, young Yussuf Fazil took the bird into his hands. He stroked it tenderly, cooing slightly as he raised it to his lips and kissed its shiny black head. Lowering it, he said, "Turn the other way, Ibrahim. You should not see this."

That had been thirty-five years ago. Yet for Ibrahim el-Magd the lesson was as clear as if it had been yesterday. They continued down the hallway — Ibrahim, Yussuf, and their two armed bodyguards. Before him was a task which he hated. Hated with all of his heart. But there was the face ... the terrifying reminder of the holy God they served. And the understanding that compromise must not be tolerated. Examples must be made. Justice must be served.

From classrooms on either side of the hall, echoing voices of instructors could be heard, their accents so thick and varied that they were not always easy to understand. Ukrainian chemists, Iraqi intelligence officers, Arab Afghans who had served against both the Russians and the Americans — each teaching from their area of expertise: document forgery, bomb making, encryption, the handling of radioactive material.

He slowed as they passed the last classroom. The young men and women seated around the lab benches could pass for students of any high school chemistry class. But high school chemistry students do not study the handling and manufacturing of chemical and biological weapons. The samples they examined came from around the world: botulism from Czechoslovakia, anthrax from Iraq, their own homegrown sarin, and of course from Russia, smallpox — the deadliest killer, the one that would very shortly return to the world scene.

But for now there was the other matter to attend to. "Where is the boy?" Ibrahim asked.

"In the next building," Yussuf answered. "They are waiting."

With a heavy sigh Ibrahim nodded. He did truly hate this. But sacrifices must be made. They approached the door, and he adjusted his robes in preparation for the harsh, blowing *haboob*. They stepped outside. The wind whipped and tore at his turban, blowing and slapping his galabiya. Although the buildings were only a few meters apart, the fine desert sand quickly worked its way into his beard and the creases of his skin.

They entered the next building and its silence.

"In here." Yussuf Fazil motioned to the second room on their right. They approached, arrived, and stepped inside.

It was a classroom like the others, but all the desks and chairs had been removed. All but one set. They remained in the middle of the room. Around them one to two inches of sand had been spread in a perfect circle about three meters in diameter. Beside the desk and chair sat a small plastic tub, a dish basin. And tied to the chair, with his right arm strapped up on the desk, his head bowed, sat a young man, seventeen years old. His face was coated in sweat and he was shivering.

At the sound of Ibrahim's entrance his head snapped up. His eyes were wide and afraid. He had been crying.

Sheikh Salad Habib, as well as a half dozen leaders of the camp, stood off to one side in grim silence. When Ibrahim el-Magd appeared, they stiffened with tension and respect. But Ibrahim did not look at them, nor did he break his gate. Instead he walked directly toward the lad. The boy gave an involuntary shudder but did not, could not, look away. Ibrahim slowed as he arrived, then squatted to join him.

"What is your name, son?"

The boy tried to speak but could only cough. His trembling grew worse.

"It is okay," Ibrahim said softly. "Do not fear. Are you Asad Sharif?"

The boy nodded.

"Have you admitted your offense?"

Again he nodded.

"Tell me."

"I ..." More coughing, more trembling.

Ibrahim motioned to one of the leaders. Immediately a water-skin was produced. Ibrahim took it into his hands, opened it, and held it to the boy's mouth. He drank cautiously, then greedily. When he had finished, Ibrahim handed back the skin and quietly repeated, "Tell me. What is your offense?"

"I took a Walkman ..." He coughed and tried again. "I stole a CD player from one of my friends."

"A friend, you say?"

The boy looked at him, unsure how he should respond.

Ibrahim nodded, trying to make it as easy for him as possible. "And what is the punishment for stealing?"

"To lose one's hand."

Ibrahim nodded again, more sadly. "Yes." Then he asked, "Tell me, what should be done?"

"Justice."

"Yes." Ibrahim's voice was a husky whisper. This was harder than he had thought. "Do you understand that this discipline is for the good of the group? Do you understand that it is not from anger or revenge? That we take no pleasure in it?"

The boy nodded.

"And Allah is merciful?"

"Yes," the boy croaked. "Allah is merciful."

"And to be praised?"

"And to be praised."

"And justice must be served?"

By now the boy trembled so violently that his entire desk started to shake. His eyes dropped to the floor in both fear and embarrassment. Ibrahim reached out and gently placed his hand on the lad's shoulders. The trembling slowly subsided. After a moment Ibrahim repeated, "And justice must be served?"

The boy still could not look up.

"And justice must be served?"

Slowly, hesitantly, his eyes rose, locking onto Ibrahim's. They seemed to draw strength from him. "Yes," he finally croaked. "Justice must be served."

Ibrahim gave a sad, reassuring smile.

The boy's wet face tried to return it.

Ibrahim patted his shoulder in encouragement and slowly stood. He glanced to Sheikh Salad Habib, hoping for some reprieve, for some insight he had missed. But Sheikh Habib, who knew his heart and soul, was already shaking his head. Justice must be served, examples must be made. Ibrahim turned from the youth and walked toward the group. He heard the desk begin to vibrate, heard the boy gag once, twice, then heave — vomit splashing onto his desk, onto the floor. As Ibrahim joined the group, he could already smell the sour, acrid odor. When he turned, he saw the boy's shirt, now wet with food. But the youth was no longer weeping. And his trembling was coming to a stop. He had raised his eyes to meet Ibrahim's. And now he waited ... prepared to meet Allah's justice like a man.

Sheikh Salad Habib nodded to one of the leaders. A large saber was produced. Holding it in both hands, the leader approached the youth, who watched his every move. Although his eyes were wide, there was no missing the boy's growing resolution. He would make a fine member of jihad, even with one hand. The man unsheathed the saber and took his position over the boy. The lad's chest heaved faster.

Ibrahim glanced at a nearby doctor, who stood with towels, first-aid materials ... and a plastic garbage bag.

The man raised his sword. He took a breath to steady himself, perhaps to strengthen his own resolve.

The boy did not cower, nor did he flinch. Instead, with a deep strength from within, he shouted, "Justice is served! Allah be praised!" as the saber came down.

It was Helen's third cup of Nescafé. But even caffeine failed to do the trick. After eighty-some hours of nonstop work, she definitely needed sleep. She'd already reached the wall of nonproductivity —

that place where it takes more time to fix the mistake than to get the sleep to avoid it in the first place. But there was little time to change that now. Now it was a matter of securing the equipment, securing the crew, and finalizing the thousand and one details to dig within the city, while she wet-nursed some middle-aged Bible thumper from America.

She set the Nescafé on the wooden dresser and stood back to look in the mirror. A little stockier than she was in college, she still had a decent figure. And with the right clothes, that extra thickness usually passed for muscle ... usually. She reached over to the khaki slacks on the unmade bed and held them to her waist. They were crumpled and a little baggy but still flattering.

She blew the sweaty bangs from her eyes and glanced at the clock. Eleven-ten p.m. and the temp was still in the mid-eighties. It was going to be one hot, miserable ride. She'd already called for a driver. Abu, her usual, was not available, but he had recommended someone he swore knew the roads, had air-conditioning that actually worked, and could be trusted with her. Not that she was concerned over the last issue. Wherever she traveled, she kept an ample supply of pepper spray and a workable knowledge of tae kwon do. After all, American women were always thought to be easy, even when they didn't want to be.

She tossed the slacks on the bed and walked back to the dresser. Taking another lukewarm gulp of Nescafé, she searched the drawers until she saw a pair of white shorts. They were cut a bit skimpy by Mideast standards, but nothing too shocking for Americans.

Her mind drifted back to Brent Appleton's instructions. Regardless of whether the stone was legitimate (and she had no reason to believe it would be), it was her job to stick by the preacher's side, report what he knew, and what else if anything he might find. She would have to become his friend, she knew that. His close friend. No easy task, considering he was supposed to be some knee-jerk Christian fundamentalist. Still, he was recently widowed, meaning he was single. She could endure the religious fanaticism, had certainly contended with enough of that ilk over the years. And she was certainly sorry to hear about his recent loss. But the operative word in her agenda, at least for tomorrow's initial meeting, would have to be *single*. This did not thrill her. But if it was what was necessary to survive, then she would survive. Reluctantly she reached for the shorts.

✱

Daniel knows he is dreaming, that this is some sort of continuation of Jill's earlier dream. He is wearing the high priest's garb and the breastplate she had described. He is standing upon the long, broad summit of Mount Sinai, looking down over the miles of desolation — the craggy mountains, the red, deserted plains ... but not really red. The full moon has bleached everything into dull pinks and grays.

Everything but the Light.

He hears it before he sees it, like distant thunder. But it does not crack and boom, then fade. Instead it continually rolls, like a waterfall, but growing louder every moment. He can feel it vibrating through the ground. He sees the wind around him kicking up. And when he finally turns to look, he gasps. The Light has no distinct shape, none that he can see, yet it is brighter than the sun, than a hundred suns. Still, it is more than brightness. It is a purity, a ... glory. So intense that it begins filling him with terror. And the closer the Glory approaches, the greater the terror becomes, icy cold, horrifying. He struggles to catch his breath. His heart hammers in his chest.

The ground shakes harder. Rocks and stones slip from their perches, cascading down the slopes. He tries turning from the Light to run away, but he can't move. It's as if he's paralyzed. The wind increases until it is blowing at gale force. He can barely stand against it. All around him the boulders, the bluffs, the rock formations begin to crumble, disintegrating, liquefying into dust. Even the stars and the moon above him are blurring, smearing, as if all of creation is melting.

The roar grows deafening. The Light is so intense that with great effort he raises a hand to protect his eyes. And then he sees it ... his flesh. This is why he can't move. He is no longer made of skin and muscle and bone. Instead he is made of ... stone, like the mountain. Granite. And more amazing, the stone is covered in some sort of writing. Writing he can read. It is Scripture. From the Bible. Not one verse. Thousands of them, complete with chapters and verse numbers. They overlap one another, running in different directions, stacked in layers atop each other. And by focusing his eyes upon the different layers, he can actually read them. There is the book of Deuteronomy. Part of Leviticus. James.

His body has become words. Words carved in granite.

He looks back to the Light. It is so close that it begins to envelope him. He opens his mouth to scream but the air is sucked from his lungs. It is impossible to breathe. The ground rolls under his feet, shaking harder and harder. And as it shakes, he shakes — as inflexible as the mountain, as the granite around him. He watches in horror as pieces of his body begin breaking off, crumbling to the ground, where they furiously vibrate until they too turn to dust.

"Danny!" He barely hears the voice over the roar. "Danny!"

He turns his head, straining to see. At last he spots her, there on a spill of boulders. It's Jill! She's wearing her wedding dress, its train and veil flapping and snapping in the wind.

"Your hand!" she cries. "It's in your hand!"

He doesn't understand.

"Look in your hand!"

He looks at the stony hand he'd been using to shield his face. He can no longer move it, not even open it. He turns to the other and to his surprise sees it is still flesh. In fact, it is the only part of his body that has remained flesh. He easily opens it and there in his palm is the stone, the Levi Stone. It glows brilliantly.

"Hold it to the breastplate!" she shouts.

The Light continues to swallow him as more and more of his body shakes loose — falling, shattering. He will be destroyed. In seconds. Like everything else, reduced to dust.

"Hold the stone to your heart!" Jill shouts. "Hold the stone to your heart!"

Using all his effort, he strains to raise his arm of rock toward the breastplate. He can feel stone grating against stone, rock against rock, as he slowly makes progress. The pain is excruciating, but at last he has raised his hand and presses the Levi Stone to his chest.

Immediately the breastplate glows. As it does, he feels a surge of energy, a type of heat. It passes through his chest, into his body. His rock body is heating up. As it does, it slowly begins to change, to return to flesh. Not quickly . . . but enough so he can move.

By now the Light has completely engulfed him. In its center he sees a form, human yet not human, impossible to distinguish from the surrounding brightness and glory. It is a dozen feet away, walk-

ing toward him. With all his strength he turns and starts to run. His rock body is jerky, clumsy and stiff, as if he were in a body cast, but at least he is moving. At least he is getting away. But to where?

He searches for a cleft to hide in, boulders to cower behind, but everything is turning to dust. Everything but ... there, up ahead! It looks like a pool cut into the rock. How strange; there hasn't been a drop of water on this mountain, and now there is a pool? Perhaps he can hide in it until the Light passes. Perhaps he can—

"Run, Danny! Run!"

He hobbles and staggers toward the pool as the center of the Light continues its approach.

"RUN!"

He is practically there. Just a few more steps, just two more, just ... and then he stumbles and falls. He hits the ground hard, breaking off more pieces of his body.

And still the Light approaches. And still the roar grows, filling his mind, his entire being.

He raises his head. The pool is inches away. Gasping, grimacing with pain and determination, he stretches out his stone arms, grips with his hands, and begins pulling his body. The pool's surface comes into view. It is only then that he realizes it is red. In it he sees the reflection of a face. But it isn't his face. Or is it? He can't tell. It is so beaten and bloody that it is impossible to recognize.

"Help me ...," he cries. "Help me!"

The image in the pool shifted and wavered as Daniel Lawson stirred from his sleep. He gave a shiver, then noticed how wet he was with perspiration and how hard he was breathing. But he was awake. The dream was over. He looked around him. Several yards away, under a blanket, slept Nayra. A little farther away in his sleeping bag was Tyler.

Daniel had not intended to fall sleep. He had wanted to spend the night praying and reading the Word. But apparently his body had other plans. He didn't understand the dream any more than when Jill had described it. Yet even now he suspected it was not the end. Even now he suspected there would be more. He looked out across the forsaken, stony wilderness. Off in the east the horizon glowed with the first hue of pink, the promise of another day about to begin.

*

Tyler was grateful that it was easier hiking down the mountain than up. Of the three of them, he should have been in the best shape. But the months of couch potatoing had definitely taken their toll. Although he had tried to hide it, he had sucked air most of yesterday. And this morning he was suffering from the burning stiffness of overworked calf and thigh muscles. Still, by comparison today was a cakewalk, which gave him plenty of opportunity to impress others of the group with his manly prowess. Particularly those of the female persuasion.

"Be careful, this one is steep," he said, reaching back to offer Nayra his hand. Like a mighty deer — no, make that a mighty stag — he'd just negotiated it himself. But instead of taking his hand, Nayra stopped and simply looked at it.

"What?" he asked.

"Is this sexual harassment?"

Tyler blinked. "I'm sorry, what?"

"You think we do not know of such things?"

Trying to understand, Tyler stuttered, "Uh ... I ..."

"We have seen your *General Hospital*, your *60 Minutes*."

"I was just trying to —"

"You may keep your hands to yourself, Tyler Lawson."

"What? What are you talk —"

Before he had finished, she leaped to a group of rocks off the trail and easily circumvented him.

Again he blinked, then tried to recover. "Look, I was just trying to help."

She gave no answer but continued down the trail ahead of him, directly behind his father.

"I was just ... Nayra ..." He sighed wearily. Shot down again. It seemed every time he opened his mouth around this woman, he was going down in flames. It was enough to make a less assured man nervous and self-conscious. Fortunately for him, that was not a problem.

Dad had been strangely quiet all morning. It was more than his sadness about Mom. That he usually hid ... well, from everyone but Tyler. Because Tyler knew his father like a book. He knew all the socially expected manners, the condescending smiles, the empty civilities that a "man of God" was supposed to follow. Yes sir, Tyler knew everything about his dad, which is why he so deeply ... well, *hated* was too strong a word. But *resented* would do. Still, he had to admit that quitting his job and going on some Indiana Jones field trip showed there was some hope for the guy.

But why was he, Tyler Lawson, here? Did he really think they'd find those other two stones, that they'd really hear the voice of God? Maybe. Maybe not. But if the Urim and Thummim were actually out there, why couldn't they? Think of it ... the voice of God. Imagine having all your questions answered, all your confusion cleared up, your future laid out. Not that he'd use God as some sort of fortune-teller or anything. Somehow Tyler suspected the Almighty wouldn't be giving inside-trader information on the stock market. But what better way to know why we're here? What better way to learn your real purpose in life, to figure out what you should be doing with it?

Of course there was another reason he was there ... Mom. So much of her last year had been spent trying to bring him and his dad back together, to make peace between them. Of course it never happened and never would. His father was too set in his ways. Maybe that's why Tyler was here, to prove to himself — to prove to *her* — that it wasn't his fault. Maybe he was here to once and for all rid himself of the guilt that seemed to dog him day and night.

Mom ... Thinking of her still made his throat ache. How deeply he missed her. Their long talks, her quiet understanding, her ability to reach inside him and —

"Hello ..."

He glanced from the wall they were descending to see a woman twenty or thirty feet below. Even from this distance he could tell she was a babe — healthy tan, good figure, nice legs that stretched into a pair of good-looking shorts. Granted, she was a good fifteen years older than he, but she was still definitely hot. He noticed she held a steel or aluminum briefcase in one hand.

Looking up at them, she called, "Are you Pastor Lawson?"

His father came to a stop. "Yes, uh, I'm Daniel Lawson."

"I'm Dr. Zimmerman." She broke into a smile, dazzling even from this distance. "Helen Zimmerman."

"The archaeologist?" Tyler asked.

She turned to him. "Yes, and you're ... Tyler?"

"Yes ma'am." He regretted the "ma'am" part, but it came out before he could stop it.

91

"Sorry I missed you," she said. "We've been working nonstop the last three or four days, hitting some snags with my new dig in Jerusalem."

"You came all the way out here just for us?" Daniel asked. He started down the path to join her. Tyler and Nayra followed.

"Dr. Hermann said you may have an authentic—" She threw a look to Nayra, then continued. "He said you may have something of interest. And after standing you up at the airport, I figured this was the least I could do. And a good thing, too."

"Why's that?" Daniel asked as they continued working their way down to her.

"You come out in that Land Cruiser?"

"Yes."

"Quite a hunk of junk. Where did you get it?"

Before Daniel could answer, Nayra replied, "That's my hunk of junk."

"And you're ..."

"This is Nayra, our friend ... from Egypt," Daniel said.

Helen paused, looking her over.

But Nayra refused to be scrutinized. "You have a difficulty with my vehicle?"

"Not really," Helen said, chuckling good-naturedly. "I have no difficulty. I'm just surprised you were able to make it all the way out here. As to your chances of making it back ... well, I'm not a betting woman, but—"

"The vehicle had no problem bringing us here, and it will have no problem returning us."

Tyler mused at the sparks between them. The woman had strength, there was no doubt about it. But Nayra was no pushover, either, and he was impressed to see the way the girl stood up to her. Even more importantly, he was grateful that someone else had strolled into Nayra's crosshairs to take the fire for a while.

When they finally reached her level, greetings were again exchanged and hands shaken. Up close, Dr. Helen Zimmerman was even more impressive—brains, self-assured, and definitely beautiful, though she did look as if she could use a couple nights' sleep. Of course Daniel was completely oblivious to the good doctor's gifts. Tyler grinned. The man had definitely been out of circulation for a while.

As they descended the mountain, they discussed her work, her findings, and her areas of interest. No mention was made yet of the Urim and Thummim, nor of the Levi Stone. That would come later. Interestingly enough, Nayra was quiet throughout all this time. Was it jealousy? Tyler doubted it. She'd probably just been put off by the initial meeting and, whether she admitted it or not, was a little intimidated by the woman.

They arrived at the monastery and followed the rocky path around it to the parking lot.

"So you drove that big ol' Land Bruiser all by yourself?" Helen asked as Nayra's Land Cruiser came into view.

"That is correct," Nayra answered.

"Well, maybe we should follow you back, just in case you have trouble."

"Trouble?"

"You know, in case something breaks down or important pieces start falling off." She laughed to soften the jab but Nayra saw no humor.

"So you want us to ride back with you?" Daniel asked the doctor.

"Unless you have something against air-conditioning, tinted windows, custom shocks, and a great sound system." She threw Tyler a grin. He couldn't help returning it. "It's the best vehicle and driver you can rent. Of course I put it on the university tab." Another smile.

More smiles returned.

"And where exactly is this bastion of luxury?" Nayra asked.

Helen turned back to the parking lot. "It's right over ..." She came to a stop. "It's right ..."

"Yes?" Nayra asked, surveying the lot. This early in the morning, the Land Cruiser was the only vehicle present.

Helen searched the area, her concern growing. "I don't understand. I told the driver to wait right here." The bright sun forced her to shield her tired eyes.

Tyler and Daniel exchanged looks, then traded them with Nayra.

Helen's frustration continued rising. "I told him to wait right here, that I'd be back in a couple hours. I told him to wait. I even paid him in advance."

Nayra turned to her incredulously. "You paid him in advance?"

"Well, yes, so that he'd know that I ... that we ..." Helen came to a stop, suddenly realizing what she'd done.

"So you paid your driver in advance, expecting him to stay," Nayra said, allowing the foolishness to register with the others.

Again Helen scanned the parking lot — "I, uh …" — then the road, then the horizon. Not a vehicle was in sight. Finally she turned to Nayra and gave a nervous laugh. "It's been some long days; guess I wasn't thinking too clearly."

Without missing a beat, Nayra headed for the Land Cruiser. "You are welcome to ride with us," she said. The group followed behind. "I apologize that we have no air-conditioning, but sitting in the back, you will have plenty of fresh air. Oh, and I apologize that we have no more seat cushions to share."

chapter five

"So you're saying that Moses and the whole Exodus account never happened?" Daniel shouted back to Helen as they bounced around inside the Land Cruiser.

"That's right," she yelled, "according to most recent evidence." She saw disappointment flicker across his face and felt a little sorry for him. Still, it was time for Bible-touting fundamentalists to get their wake-up call. Unfortunately, he wasn't the only "fundy" in the vehicle.

"That's absurd," Nayra called back to her from behind the steering wheel.

"Pardon me?"

"You cannot use lack of evidence to prove lack of existence."

Helen frowned, not sure she'd heard correctly. To be honest, it was hard to hear anything from the backseat. And though she couldn't prove it, her suspicions were rising that the kid was purposely hitting every rut and pothole between Mount Sinai and Jerusalem. Earlier the preacher had offered, insisted, that he take the backseat. Of course she turned him down, making it clear that she did not need such preferential treatment . . . though at this moment she wasn't exactly sure why.

Nayra continued. "You cannot disprove the holy books of God by saying you cannot prove them. That is the logic of a child."

Helen threw a look at the preacher, who listened quietly. Although she found the girl a constant source of irritation, she knew it was best to stay in good humor. One bad first impression was enough. "So what are you," she asked Nayra with a chuckle, "a law student?"

"Actually," Tyler corrected from behind his video camera, "she's a student of Middle East history."

Helen smiled tightly at the camera while thinking, *Great . . . Preacher Man hasn't given me a second look. Video Boy won't stop looking. And I've got some know-it-all Arab to contend with.*

Nayra glanced at her in the mirror, continuing to shout over the noise. "Just because your science is not yet sophisticated enough to verify that something exists does not mean it does not exist. What was it the great British archaeologist Dame Kenyon said in 1967? 'The archaeology in Jerusalem is finished; there is nothing more to find'?"

"Well, yes — "

"And now is it not the most excavated city in the world?"

"That's correct, because of our improvement of procedure and technology."

"Precisely. And your improvement will continue until someday you will catch up with the historical accuracy of the Bible."

Helen looked at her. Was that a smile? She couldn't tell. Suddenly they hit another series of potholes, slamming her head into the vehicle's roof.

"Sorry," Nayra called.

"You okay?" the preacher asked. There was no missing the concern in his voice.

Helen nodded, rubbing her head. "Nothing a handful of Tylenol won't help."

"You sure you don't want me to — "

"I said I'm fine." Hearing the irritation in her voice, she tried to soften it. "Thanks, though." She glanced toward Video Boy. He was certainly getting his money's worth. "Do you really need to be taping all this?" she asked.

"Does it bother you?" he said, not taking his eye from the viewfinder.

"Well, no," she lied. "It's just, uh . . . do whatever you like." Turning her attention back to Nayra, she asked, "I thought you were Egyptian?"

"I am."

"So why are you interested in defending the Jewish Scriptures — particularly when it involves disputed Israeli territory?"

"As Muslims, we put great emphasis on the truth of Scripture. Particularly when we have to defend it from the lies of man."

"Excuse me?" Helen's irritation resurfaced before she could catch it. She threw a quick glance at the preacher to see if he had noticed. He gave no indication one way or the other. She restrained herself from checking on Video Boy. Turning back to Nayra, she asked, "Are you saying we distort facts?"

"I am saying your science is still in its infancy. Less than one hundred years ago you were nothing more than elaborate grave robbers."

Unbelievable. Here she was, defending her occupation to some kid. A *kid*. Any other time she would have shredded such sophomoric thinking to pieces. But she was supposed to be on her best behavior here, the civilized grown-up. Unfortunately, the brat up front didn't have that handicap.

"While at the same time," Nayra continued, "in the nineteenth century Edward Robinson used only the Bible to discover two hundred lost biblical sites — "

"Edward Robinson was no archaeologist."

"My point exactly."

"And men like him, with their antiscientific, biblical bias, have done more to distort truth than anyone in our field." She wasn't sure what Preacher Man thought of her slam but, like it or not, the gloves were coming off.

Nayra responded in kind. "And so you push the pendulum the other way, even questioning men like Amon Ben-Tor at the Hebrew University of Jerusalem — "

"Amon Ben-Tor is a great archaeologist!"

"Yet do not some in your field secretly suspect him of having orthodox tendencies?"

"That's absurd! Why, because of his work at Hazor?"

"Because he insists that the evidence points to the city being burned with fire, just as was described in the holy book of Joshua."

"Listen, my friend, just because you know a few — " They hit another series of bumps, longer and more brutal than the last. Fortunately, it provided a suitable pause, allowing Helen to cool down. She stole another glance at the preacher. He wore a quizzical, almost amused look. *Great*, she thought. *Not only does he think I'm a moron for losing the car, but now I'm a hothead. And Video Boy, there ... turn off the stupid camera! This is not Jerry Springer!*

Using her last ounce of self-control, Helen settled back into her seat, vowing that if Nayra continued the argument, she would have to continue it on her own. She stretched out her hand and rested it on the briefcase beside her. At her insistence they had removed the stone from the preacher's pocket (an unbelievable place to store such an article), unwrapped it from its only protection, a handkerchief (even more unbelievable), and placed it inside the foam-lined case, where it would be considerably safer. She was not crazy about handling it even this much in front of the inquisitive eyes of the girl. It was a treacherous world out there, and the fewer people who knew of the so-called discovery, the safer everyone would be.

There would be much to examine and discuss, including their ridiculous hopes of finding the Urim and Thummim. But not now. Not with this part–Johnny Cochran, part–Evil Knievel behind the wheel. No, she would wait until they were alone. Until she had better control of the situation. She blew at her bangs and stole another look toward Preacher Man. She'd lost some ground with him, no doubt. But that was okay; she'd regain it — and more. She had to.

✳

"Sir?" The young man rose respectfully to his feet. In the flickering candles on the table, he looked no older than eighteen, nineteen at most. "Ibrahim el-Magd?"

"Yes."

"With the greatest respect ..." He hesitated, unsure how to continue.

"Please, go ahead."

"Are you absolutely sure ... that is, are you certain we must wait?"

Ibrahim did not blame the boy. He supposed the question was planted into the youth's head by members of the Shura. Yes, they had soiled even these young heroes, polluting even their minds with doubt and division. Ibrahim el-Magd pulled back his sleeve and dipped his bread into the *hummus*. "Are you in such a hurry to enter paradise, my friend?"

The truth of the comment was far greater than its humor, and there were only polite smiles ... at least for tonight. For tonight all seven of the heroes sat about the eating table of the great Ibrahim el-Magd in somber reverence. Not in fear of the man but in respect for what they were about to accomplish.

The youth threw a nervous glance to his companions and cleared his throat.

"Please," Ibrahim motioned. "Speak what is on your mind."

At last he obeyed. "Sir, if the smallpox is ready for placement . . . and if the briefcases are ready to be armed . . . is not every day we wait an endangerment to our mission?"

Although he resented the young man being manipulated, Ibrahim el-Magd did not resent his question. Open and frank discussion was what he had requested. It was what they deserved. If these seven men — boys, really, as not one was beyond twenty-five years of age — were about to sacrifice their lives for the final outpouring of Allah's wrath, it was important that all their questions be put to rest.

"What is your name, son?"

"Abdul-Hadi Dargahi," he answered.

"The hero from Iraq?" Ibrahim asked. He called them all heroes. For they were. From the moment they had passed the final screening and entered the training program nine months earlier, they were referred to as such.

"Yes sir," the youth answered.

"Abdul-Hadi Dargahi, I know you understand the importance of cleansing our world of infidels. As it says in Surat al-Taubah 9:29, we are to 'fight against those who believe not in Allah.'"

"Yes sir, I believe and agree."

"And you believe and agree how fierce such warfare and destruction must be."

"Yes sir."

"Then you can appreciate why we must be absolutely certain of both the time and execution of this great and terrifying event."

There was a gentle knock at the doorway. Ibrahim turned and called, "Yes?"

Dalal entered through the curtain. "I apologize for the interruption," she said, gliding across the room and handing Ibrahim a piece of paper.

He received the note and unfolded it. It was from the hospital. From Sarah. There were only three words, written in a shaking scrawl:

Muhammad is dead.

The news struck Ibrahim hard, a powerful blow to his stomach. For a moment he could not breathe. He closed his eyes, fighting for composure. This was not the time. There would be time for grief later. There would be a suitable period for mourning. Muhammad deserved that. His wife deserved that. But not now. Now, as impossible as it felt, he must continue. The meeting was too critical, his service to Allah too important.

At last he opened his eyes and looked about the group. Then he turned to Dalal. Her dark, sensitive gaze remained fixed on his. He gave the slightest nod. "Thank you," was all he said. "I will take care of this matter once we have shared our meal."

Dalal nodded. Like Ibrahim, she knew and appreciated the importance of this gathering. She was a strong woman who knew of the sacrifices that must be made. He watched as she turned and gracefully exited the room.

He returned his attention to the young man. It took a moment to recall the question. When he had, he addressed it. "We are waiting, my young friend, because a means has been secured in which we will be able to hear the voice of Allah."

"You mean" — the youth cleared his throat — "we will know his will through the Qur'an."

"No. I mean we will soon be able to hear the audible voice of Allah himself."

The heroes ceased eating and turned to him in disbelief.

He nodded to them in silent confirmation.

Amazement grew. They looked at one another. Was such a thing possible?

Again he nodded. "You have heard correctly."

"Sir ..." It was the young hero from Afghanistan. "Not even the prophet Muhammad, may his name be praised, heard the actual voice of Allah."

Ibrahim nodded.

"This ..." Abdul-Hadi Dargahi looked for the words. "If it is true, this is a marvelous thing, a most holy thing."

Ibrahim nodded. "It is true. It is divine confirmation. It is proof that our course has been set and approved by the Almighty himself." He waited a moment before continuing. "And to ensure that both our course and our timing are in his perfect will, it has been my decision that we wait until we hear his voice. That we wait until he speaks directly to us. Then we will know the precise detail and moment in which we are to pour out his great and terrible wrath."

The heroes exchanged comments, their excitement growing.

Ibrahim watched as a certain sadness crept in. For soon, within a very short time, each of their lives would be sacrificed, each of them would leave this world as martyrs and enter paradise. The decision had been reached nearly three years earlier. The mission was far too important to rely upon radio-controlled or timing devices. No. Each hero was to detonate his nuclear briefcase by hand—one in New York, another in Los Angeles, others in London, Munich, Saint Petersburg, Tokyo, and Hong Kong. Seven locations strategically selected, not only because of the size of the cities but because of their proximity to the jet stream and other wind currents. Yet none were to be detonated in locations that would endanger such Islamic centers as Afghanistan, India, Malaysia, Africa, and the Middle East.

Abdul-Hadi Dargahi was correct. The smallpox had been cultivated and was ready to be placed. The position of each canister had been calculated and recalculated by expert physicists until all were in absolute agreement. It was imperative that each container be far enough from the blast sight so its contents would not be killed by the heat or radiation, yet close enough for the liquid to be propelled into the atmosphere as vapor.

Everything was ready to go, worked out to the finest detail. Nothing, absolutely nothing, had been left to chance. Now there was only the waiting. Ibrahim el-Magd fingered the folded note in his hands as he looked about the table at the seven young men. There was only the waiting . . . until they joined his son in paradise.

Daniel slipped off his shoes and followed Nayra and Tyler into the dim coolness of the Dome of the Rock. As magnificent as the building appeared on the outside, with its bright roof of brass dominating Old Jerusalem's skyline, the inside was even more spectacular. He'd been here several times with the church tours, and each time he entered, he was taken aback by the absolute beauty and reverence. Green oriental carpet lined the octagonal floor's border, while deep red carpeting filled the center. Huge pillars of green marble alternating with giant blocks of white, and inlaid with gold, rose dozens of feet to a multiple-arched ceiling crowded with dazzling and intricate mosaic patterns.

Daniel had always found it difficult to put such beauty into words. Not Tyler. "Cool," was all he said as he took in the structure. Without missing a beat, he returned to the discussion he and Nayra had been having. "So basically Christianity and Islam are pretty much the same."

"In some ways yes. In many ways not at all."

"Sure they are. We both believe in God. The rest is just fine print, right?"

Nayra shook her head in disdain and rolled her eyes.

Daniel smiled, realizing the gesture was no longer limited to Western society. Maybe the fundamentalists were right — maybe we really were polluting their culture. The two kids moved off, continuing their whispered debate as Daniel lagged behind, partially to give them their space but also because of the sadness. Try as he might to ignore and overcome it, everything on the trip registered as miniature anniversaries. *The last time I did this was with Jill ... This is the first time I've done this without Jill ...* and so on. Indulgent and self-pitying, he knew that. But just as human history was divided into B.C. and A.D., his life seemed divided into "before Jill's death" and "after it."

He looked ahead, watching Tyler and Nayra. His son was attracted to the girl; there was little doubt. Why else would he be strutting around so? And since he didn't have the video camera to hide behind (they made him check it at the door), he was even more self-conscious, which made him even more obnoxious. And Nayra? As far as he could tell, she wasn't giving him the time of day — which, as best as Daniel understood the female mind, meant she either hated him or was very interested; it was impossible to tell the difference.

He and Tyler were supposed to have met Helen in their hotel lobby at eight this morning, then go up to the room to discuss the Levi Stone and the various rumored locations of the Urim and Thummim. But that had been nearly — he looked at his watch — three hours ago. And since she hadn't shown, and since Tyler had somehow finessed the phone number to the place where Nayra was staying, and since Nayra had said she'd be happy to show them around Jerusalem … well, here they were.

Shaking his head, he mused a moment over Helen. What an unusual woman. Oh, she was attractive, he'd give her that — though she didn't have to work quite so hard to advertise it. But it was funny: on the one hand she was so intelligent and self-assured, not unlike Linda Grossman at church — who, by the way, he did not miss in the slightest — while on the other hand she came off as some sort of ditzy klutz. It would be a long time before he forgot the sound of her head continually slamming into the Land Cruiser's roof. Then there was the matter of losing both her car and her driver. Again Daniel shook his head. What an unusual woman.

He approached Tyler and Nayra, who had stopped and were staring up at the large mosaic of Arab writing that encircled the ceiling. Nayra was translating. "'Oh, you people of the Book —'"

"'People of the Book,'" Tyler interrupted. "You said that's what Muhammad called Christians, right?"

Nayra nodded and continued to read. "'Don't go overboard about your faith. Don't tell lies about God. Jesus Christ, the son of Mary, is indeed a messenger of God.'"

Tyler shrugged. "Sounds good to me."

She read quietly a moment, then out loud. "'So believe in God and his messengers and quit talking about a Trinity.'"

"Where does it say that?"

"Right there," she said, pointing. Then she continued. "'Speak only the truth about this Jesus who you are arguing about. He is the son of Mary. It is not appropriate that God should give birth or that he should be the father of a child.'"

"It really says all that?"

She gave a nod.

"So you guys believe Jesus was a good teacher but not the Son of God."

"Why should we believe otherwise?"

"Because he said he was. Over and over again he claimed to be God the Son."

"So your Scriptures say."

"But you said our Scriptures are holy and to be trusted."

"Only to a point."

"Whose point?"

Nayra ignored his question. "That is why the Qur'an was given to the Prophet six hundred years after the Gospels. To clear up questions and imperfections. It is the final revelation of God."

"So the Qur'an points out where the Bible is wrong."

"It removes the errors that have been put in by man."

Tyler threw a look to Daniel, who made it clear his son was on his own.

But before he could respond, Nayra motioned and said, "Come, there is something you must see."

The two followed her toward the center of the building. It was dominated by a large gray outcropping of rock. It rose nearly six feet above the floor and was surrounded by dark, wooden partitions. They walked around several of the ornately carved panels until they arrived at a small viewing area. And there, past a handful of other spectators, lay a dozen yards of uneven rock, so barren that it could have passed for the moon.

"What is it?" Tyler asked.

"*Es-Sakhra,*" Nayra whispered. "It is where the prophet Muhammad's feet touched before he went on his night journey to heaven."

"Oh," Tyler said, trying his best to sound interested.

"Of course the Jews have twisted the Scriptures to say this is also the place where Abraham presented Isaac as a sacrifice."

"You don't buy that?" Tyler asked.

She gave him a look. "Ishmael was the one who was presented as a sacrifice, and it was in Mecca, not here."

Tyler threw another glance to Daniel, who raised an eyebrow over this new revelation. The group in front of them stepped aside and they moved in for a better look.

"But there is one other item you will find of interest pertaining to es-Sakhra. Particularly in regard to the quest you and your father have undertaken."

"What's that?"

"Many believe that it was upon this rock that the Jews' Holy of Holies was located."

"Holy of Holies?" Tyler asked.

"Yes. The most sacred part of the ancient temple. The very place where God's holy presence dwelled, hovering over the ark of the covenant. A presence so pure that the people had to weave a thick curtain to shield themselves so they would not die from being exposed to him."

Tyler turned to his father. "Kinda sounds like Mount Sinai, doesn't it?"

Daniel nodded.

"So this was where they kept the ark?" Tyler asked. "The *Raiders of the Lost Ark* kind of ark?"

"The ark of the covenant," Nayra repeated. "The high priest would come back here only once a year to intercede for the people before God. When he did, they tied a rope around his ankle in case the holiness killed him. That way they could pull him out and not go in after him and risk dying themselves."

"The high priest ... as in the guy who wore that breastplate with the stones on it?" Tyler asked.

"Exactly. And the one who kept the Urim and Thummim you two have been talking about." Nayra pointed toward the left side of the rock. "And do you see that indentation over there?"

Tyler squinted. "There are plenty of indentations."

"No, that rectangle over there that's been cut into the rock. Do you see it?"

"Yes, barely."

"It is exactly four feet four inches by two feet seven inches."

"Meaning ..."

"Those are the precise dimensions the Bible gives for the ark of the covenant."

Both men fell silent. This was news, even to Daniel.

"You mean," Tyler finally asked, "that's where it sat? The ark of the covenant sat right there?"

"There's actually no way of verifying that" — all three gave a start and turned to see Helen Zimmerman speaking directly behind them — "although the coincidence is somewhat interesting."

"Doc," Tyler greeted her.

She turned to Daniel. "I got your message at the desk. Sorry I was late."

"We waited over an hour, and when nobody showed — "

"I know, I know ..." She ran her hand through her hair, obviously trying to hide her frustration. "We got hung up in traffic."

Daniel nodded. "Yes, that can sometimes be a — "

"Another suicide bombing," she interrupted. "They've got that whole west side shut down." Throwing a look at Nayra, she added, "I'm surprised the girl here didn't tell you."

Nayra simply shrugged and turned back to the rock. "My name is Nayra."

"Yes, well, if you'll excuse us, Nayra, the three of us have some important business to discuss." She turned and started to leave. "So if you don't mind, we'll have to end your little sight-seeing excursion and — augh!" In her haste Helen had not seen the small woman who had pushed in behind her. She stumbled over her, trying not to step on her while trying to keep her balance . . . and failed on both accounts. The woman let out a shriek as Helen twisted to the left, then to the right, managing to throw herself into one of the side partitions. As she fell, she groped for something, anything. Unfortunately, the only something she could grab was the wooden partition, which gave little support as she dragged it down with her.

It was like a slow-motion movie as Helen fell backward, out of control, arms flailing. For the briefest second her eyes connected with Daniel's, and for the briefest second he saw her amazement — and helplessness.

She hit the ground an instant before the wooden partition, though it was the partition that created most of the racket and drew everyone's attention. As best as Daniel could tell, she only lost consciousness for a moment, but that was long enough for the caretakers to decide upon the extra precaution of calling an ambulance.

And despite her protests, her embarrassment, and apologies for the inconvenience, Dr. Helen Zimmerman was hustled out of the Dome of the Rock, across the courtyard, and into an arriving ambulance. All this as Daniel did his best to assure her that it was okay, that it could happen to anybody.

But even as the ambulance pulled away, he found himself shaking his head and musing. What an incredibly peculiar woman.

"Doctor Zimmerman? Helen?"

She froze at the sound of his voice. It couldn't be. Not here, not now. But it was. Preacher Man had stuck his head through the doorway of her hospital room and was now smiling. "There you are. How are you feeling?"

Instinctively she pulled the sheet up higher to cover her pathetic hospital gown. "Aren't visiting hours over? How'd you get in?"

His smile broadened. "I'm clergy, remember?"

"Of course," she muttered as he stepped into the room. "How could I forget."

"Are you okay? I thought you'd be out by — "

"I'm fine, I'm fine," she said, checking her hair. "They've just lost the paperwork, that's all. As soon as they find it, they can release me."

"Ah," he said, nodding.

She wasn't entirely sure he believed her. And why should he, after her performance the last couple of days? "Look," she tried to explain, "I know you think I'm completely incompetent, but — "

"I've never said — "

"You don't have to. I see it every time you look at me." Catching herself, she confessed, "Actually, I see it every time *I* look at me. I don't know what's going on, but it's important you understand that I'm really quite efficient and very capable."

"I'm sure you are."

"I am."

Again he nodded.

"As you may know, I'm considered one of the leading archaeologists in Israel."

"So I've heard."

"Some would say the entire Middle East."

"That's very impressive."

Frustrated, she looked away and blew the bangs out of her eyes. Now he had her defending herself. What was she doing? There was no need for this! Especially in front of him. It was time to change gears. She turned back and said, "We've run the preliminary tests on that stone of yours."

"And?"

"Dr. Hermann was right: though it's impossible to know for certain at this stage, there is a possibility it's authentic. It's the right gem, the right size, and the correct script. It could very well indeed be the stone used to represent the priestly tribe of Levi."

He nodded once more, taking a moment to think. Folding his arms, he asked, "So . . . where do we go from here?"

"You're still set on trying to find the Urim and Thummim?"

He gave that quizzical smile of his. "You still think we're crazy?"

"Of course. Not only crazy but incredibly egocentric." *What? What did I say that for? Why can't I just be nice?* But she'd already committed herself, so she continued. "I mean, look at the situation objectively. After all these centuries of being lost, to think that they would just happen to resurface now and that you would just happen to be the ones to find them. Doesn't that seem, oh, just a bit self-centered?"

He shrugged good-naturedly. "It happened with the Levi Stone."

"And you think lightning will strike twice?"

"Stranger things have happened."

There was that smile again. For the briefest second she lost her train of thought. She glanced away to regroup, then turned back to him. "You do have one thing going for you, though."

"What's that?"

"Over the past several months there have been various rumored sightings."

"That's what Dr. Hermann said. Are they around here?"

She shook her head. "No, the most credible come from France."

"France?"

"Avignon, to be exact. The Palace of the Popes." He frowned and she felt a wave of satisfaction. Good. Now it was his turn to play catch-up for a change. She continued. "You may or may not have heard stories about how, back in the twelfth century, the Knights of the Templar excavated the temple site here in Jerusalem and supposedly found all sorts of temple artifacts — the ark of the covenant, the Holy Grail, the high priest's vestments — all items that the Jews were rumored to have hid under the temple when it was destroyed by the Babylonians."

He gave a half nod. "What does that have to do with Avignon?"

"Two hundred years later when the pope moved to France and the King of France turned up the heat to persecute the Templars, legend has it that the Templars tried to bribe the papacy with special, holy articles."

"Like some of the priestly vestments."

"Like the Urim and Thummim."

He paused a moment, then asked, "Is there any substance to these legends?"

She laughed. "Of course not. Though there are two events whose timing is interesting. First, when the pope—I believe it was Clement VI—finally agreed to receive some of the 'gifts,' the black plague immediately struck the city, killing half its inhabitancy. Fifteen thousand men, women, and children."

Preacher Man winced at the figure.

"But it's the second event that you'll find more interesting. Again, these are only rumors, you understand?"

"I understand."

"When the stones were supposedly rediscovered in 1413, right there in the palace, and brought alongside a newer gift, the high priest's breastplate with its twelve additional stones ... well, a terrible fire ignited."

"Fire?"

"Supposedly a 'holy, unquenchable fire' created by the presence of God."

The preacher's frown deepened. Then in quiet reflection he asked, "That was a long time ago; do you really think they're still there, in Avignon?"

"I doubt they ever were. But the story goes on to say that the breastplate stones were quickly divided and dispersed so they would never again come together to create such a disaster."

"Dispersed to ..."

"Various areas, some as far away as Africa. Or as may be in your case, Rockford, Illinois."

"And the Urim and Thummim?"

"I'm afraid the rumor gets even stranger."

He nodded, waiting for more.

She obliged. "It seems they were passed down from one group to another until they came into the hands of gypsies."

"Gypsies?"

"Yes. They're quite prevalent in that region. If fact, to this day they hold an annual reunion there."

"In Avignon?"

"Nearby, in Camargue."

Once again the man fell silent. *Finally,* Helen thought. *This is the way it's supposed to be. I'm the professional; he's the civilian. I'm the teacher; he's the pupil.* Encouraged and on a roll, she continued. "There is, however, a slightly more believable story ... and one much closer to home."

He looked up. "Where's that?"

"Right here in Israel. Mizpah, Tell en-Nasbeh. Just a few miles north of Jerusalem. As best as we can tell, it was some type of head-quarters for the Babylonian army when they destroyed the city."

"Back when Jerusalem and the temple were sacked?"

"That's right. For about five years in the twenties and thirties William Bade, an American archaeologist, dug there. Initially he found nothing of the Babylonian occupation."

"Initially?"

She nodded. "But sixty years later Jeffrey Zorn went through the old records and found an entire layer that had been overlooked as belonging to that period. He also went back and identified arti-facts that we now know belonged to that era — jars with stamped impressions, pieces of a ceramic coffin unique to the Mesopotamian region. He even found a bronze vase, given to the Rockefeller Museum in Jerusalem, that is believed to be Babylonian."

"So they reopened the dig?"

She shook her head. "Insufficient funds. And the fact that it's in the West Bank makes it difficult to secure permission and coop-eration. For years it's simply been open to the public, to anybody who wants to stroll through. And rumor has it that the local Pales-tinians have occasionally found items associated with the First Temple Era."

"Items?"

"Implements used in temple worship, perhaps some of the priestly vestments. And ..." — she threw him a look — "the Urim and Thummim."

"Have you looked into those rumors?"

"I did mention it's in the West Bank, didn't I? And that they were found by Palestinians?"

"Yes."

"And since all artifacts are property of the Israeli government, and since many of the Palestinians are not exactly friends of the government ..."

"They've been uncooperative."

"To say the least."

"Would it be possible ... I mean, could you arrange for us to go up there?"

Helen felt another wave of satisfaction. "I already have. I'll pick up you and your son at your hotel tomorrow morning. How does seven o'clock sound?"

"Great." Once again he broke into that smile of his. "Thanks." The smile broadened. "That will be great."

Helen shrugged. It was all part of her job. And to be candid, it was about time she started doing it correctly. "Now, if you'll excuse me," she said, returning to the notebook on her bed table, "I've got some work to finish."

"Certainly. I'll see you at seven, then."

She nodded.

He headed toward the door, then turned to her. "Thanks, Helen. I really appreciate it."

She smiled politely and waved him on. He disappeared through the doorway, and she reached for the plastic water pitcher on the table before her. She didn't know what had happened the past forty-eight hours, but it felt good to return to the competent Dr. Helen Zimmerman that everyone knew and respected. She would have felt a bit more competent if she'd remembered to remove the cellophane wrapper from her glass before she poured. The icy water rolled off the cellophane and spilled onto her lap, so startling her that she fumbled with the pitcher and accidentally dumped its entire contents on herself. She let out a whoop and cried, "Nurse!"

The nurse did not appear. Unfortunately, Preacher Man did. "Are you all right?" he asked, racing back in.

"Yes! I'm all right," she said, futilely dabbing at the water with a tiny napkin.

"You sure? Here, let me get you—"

"No. I'm sure! I'm sure! I'll see you at seven!"

"But—"

"Seven!"

"Right . . ."

He hesitated and stared until she looked up at him and glared.

"Right," he repeated. "Seven." Thankfully, mercifully, he turned and exited into the hallway.

"Nurse!" Helen continued dabbing at the ice water, blowing the hair out of her face. "Nurse!"

chapter six

Daniel should have suspected there would be trouble. As early as their crossing the Israeli checkpoint into the West Bank, things hadn't gone right.

"Turn off the camera," the guard had said, motioning through the window to Tyler, who sat in the backseat of Helen's rented Mercedes.

But Tyler pretended not to hear and continued to videotape.

"Better do what he says," Helen called from behind the wheel. "They don't mess around here."

Not taking his face from the viewfinder, and positioning himself for a better angle, Tyler asked, "Why, they got something to hide?"

Again the guard motioned. "Turn off the camera."

He pretended not to notice.

"Tyler," Daniel warned.

"Do as he says." Helen's voice grew firm. "With yesterday's bombing, things are pretty hot right now, and—"

The rap on the glass startled all three of them. Tyler lowered the camera from his eye to see the guard, a kid no older than himself, glowering down at him, motioning for him to roll down his window.

"Do what he says," Helen ordered while rolling down her own window.

Tyler obeyed.

Holding out his hand, the kid ordered, "Let me have it, please."

"Excuse me." Helen turned to the guard and smiled. "Excuse me?" She shaded her eyes from the early-morning sun. "I'm afraid he didn't understand you."

"Hand it over, please."

"Excuse me? Excuse me?" She finally got the guard's attention and he moved up to her window. "I need it for my work," she said. Reaching into her canvas bag, she produced a handful of papers. "I'm Dr. Helen Zimmerman, an archaeologist from America. A guest of your government." She thrust the papers toward him. "I need the camera for my work. He did not know. He did not understand."

The boy took the papers and with grave earnestness began studying each page. Daniel exchanged looks with his son, who slowly lowered the camera out of sight.

"We are going to Tell en-Nasbeh," Helen explained. "We are taking some videos of the ruins. For my work. To study later. Tell en-Nasbeh."

After an excruciating length of time the young man finally shoved the papers back through the window at her. "Go." He lowered his head to better see Tyler and ordered, "No photos of checkpoints. No pictures of military or bridges. Do you understand?"

Tyler nodded.

Helen turned up her grin. "Thank you, sir. Thank you very much."

The guard gave no response but motioned them forward with indifference while directing his attention to the next car.

As the Mercedes pulled away, Tyler teased, "Thank you, sir. Yes sir. Whatever you say, sir."

Rolling up her window, Helen replied, "This isn't some Hollywood movie, kiddo. They play for keeps here."

Tyler said nothing, pretending to ignore the admonition. But Daniel, thinking it best to show some manners, thanked her. She shrugged as they picked up speed. Eventually Daniel settled back into the tan leather seat and watched the passing countryside. It was mostly rolling fields of rock, grass, and weeds. Scattered here and there were small homes of rock with corrugated roofs. Even with the air-conditioning on, there was no missing the smell of diesel, dust, and hot asphalt, all mixed in with the summer-sweet smell of grass. Not far away he spotted a Bedouin camp with its makeshift tents of cloth and plastic tarp. A wizened old woman — she could have been forty; she could have been eighty — squatted beside an open fire, cooking as she waved off flies with a piece of cardboard. Nearby children played with the pieces of a rusting bicycle. And beyond them, down the hill, lay Ramallah, the closest city to Tell en-Nasbeh.

Daniel stole another look over at Helen. She certainly had strength; he'd give her that. For a woman to survive on her own in these parts took more than a little courage. And by the look of things, she not only survived; she was flourishing. Oh, she still had those Linda Grossman qualities he found so annoying — that independent assertiveness — not to mention a somewhat defensive shell. But now at least he was beginning to understand the need for those qualities. Just as importantly, he was beginning to appreciate the vulnerable human he saw underneath them.

Of course she didn't take very well the news that Nayra would be meeting them. But since Tyler had insisted upon calling Nayra with last night's information, and since Nayra had some relatives in the area who she said could help, and since Tyler had agreed to meet her at some restaurant ... well, what could be done? To Helen's frustration, not much.

Twenty-five minutes after the checkpoint, they pulled to a stop in front of a dilapidated restaurant on the outskirts of Ramallah.

"Are you sure this is the place?" Daniel asked.

"313 Nirim Road," Helen said, comparing the slip of paper in her hands with the number on the building.

From the open doorway a brown, crinkle-faced man emerged and approached the car. His clothes were as worn and tattered as the buildings that surrounded him. At first Daniel thought he might be a beggar, until he leaned down and called through the window, "Are you the pastor?"

"Uh, yes," Daniel said, fumbling with the door handle until he finally got it open.

The man broke into a cordial grin of uneven, rotting teeth. "My name is Abou Madani. I am the owner." He stretched out his hand. "Please, welcome."

"Thank you," Daniel said, shaking it.

"Did you see any troops?"

"Troops?" Daniel asked.

"Revenge for yesterday's bombing. There are rumors that — "

"There are no troops," Helen interrupted as she stepped out from her side of the car. "Everybody's a little tense but we saw no troops."

The owner looked at her, his eyes widening. He was no doubt struck by her beauty. And she was beautiful, Daniel thought. The way the morning sun backlit her hair, making it glow, the way it outlined her figure, her trim waist, her —

He scolded himself and glanced away.

But not the owner. "You are certain?" the man asked, continuing to stare. "About the troops?"

"As certain as one can be," Helen answered. "Where's the girl?"

"Inside. Please come. Come."

"We were supposed to meet her — "

"Yes, I know. Please come inside." He turned for the restaurant.

Helen followed, then Tyler, with Daniel bringing up the rear. They moved across the broken sidewalk and through the open doorway, which was void of any screen. No worry of flies, though — the room's thick smoke kept them away. As his eyes adjusted to the dimness, Daniel counted at least a dozen patrons. All men. Some sat at tables, eating; others stood, smoking cigarettes or sipping coffee. At the moment all had turned to stare at them. Well, not really at them — more likely at Helen. And instead of glancing away or dropping her eyes to the ground in submissive meekness, she looked right back at them, holding their stares until one by one they looked away.

Daniel smiled. She *was* a remarkable woman.

"This way, come," the owner said, motioning. "Come."

They passed a yellowed linoleum counter full of cut marks. On it lay plates of freshly sliced cucumbers, tomatoes, leeks, and bottles of various oils and sauces. At the end of the counter a shank of skewered lamb turned on a rotisserie. It was warmed by a single infrared bulb.

"There you are."

Daniel turned to see Nayra enter through a curtain of clicking beads.

"What's going on?" Helen asked. "Why are we here?"

Ignoring her question, Nayra turned to Tyler. "They brought him here about an hour ago. He's been waiting."

"Who's waiting?" Helen demanded.

Nayra frowned, motioning to the customers within listening distance.

"Who's waiting?" Helen repeated.

Nayra lowered her voice. "Tyler said you thought the . . ." — she glanced around, then continued — "he said you thought those two stones might be somewhere around here. That the local people might know something."

"I said there were rumors."

"Yes." Keeping her eyes on the patrons, she continued. "After Tyler phoned, I called friends in this area. They have friends. Friends of friends."

"And . . ."

"I think you will find what he has to be most interesting."

"What who has? Who is he?" Helen asked.

Without a word Nayra stepped aside, momentarily blocking Helen while motioning for Daniel to enter through the beads.

He hesitated.

"It is okay," Nayra insisted. "They are friends. It is okay."

Daniel turned to his son, who nodded. Then to Helen, who indicated it was his call. Steeling his resolve, he turned and entered the darkened room. Tyler and the owner followed. But when Helen tried to enter, Nayra remained in front of the woman, her small frame blocking Helen's larger one. "You must wait here."

"What?"

"Your presence is not welcome."

"What do you — "

"You are a Jew; you are not welcome."

The tension between them was palpable. And for a moment it seemed uncertain whether Helen would back down or not. Then reluctantly she agreed. But she would not leave the doorway. Apparently, she was going to stand right there and wait. Just she and the two dozen pair of eyes stealing peeks at her.

Inside, an old man greeted them. He sat on a rug and appeared even less conscious of dental hygiene than did the restaurant's owner. His mouth worked the end of a plastic tube that led to a *hookah* water pipe. The air was full of pungent, sweet smoke. Not far away two or three younger men stood, slouched in the shadows behind him.

He turned and spoke to Nayra. She nodded and translated. "Please, sit." She motioned Daniel toward the cushions in front of him.

"Tell him we will stand," Daniel said.

Nayra spoke to the old man in Arabic. He shrugged, then said something else.

"He would like you to come closer," Nayra said. "His eyes are no longer good, and he would like to see your face."

Daniel turned to Tyler, who nodded. He moved forward until he was directly under the light of a bare bulb that hung from the ceiling.

The man grinned broadly. *"Shukran, shukran."* Then he spoke something else.

"He would like to see the stone," Nayra said.

"Stone?"

"The Levi Stone."

Daniel kept his eyes on the old man's. Even in the shadows he could see the milky cataracts. "Tell him ..." — he cleared his throat — "tell him it is in good hands."

More Arabic was exchanged.

"Your hands?" Nayra asked.

"Perhaps."

The old man chuckled, then asked something else in Arabic.

Nayra translated. "He wants to know if you have had any dreams?"

Daniel tried not to stiffen. "We all dream."

The man grinned again, obviously enjoying the repartee. He answered and Nayra translated. "Yes, but how many of us dream of ..." — she turned back to the old man to confirm what she'd heard, then returned to Daniel — "how many of us dream of the face of God?"

Daniel felt the blood drain from his cheeks. The old man saw it and cackled softly. Apparently, he had his answer. Turning to his companions, he gave a curt order. One of the young men obeyed, producing a small box of olive wood inlaid with mother-of-pearl. Holding it with great care, he approached the old man. It was only then that Daniel noticed the rifle dangling from the boy's shoulder. As he stepped into the light, his two associates moved forward, making it clear that everything was being carefully observed and carefully protected.

The old man took the box into his knotted, arthritic hands. He spoke again and Nayra translated. "I too have had dreams, Pastor. The dream of a face. But unlike your dream, mine is the face of a — "

The explosion shook the room with such force that Daniel nearly lost his balance. He heard the old man cry out but his voice was lost in another explosion. And another.

"Rockets!" the owner's voice shouted. "Helicopter gunships!"

Adrenaline surged through Daniel as another explosion pounded the room, knocking him to his knees. The light was gone but he could hear the plaster and concrete falling around him, felt smaller chunks bouncing off his shoulders and head. Dust filled the room, making it nearly impossible to breathe.

"Outside!" the owner shouted and coughed. A back door was suddenly kicked open and blinding light stabbed Daniel's eyes. "Everybody outside!"

He staggered to his feet. To his left he saw the boy with the rifle helping the old man do the same. More explosions shattered the room. Pounding, deafening, throwing Daniel into Tyler. Somehow they kept their balance and stumbled toward the light. Coughing and gagging, they emerged into a narrow street, one end already blocked by smoke.

"This way!" one of the young men shouted, waving. "This way!" Everyone turned and started to follow. Everyone but Daniel.

"Dad!" Tyler yelled over his shoulder. "Come on!"

"Where is he!" Daniel shouted, straining to see through the dust. "Where is the old man?"

"What?"

"The old man!"

Tyler spotted him at the door. "Right there, behind you!"

He spun around to see the old man emerge into the light, clutching the wooden box, leaning heavily upon his young assistant. Daniel heard the rocket coming but had no time to cover his face before the apartment next door exploded. The concussion threw him backward, pelting his skin with rock and concrete as he landed hard on the ground. But he only remained a moment. Even as the debris rained around him, he scrambled to his feet. "Tyler!" he shouted. "Tyler!" He squinted through the billowing dust, choking, his throat on fire. "Tyler!"

"Here!" his son cried, coughing. "Over here!"

He turned to see Tyler staggering to his feet, helping Nayra to hers. The debris stopped falling and was replaced by the distant pop of automatic gunfire and panicked cries.

"He's hurt!" Nayra shouted. She motioned to the old man, who lay under his young assistant. She raced toward them and Tyler followed. But it wasn't the old man who was hurt. It was the aide. He did not move. And by the way his body was sprawled in the dirt, his neck grotesquely twisted, his eyes staring lifelessly, Daniel knew he would not move again.

The old man was struggling to crawl out from under him, shouting orders.

Nayra nodded and yelled to Tyler, "Get his gun! Get his gun!"

But Tyler had frozen. All he could do was stare at the young man. As far as Daniel knew, his son had never seen death before — except in movies or video games.

The gunfire grew closer.

Again the old man shouted and again Nayra translated. "Get the rifle!"

But Tyler could not move. With some effort Nayra pushed the aide aside and pulled the rifle off his shoulder. The movement shamed Tyler back into action. He reached for the old man and helped him to his feet.

"We must leave here!" Nayra shouted.

Tyler nodded and, allowing the old man to lean on him, started off in the only clear direction.

Daniel had just moved to join them when a soldier suddenly came into view. Another youngster. Younger than Tyler. He shouted something in Hebrew, an obvious order for them to stop. Daniel slowed but Tyler did not. Instead he turned and began hobbling in the opposite direction.

"Tyler!" Daniel yelled.

Again the soldier shouted.

"Tyler, stop!"

The soldier raised his rifle.

"Tyler!" Gripped with fear, Daniel started toward the soldier, trying to explain, trying to draw his attention.

But the soldier ignored him and took aim.

"No!" Daniel twirled to Tyler. "Tyler, no!" Then back to the soldier. "No!" He started running at him. "No! *No!*"

The soldier fired.

Daniel spun around just in time to see the old man go limp in Tyler's arms. But Tyler did not stop. In fear and panic he dragged the man faster.

"Tyler!"

The soldier aimed again.

Seeing no alternative, Daniel leaped between them, waving his arms, as a second shot was fired. Only it did not hit Tyler. Nor did it hit Daniel. Instead it was the young soldier who crumbled to the ground.

Confused, Daniel turned. He spotted Nayra lowering her rifle. She stared at it as if it were some strange creature as she tried to fathom what it had just done, what she had just done.

Three armed soldiers rounded the corner. They spotted their comrade, then Nayra, and immediately shouted, demanding that she drop the rifle. She held it at arm's length, like a poisonous snake, and released it. It clattered onto the road. The soldiers started toward her.

Suddenly a white Mercedes slid around the corner, accelerating, barreling down on them. Having no time to take aim, the soldiers realized it would be smarter to leap for their lives. They weren't wrong. The driver missed them by inches. The car fishtailed, avoiding the fallen soldier, then skidded to a stop directly beside Nayra.

"Get in!" a voice shouted.

Nayra stood paralyzed, still in shock.

The driver reached over and opened the passenger door. The sun's reflection off the windshield made it impossible to recognize the face, but Daniel knew the voice.

"Get in!"

Woodenly Nayra obeyed. She had barely entered before the tires spun furiously. The car slid to another stop between Daniel and Tyler.

"Hurry!" Helen shouted. "Get in! Get in!"

Daniel turned to help Tyler, who had kneeled down with the man. But the dark, widening circle in the old-timer's back, and the ashen look on Tyler's face, made it clear that his son had just witnessed his second death in as many minutes.

The soldiers behind them were scrambling to their feet, shouting, raising their rifles.

"Get in!" Helen yelled.

Daniel obeyed. But not Tyler. Not before the boy spotted the box near the old man's hand and tentatively reached for it.

"Get in!"

The first bullet sank into the Mercedes' left rear fender with a sickening thud. The second missed the car, sending up a cloud of dust inches from Tyler's feet. He did not have to be told again. He grabbed the box, leaped up, and raced to the car. More shots were fired as he tumbled into the backseat, as the Mercedes sped off, as he tried more than once to grab the back door until he finally slammed it shut.

Helen didn't say a word until they hit the main street. She took a hard left, accelerated, and raced from the city. When she finally spoke, she kept her attention divided between the road and the rearview mirror. "Well now, that could have gone better."

Daniel looked over his shoulder to see a rising pillar of gray and black smoke.

"What do we do now?" Tyler asked, his voice thin and shaky.

"They probably got a look at your faces."

No one disagreed.

"And they'll have no problem tracking me down with the car."

"So we turn ourselves in," Daniel concluded.

"We could do that," Helen agreed.

Daniel nodded. "Tell them that it was all an accident, a misunderstanding."

Helen added, "That we really didn't mean to be visiting members of the Hamas, that we really didn't mean to be fleeing arrest, that we really didn't mean to shoot down one of their soldiers in cold blood and nearly kill two others ... yeah, that could work."

"What else can we do?" Daniel asked.

She glanced at him in the mirror. "I've got another suggestion."

✳

"And did you find your stay in Israel enjoyable?"

"Yeah," Tyler said, forcing a grin at the airport official. "Way too short, though. But it was cool."

The official nodded. He was another kid about Tyler's age. "Perhaps you may come back another time."

"You bet," Tyler agreed. In an attempt to establish camaraderie, he added, "I mean, you got yourself some pretty hot babes here, if you know what I mean." It was supposed to assure the guy that he was one of them, that he could be trusted, but Tyler immediately recognized his mistake. He was trying too hard. More importantly, he knew the guy knew.

The officer looked at him a moment, neither smiling nor acknowledging the comment. Returning to the interview, he said, "Now, if you don't mind, I must ask you some of the same questions my colleague did a moment ago."

"Sure."

"That way we are certain we have covered everything. For your own safety, you understand."

"Got it." Tyler shifted his weight. He'd been standing in this airport security line for fifty minutes. First with one guy and now, by the look of things, he was going to do it all over again with this one. He tried his best to hide it but the stress was starting to take its toll.

"Where all did you visit?"

Tyler lied as easily as he had with the first official. "Just Jerusalem."

Earlier, in the car, Doc had made it clear that they were not to mention they'd been to the West Bank or that they had spoken with any of its citizens. "It would only raise suspicion," she had said, "waste precious time. And that, my friends, we have very little of."

"I thought you said you were Christian?" the young officer asked.

"You bet."

"And you did not go to Bethlehem or Galilee or any of the other religious sites?"

Tyler shrugged. "Wish I had." He motioned to his father, who stood in the next line, undergoing the same questions. "I mean, my dad's a pastor and everything but we just ran out of time."

"That is your father?" the official asked with some interest.

Pleased that he'd finally made a connection, Tyler pressed it further by calling over, "How you doing there, Dad?"

His father looked up. "Not bad. How about you?"

Tyler turned back to his officer and smiled. "How we doin'?"

The kid gave a slight nod.

"Not bad," Tyler called back.

When he turned to the officer, the guy was motioning to him with upturned palms. "May I?"

"Hm?" Realizing he wanted to search him, Tyler answered, "Oh, sure." He raised his arms and for the briefest moment thought of commenting about it being like a TV cop show. Fortunately, he had the good sense to restrain himself.

As the official patted him down, Tyler stole a look toward Nayra. She stood four lines over, undergoing a similar interview. Even from this distance she looked sullen and pale. The shooting had taken a lot out of her. She had remained silent during the trip to the hotel and then to the airport. But now as she answered the questions, she seemed to at least be holding her own. After Doc had secured tickets for the next flight out of Israel (to where, he'd already forgotten), she had warned them to avoid all contact with Nayra until they were on the plane. As an Arab, she would be under more suspicion, and the interrogations and searches she underwent would be more extensive.

"What is this?"

"Huh?"

"In your pocket; may I see it, please?"

Tyler went cold. "Oh, sure." He tried to appear casual as he reached into his jeans pocket and pulled out the Levi Stone. Back at the hotel, as they quickly packed, they had decided not to bring it in the aluminum briefcase; it would only draw attention.

The official took the stone into his hands. "It is jewelry?" he asked. "Some sort of gem?"

"I wish," Tyler said, pretending to sigh. "It's just a good-luck piece."

"It looks very old."

"It was my mother's. She passed it on to me before she died a few months back."

"Your mother, she has recently died?"

Tyler nodded, grateful to play the sympathy card. "Yeah, last spring. Still feels like yesterday, though, if you know what I mean."

"I am sorry."

"Yeah." Motioning to his dad, Tyler continued. "We kinda came here as a father-son thing — you know, to try and get over it."

"I understand." The official handed the stone back to him. "Do you mind if I go through your suitcases again? For your own safety, you understand."

"Sure. You gotta do what you gotta do," Tyler said, grinning just a little too hard. Trying to compensate, he added, "I mean, that's why they pay you the big bucks, right?"

The officer simply looked at him.

Tyler turned his grin up higher.

"Yes," the officer finally answered, returning to the suitcases, "that is why they pay me the big bucks."

✳

Ibrahim el-Magd opened the roof's door and started back down the stairway. He did not trust elevators, their cramped quarters, their confinement. And since he'd dismissed his bodyguards for some solitude upon the roof, he saw no reason for further risks.

It had been another long meeting of the Shura. Exacting questions asked, exacting answers given.

Of course it had begun with their usual impatience. How much longer must they wait? Were not the stones he'd already secured good enough? What assurance did they have that the others would even appear? It had taken great skill, but once again Ibrahim el-Magd had used his powers of influence to convince them to wait. Did they not have nearly two dozen brothers diligently searching the globe for the remaining stones? And every day were they not making greater and greater progress, coming closer and closer to success? The argument was powerful but this time even he had to make concessions. A fortnight. That is all they would give him. Just fourteen more days. If the remaining stones had not been secured within that time, he would agree to carry out the operation — regardless of whether or not they heard Allah's voice. Yet even that concession did not appease them all, including his brother-in-law. "Every day we wait is another day of risking discovery," Yussuf Fazil had complained. Yet fourteen days had been Ibrahim's concession, and fourteen days it would be.

Other details had also been covered, particularly the incubation and transportation of the virus. Detailed explanations were made as to how the dried smallpox, smuggled out of the Russian State Research Center of Virology and Biotechnology (better known as Vector), near Koltsovo, Novosibirsk, had been incubated and grown. Then they had carefully covered every detail of its transportation. Since the World Trade Center victory, airport security had increased many fold. Yet while the infidels were busy searching for box cutters and exploding tennis shoes, confiscating everything from fingernail files to chopsticks, they would pay little attention to canisters disguised as bottles of prepackaged fruit juice that each hero carried. Canisters which in reality contained billions upon billions of the viral particles.

And the nuclear briefcases? Again, much of the technology, not to mention the plutonium, had come courtesy of lax Russian security. Once obtained, the materials were smuggled in bits and pieces by cargo ships to their locations and assembled on site. The resulting weapons were not extremely sophisticated — "dirty bombs," they were called — but they would do the trick.

But afterward, after the detonation of the briefcases and the dispersion of the virus, what could they expect?

Sharif Abdu Massud, head of the manufacturing and distribution team, had pushed up his glasses and answered. Initially opposed to smallpox because of the inability to control the spread of the disease, he had originally planned to use anthrax. But after the anthrax scare in America and the mass manufacturing of ciprofloxacin and other antibiotics, they were forced to resort to the more communicable disease.

"The briefcases will be detonated as the sun sets over each city, giving the maximum amount of time to spread the virus before sunrise," Sharif Abdu Massud had explained.

"What will the people see? What will they smell?" Yussuf had asked.

"Nothing. Once the blast vaporizes the liquid, the particles floating in the air will be less than a micrometer across, nearly impossible to detect."

"And the effects?"

"From the smallpox, nothing at first. For two weeks the victims will silently spread the disease from one to another. During this time the virus is quietly replicating itself within each carrier's lymph cells. Only after ten to fourteen days will they begin experiencing headaches, backaches, vomiting, and fever. Those who go to their doctors will be diagnosed as having either the flu or, for those closer to the blast site, radiation sickness."

"When will the health officials know the truth?" young Mustafa Muhammad Dahab had inquired.

"Tests will be taken. The high white blood count will indicate some sort of viral infection but nothing definitive. A pale rash will begin to form — often on the face — which quickly turns to tiny blisters. Delirium will set in as the blisters turn to hard pustules. Only then will the officials realize what has happened. Only then will they begin quarantining and vaccinating the population. And by then it will be too late. The disease will have spread from many persons to many persons several times over."

"What is the final outcome?" Yussuf had asked.

"A third of those exposed will die. The survivors will be covered in hideous scars for the rest of their lives."

"The mark of Cain," Mustafa had suggested.

"And you are certain the governments will have no clue until the disease begins spreading?"

Sharif Abdu Massud had smiled. "That is the genius of the nuclear briefcases. Our enemy will focus upon that aspect of the attack. In his arrogance he will think that is our plan. He will have no idea that the briefcases are only a cloak. Yes, they will serve some purpose but they will serve more as a veil. A veil to disguise the true sword of Allah, whose vengeance will fall swiftly and terribly fourteen days later."

The men around the table had nodded. But Ibrahim had one more question. One he hoped was in the back of each man's mind. "And the death rate?" he asked. "What will be the final toll of those who die?"

"Much of that will depend upon the wind conditions, as well as how quickly the disease is diagnosed and those infected quarantined."

"I understand."

"There is also the matter of how quickly the people can be vaccinated."

"How many?" Ibrahim had repeated.

"I do not think it is an exaggeration to say that when all is finished, we are speaking of between one hundred to three hundred million fatalities."

The group had sat in absolute, stunned silence.

And it was that figure which lingered in Ibrahim's mind as he paced the roof of the building, as he eventually headed down the stairway to his waiting car. So much death, so much wrath. Still, it was Allah's way. He was a God of justice. Sin was sin and justice was justice. Once again Ibrahim thought of his dreams, of the face of Allah — that vengeful face covered in his enemy's blood. And there would be bloodshed, more than the world had ever seen.

Three hundred million. That is why the stones must be found. That is why they must hear his voice. To be sure. To confirm. But time was running out.

He thought of the young heroes he'd dined with earlier that week, who were now making their way across the globe to their assigned targets. Soon the canisters of smallpox would be strategically placed upwind of each city to assure its maximum distribution across the population. From the heroes his mind drifted to little Muhammad. He thought of him as he had a thousand times a day since his death, since the attack on their headquarters, since the obvious breach of security. And he thought again of his attacker. Someone had known. Someone in his inner circle had betrayed not only himself but his family.

He arrived at the door leading to the street. It moaned in protest as he pushed it open. The sun had just set, and the air smelled of jasmine and the spices of cooking meat as families prepared their suppers. The smell made him both hungry and nostalgic. He thought of his youth. He had been just a few years older than young Muhammad when he had stood before his father, proclaiming that he was committing all that he had and all that he would become to Allah. He remembered the delight upon his father's face. And he remembered the discipline, more diligent than most, as he pursued such a dream. Yet even at that, who would have thought? In such a few years, who would have thought that he'd be given such an awesome honor, such unfathomable responsibility?

"Ibrahim?"

He looked up to see Dalal standing at the door of his car. She appeared more lovely than ever. There was no doubt he found her attractive, but it was more than that. He also enjoyed her mind and her spirit. Such strength she had. Such peace. He knew the attraction was mutual. It had to be. Why else, when he glanced up, did he occasionally catch those deep, dark eyes looking away in embarrassment? They were captivating eyes, endless in their depth — inviting pools of refreshment amid his endless duties of leadership.

"Where is Yussuf Fazil?" he called. "Where is my brother-in-law?"

"He had to leave early. He said it was urgent. He has asked that I drive you."

Ibrahim stared. "You," he teased, "you are but a girl."

It was good-natured and he saw her eyes crinkle into a smile above the veil. He knew she enjoyed the barb. And he knew she had the spunk to return it.

"Ibrahim el-Magd, in spite of my youth, I am certain you will find both my wisdom and experience more than adequate."

He returned the smile. But she was not finished.

"Your brother-in-law suggested that I drive only as far as Tegal tonight."

"Because of your driving skills?" Ibrahim teased.

Once again her eyes crinkled. "No, because of the car. He does not entirely trust it. He asked a mechanic to examine it earlier. He will send a driver for us tomorrow." She motioned toward the car. "So for tonight I am afraid you have only my skills and my company to contend with." She held his eyes just a fraction longer than necessary — long enough to underline the deeper meaning and possibilities without compromising either her honor or her modesty.

Now Ibrahim el-Magd understood. His brother-in-law was an observant man. He had obviously sensed their attraction. And as was his way, he was again doing his best to accommodate Ibrahim with all possible comforts. Yes, they were still the best of friends. Despite his impatience Yussuf was a good man, a great man. Yet deep in his soul Ibrahim el-Magd knew this action was not correct. As much as he appreciated the gesture, he knew it was inappropriate for a man of his calling.

"Is there a problem?" Dalal asked.

Ibrahim hesitated. Why should there be a problem? Were they not in the middle of jihad? And were not such things acceptable, especially for leaders? Did not greater pressure call for greater pleasures? Besides, did not the Qur'an itself say a man could have up to four wives?

But even as the arguments surfaced, he knew they were false. Dalal was not a wife. Maybe in the future, maybe after Allah's wrath had been administered. But not now. Not in these most holy and sacred of times.

"Is there a problem?" Dalal repeated.

"There is no problem. I will wait to ride with Sheikh Habib or Mustafa. I will see to it that one of the secretaries rides with you."

"I do not understand."

"I apologize to you, Dalal. This is simply not the correct time."

Her eyes searched his a moment, trying to understand. Then she looked away. He had shamed her. It had not been his intention, nor Yussuf's, but it had been done. Without a word she slowly lowered herself into the driver's seat and shut the door, where she would wait. Ibrahim hurt for her. He could feel her embarrassment. But he knew his actions were correct. He heard the voices of the other men and looked as they emerged from the building. He glanced back at her as she turned the car's ignition.

The flash of light was blinding. The concussion from the explosion knocked him to the ground, sending a thousand pieces of glass and metal high into the air. For the briefest second he lost consciousness. When he awoke, debris was raining and clattering around him. But even as his mind cleared, even as the pieces fell and the men raced toward him, Ibrahim el-Magd knew that security had once again been breached. Even more importantly, he knew by whom. And it was that knowledge that broke his heart.

"Marseilles?" Daniel asked. "I've just spent twenty-one hundred dollars to go to Marseilles?"

"Twenty-eight hundred," Helen corrected. "You're paying for my flight, too."

Daniel sat back in the seat and slowly let out a sigh. They'd been in the air ten minutes, and with every passing minute he felt a little safer — and a little poorer.

"I told you it had to be the first flight out of there. Though if you wanted, we could have stuck around for a few weeks of Q and A with the government. Of course it might have taken a bit longer than that for your little friend over there."

Daniel looked across the aisle to Nayra, who sat flipping mechanically through the airline magazine. He doubted she was reading; she probably wasn't even seeing the pages. Beside her sat Tyler, pillow against the window, eyes closed and mouth starting to sag.

"You think she'll be okay?" Daniel asked.

"I don't know; I've never killed anybody before."

The words were harsh and Daniel gave her a look. Realizing she'd been too strident, she shrugged a type of apology. Reaching for a magazine, she fumbled with it slightly and self-consciously started to turn the pages. Yes, it was growing easier to see through her bluff and bluster and to appreciate whom he saw underneath.

He cleared his throat. "That was, uh . . . that was quite a sacrifice you made for her . . . for us."

"If there was any other way, I would have done it."

He looked at her, not at all convinced. "Will it be tough for you to get back in?" he asked. "To return to work?"

"Tougher than nails." She continued flipping the pages. "But I've chewed my fair share of nails."

Daniel nodded, once again feeling his admiration growing. "Marseilles . . . Isn't that, like, on the French Riviera?" he asked.

"Yup."

"Does that mean I have to buy a pair of Speedos?"

The phrase stopped her cold and she worked not to smile. Quickly recovering, she replied, "You'd be doing us all a favor if you didn't." Glancing at him, she added, "Trust me."

It was his turn to smile.

"There is one bit of good news, though," she said.

"What's that?"

"Marseilles isn't that far from Avignon."

"Avignon . . . the Palace of the Popes?"

She nodded. "I have a contact there we can meet."

"Haven't you done enough already?"

"I've done more than enough," she said, finally closing the magazine. "But since we're going to be there anyway . . ."

Daniel looked on, again surprised at the depth of this woman's selflessness.

The seat belt sign dinged and went off. Without a word she unbuckled, rose from her seat, and indicated that she needed to get by him into the aisle. Daniel unbuckled and half rose, allowing her to pass. Once in the aisle she reached up and unlatched the overhead bin. For the second time that day he noticed her figure, and for the second time that day he glanced away, admonishing himself.

She rummaged through one of the carry-ons for several moments until she finally found something. "Here we go," she said. Zipping up the bag, she shut the overhead compartment. In her hand was the small olive wood box the old man had been holding when he was shot.

Once again Daniel rose as she passed. This time, however, there was a jolt of turbulence, causing Helen to fall clumsily into him.

"Sorry," she apologized. Before she could recover, a much harder jolt sent them both tumbling into his seat. Well, he was in his seat; she was now sitting on his lap, from which she leaped up as if it were a hot stove. But she did so a little too fast and a little too hard, banging her head into the overhead console. She swore as she half spun, half fell into her own seat just as the seat belt sign dinged back on.

"Are you okay?" he asked.

"Yeah," she muttered, rubbing her head. "Sorry."

"About what?"

"My mouth."

"Don't worry about it," he chuckled. "I've heard worse." Suddenly the cabin seemed much warmer, and he reached up to turn on the AC above his seat.

"Stupid plane," she said, still rubbing her head. "Why do they turn off the stupid seat belt sign if there's still the stupid turbulence?"

"Don't worry about it," he repeated. "It could happen to anyone." However, he had his doubts.

She blew the hair out of her eyes and reached up to turn on her own AC.

Changing subjects, he motioned to the box in her hand. "So . . . did you have a chance to look inside?"

"Not yet." She handed it to him. "Thought I'd save you the honors."

He stared at it. It was half the size of a cigar box and just as deep. In the front was a rusting metal latch. Carefully he unhooked it. Then slowly, cautiously, he opened the lid. Inside was yellowed paper, thick and coarse, like that used for watercolor. But it served only as a wrapper and padding.

He pulled the contents from the box. Helen leaned closer. He began unwrapping it. There were pencil markings on the inside of the paper, some sort of sketch. But he'd investigate that later. Right now there was something more important to look at. He pulled the last of the paper aside to reveal . . .

"It's another stone," Helen said. "Like the Levi Stone."

Not quite. Daniel could already see the difference. Though it was the same size as his stone and about the same weight, the color was different. The Levi Stone was a dark, opaque green. This was also green but much more transparent. Turning it over, he saw another difference. Like the Levi Stone, this one also had engraving upon it. It was nearly worn off and as far as he could tell, it was also in Hebrew. But the letters were different.

"Can you make out what it says?" he asked.

She leaned closer, then reached out to take it in her hands for a better look. While she examined it, Daniel turned to the wrapping paper and began straightening it on his lap.

"Benjamin," she finally said.

He looked to her. "What?"

Carefully tracing the inscription with her finger, she said, "It's the name Benjamin."

He stared at it. "That's another one of the twelve tribes of Israel."

She nodded.

"Do you think it's another stone? From the high priest's breastplate?"

"Could be."

The two sat without talking. For how long Daniel wasn't certain. It was only when Helen glanced at the paper on his lap that they continued. "What do you have there?" she asked.

"I'm not sure." He resumed straightening it. "It looks like some sort of drawing."

"It's a face," she observed. "A sketch of someone's face."

Daniel felt himself growing cold. She was right, of course. But it wasn't just any face. He noticed his hands beginning to tremble.

"Daniel . . . are you all right?"

He nodded but did not speak. He finished smoothing the paper. There it was — cut, bleeding, swollen from beatings, twisted in agony . . . a sketch identical to the face Jill had described in her dream . . . identical to the one he'd seen atop Mount Sinai.

part
three

chapter seven

"So this was where the big fire broke out?" Tyler asked, looking through his camera's viewfinder.

Daniel glanced at the tour book. "That's what it says. 'The Hall of Consistory, 1413.' This is where the pope would hold audience."

"So the pope is sitting here with the Urim and Thummim — "

"If his predecessor, Clement VI, actually received it."

"Right. So he's sitting in this room with the Urim and Thummim, and some guy comes in, presents him with the other stones from the breastplate, and — poof! — big-time fire."

"That's one theory."

Tyler continued. "Bringing them all together in this one room created some sort of holy critical mass . . . like the stuff you read to us back at Mount Sinai."

"Critical mass?" Nayra asked.

Although no expert in nuclear physics, Tyler was grateful to share his expertise. "Critical mass is what happens when you bring too much radioactive material together in one place. If you're not careful, it's nuclear fusion time."

"Like what you did to Hiroshima and Nagasaki?" Nayra asked.

"Uh . . . well, yeah, I guess." He stole a peek at her from the viewfinder. She was getting her spunk back and for the most part he was grateful. For the most part. They'd been in the Provence region of France two days now, staying in Nimes — as in the City de Nimes, as in "de nim," as in the place they invented denim, the cloth to make blue jeans. Fortunately for Tyler, it had more going for it than that bit of historical trivia. Such as a giant, multilevel Roman aqueduct and a nineteen-hundred-year-old amphitheater where gladiators fought. Then there were the incredible water gardens, acres and acres of water gardens. What a great place for taking long evening strolls to help Nayra overcome her depression — and for falling in love. He hated to admit it but facts were facts. He didn't know what she thought of him — not much, he supposed — but there was something about her focus, her iron resolve, her belief in absolutes, that drew him like a magnet. He'd give anything to have that type of strength, that type of faith.

Doc had hooked up with her friend, Jean Mark Something-or-Other, who had found them a pretty cheap pension. He was a good-looking French guy she was obviously attracted to — though it seemed her attraction was a lot stronger whenever the two of them got around Daniel. Jean Mark had offered to take the day off and drive them to Avignon, the ancient walled city that housed the Palace of the Popes. They'd left early that morning, passing through miles upon miles of orchards and fields, which were divided every few hundred yards by a row of poplars. Then there were the sunflowers, miles and miles of sunflowers. They even passed the city where Vincent van Gogh had lived and painted.

Knowing Daniel was a pastor, Jean Mark had thought it would be interesting to share some of the area's religious history — such as the one or two million people who were killed a few centuries back for being "book owners," folks caught in the sinister act of owning their own Bible. Apparently, the religious establishment wasn't too pleased about just any ol' person reading God's Word, so they started burning them at the stake. They usually used the victim's own Bible to fuel the flames — but not before forcing them to watch their children being tortured by dunking them upside down into burning chimneys. Nice guys. All part of the religious establishment, doing it all in the name of religion.

Religion. That's all his dad and Nayra seemed to care about. Not that Tyler begrudged their believing; as admitted, he'd do anything to have their unshakable resolve — anything but be religious. Unfortunately, there seemed to be little relief from the subject, especially here inside the Palace of the Popes. It was barely noon and already one vaulted ceiling had started to look like another, as did the hundreds of faded paintings, frescoes, and tapestries, not to mention all the gaudy statues and gaudier altars.

Doc and Jean Mark had the good sense to wait for them down in the courtyard, where they sipped espresso and caught up on old times. But not Dad, Nayra, or himself. No sir, the three of them were examining everything. And for Tyler, examining meant videotaping. It was difficult to explain, but life seemed more accessible when seen through a viewfinder. It was easier to break down and get ahold of.

They moved through the halls and eventually entered St. John's Chapel, where the artist Matteo Giovanetti had painted religious scenes on the walls and ceiling. More from habit than desire, Tyler raised his camera and once again began to tape.

"Pretty amazing, isn't it?" Daniel said.

"What's that?"

"All these rooms, all this art, all this opulence . . . and for what?" There was no missing the sadness in his voice. "I mean, honestly, did any of this stuff draw the people one inch closer to God?"

Tyler turned the camera on his father. "What do you mean?"

"I mean all of this . . . these statues and altars and gold and paintings. This isn't what God is about."

"Go on," Tyler encouraged. He watched his father rub his forehead, struggling to find the words.

"Think of it, Ty. You got this Giovanetti fellow creating all these gorgeous paintings, making everything nice and pretty for the religious aristocracy, while about the same time, just a few hundred yards from here, out in the streets, people are dropping like flies from the black plague."

"Religion at its finest," Tyler said.

"What's that?"

He zoomed tighter on his father's face. "Couldn't you say the same thing about your own church?"

Daniel frowned. "What do you mean?"

"How's this any different from your cushy theater seats or your big-screen projectors or your plush carpeting?"

"I'm not sure I follow."

But he did follow; Tyler could see it through the viewfinder. "Religion is religion, Dad. It doesn't matter how you disguise it. It's all about guys in charge wanting to stay in charge. Get your little God machine built, stay as comfortable as possible, keep it running as long as possible."

"Son, I don't think that's entirely — "

"I am afraid he has a point," Nayra agreed. Tyler turned to bring her into a close-up. "Christianity is full of people killing and torturing others so they can stay in power. You heard what Jean Mark said in the car about those poor people who simply wanted to own a Bible. And what about the Inquisition or the Crusades or the — "

"Whoa, wait a minute," Tyler said, zooming out to include both of them in his shot. "What makes Islam any better than Christianity? What about the millions the Muslims have killed, the people they're killing today? What about the wackos who bombed the embassies, who destroyed the World Trade Center, who are blowing themselves up in suicide — "

"That is a fringe minority."

"Is it? What about the million you wiped out in Turkey, or the Christians you wiped out during the Middle Ages, or — "

"We were defending truth."

"Whose truth?" Things had heated up. Tyler didn't want to offend Nayra, particularly given the ground they'd gained the last few days, but if she could dish it out, she ought to be able to take it. "Seems to me, God is big enough to protect his own truth, don't you think?"

"Certainly," Daniel agreed, "but we have a responsibility to the people — "

"The people?" Tyler almost laughed. "Religion doesn't care about people. Protestants, Catholics, Muslims — it's all the same. All religion cares about is being right and being in charge."

"Tyler — "

"Being in charge and making sure everyone who disagrees is either converted or destroyed." The outburst surprised Tyler almost as much as it did the other two. "Anyway ..." — he backtracked to soften the blow, particularly for Nayra — "that's *my* version of the truth." He glanced up, giving them a wry little smile to assure them he wasn't taking himself too seriously, then returned to the camera, bracing for a rebuttal. Fortunately, they were interrupted before it came.

"There you guys are."

He looked up to see Doc and Jean Mark approach, holding hands, of all things. He threw a glance to his dad, who did his best not to notice.

"Sorry we're so slow ...," Daniel said.

"That's all right." Doc smiled. "I figured Video Boy here was covering every square inch of the place."

"You've got that right," Daniel said, chuckling.

"With commentary," Nayra added under her breath.

"Anyway, we're in luck. I was telling Jean Mark the stories about the gypsies being given the Urim and Thummim, and he says they're meeting in Les Saintes Maries for their annual pilgrimage."

"Their what?" Tyler asked.

Jean Mark explained. "It is a three-day festival where the gypsies, they come from all around the world to celebrate. It is on the coast, not far from here."

Doc nodded. "What better place to track down all the rumors than from there?"

"But we must hurry," Jean Mark added. "Particularly if we want to see the taking down of the reliquaries."

"The what?" Daniel asked.

"It is the high point of the festival. It is where they take down the ancient bones of the sister saints, then carry their statues out to sea. It is a marvelous ceremony you will not wish to miss. But come, we must hurry."

With that he turned, guiding Doc through the crowd with a hand in the small of her back. It was a thoughtful gesture, impossible for his dad to miss. And for the briefest second Tyler thought of trying it with Nayra ... until he realized the need to keep both hands operational and unbroken.

"It is true! By all that is pure and holy, it is true! I do not know where he is. I swear!"

Ibrahim el-Magd let out a weary sigh. Slowly he walked across the large blue and green tiles of the living room to sit beside his sister. As he lowered himself onto the sofa and gathered his robes, he noted her pulling away from him. The fear made him sad. Though it would make his task easier, it still grieved him. Was there anything Allah would not ask of him? Still, it had to be done. "You were never good at telling falsehoods, my little Dunya. Not even as a child."

"Ibrahim, I swear to you, I do not—"

He held up a finger. "Please, no more lies."

"I am telling you the truth. I am —"

"No more lies!" The outburst echoed against the plastered walls and small domed ceiling, forcing Dunya into silence. In the next room the baby began to cry. Hearing her, Dunya rose to her feet.

"Sit."

"But she is —"

"Sit!"

Slowly, fearfully, Dunya sat. She was a small woman in her early twenties, the youngest of his eight sisters.

Regaining his composure, Ibrahim continued. "Your child, she is well?"

"Yes, she is fine."

The baby continued crying.

Ibrahim cocked his head. "I am not so sure. Her cries, they sound . . . they do not sound so healthy."

His sister fidgeted. "She is fine; she just needs —"

Ibrahim turned to one of his two bodyguards. "Does she sound well to you?" The young man did not understand. Ibrahim rephrased the question. "She does not sound so well, does she?"

Taking his cue, the guard shook his head.

The baby continued to cry.

Again Dunya started to rise. "She just needs me to go in and —"

He held up his finger and she came to a stop. He rose from the sofa. "Perhaps she should see a doctor."

Immediately Dunya was at his side. "She does not need a doctor."

"I would not be so certain. Surely Yussuf would expect your brother to look after his family while he is away. It is the proper thing to do." He paused as the baby continued to bawl.

"What are you saying?"

He could hear the trembling in her voice. Good. She was beginning to understand.

"I know a good doctor. At the hospital in Khartoum."

"Ibrahim —"

"I know it is very far away, several days' journey from here. But I assure you, you could make the trip and visit her from time to time."

"What are you — "

He turned to the guard and ordered, "Bring the child."

"No!" Dunya started toward the door but was blocked by the second guard. "No!" Spinning back to Ibrahim, she cried, "Why are you doing this to me! Why?"

"I am only looking out for your interests."

"Why?"

"Since your husband is away, since we do not know where he is, it is my duty to look after my baby niece."

The guard entered, holding the baby, who was crying much more loudly.

"Suda!" Dunya started for her child and again was blocked. "Suda!" She began to cry. Not looking at him, she pleaded, "Please, Ibrahim, please do not take my baby." She started choking on the words — "Please ... please ..." — until she was overcome by tears.

Quietly he approached and stood by her side.

"Please, Ibrahim ... please ..."

Tenderly he stretched out his hand to her.

Again she pulled back. "Please ... not my baby ..."

He continued reaching out, gently touching her shoulder, persisting, until finally she allowed him to pull her into an embrace.

"Please ... she is all I have left ... you do not understand ..."

"Shh," he whispered. "I understand, I understand."

"... please ..."

He felt her body trembling against his chest. He allowed another moment to pass before he spoke. "I do not wish to take your baby. Believe me. She may not have to leave. But unless I talk to your husband ..."

"I promised, I promised ..."

"That is a good thing, to protect your husband. A very good thing. And that is why I must speak to him. To protect him, to warn him."

She continued to weep against him. The baby continued to cry.

"Tell me, Dunya ... where is your husband? Where is Yussuf Fazil, my brother-in-law?"

She sniffed, then spoke into his chest. "He said I was to tell no one."

"Of course. I understand. But I am family. I am your brother."

She nodded. "Yes, but — "

"Tell me." He spoke delicately, tenderly, as a father to a little child. "Tell me where he is."

She hesitated.

"Tell me, Dunya." He lifted her chin to face him. Her eyes were red and swollen. "Tell me, little sister. Tell me where my brother is."

Her eyes searched his, looking for the honesty, the sincerity.

"Tell me."

At last the answer came. A whisper, barely audible over the baby's cries. "Cairo."

"Cairo, you say?"

She nodded.

"To see his first wife?"

"I do not — "

"To see his first wife?"

She nodded. "There was an incident with his firstborn in Jerusalem."

"With Nayra?" Concern filled his mind. "Is she all right?"

"She shot a Jew. A soldier. She has fled the country."

The news surprised him. Little Bird — his Little Bird had shot a Jew? "Where?" he asked. "Where has she gone?"

Dunya shook her head.

Ibrahim grew more insistent. "Where!"

"I did not hear; he did not say."

He looked up to the soldier with the crying baby, then motioned for him to start for the door.

Spotting the move, Dunya cried, "I swear it, Ibrahim!" She grabbed the folds of his galabiya. "Please, I do not know! I swear, I do not know, I do not know, I ... do not ..." Once again her words were swallowed in tears. And as Ibrahim watched, he knew she was telling the truth.

"It is okay," he said. He took her hands and held them. "I believe you." He motioned for the guard to approach and hand her the baby. He obeyed.

Greedily she took the child into her arms and immediately the baby began to quiet.

"There," Ibrahim said gently. "See, she is better already."

Adjusting the blanket, Dunya kissed the baby again and again. Then she turned to Ibrahim, sobbing. "Thank you ... thank you ..."

"Of course," he said, smiling. "You are my sister." He bent down and gently kissed her on the forehead. "It is late. You two should return to bed and rest."

She nodded.

"Go now."

Dunya turned and started for the room as Ibrahim watched, his mind racing. Time was so short and now this. He understood Yussuf fleeing the country. After the failed assassination he would be a fool to remain. And the escape to Cairo made sense. But what of this news of Nayra? Had her father divulged their deeper plans? Warned her of his failed treachery? What of the stone? Had she stolen it from the pastor? Found others? Taken them and fled to also become a traitor? So many questions and so little time for answers. But by the grace of Allah they would be answered. One at a time. But first there was the matter of Yussuf Fazil. After that, his daughter . . .

Pastor Daniel Lawson stood knee-deep in the Mediterranean Sea, unsure what to think. All around him the crowd clapped and cheered in the late-afternoon sun as the replica of a boat with two wooden statues standing in it was carried into the water. Statues of two saints — Mary-Jacobe and Mary Salome, the supposed sisters of Mary, the mother of Jesus. Earlier he had watched a large wooden box containing their bones being lowered from the church's balcony — a church crammed with these same people praying, lighting candles, and weeping.

So much feeling here. So much superstition mixed with sincere reverence. Was it emotional? Yes. Did it make him nervous? You bet. He couldn't help thinking how well Charlie Rue, from his own church, would fit in here. All mystical and feelings. It was as if he were surrounded by a thousand Charlie Rues, singing, dancing, and clapping. Who cared if their theology was a shambles, as long as they felt something, as long as their emotions were whipped up?

Yet there was another part of him that envied what he saw . . . that was jealous of their joy. It was a joy he often preached about, a joy he'd read of in the Scriptures, but it was a joy that, even before Jill's death, he seemed to be experiencing less and less of. His had become a faith of theory, a faith simply of words. And that's definitely not what he saw here. Here, in the small coastal city of Saintes Maries de la Mer, amid the salty spray, the sticky wet sand, and the sweating throng, there was another type of faith — a faith of raw, unfettered humanity, a faith that celebrated both life and its Creator.

Yes, their theology was wrong; there was no doubt about it. And yet ... and yet ... *"Yet I hold this against you: You have forsaken your first love."* The words from Revelation bubbled up in his mind as they had a hundred times since he'd spoken them in church. But surely they didn't apply here ... did they?

"Hey, Preacher Man."

He turned to see Helen sloshing through the water toward him. She'd changed to a longer dress out of reverence for the occasion ... though the purpose was somewhat defeated by the way the gauzy material clung to her legs as she moved through the water.

"So what do you think?"

He glanced around. "I think they're one happy crowd."

"I think you're right," she agreed.

"And you say they're all gypsies?"

Helen nodded. "According to Jean Mark. They come from all over the world to celebrate the landing of the two sisters from the Holy Land."

"Is there any truth to the story?"

She shrugged. "Who knows?"

The crowd had started singing again. He didn't recognize the song, but it was upbeat and he did recognize some of the words — *Jesus ... Gloria ... Alleluia ...,* all in a hodgepodge of European accents. He looked out across the people, who stretched a hundred yards up and down the beach. All worshiping in unashamed and unrestrained joy.

"You look good in a smile."

He turned to her. "Pardon me?"

"It's the first time I've really seen you enjoy yourself."

His grin broadened. "It must be contagious."

She nodded and looked out across the crowd. After a moment, a little more quietly she added, "It must be hard ..." She hesitated. Keeping her gaze averted, she continued. "Losing someone, I mean ... After all those years."

He glanced down at the water. If she only knew. Because he hadn't just lost his wife; he'd lost everything he believed in. Not about God or Christ. No, that would never change. But what he believed about his belief. Something was happening. He couldn't put his finger on it, but — *"You'll hear his voice, Danny ... You'll hear his voice and you'll love him"* — something was happening.

Then of course there was Tyler's accusation. *"All religion cares about is being in charge."* In one sense he had a point. Daniel wasn't sure when it had happened, but somehow it had crept in, this greater concern for maintaining the machine than for serving the people. And if that was true, then how did that make him any different from the Pharisees or the Sadducees? *"It's what nailed Jesus to the cross,"* Tyler had said. *"Not the Romans. Not the Jews. Religion."* If Daniel had lived back then and Jesus had threatened his machine, what would have prevented him from standing in line to drive the nails?

And Helen. Two weeks ago he would have written her off as some atheistic feminist. Oh sure, he would have been civil, but as far as thinking of her as an actual human being or even a friend? That would never have happened. Until now ...

He glanced up and saw she was staring at him. He coughed slightly, trying to remember the thread of the conversation. "So where is ... where's Jean Mark?"

"He's working out the details."

"Details?"

"I think he's found us a contact."

Daniel raised an eyebrow.

"Some gypsy king. But he's suspicious — as nervous about meeting you as you should be about meeting him. Jean Mark is trying to negotiate a safe location for tonight, someplace where everyone will feel comfortable."

"You think it could be dangerous?"

"It *will* be dangerous," she said. "Where are the kids?"

"Sight-seeing. We're meeting up at the café." He motioned toward a building next to the beach. "About five o'clock."

Helen glanced at her watch. "Good. Jean Mark should have his answer by then. Let's all meet there at five." With that she turned and started back through the water.

"Helen ... Helen?"

145

She stopped and turned to him.

"Thanks. For what you're doing, I mean. I'm ... grateful."

She hesitated a moment, then nodded. Without waiting for a response, she turned and continued walking.

Daniel watched until she had completely disappeared into the singing crowd.

✳

No matter how hard he tried to put aside his prejudices, Daniel found Guido, the gypsy king, anything but trustworthy. Maybe it was because they were eating at a marble table, surrounded by marble columns, beside a marble pool and a marble spa ... and when asked what he did for a living, the man simply shrugged and said, "My family, they used to be horse traders." Not that Daniel expected him to be living in a gypsy wagon and traveling in a caravan. But this?

Then there was his exhausting personality. The scrappy old-timer — Daniel guessed he was in his seventies — was "on" every moment of every second, a bundle of energy barely pausing to take a breath. It was as if all the emotion Daniel had experienced on the beach was compressed into this one wiry bundle of humanity. He went by the name of Guido Sanchez ... but in Daniel's part of the world he could just as well have been known as Charlie Rue.

Jean Mark had tried to find a more neutral location, but the gypsy king had been insistent. The meeting was to be at his place or no place at all. Neither Helen nor Jean Mark liked the idea, but they left the final decision with Daniel. And after careful consideration he decided to go. Of course he'd tried to convince Tyler and Nayra to stay behind, but they would have none of it. Nor for that matter would Helen and Jean Mark. So now they all sat about the marble dinner table near the marble pool, entirely at Guido's mercy.

At the moment the old man was working his charms on Helen. "We too know what it was like to suffer under the hands of the Nazis." With his mouth already at overflow capacity, he took another bite of stew and continued. "'Irredeemable criminals,' that's what he called us, with five hundred thousand — you can check the figures if you like — with five hundred thousand of us sacrificed in Dachau, Auschwitz, Buchenwald, Birkenau." Turning back to Daniel, he motioned broadly. "Please, eat, eat."

Daniel looked down at the dish before him. He'd already had a try at something called *escoude,* a pork belly and bean concoction. But this meat in front of him was an entirely different matter.

"You have never had barbecued hedgehog?" Guido asked, grinning, as he stabbed another piece with his fork and shoved it into his mouth.

"Hedgehog?" Tyler asked with concern.

"Yes, an animal similar to but smaller than your American porcupine."

Daniel looked back at the plate, his appetite not increasing.

"As you no doubt imagine, it can be most difficult to remove the spines from the creature."

"Yes," Daniel said, nodding, while making a quick double check to ensure they'd succeeded at the task.

"So before barbecuing it, we take a bicycle pump and inflate the creature." Turning to the others, he said, "No, no, it is true. Just like a bicycle tire, we pump him up — kwoosh, kwoosh, kwoosh." As he spoke, he inflated himself, puffing out his cheeks and expanding his chest larger and larger. "And then, just before the animal explodes" — he performed a flicking, shaving motion with his hands — "zip, zip, zip, zip, we remove all of his spines. Just so. Trust me, it is actually very easy, yes it is. Very easy."

"I see," Daniel said, forcing a smile.

"Of course the trick is not to overinflate the animal, or — Kaboom! Splish! — hedgehog all over the room. Quite the mess, as you can imagine."

Daniel's smile wilted slightly.

"Joke!" Guido burst out laughing, wiping orange-colored grease from the corners of his mouth. "I tell you a joke!"

Daniel relaxed slightly. "So what is it really?" he asked, scooping the meat onto his fork with a piece of bread. "I'm guessing rabbit?"

Guido looked up from his plate. "Oh no, it is hedgehog. The explosion, that is the joke. Kaboom! Splish!" He laughed again.

"Ah ..." Once again Daniel's appetite waned.

But not Guido's energy. "So, you two" — he motioned toward Tyler and Nayra — "you are engaged?"

They looked up, startled. Nayra frowned. "No, not at all."

"You are certain?"

"Yes," Tyler assured him, "we are certain."

"Hm . . . I am not usually wrong about such things." He tapped the center of his forehead with his index finger. "Such things I usually see. Perhaps it is true, but for later."

"We are simply good friends on holiday," Nayra said.

"Ah." Guido laughed, opening his mouth wide enough for them to see both his food and part of his gold bridgework. "Well, be careful, you two. Many babies come from such friendship." He gave a friendly wink and without missing a beat turned to Daniel. "And you three," he said, motioning to include Helen and Jean Mark. "Which of you three are just good friends?"

Helen's reply was cordial but cool. "We are simply colleagues."

"Of course, good friends and simply colleagues . . . all out on holiday. Who just happen to be looking for two very important stones."

Daniel felt a sense of relief. It had been ninety minutes of non-stop "entertainment," and he was beginning to fear they might never get to the point. Now at last it had arrived. He adjusted his position in the chair and answered, "Actually, it's a bit more complicated than that."

"It always is," Guido said, chuckling. "It always is. So, do you have them with you?"

"Them?" Daniel asked.

"Your two stones from the breastplate? The Levi and Benjamin Stones?"

"Who told you we had those?"

Jean Mark spoke up. "It was the only way he would see you."

Daniel nodded and turned to Guido. "No, they are safe and secure, under lock and key."

"You did not feel it was safe to bring them here, into the gypsy king's home?"

"No," Helen replied.

He turned to her and grinned. "A wise choice, my friends, a very wise choice."

"Papa . . . ," a voice called from the shadows of the doorway. "Are you ready for café?" She was a slender woman in her thirties. Dark skin like her father, and long raven hair. For the briefest second Daniel caught the profile of her face. Although not pretty, she had a classic nobility . . . except for her nose. It was severely misshapen.

"No, child, not tonight. Tomorrow will be an early morning and I will need my rest."

The woman nodded and disappeared into the house.

Turning back to the group, Guido stated, "She was pretty once . . . until the accident."

"Accident?" Helen asked.

Guido nodded and leaned toward her. "My daughter, she was caught in the act of adultery. Before divorcing her, the husband had only one request." He gave a slicing motion to his nostril.

Helen recoiled.

The gypsy king shrugged. "Being a man of justice, how could I deny him? Unfortunately, her lover, he did not fare nearly so well."

The group exchanged glances but no one ventured to speak. Guido seemed disappointed. He turned back to Daniel. "So you see, Pastor, despite the rumors we are a moral people. And we can be trusted."

Daniel nodded, searching for the correct response.

Not Tyler. He leaped right in. "Is that why the pope chose to give you guys the Urim and Thummim — because you could be trusted?"

Guido looked at him, then at Helen, then at Daniel. "I see you have done your research."

"It's no great secret," Helen said. "The rumors have been around for centuries."

"Is it true?" Tyler asked.

Ignoring him, the gypsy king turned back to Daniel. "As a man of God, as one Christian to another, I have your word that you possess the stones of Levi and Benjamin?"

Daniel held his look a moment. He did not trust Guido but he had no reason to lie. "Yes."

"Then be very careful, my friend." Guido lowered his voice. "There are people not nearly as moral as you or I. People who would do anything to get their hands on them."

"You're speaking from experience?" Helen asked.

"Yes. More than once. In the past several months notorious people" — he looked at Nayra — "some of your faith, some not, they have threatened me, they have nearly taken my life." He motioned to the three large men lurking around the edges of the patio. "That is why my nephews . . . why they are meeting with us."

Daniel glanced at them and nodded, still not feeling all that secure.

"And not just me," he continued. "The same is true with my father and the Nazis, his father and the Russians, and then Napoleon ... and the list, it goes on."

"Why?" Helen asked. "Why was it so important to them?"

Guido shrugged. "Why is it important to you?"

She gave no answer.

He turned back to Nayra. "I was able to persuade them that such stories were rumors with no substance. But you ..." — he looked at Daniel — "I am not so certain I can convince you."

Daniel frowned, not understanding.

Guido let the silence hang.

Finally Daniel cleared his throat. "I'm sorry, I don't — "

"Meet me here at five o'clock tomorrow morning. We will take my van."

"Why? Where are we going?" Helen asked.

Ignoring her, Guido leaned toward Tyler. "You ... have you had experience diving?"

"Me?"

"In the sea, with scuba gear?"

"Well, no, not really, but I can learn. I mean, I can — "

"You are a strong swimmer?"

"Yes."

"Good, good."

"Where are we going?" Helen repeated.

"The Calanques."

"The Calanques," Jean Mark replied, "they are a hundred kilometers from here."

"More than that," Guido said. "And another hour of hiking once we arrive."

"Is that where the stones are?" Helen asked.

Looking back at the group, he repeated, "Five o'clock." Rising from the table, he added, "Now, if you will excuse me. I am an old man; I will need my rest."

"Wait," Helen persisted. "Are you saying the Calanques are where the Urim and Thummim are?"

He said nothing but turned and started for the house.

Helen grew insistent. "You expect us to travel all the way to the Calanques with you? What assurance do we have that you are telling the truth, that this isn't some sort of trick?"

Guido stopped and turned. "None. You, my dear woman, have absolutely no assurance. But you ..." — he looked toward Daniel — "you have the assurance."

Daniel frowned. "What do you mean?"

"Christian to Christian, you have my word."

Daniel was unable to hide his skepticism.

Spotting it, Guido added, "And you have your dreams."

A chill crept over Daniel. "I don't understand."

Guido turned and resumed his exit. "I think you do."

Daniel persisted. "No, I don't. And you, how do you know you can trust us?"

The old man paused and turned. "Because I know you, Pastor ..." Once again he tapped the center of his forehead with his index finger. Then he pointed it directly at Daniel. "And you will know me."

Silence filled the room.

Turning to the others one last time, he concluded. "Good night, my just friends and simply colleagues. I will see you in the morning." He bowed graciously, then turned and left the room.

chapter eight

It was time to stop. Enough was enough.

Daniel Lawson rolled onto his back and stared up at the cracks in the plaster ceiling above his bed. It was a little after two in the morning. Light filtered into their tiny French pension from a nearby street lamp. Except for a barking dog in the distance, all he could hear was Tyler's deep, rhythmic breathing. The same breathing he'd been hearing for the last several hours as he prayed and wrestled with the decision.

What was he thinking, heading off like some Bilbo Baggins, traversing the globe in search of magical trinkets? He was a pastor, for crying out loud, a teacher of God's Word, who —

"If I can't hear his voice, I am no longer qualified to teach his Word."

The phrase startled him, though he recognized it immediately. It came from his last address, his farewell sermon. Somewhat troubled, he pushed it from his mind and returned to his thoughts.

The meeting with Guido the gypsy king had been unsettling enough by itself. Then there was the matter of these others, these ruthless men who were supposedly seeking the very same stones. Not only was he being a fool, now he was endangering everyone's life in the process. And let's not overlook that at least one of their party was currently wanted for murder by the Israeli government. And now he'd agreed to go on some diving trip with a nutcase?

What *was* he thinking? No, enough was enough. It was time to stop. It was time to end this little field trip through insanity and —

"You will hear his voice, Danny, and you'll love him."

No. He closed his eyes against the memory. *I love him now!*

"You love serving him ... "

You're wrong!

"You used to love like that, Danny ... but that was a long time ago."

No, I ...

"Yet I hold this against you: You have forsaken your first love."

No!

"Repent and do the things you did at first."

No! No!

"You have forsaken your first love."

No!

And so the wrestling match resumed—Daniel's clear-cut rationale against ... against ... well, he wasn't quite sure what it was against. Nor was he sure at what time he finally drifted off to sleep. But it wasn't a restful sleep. It gave him no peace. Because with his sleep came the dream ...

He is running again. He looks over his shoulder and sees Jill standing in her wedding gown, a mere silhouette in the approaching Light—the horrifying, impossibly pure Light. He continues forward, hobbling and limping, forcing his body of rock and stone and Scripture toward the pool.

"Run, Danny! Run!"

He still wears the high priest's vest, still clutches the Levi Stone.

"Run!"

He is practically there. Just a few more steps, just two more, just ... He stumbles and falls, hitting the ground so hard that, as before, pieces of his body break off.

And still the Light approaches. And still the roar grows, filling his thoughts, his entire being.

Once again he reaches out and drags himself toward the pool until its red surface comes into view. And there it is, the reflection of the face, the one from the dreams and the sketch—beaten, bloody.

"Help me ... ," he cries to the image. "Help—"

Suddenly the bank gives way and he tumbles headfirst into the pool. Because he is rock, he sinks hard and fast. Deeper and deeper he falls. And the deeper he falls, the more warmth he feels. It is similar to the warmth of the Levi Stone and of the glowing breastplate, only it completely surrounds him. It comes from the liquid. It is soaking through his stone skin, into his rock muscles. As it does, he feels the hardness of his body begin to soften. He is no longer made of granite and words. He is returning to flesh. Yet it is a softer, more supple flesh. The flesh of a newborn.

At last he lands on the floor of the pool. But it is not the floor. Instead he is standing on the bank again. With the Light. The Light that begins to engulf him, to absorb him. But there is no shaking now, no falling to the ground. The rock body is gone. Completely. There is no longer the destruction or the terror. Instead there is only the Light as it wraps itself about him . . . warmly, tenderly. Like the liquid from the pool, its warmth soaks into him, through his pores, saturating his body, his mind, filling his every thought with . . . There are no other words for it except absolute peace, overwhelming love. He has never felt such acceptance. Such compassion. All of it directed at him. His throat aches; his eyes brim with tears. It is an embrace. He is experiencing some sort of cosmic embrace.

The love soaks deeper, working its way into his very soul . . . until, ever so slightly, the trembling returns. But this time it is only confined to his chest, to the center of his chest. His heart. Persistent, relentless, it grows until he begins to cough. Something is lodged there, stuck inside. He bends over, coughing harder. Something that must be expelled.

He lowers to his knees, continuing to cough, but nothing will come. He drops to all fours, leaning over the red pool, seeing the beaten face, as he coughs and gags until finally something comes from his throat and splashes into the liquid. It's the stone! The Levi Stone. No, wait. He still holds that stone in his hand. This is a different stone. It is the same shape and size but the color is a lighter green. Of course! It is the Benjamin Stone, the one they retrieved from the old man in Israel. But it does not sink. Instead it floats. As it does, it changes the reflection of the face in the pool. It is no longer the face from his dream but is now the face of one of his congregation members—the strident, outspoken Linda Grossman. But it isn't just Linda Grossman. It shimmers into another—the face of Dr. Helen Zimmerman. Somehow the two ripple into one, becoming the same. The image surprises him. Yes, he'd noted the similarities between the two women, but what does their similarity have to do with this stone?

Before he can react, he convulses again and coughs up a second stone that splashes into the pool. This one is crystal clear, like a dia-

mond. As he stares, the face reflected in the pool shifts and wavers into yet another member of his congregation — Charlie Rue. The same Charlie Rue he had so closely associated with yesterday's gypsies and with Guido, the self-proclaimed king of the gypsies. The image ripples and, sure enough, it turns to Guido himself. Again, two men of similar character somehow connected to a stone.

He stares, trying to understand. Two stones … three if you count the Levi Stone he still clutches in his hand …

And it is the image of these stones and their faces — Linda Grossman and Helen Zimmerman, Charlie Rue and Guido Sanchez — that remain with him as he starts awake.

Daniel Lawson stared up at the cracked ceiling and took a deep breath. Some of the images were new. Others were just as haunting as when he'd first dreamed them on Mount Sinai … as when Jill had shared them with him in Istanbul. What had the old man in Israel said? *"Have you had any dreams lately?"* And now the gypsy king? *"You have your dreams."*

Coincidence? Maybe in the beginning but now he wasn't so sure. He knew most dreams were usually the unconscious mind venting … not so much the supernatural as the work of too many green peppers on a late-night pizza (or in this case, barbecued hedgehog). But he also knew there were exceptions, like those in the Bible — Joseph, Paul, Pilate's wife, from the New Testament; Jacob, Joseph, and his own namesake, Daniel, from the Old Testament.

And what was it the book of Job said? *"God does speak … in a dream, in a vision of the night, when deep sleep falls on men …"*

Not that Daniel would put himself in the same category as these great people. But this dream … coming a second time, a third if you counted Jill's. So vivid, so filled with images and symbolism. Could it be? And if it *was* somehow from God, what was he saying?

As before, the beads lay scattered on a table. Only this time he could find no order, no strand to attach them. No strand except Jill's final words: *"He promised. You'll hear his voice, Danny, and you'll love him."*

Daniel Lawson turned onto his side and stared out the window. He would pray some more, he would reason some more, but he suspected it would do no good. He suspected he'd already received his answer. It was not the one he wanted. But it was one he would obey.

He glanced at the travel alarm. Three twenty-five. In ninety minutes they would again meet up with the king of the gypsies.

✳

"No, he's not going."

"Dad — "

"You didn't say anything about cave diving."

"Forty, fifty meters at most," Guido said. "It is not far."

"You can die in one meter."

"That is nonsense."

"That is a fact."

Guido raised his palms in supplication. With his shirt off, Helen could see the saggy skin of age. Yet underneath there was still hard muscle and steel-cable tendons. He tried to explain. "As a child, my father and I, we would swim these caves even without the air tanks. We would work our way along the pockets of air in the ceiling."

"See," Tyler said, hoisting the diving tank to his shoulders. His shirt was also off, his skin already glowing red from the relentless sun of southern France. They had just finished an hour hike from the town of Cassis, winding their way down the white limestone cliffs to the rocky beach and crystalline water. Like miniature fjords with fingerlike inlets, the Calanques were a favorite destination for yachts, sailboats, and as in their case, the occasional diver.

"You're not going," Daniel repeated.

"Dad, I'm old enough to go on my own . . . I don't need your permission."

"Don't test me on this."

"I'm not testing you; I'm telling you. I'm going."

"And I say you're not."

The tension between these two was not new. Helen had seen it every day they'd been together — two bulls pulling in opposite directions. And when she didn't want to shake Tyler for his disrespect, she wanted to shout at his father to let him go. It was so painful to watch these two people, who so desperately needed and loved each other, tear at each other so continually.

"You still do not trust me, do you?" the gypsy king said to Daniel. "After these many hours you still do not trust."

"My son is not going to risk his life with someone we barely know, looking for something we're not even sure exists."

"My words," the gypsy repeated, "they still mean nothing to you."

Helen watched as Preacher Man looked out over the water. The glare of the morning sun outlined a strong chin and rugged features. He was good-looking and still in great shape, there was no doubting it. And what made him even more appealing was that he didn't seem to know it. *So much talent wasted,* she mused. Not that it mattered. She certainly wasn't interested. How could she be? But getting a man's attention and keeping him a little off balance was one of the ways she'd learned to operate in their world. The least he could do was show a little interest.

The situation with Jean Mark was the perfect example. The two of them had gotten into a doozy of a spat — so bad that Jean Mark opted to hang back in Cassis and wait for their return. He had wanted to revisit the Calanques for years, but now he chose to stay back at some café and sulk. It was stupid. Completely illogical. Upon hearing the news, Guido had only chuckled. "Sometimes in matters of the heart the brain does not matter." And Preacher Man's response? Instead of seeing this as an opportunity to move in, to make up for lost ground, he actually tried to convince Jean Mark to come along, to try to make peace between them. Not exactly the reaction she'd expected . . . or preferred.

She returned her attention to the argument.

"So you'll go in without me?" Tyler was asking.

"At my age?" Guido shook his head. "No. Though your father thinks me a fool, even I would not do such a thing on my own. However . . ." — he reached into his baggy blue nylon pants — "I have something which I have been waiting to share. And since my credibility seems in question, perhaps this is the time." He removed an item from his pocket, careful to keep it hidden in his palm.

"What is it?" Tyler asked.

Always the showman, Guido motioned to them. "Come, come. You will all want to see this."

Tyler, Nayra, Helen, and eventually Daniel gathered around him in the bright sunlight. When he was sure he had their undivided attention, he held out his hand and slowly opened it.

It was a small, rectangular stone, identical in size to the Levi and Benjamin Stones, which were still safely locked away at the pension. Helen threw a look to Daniel. Even in the harsh sunlight she could see he had noticeably paled.

The gypsy king saw it as well and broke into a smile. "It looks familiar?"

Daniel could only stare.

Helen moved in for a better look.

"Is it . . ." — Tyler swallowed — "is it a diamond?"

Guido continued to smile.

Noticing an inscription on its face, Helen asked, "May I see it?"

"Certainly." He carefully placed it into her hands. "After all, we are all friends here. We all trust one another."

The inscription was Hebrew, just as with the other two stones. And just as worn. Turning it to get the right angle of light, she was finally able to read it. "Naphtali," she quietly whispered.

"What?" Daniel asked hoarsely.

"Naphtali . . . another one of the twelve tribes."

A moment of awe hung over the group.

Unable to endure any silence for long, Guido spoke up. "I am told the Naphtali tribe, they were somewhat impulsive, swift to act."

"Where did you get this?" Daniel asked.

Ignoring the question, Guido continued. "That is why perhaps it was given to my family, to my people . . . because we are impulsive, swift to act, like Naphtali. For many generations we have had it."

"Are there . . . are there others?" Daniel asked.

The gypsy king shrugged, then grinned. "I know of at least two more, don't you?"

Daniel said nothing.

"And the others, they may be in several places. Many, like myself, believe they are safe and secure inside the ark of the covenant."

"Ark of the covenant?" Tyler asked, then glanced at Nayra.

Guido nodded. "Yes."

The entire group stared in silence at the stone. Helen turned it over in her hands, allowing it to reflect and refract the light.

"So what do you say, Pastor?" Guido finally asked.

Daniel remained silent.

"Dad . . ."

"We must hurry and decide," Guido said. "The tide, it will change soon."

Helen looked on, waiting for a decision, hoping Preacher Man would go against his better judgment. Yes, he loved his son. And yes, she respected that love. But the chances of this being a legitimate opportunity had just increased several fold.

"Dad, we're this close . . . we just can't walk away now."

More silence as he continued to struggle. Helen knew it was a lose-lose decision for him. On the one hand he would hate himself for crumbling and giving in; what type of father would allow his son to be endangered? On the other he would hate himself for being so stubborn and cowardly. She felt bad for him, even wondered if she should somehow step in, when—

"Okay," he said softly.

"All right!" Tyler whooped.

"But not my son."

"What?" Tyler croaked.

"No."

"Then who . . . ," Guido asked. Suddenly his face filled with incredulity. "Not you?"

"Yes."

"You?" Helen asked.

"But you are so old," Guido argued.

"And you're not?"

"Dad, you don't know the first thing about diving."

"Actually, I do, a little. As a kid, we used to borrow my uncle's scuba gear to dive for fishing lures in the river."

"I am afraid diving in a river is much different than diving in a cave."

"I know. But you were going to teach Tyler; now you're going to teach me."

The gypsy king looked first at Daniel, then at Helen, then back at Daniel. "You may find it quite stressful."

Daniel gave a slow nod but would not look away.

"We have very much to cover and not so very much time."

"Then we'd better hurry," was all he said.

Helen looked on as Tyler grumbled, then grudgingly passed the scuba gear to his father. Preacher Man was afraid, there was no doubt, but he would not back down. Not only did the man have compassion, he also had courage. And honesty and sensitivity and . . . The list could go on if she let it. But she would not let it. Each day it took a little more effort on her part, but she would not let it.

✳

The water was clear and cold. Daniel would have given anything for a wet suit, but not thirty minutes earlier Guido had lectured him on how spoiled Americans were and how such indulgences were unnecessary. "After all, Pastor, this is the Mediterranean."

Well, Mediterranean or not, he was freezing. And he was frightened. Very frightened. As they drifted just below the surface in this unknown world, all he heard was the pounding of his heart and the perpetual stream of bubbles from his regulator. He was breathing too fast, he knew that, but Guido had assured him he didn't have to worry. He'd have plenty of air.

"How will I know if I'm running out?" Daniel had asked when they were practicing on the beach. "I mean, if I don't have a gage or anything. Shouldn't we have gages?"

"You will not run out of air, my friend."

Daniel persisted. Despite the Naphtali Stone, he still didn't look upon honesty as Guido's strong suit. "But if I start to run out . . . I mean, if we're in that cave and I start to run out . . . it's not like I can just pop up to the surface."

"This is true. If you find it difficult to suck air from your tank, then you should begin to hurry out."

"How much time would I have?"

"Much time."

"How much?"

"I don't know. Seven, maybe eight breaths."

Daniel gave him a look.

"You will not run out of air, trust me. Besides, we have a reserve. Something you Americans call a 'J valve.'" He pointed to a small handle at the top of the tank. "It gives you a false alarm; it makes you feel like you are running out of air before you do. If the breathing should become difficult, reach up like so and pull it down." He gave the shiny, spring-loaded lever a yank. "It will give you an extra three or so minutes."

"So if the breathing becomes difficult —"

160

"Pull down the J valve and you will have three more minutes."

"And if it becomes difficult after that?"

"Then I would hurry faster."

The knowledge gave Daniel a vague sort of comfort. If he should die, it was nice to know the details.

The lesson on the beach had started nearly ninety minutes earlier. Now the two of them swam along the base of the towering cliffs of white limestone, as brilliant under the water as above. Guido had taken the lead. Daniel followed close behind, staying within a yard or two of his guide's waving fins. The water was crystal, so clear that the sun cast sharp shadows of their figures drifting across the rocks below. Among the cracks and crevices Daniel noticed a violet black sea urchin, its bristly spines bringing back memories of last night's cuisine.

Guido slowed and motioned to a small indentation in the rock to his right. At first Daniel saw nothing, until Guido waved his hand close to the opening and an invisible octopus suddenly turned bright red with anger. Guido removed his hand, allowing the creature to scurry off for a safer shelter. The gypsy king looked up, his eyes squinting in a grin, then gave a thumbs-up. Daniel found himself returning the gesture. The place was beautiful. Fascinating. And despite the cold and the fear and the rapid breathing and the pounding of his heart ... there was a certain peace here, a tranquillity.

Guido pushed off from the wall of rock and Daniel followed. He noticed his breathing had slowed a little. Not much but a little. He wished the same were true for his heart. Moments later they came upon the opening—a dark shadow, no more than two yards across, easy for an untrained eye to miss. Guido motioned for him to wait as he tied a white nylon cord to an outcropping of rock.

"It is not a simple cave," he had explained earlier. "There are many passages and tributaries. The line will be for our return, so we will not get lost coming out."

Daniel nodded.

"Also, there is much silt at the bottom. If you should touch it or stir it up with your fins, it has no place to go. It will fill the cave, making it completely black. Even our lights will be useless. If this should happen, do not let go of the line. It is your only point of reference. Swim with your hand wrapped around it like so" — he had made an okay sign with his thumb and index finger — "touching the line as lightly as possible so you do not dislodge it but so you always know where it is."

Daniel watched as Guido tied off the line. When he was finished, he turned and motioned that they snap on their lights. Daniel obeyed and turned on his three-cell, waterproof flashlight. Squinting his eyes into another smile, Guido turned and entered the cave. Daniel followed, his heart pounding even harder.

Instantly it became dark. The sun disappeared. So had the surface. Now there was only blackness and rock. They could no longer end the dive by simply popping up to the surface. Once again Daniel's breathing rate increased.

The rock walls quickly narrowed, so close that he could reach out to either side and touch them. So close that if he needed to escape, he could not turn around.

Claustrophobia began closing in, trying to take hold. He managed to keep it at bay. Just barely.

He directed his light to the ceiling. It hovered eighteen inches above his head and was covered with small, daggerlike stalactites — something Guido had warned him would be present, since the roof was exposed at low tide. He glanced down at the floor, another eighteen inches away, with its velvety smooth silt that must never be touched.

Earlier Guido had explained how to stay at the proper height, neither hitting the stalactites above nor disturbing the silt below. "It is all a matter of buoyancy," he had said. "If you wish to rise, fill your lungs with more air. If you wish to sink, take shallower breaths. It is really quite simple."

Well, "quite simple" for Guido was becoming less and less simple for Daniel. Besides his rapid breathing, he now had to consciously think about how deep to take each breath — a problem further complicated in that it took two to three seconds for his body to adjust its height after each breath. Consequently, Daniel found himself panting even faster, taking even more rapid, shallower breaths as he searched for the right amount of air to breathe, while forgetting that he'd always be two or three seconds behind. Afraid to exhale and hit the bottom, he held the old air in his lungs, only topping it off with fractions of new, until suddenly his body began crying for oxygen. He had to exhale, but he couldn't or he'd hit the floor. He had to inhale, but he couldn't or he'd hit the ceiling. His breaths continued, rapid, incremental ... and useless. He had to breathe but there was nothing he could do. He was beginning to suffocate. He was trapped. He was suffocating and trapped and there was nothing he could do. His lungs began to burn. He had to cool them. He had to fill them with something, anything ... even if it meant the soothing cold water around him. He had to breathe. He had to spit out the mouthpiece and fill his lungs. It was panic, he knew it, but he had to breathe. Something. Anything. He had to get out but he couldn't. Not up, not down, not back. He was trapped! Suffocating and trapped! Suffocating and trapped and —

Stop it! he ordered himself. *Take control!*

I need to breathe! I need to —

Stop it! He forced the words into his mind, jamming them in until they stuck. *Slow down. Take a breath ... slow down ... take it easy ... take a breath ...*

Somehow he heard and was able to obey.

Good. Now exhale.

But I —

Exhale!

He breathed out.

Slowly, slowly ... now breathe again ...

Gradually, second after torturous second, he began taking control. Not completely but enough. Ahead he saw Guido spooling off the line, just a few feet in front of him. No, he was yards in front of him. No, he was practically on top of him and they were going to collide. No, he was too far. Too close, too far, both at the same time! *What's happening! What's —*

Hallucination! ... Slow down ... breathe in ...

What's happening! What's —

Exhale.

What's —

Halocline. The word swelled into his consciousness. *Yes, halocline.* Guido had warned him of this as well. When fresh water from the cave's river enters the salty water of the Mediterranean, the two densities lie on top of each other, unless they are mixed together by something or someone ... like a passing diver ... like Guido. If that happens, depth perception will distort — like looking through clear, swirling syrup, a nightmare of Coke bottle

163

glasses and fun house mirrors, making it impossible to judge any distance correctly.

What do I do? What do I —

What did Guido say?

I don't —

Think! Breathe ... easy ... easy ...

I don't rememb —

Think! Guido said ... Guido said ...

"Let it clear!"

Yes! Exhale ... slowly ... slow ...

"Let it clear before you follow!"

Yes! Breathe ... easy ... easy ...

Daniel slowed to a stop, swimming just enough to hold himself against the current flowing out of the cave. He watched, fighting back the panic, as Guido continued to move ahead.

He's deserting you!

Let it clear ... let it clear ...

The swirling distortions began to decrease as Guido continued moving farther and farther ahead.

He's getting away! He's —

Let it clear ... exhale ... take it easy —

But he's —

... nice and easy ... let it clear ...

The farther Guido moved away, the more isolated and desperate Daniel grew. Yes, he still had his light ... and he still had Guido's nylon cord between his fingers, but ...

He's getting away, he's —

... let it clear ... breathe ... let it clear ...

He's getting —

Wait ... exhale ... easy ...

Guido's image twisted less and less — *wait ... wait ... breathe —* until the gypsy started around a curve in the tunnel and disappeared altogether.

He's gone! Daniel's stomach knotted. *I'm alone! Deserted!* He began to hyperventilate.

Slow down! Slow down!

He's gone, he's —

Slow!

But —

164

Slow down! He thought of counting. He wasn't sure why, but it was his only reality, the only thing he could cling to.

One ... two ...

But he's —

Breathe! Three ... four ...

But —

Easy ... a little deeper ... one ... exhale ... slower, slower ... two ... three ... breathe ... four ...

Moments passed. The distortions had not entirely cleared, but they were good enough. Finally he pushed off. Clutching his light with one hand, keeping his fingers around the cord with the other, he continued through the underwater crypt.

One ... two ...

To his left was another passage and beyond that another. But he had his cord and he had his light and he had his counting.

Breathe ... three ... four ...

He followed the bend in the tunnel.

One ...

At last Guido's light came into view. Then his body. But it was only half his body! The lower half! The upper half was completely gone! Had he been attacked? Was it a shark? There was no blood, but —

Exhale ... exhale!

Then he saw that the legs were still moving. So was the light! He was alive!

Easy ... easy ...

Now he saw the upper half of the body; he was divided by the surface refraction. *Surface!* Guido was out of the water! He was at the surface!

Daniel swam faster, forgetting to count, forgetting to breathe. It didn't matter; they were safe. With overwhelming relief he took several deep breaths and quickly rose. He broke through the surface and immediately spit out his mouthpiece, gasping, gulping in the dank, moist air. He was alive — he had made it and he was alive!

"See?" Guido said, grinning at him. "A piece of cake."

Daniel said nothing but continued to gulp air. Eventually he glanced about the cave. It was small and saucerlike, no more than six feet high and ten, maybe fifteen feet across.

Guido hoisted himself onto the rocky shelf and reached up to a small, unseen niche in the ceiling. There was a moment of silence as his fingers searched in the darkness.

"It has been many years …," he said, continuing to look. "Many — ah …" His face lit up. "Here we go." He pulled a small metal box from the ceiling. It may have been beautiful once, even ornate. But now the metal had corroded, breaking off in layers in his hands. Sporting his trademark grin, he produced a plastic supermarket bag and carefully lowered the prized box inside it.

"You're taking it out?" Daniel managed between breaths.

Guido nodded. "For now. But we must hurry, while the tide is still in our favor." He carefully pressed the air out of the bag, knotted it, and lowered himself back into the water. "Are we ready?"

"Just give … give me another minute."

"Of course, Pastor; whatever you say. We have waited these many years … we can wait another minute."

"But we can make him well."

"He will contaminate the others. If we do not kill him, he will make his brothers and sisters sick. We do not want that, do we, Ibrahim? We do not want them to catch his sickness?"

The tears fell from Ibrahim's eyes, one splattering onto the gasping bird's breast.

"We do not want that, do we, Ibrahim? Do we?"

Little Ibrahim shook his head.

"You do not have to stay," Yussuf said. "You may go to the house."

Fighting back the emotions, Ibrahim wiped his tears and again shook his head. He would stay until the deed was done.

Yussuf Fazil took the pigeon from Ibrahim's hand. He stroked the creature, cooing to it as he lifted it to his lips and kissed its shiny black head. Lowering it, he said, "Turn the other way, Ibrahim. You should not see this."

But Ibrahim would not turn away. He stood with resolve and watched. He stood, unmoving, as Yussuf produced a small knife. He stared, unblinking, as Yussuf firmly held the bird to the wooden board with one hand while placing the knife to its neck with the other.

"Farewell, my friend," Yussuf Fazil said quietly, obviously struggling with his own emotions. *"Until this time you have been good to us."* He drew the knife across the bird's neck, cutting through the feathers, then drawing blood as he sawed back and forth. The pigeon struggled and fought as blood gushed, but only for a moment. Soon the head was severed. *"Farewell."*

Alone with only his memories, Ibrahim el-Magd sat against the wall of the long council room. Outside, the desert haboob whistled, relentlessly smoothing the compound's walls with its blasting sand. He mused silently. How like the wind had his own life become — knowing the will of Allah and steadily, persistently, setting out to accomplish it, regardless of the difficulties, regardless of the obstacles. He would win; there was no doubt about it. Like the haboob, he would eventually have his way. But the cost — oh, the terrible cost . . .

In just a few hours he would board a chartered jet to Cairo. From there he must find Yussuf Fazil, his brother-in-law and best friend. (Even now he thought of him as his friend.) And once he was found, Ibrahim el-Magd must not hesitate to administer Allah's justice. Yussuf Fazil had not merely betrayed their love and friendship — for that he could be forgiven. Someday Ibrahim could even forgive him for the betrayal that led to the death of his son. Even that, as horrific as it may be, was not the offense to which Yussuf must answer. No, his offense was something far greater. He had betrayed Allah. And for that there was no course but justice. Not revenge, not retribution. Justice.

One plus one equals two. That is how Sheikh Salad Habib so often explained Allah to them. Logical. Cause and effect. A specific action leads to a specific reaction. That is how Allah runs the universe. *One plus one equals two.* His laws of morality are no different from his laws of nature. One cannot jump off a cliff and expect the law of gravity to cease. Neither can one commit heresy and expect no retribution. *One plus one equals two.* Cause and effect. That is how he must now deal with Yussuf Fazil. For Ibrahim to do any less would mean his own refusal of the law, his own betrayal of Allah.

The thought forced Ibrahim to take a breath and release it in a long, heavy sigh. He looked to the velvet pillow before him, to the four stones that lay upon it. Minutes earlier he had removed them from the vault and carefully laid them out. Four stones, each with faded inscriptions that experts claimed were Hebrew. Inscriptions that spelled out the names of the various tribes of Israel. The first was a translucent, bloodred jasper. On it was written the name Reuben — the tribe descended from Jacob's firstborn. Next was an onyx made of white and brown layers. Its inscription read, "Joseph" — a tribe whose founder was praised for his trust in God despite many obstacles. Next was a fiery yellow crystal made of jacinth, the stone representing Gad — a tribe famous for their fierce fighting. And last there was a clear yellow stone made of citrine. It represented Zebulun, a tribe renowned for their unwavering allegiance.

Firstborn, truster of God, fierce fighter, unwavering allegiance … The symbolism was not lost on Ibrahim. Besides the four tribes of Israel, he sensed — he knew — that each stone also represented an aspect of his own personality: firstborn, steadfast believer, fierce warrior, follower to the end. Was such coincidence an accident? No, nothing with Allah was accident.

And soon, with the help of others, the remaining stones would be retrieved as well. They must. Time was quickly running out. Very soon he would hear the voice of Allah. Very soon that vengeful face, splattered with the blood of his enemies, would speak. And after that … his great and terrible wrath.

Until then Ibrahim el-Magd must be faithful in these smaller matters. For the wrath of Allah is the wrath of Allah … whether it be poured out upon millions or poured out upon one. And it made no difference how close to Ibrahim's heart the one may be. It made no difference that he loved Yussuf Fazil more deeply than a brother. For it was simply another test. *One plus one equals two.* Cause and effect. If he could carry out this justice, he could carry out any justice. If he was faithful with this thing, he would be entrusted with the greater.

*

The trip out of the cavern was easier than the trip in. At least at the beginning …

Knowing what to expect, Daniel was better able to control his breathing, though he knew he was still using too much air. After hearing about the halocline, Guido had suggested that Daniel go first. "Just follow the cord and there will be no problem." Daniel was more than grateful to accept. The last thing he wanted was to experience that awful feeling of abandonment again.

He had reentered the water, exhaled a little, and sunk into the tunnel. With the tide heading out, there was less need to swim, so he drifted along, only kicking his feet from time to time while keeping his thumb and index finger circled about the nylon cord. Because his tank had less air than when he started, it was lighter ... which meant he floated higher ... which meant more than one head-banging into the top of the cave. Painful, yes. Terminal, not likely. But with each impact he froze, listening for a surge of streaming bubbles which would mean he had snapped off his regulator valve and was rapidly emptying his tank.

Fortunately, he heard no such sound. And once again giving himself commands, he took shallower breaths until he hovered closer to the floor.

Breathe ... easy, easy ... exhale ...

He passed a fork in the cave that branched off to his left and then another to the right. And with each passing fork he was grateful to Guido for marking the route with the cord. He had gone about twenty feet or so when the line suddenly pulled tight against his palm. At the same instant something grabbed his right foot. Instinctively he tried to pull his foot away, but whatever had grabbed him held on tight. His mind raced. Was it a fish, a giant octopus, some cave monster? He had seen nothing as he passed, but who knew what lurked in the shadows of those tributaries?

He turned to investigate. Shining his light on his foot, he was relieved to see that the problem was simply his swim fin. Somehow its strap had tangled itself up in the guide line. He tried to shake it off but was unsuccessful. He reached back to undo it with his hand, but for some reason it pulled away. He tried again, drawing up his knee until he finally realized the problem. The line had also become entangled in the valves atop his tank. Inadvertently he had managed to hog-tie himself.

He reached up and felt the cord around the valve. But since he could not see it, he had no idea how to untangle it. He tucked in, turning to his right, then to his left, trying to get more of a view. That's when his free fin accidentally dug into the tunnel's floor and kicked up the silt. A black cloud rose, darkening the tunnel as quickly and thoroughly as if someone had dumped in a truckload of instant coffee.

As the darkness rose and swallowed him, Daniel breathed deeper, faster, until he suddenly crashed into the top of the tunnel, stalactites jabbing into his ribs. *His ribs?* Why not his head? Had he turned that much? He raised his light but it was only a dull, brown orb in the blackness. He began fighting the cord, struggling to get free. Desperation grew. A stalactite dug into his belly, another into his thigh. He had to get free. He had to get out! As he fought, he realized he was sucking hard on his respirator. Too hard. The tank was running out of air, he was going to suffocate, he was going to —

No! The voice of reason shouted over his panic. *The J valve. That's why you have the J valve!*

He reached to the top of his tank, groping for the spring-loaded lever. Guido had said that by pulling it down, he would have three extra minutes of air. There. He'd found it.

Good. Now all I have to do is —

It's already down! It's already pulled down!

No, that's not possible. He reached for a better grip and tried again. But it was true; it had already been pulled.

The ceiling! You opened it when you hit the ceiling!

Once again panic seized him. He squirmed, tugging harder, sucking harder, but getting less and less air.

Seven, eight breaths, that's all Guido said!

He sucked but then there was nothing.

Get free! Free of the line! Get —

Cut it! Cut the line!

Yes! Yes! He reached down for the knife that was strapped to his leg. He could see nothing. Everything was by touch but he found the strap. He unsnapped it and pulled out the blade.

Get free! Cut it!

What about Guido? How will he get out if —

Cut it! Get free! Cut it and breathe!

How will Guido get —

He knows the cave; he knows the way —

Not without the line! Not with this silt!

Cut it!

He won't be able —

170

Cut it! Cut it!
By now Daniel's lungs were on fire, burning for air.
CUT IT!
But —
CUT IT! CUT IT!
Panic consumed his thoughts. He could no longer see, he could no longer breathe, he could no longer reason.
CUT IT! CUT IT! CUT IT!
With the knife in his hand he reached for the line. He stretched out the blade, straining to feel for the resistance of the cord against the serrated edge. It was there somewhere, if he could just —

Suddenly a light flared in his eyes. He turned to see Guido's face appear through the blackness. The gypsy instantly recognized the problem. He pulled the regulator from his own mouth and motioned for Daniel to take it.

Daniel grabbed it greedily and shoved it into his mouth. He took one, two, three breaths — deep and purging. Once again he rose and banged hard into the ceiling. Some of the panic began to subside. Guido motioned for the mouthpiece. After taking another breath, Daniel handed it to him. The gypsy took one breath and handed it back.

Daniel took two more breaths, feeling more and more in control, pushing the panic farther and farther away. He handed the respirator to Guido, who took another single breath before returning it to him. Guido then reached out to the line directly in front of them, the part Daniel had not yet tangled. He motioned for Daniel to take it and wrap it around his hand several times. He was not to let go. Regardless of the reason, he was not to let go.

Daniel nodded in understanding.

Guido took the respirator for another breath, then handed it back to him. He motioned that Daniel should take several more breaths and hold the last. Daniel obeyed and passed it back. Guido took it, then pulled out his own knife and in a single slice cut the line off Daniel's fin. That done, he drifted to the top of Daniel's tank and cut away the cord tangled there. When he had finished, he returned to Daniel and handed him the mouthpiece.

Daniel exhaled and gratefully took in two more breaths.

Guido motioned to the straps and buckle holding Daniel's tank. It took a moment before Daniel understood that he was to shed the useless gear. Since it was empty and they now shared Guido's, his tank no longer served a purpose. But there was more. As Daniel unbuckled and slipped out of his tank, Guido began doing the same with his. What was he doing? What was going on? Daniel had no sooner released his tank, letting it slip to the ground, before Guido was handing him his own.

Daniel shook his head, motioning for Guido to keep it.

But Guido was insistent, refusing to take no for an answer. Finally Daniel complied. As they continued sharing the mouthpiece, the gypsy taking one breath for every two or three of Daniel's, they slipped the tank onto Daniel's back and buckled it around his waist. He was still frightened, no doubt about it, but working in such close proximity with another person gave Daniel enough security to continue. Unfortunately, that security was short-lived.

When they finished, Guido tapped his chest and motioned down the tunnel. He tapped his chest again and motioned.

Thinking he understood, that they would go together through the passage, sharing the remaining tank, Daniel nodded.

But Guido shook his head and pointed to his watch. There was not enough time. He pointed to the tank and shook his head, indicating there was not enough air. Then he tapped his chest again and motioned that he would go on his own.

Daniel shook his head. Without air? Was he crazy?

Guido reached for the mouthpiece and took another breath. Handing it back to Daniel, he motioned for them to head up to the tunnel's ceiling.

Daniel obeyed and the two drifted the twelve or so inches until they were staring at each other through the stalactites. Using his light, Guido pointed to the pockets of air trapped against the ceiling—some up to three inches deep. He motioned that he would move along the tunnel, breathing from these pockets, just as he had done as a little boy.

Daniel shook his head. He was no fool. He knew these air pockets were from their own expelled air.

Guido disagreed, motioning his arms, indicating that as the tide went out, there would be more pockets and they would be almost as deep. Again he indicated that Daniel needed to hold the nylon line tight. It was imperative he not release it but keep it taut so

Guido wouldn't have to fumble with it as he made his dash through the tunnel.

Before Daniel could argue further, Guido again motioned for the mouthpiece. Daniel gave it to him and watched as the man took one, two, three deep breaths. He knew what the gypsy was doing but he didn't know how to stop him. As Guido breathed, he motioned up. At first Daniel thought it was to the ceiling. Then he understood it was to God. He nodded. Yes, he would pray.

Guido's eyes squinted into another grin as he took the final breath and clasped Daniel on the shoulder. Dropping the mouthpiece, he pushed away, swimming quickly and smoothly. It took a moment for Daniel to find the mouthpiece. Fumbling for the hose and tracing it, he was finally able to get it back into his mouth and start breathing. As he did, he looked down the cave. The silt and darkness had already swallowed the gypsy.

Once again the feeling of isolation rose within him. Only now it was coupled with guilt. What had he let the man do? The very person he was going to leave behind and let die was now risking his own life to save him? Talk about courage. But it was more than courage. Wasn't it also love? Sure, the gypsy's integrity was a little rough around the edges, as was his theology ... but which of the two men was acting more as Christ commanded? Which of the two was really living out the love of God? Unfortunately, the answer was clear in Daniel's mind.

Taking a moment to push aside the guilt and build his courage, Daniel finally started forward. But as he pushed off, the line in his hand slackened and he had to stop and pull it taut. Guido could not waste valuable seconds fumbling for a loose line. Daniel started forward again, this time more slowly, pulling and retrieving the line, keeping it tight as the current carried him forward.

The going was torturously slow but he would move no faster. The silt he had stirred up continued moving with the current, maintaining a brown cloud about him. Some of it had settled, but not much. Eventually he came to a bend in the tunnel and slowly rounded it. Guido was nowhere to be seen.

Daniel continued forward, foot by foot, each second turning into a minute, each minute an eternity. He no longer counted to himself; he no longer gave orders. Instead he occupied himself with something far more important.

Please, God … protect him. Help him get out. Be with him.

As he prayed, Daniel again noticed his breathing was growing more difficult. He was sucking harder on the mouthpiece. With a head more clear than the last time, he reached up and pulled down the J valve. Immediately the air came easier. But he only had three minutes. Three minutes to follow Guido out of the cave and head to the surface.

Although he picked up some speed, he never let the line slacken. Time dragged as precious breaths were wasted, but he would go no faster. He would not endanger Guido again. And then, through the thinning brown haze, he saw it — Guido's light. He closed in until he saw Guido himself, his head at the top of the tunnel, no doubt drawing in air.

Daniel moved faster, letting the line slacken some, promising himself he would tighten it in a moment. When he arrived, he patted Guido's thigh for his attention. But Guido ignored him, keeping his face pressed to the ceiling. Drifting up to join him, Daniel tapped his shoulder, preparing to remove his mouthpiece. Guido still did not respond. Daniel moved to his face. It was turned slightly and pointed toward the ceiling.

It was only then that Daniel saw there were virtually no air pockets in this portion of the tunnel. Instead Guido's upturned face floated, pressing and banging into the roof of the cave. He was no longer breathing.

No … Dear God, no!

Daniel ripped out his mouthpiece and pulled Guido's head toward him. That's when he saw the eyes, vacant and staring.

Dear Jesus …

He opened Guido's mouth, shoved the respirator inside it.

Breathe …, he willed. *Breath!*

But the gypsy did not breathe.

Daniel reached down to the man's chest, trying to press it, trying to perform some clumsy sort of CPR. But it did no good; the mouthpiece popped out. He shoved it into the mouth, anchoring it more firmly, and pressed the chest again.

Breathe … Breathe!

Nothing.

He pulled out the mouthpiece, filled his own lungs with air, then pulled Guido's mouth toward his. The face masks made it difficult,

174

but at last he was able to clamp his lips around Guido's and blow. At first the air bubbled through the nose, until he plugged it and blew again. Some air filled his lungs but not enough. He tried again.

Breathe! BREATHE!

But Guido did not breathe. He did not cough; he did not move. Instead he stared unblinking as the air bubbled out of his mouth.

Daniel's mind reeled. He had no choice. He dropped down, grabbed Guido's waist, and pulled him from the ceiling. They'd have to make a run for it. He'd have to get him to the surface and perform CPR there — and fast.

Help us. Dear God, help us!

He swam forward, this time with all his might. He no longer worried about keeping the line tight. Now he just had to get out of there as fast as possible. He kept the man from the ceiling and its rocky spikes while doing his best to hold the line and stay out of the silt. It grew harder to breathe. It was either the extra exertion or the emptying tank. Daniel suspected both.

Dear Jesus . . .

Then he saw it, through the brown haze. A faint glow. He swam harder, sucking up the precious air, his fins hitting the floor, kicking up more silt, but it didn't matter. Nothing mattered except getting out.

Jesus . . .

The tunnel grew brighter, the opening wider, until suddenly they exploded from the brown murk and into light — beautiful, blinding light. Daniel let go of the line and swam toward the surface with one arm while clinging to Guido with the other, kicking his feet and clawing with his free hand. His mind screamed with prayer; his lungs burned for air . . . until finally, finally he broke through to the surface.

He spit out his mouthpiece and gasped. "Help —," he cried and choked. "Somebody . . ." Another gasp. "Somebody help us!"

He heard Tyler shout and turned toward the voice. The group was a hundred yards away on the shore.

"Help . . ." More coughing. He reached back, pulling Guido's face out of the water. He ripped off his mask, then Guido's, as he gulped in the air. He grabbed Guido's chin and pulled it to his own, this time remembering to clamp the nose before pressing the man's lips to his and blowing.

There was no response.

"Dad . . ."

He could hear splashing. Tyler was in the water. Swimming toward them.

"Dad, hang on!"

Again Daniel took a gulp of air, and again he blew it into the lifeless mouth.

Again there was no response.

Dear God . . . no . . . no . . .

But even as Daniel prayed, even as he pleaded, the mind-numbing truth began to take hold. This was one request God was not going to grant.

chapter nine

"Maybe they have to be lined up a certain way," Tyler suggested.

Daniel shook his head. "I've tried everything. Lining them up, stacking them up, putting them in the sun, keeping them in the darkness, holding them to my chest, my forehead, my ear. Nothing works."

The group sat in the cramped pension, staring at the two rocks sitting on the table. They were a bit smaller and rounder than the Levi, Benjamin, and Naphtali Stones, and much plainer. As far as Daniel could see, they had no writing or distinguishing marks of any kind, which nixed the idea that they could spell out words or be used to cast lots. No, they were simply two rocks made from what appeared to be the same red granite as Mount Sinai. And there was no voice, no hocus-pocus, no supernatural communication of any kind.

"Are you certain they are the actual stones, the ones he believed to be the Urim and Thummim?" Nayra asked. "Are you certain he was being honest with you?"

Daniel nodded. Truth be told, he was more than certain. He trusted Guido's integrity as much as his own. Maybe more. Would he have risked his life to save another? Particularly some stranger from a foreign country? He had his doubts. In fact, hadn't he already proved that, back when he was about to cut the line and leave Guido to fend for himself in the cave? There would have been no way the man could have survived if he'd cut it, not with the thick silt and multiple tributaries. Yet moments later the gypsy had done just the opposite, had given up his life for Daniel's. A *gypsy*.

An impulsive, heretical, superstitious vagabond … who proved he knew more about Christ's love than Daniel ever dreamed of.

The police had asked only a few questions, apparently exercising the same prejudice toward Guido that Daniel had shown earlier. And his daughter? Although saddened and depressed at the news, part of her seemed relieved. The fact that she was sole heir to the house and estate may have been of some help. That type of money could make even a person with a deformed face very attractive.

Interestingly enough, she did not want the stones. "No," she had told Daniel when he presented them to her. "They have hurt my family for too many generations. My grandfather suffered over them, as did his father. And now my own father, he dies because of them. No. If you wish for them, they are yours. If not, I suggest you rid yourself of them as quickly as possible."

Back in the pension Nayra rephrased her question. "Are you certain?" she asked. "About his integrity, I mean?"

Tyler answered. "He sure went through a lot just to be pulling our leg. I mean, in one sense the guy died for these, didn't he?" He reached across the rickety wooden table to the clear Naphtali Stone. "Then there's the matter of him having this extra little — Ow!" He dropped the stone and it clattered to the table.

"What's the matter?" Nayra asked.

"The stupid thing burned me!"

"Burned you," Helen scoffed. "How could it burn you?"

"See for yourself," Tyler said, sucking his fingers.

Helen reached for the stone. But instead of picking it up, she held her fingertips just above its surface. She turned to Daniel in surprise. "He's right. The thing's warm."

"Warm, nothing," Tyler whined. "It's on fire."

Daniel frowned, staring at the stone, then at the other two beside it. Reading his mind, Helen reached out to the Benjamin Stone, holding her fingertips just above it. She looked at him and slowly nodded. It was hot as well. She reached for the Levi Stone. This time, however, she shook her head. "Not this one," she said. She picked it up. "It's perfectly cool."

Daniel stretched out his hand to test the stones himself. The Benjamin and Naphtali Stones were definitely warm. But when

Helen handed him the Levi Stone, it was completely cool. He looked at her, his frown deepening. "What's going on?" he asked.

"I don't know. Unless . . . unless when they're together, they create some sort of energy."

"They're just stones."

"I understand that, but you can feel for yourself the heat being generated."

"Like the fire at Avignon," Tyler said. They turned to him. "Remember what happened when they brought the Urim and Thummim together with the other twelve stones?"

Daniel looked back at the nondescript pair of rocks. More than ever he was certain of their authenticity.

"Do you think that is why nothing is happening?" Nayra asked. "Do we need all of the other twelve stones for these two to work?"

Daniel turned to Helen, who continued staring at the stones. "This is way out of my league," she conceded. "But you're right about one thing. Whenever the high priest used the Urim and Thummim, he always wore the breastplate, which meant he was also in contact with the other twelve stones."

Daniel thought back to his dream — to Jill's dream. Oddly enough, not once did he remember seeing the Urim and Thummim. No, it was always the other stones. First the Levi Stone, then the Benjamin, and finally the Naphtali, but never the Urim and Thummim. Never.

A deeper, unsettling thought began to rise within him. Was it possible? Did God expect him to retrieve all twelve stones? Were all twelve needed, *plus* the Urim and Thummim, to hear God speak? He felt himself growing cold. So much death and killing already, and that was only for these first few. If they were to continue, how much more violence would follow? What had Guido's daughter said? *"They have hurt my family for too many generations."*

How could he continue a journey with so much risk and danger? Then again, if this was something God had called him to . . . if, as strange as it seemed, this was the only way for him to rekindle his first love . . . and if this was what Jill had dreamed, what she had meant when she died, then how could he do anything less?

✳

Maybe it was Nayra's purity; Tyler wasn't sure. Or maybe it was her unwavering devotion to God, a devotion that made his own seem superficial and, yes, even hypocritical. But as he watched her studying his videotapes through the small viewfinder monitor, he couldn't help thinking that of all the girls he'd ever met, both inside and outside the church, this one knew exactly who she was. There was no ambiguity about her, no lack of focus. In short, she was everything he longed to be. She had everything he longed to possess. And for that reason — among the other incidentals, like her exotic beauty, her penetrating eyes, her intelligence, and her spunk — there was nothing he could do to shake her from his mind . . . or his heart. He thought of her most of the time now. Even when they weren't together, he seemed to be watching his every action through her eyes. Sure, her religious dogma irritated him, sometimes made him crazy. Yet there were no games with Nayra. You always knew where you stood, because she knew where she stood. Because of the rules.

Ah yes, the rules. She called them the *Shariah,* or Allah's divine law. It was a detailed code covering every aspect of her life . . . telling her how to pray (at least five times a day), what she can drink (forget anything with alcohol), what to eat, how to entertain guests, how to buy, how to sell, how to clean herself, how to go to the toilet, even how she should sleep. The list of dos and don'ts went on forever, and when confronted with this, her answer was as simple and direct as her life: "Man is imperfect. How can he possibly make such decisions on his own?"

And as far as getting physical with her? Dream on. He knew the attraction was mutual; he could see it in her eyes. He could tell by the way her voice — in fact, her entire body — seemed to soften when they talked. And that excuse of hers for staying with them because it was safer than heading back to Cairo (since Israeli intelligence had longer arms than he realized) . . . well, maybe it was true and maybe it wasn't. He hoped it wasn't, in more ways than one. He also found it interesting that not getting physical with her seemed to deepen his feelings toward her. Instead of all that planning and manipulating to get her into bed, he discovered that the talking and sharing drove her deeper into his heart.

Her interest in his video work was the perfect example. Most folks just blew it off as weirdness and eccentricity. Not Nayra.

More and more frequently she picked up his camera to review what he'd taped. And just this morning she had startled him with a deep insight.

"I think I understand what you see in this," she had said.

"What's that?"

"Through the viewfinder, when you look through it . . . it is as if you see things you do not normally see."

He turned to her in surprise. "Yes, exactly. That's it exactly." She smiled, obviously pleased with herself. He went on to explain. "It's like it filters out all the extraneous noise and images. It allows me to really see what I'm looking at."

She nodded. "So by experiencing less, you actually experience more."

"Precisely! People are always saying that I'm missing life around me, but in reality I'm seeing more than they are."

"Yes," she said, beaming. "Exactly. That is how it is with Islam."

"Huh? Run that past me again?"

"People make fun of all our rules; they say we limit our freedom, our ability to live. When in reality, by reducing our options, we more thoroughly live and enjoy the life Allah has set before us."

"Um, if you say so . . ."

"No, I am serious. Your restricted images give you greater clarity in what you see; our restricted ways give us greater clarity in what we live."

Tyler wasn't particularly fond of comparing his passion for video with her religious legalism, but he thought he understood. And he was grateful that she'd made another connection between them.

That had been this morning, and now this evening as she sat across the table from him, reviewing his footage from the Palace of the Popes, she had seen something else. "Tyler?"

"What's up?" he said, turning a page in one of the French cinema magazines he'd picked up.

"Did you see this?"

"What?"

"This."

He laid down the magazine and moved around the table to look over her shoulder — grateful for another excuse to get close. His dad was in the other room studying, and Helen, who had kissed and made up with Jean Mark, was down the hall in her room, no doubt doing more kissing and making up.

"Here is another one," Nayra said.

"One what?" he asked, moving so close to the viewfinder that they were practically cheek to cheek. If she noticed, she didn't protest.

"This painting," she said. "By Giovanetti, at the Palace of the Popes."

"What about it?"

"Like three others I have seen ... it has the ark of the covenant in it."

"Is that a big deal?" He inched a little closer.

"No," she said. "Back then the ark was quite a point of interest, especially for the Knights Templar. But this is the third time I've seen it accompanied by a woman. "

"Really ..." He moved until his face brushed against hers.

"All right," she said, pulling away. "That is enough."

He turned to her innocently. "Hm?"

"I know what you are trying to accomplish."

"I'm sorry, what?"

"You can see the screen perfectly fine from over there." She motioned behind her.

"Oh, sorry ..." Tyler retreated a foot or so. She was flustered and he was grateful to see it. "Now, what were you saying?"

"I was saying ..." She scowled, obviously trying to find her train of thought.

Tyler smiled.

"I was saying that this is the third or so picture that has been painted in which someone is transporting the ark."

"Right, but you said that was no big deal back then."

"Yes. But in each picture it is accompanied by a woman, or a woman and a young man."

"Is that so surprising?"

"No ..."

"Maybe she's some famous guy's wife or something."

"Perhaps, but ..."

"But what?"

"In each and every case the woman — well, see for yourself."

Tyler moved in closer to the viewfinder.

"In each and every case her skin, it is black. In every case she appears to be African."

∗

Allah u Akabar.
    Allah u Akabar.
    God is greater.
    God is greater.
The wavering voice rang through the minaret speakers not a hundred meters outside his hotel room. Each sound of the *Adhan,* the call to prayer, was drawn out musically, savoring every syllable. Ibrahim el-Magd glanced at his watch, surprised at how late it had become. Nearby another *Adhan* began, and a moment later a third, then a fourth, each seeming to compete with the other in their proclamation:
    I witness that there is no God but God.
Ibrahim walked to the tiny bathroom, where he removed his sandals, pulled up his robes, and sat on the edge of the tub. Turning on the water, he briefly washed his hands, his face, and his feet. You do not enter the presence of Allah soiled.
    I witness that Muhammad is the prophet of God.
Briefly drying the soles of his feet, he rose and padded to the closet, where he produced his prayer rug.
    Rise to prayer.
    Rise to felicity.
Laying it upon the floor in the direction of Mecca, Ibrahim el-Magd lowered himself to his knees, then prostrated himself until his forehead touched the ground. Other, greater men than he had small calluses in the center of their forehead from such disciplined devotion.
    God is greater.
    God is greater.
He had forgotten to close the balcony door, and already a dozen mosquitoes from the Nile had entered, whining and circling around him. But no matter, he was about to pray. And when he finished, he would rise and pay his brother-in-law and best friend a visit. It had been a dangerous move, leaving Sudan, traveling incognito without bodyguards, but it would be the quickest and surest

183

method of accomplishing his purpose. He did not relish what he had to do, but it had to be done.

There is no god but God.

The nearest *Adhan* ceased; the others soon followed, their last phrase echoing across the city before fading into the perpetual drone of street traffic. But Ibrahim el-Magd did not notice. He was already deep in prayer.

*

Daniel stared at the open Bible before him. Something Guido had said continued to haunt him. He couldn't shake it. And he sensed it was related to his recurring dream . . .

"That is why the stones were given to my people, because we are impulsive, swift to act, like Naphtali . . ."

He looked back to the notes he had been writing all evening. The words drifted in and out of focus before his exhausted eyes. It was true: each of the twelve stones represented one of the twelve tribes. And looking up the history of the tribes, it was plain to see that each had a distinct personality. Guido was right; Naphtali could best be described as impulsive and swift to act, very much like Guido himself. Very much like — and here was the connection — very much like Charlie Rue back at church, the man whose face he'd seen in the pool with Guido and the Naphtali Stone. Both men had the same emotional, impulsive personality, one that Daniel had always disdained . . . until Guido had shown what he was really made of.

Then there was the Benjamin Stone and its tribe — an aggressive, opinionated people who would tear into their own clansmen until they got the full picture and were redirected. In many ways they were identical to Linda Grossman at church, and to Dr. Helen Zimmerman — the two faces in his dream that had been connected to the Benjamin Stone. Tough, combative, all spine on the outside . . . yet on the inside courageous, giving, compassionate. As he had with Guido, he was beginning to see past his initial prejudice and, particularly in Helen's case, appreciate the person underneath. But it was more than appreciation. Truth be told, on more than one occasion he had caught himself making excuses to be in her presence. Of course there was nothing wrong with that; they were becoming friends, that's all. But until now who would have thought such a thing possible?

Finally, there was the Levi Stone — the one representing God's priests, holy men overseeing the rules and regulations, justice and order. Men like himself . . . or like he had been until Jill's death. But just as with Helen and Linda Grossman, just as with Guido Sanchez and Charlie Rue, he was seeing another side to himself as well. A side whose legalism and rigidity was far too evident, but a side that was beginning to soften and change. Not a lot but gradually, stone by stone.

Stone by stone . . .

Was that what was happening? Was the acquisition of these stones somehow changing him — not the stones themselves, though he supposed that was also possible, but the process of acquiring them? Was that what all this was about? He gave an involuntary shudder, then shook his head. He was thinking too deeply, trying too hard to find too much.

Or was he?

He closed his eyes. It was late. Already he could feel the ache in his temples and the numbness that spread across his forehead whenever he reached mental exhaustion. Wasn't this what Jill always teased him about? Thinking too hard, looking for too much meaning? For her everything came easily and instinctively. But for him it was one laborious thought built upon another. How deeply he missed her. Her ease, her faith, her love.

"You'll hear his voice, Danny, and you'll love him . . ."

His eyes welled with moisture. Time was supposed to heal all wounds, but he felt no differently now than he had the day he lost her. Yet in many ways she was still with him. In his dreams. On this trip. Somehow it kept them connected, this quest. And her promise . . .

"You'll love him again . . . but not unless I go."

Had she really left him so he could be where he was, doing what he was doing? He hated the thought. Yet somehow, some way, he *was* growing. But did it have to be so painful? And so deep . . . so gut-wrenching, bone-aching deep?

He removed his glasses and wiped his eyes with his sleeve. That was enough of that. "Please . . . ," he whispered. "How many more of these stones do I have to find? Not all twelve; I don't have the strength for that. How many . . ."

But as usual, at least for Daniel Lawson, the heavens remained silent.

So, as was often his habit, he took off his shoes, stripped to his shorts, and went to bed in the silence. Just the silence. And Jill's journal. He had debated bringing it on the trip, but now he was glad he had. He slept with it every night. Sometimes reading a page or two before he went to bed. Sometimes simply holding her to his chest as he slept.

✳

"What is wrong?"

"I don't know." Helen rolled away from Jean Mark and sat up in bed.

"Tell me?"

"Something . . ." — she rubbed her head — "something's just not right."

Scooting beside her, he softly asked, "You are not still angry with me, are you?"

She shook her head. "No, of course not."

He reached out and tenderly played with the hair over her ear. "Because I have ways of making you forget such anger."

Helen pulled his hand aside to hold it. "It's not that; it's just . . ." She stared down at his fingers. "I don't know; something's just . . ." She took a deep breath and let it out.

"It is the preacher, isn't it?"

She looked at him, startled. "What?"

"Your preacher boyfriend."

"Don't be ridiculous."

"No, no, no. I see the way you act around him."

"Please — "

"Like a little schoolgirl, so unsure. And clumsy. I tell you, it sometimes is too painful to watch."

"What are you talking about?"

"I bet you even have trouble eating, don't you?"

"What's that got to do with — "

"The great Dr. Zimmerman, finally she has fallen."

"What?"

"L'amore, my friend. L'amore."

186

"Don't be ridiculous." She released his hand and pushed it aside.

"'How hard the mighty doth fall.'"

"You think so, do you," she challenged.

"I know so. It is obvious to everyone. Well, everyone but you. And him of course. So now you find yourself starting to play by his rules."

"Rules?"

"I am no theologian but I imagine his rules, they do not include such extracurricular activities as ours?"

Helen shook her head. "Don't be absurd. It has nothing to do with his rules. It's just that I . . . I don't know . . . "

"And I tell you, you do."

"What?" she demanded in exasperation. "What do I know?"

"That you are in love."

"Why do you keep saying that?"

"Why do you keep denying it?"

"Because it's not true. I mean, the man's just lost his wife."

"And to your credit, you have hidden your feelings well — from him and yourself."

"Will you stop it!"

"It is true."

"No. It's stupid and it is absurd. And he's so . . . so . . . I mean, *him?* He's a preacher, for crying out loud."

"Worse things could happen."

She turned to him. "Name one."

He frowned. "Give me time; I am sure something will come to mind."

Helen dropped her head into her hands, then shook it. "This is too weird . . ."

Without further word he reached for his shirt.

She glanced up. "Jean Mark, I'm sorry. I . . ."

"Not to worry," he said, slipping into the shirt and buttoning it. "It can happen to the best of us. But to you . . . No offense, my friend, but I did not think such a thing was possible."

Helen took a deep, weary breath. "Neither did I," she mumbled. "Neither did I."

✳

"The queen of Sheba," Helen said. She motioned toward Tyler's viewfinder. "That's the African woman."

"Queen of Sheba?" Tyler repeated.

Helen nodded.

"From the Old Testament?" Daniel asked. "The one who visited King Solomon?"

"One and the same."

"And the young man, the kid?" Tyler asked. He indicated the picture that he'd freeze-framed on his monitor.

"Hard to say, but I imagine it's Menelik."

"Who?" Daniel asked.

"The illegitimate son of King Solomon and the queen of Sheba."

Daniel coughed on his morning coffee. "Excuse me?"

Helen knew the statement came as a shock, so she tried to soften it. "According to Ethiopian tradition, that is." Angry at herself for going easy on the man, she added, "Granted, their sexual relationship is never mentioned in the Scriptures, but Ethiopian legend insists that Menelik was the illegitimate son of King Solomon and the queen of Sheba. It says that he grew up, returned to Jerusalem, and stole the ark of the covenant."

"*Legend,*" Daniel emphasized, "not Scripture."

She threw him a glance. "Many see little difference." Immediately she chastised herself. *Stop it! Do you have to turn everything into a fight?*

Unfazed, Daniel repeated, "I'm just saying it's not in the Bible."

Helen nodded. "It's mostly Ethiopian tradition and Knights of the Templar folklore."

Tyler turned to Nayra. "You mentioned them before. Who are these knight guys?"

She answered, "Nine French noblemen who came to Palestine in A.D. 1119—twenty years after it was stolen and occupied by the European Christians."

Helen looked at the girl, impressed at her knowledge, then added, "Their primary purpose was to find the ark of the covenant. They took possession of the temple mount that we visited in Jerusalem and spent seven years excavating there, looking for the ark. Some call them the Holy Land's first archaeologists."

"Any results?" Tyler asked.

Helen shook her head.

Daniel ventured, "Because it was stolen by the Babylonians during their destruction of Jerusalem in 587 B.C."

Helen nodded. "That's one theory."

"There are others?" Tyler asked.

"Many insist it's still buried under the temple mount. Then of course there are the Templar Knight rumors, too varied to go into now. But every so often somebody claims to find clues left in the artwork of their time." She motioned to the viewfinder. "Like your painting here."

Tyler's interest grew. "So you think this is some sort of clue — telling us where they took the ark back then?"

"Not only where they took it then but where it is today."

"Today? You just said it was lost."

"*I* said it was lost. The Ethiopians, of whom Menelik was king, have a different take."

"They claim to know where it is?" Tyler asked.

Helen nodded. "Down to the city, building, and room."

"No way."

"In fact, they have a priest who devotes his entire life to protecting it. He lives, eats, and sleeps guarding it. And his last act before he dies will be to select a predecessor who will do exactly the same."

"All this is in Ethiopia?" Daniel asked.

"Yes. Saint Mary's Church in Axum."

"That's crazy," Tyler said. "Why haven't we ever heard of it before? Or seen pictures of it or something?"

"Because no one is allowed to see it."

"You mean, they say they have it, but they won't show it?"

"Precisely."

"How convenient," Nayra said. "They claim to have something but won't show it. They expect us to believe them just because they say it is so."

"Sounds like some religions I know," Helen said.

Nayra did not miss the dig. Nor did Daniel, who cleared his throat to diffuse any tension. "So the Ethiopians believe this story of Menelik being the offspring of Sheba and Solomon?"

"It's the second article of their 1955 constitution."

"And they're certain they possess the ark?"

"Every person of faith from there I've spoken to swears it's true."

Daniel gave his neck a rub. She could see he was fighting off some sort of headache. He didn't appear particularly crazy about this new information. "And what do you believe?" he finally asked.

Helen waited until he looked up. "You know me," she said. "I don't believe anything until I see it ... and even then I have my doubts."

Daniel nodded. "But you do speculate."

Still holding his gaze, she nodded.

"So what do you think?" he asked. "Is there any basis to their belief?"

"I think it is an interesting phenomena ... an entire nation convincing itself that it possesses the ark of the covenant."

"The whole nation?" Tyler asked.

"At least the Christians," Helen replied. "In fact, every church has a replica of it."

"Of the ark?"

"Yes. They're called *talbots*. On the highest holy days they take them outside their churches, keeping them covered of course, and parade them around for everyone to see — well, actually not to see, as the case may be." She turned back to Daniel. It was obvious he was struggling with something. "What's on your mind?" she asked a bit more softly.

"I'm thinking ..." — he lowered his head and rubbed his neck — "that if, as Guido believed, the other stones are still in the ark of the covenant, and if the ark could be in Ethiopia ..."

Suddenly she understood. No wonder he was asking so many questions. No wonder he was getting a headache. "You're not serious?" she asked.

"I don't know." He continued rubbing his neck. "I don't know what I am anymore. But if those things ..." — he motioned to the table, where the Urim and Thummim still sat — "if they won't work without all twelve stones ... and if we know where the rest of those twelve may be ..."

"All right!" Tyler exclaimed, seeing where his dad was going.

Daniel ignored him. "I mean, wouldn't it be foolish to come this far and stop now?"

"Do you have any idea what you'd be getting into?" Helen asked. "Ethiopia is one of the most godforsaken places on earth — mountainous deserts, drought, disease, famine . . ."

Daniel looked at the ground and nodded. "So I've heard."

"And you still want to go there?"

She waited until he slowly shook his head. "No . . . I don't want to go there at all."

Helen looked on, understanding this man more and more deeply. "But you have to," she quietly concluded.

He continued staring at the worn floorboards before him, rubbing his neck. Slowly, almost imperceptibly, he began to nod.

part
four

chapter ten

"So again I say, what's the big difference?" Tyler asked as he caught a dribble of hot sauce falling from his *injera,* a type of bitter-tasting tortilla wrap. He slurped up the part that hadn't run down the wrist of one hand, while holding his camera and zooming in on Nayra with the other. "I mean, other than you guys believing Muhammad was the last great prophet, and a few other technicalities . . . aren't we basically the same?"

"You mean, except for the fact that we live and practice our faith, whereas most Christians and Jews do not?" Nayra asked wryly.

Tyler glanced from his camera to his dad and Doc. Both pretended to ignore the comment. "Well, yeah, other than that. I mean, you said you believe in the Bible and everything, so I really don't see that big a difference."

The four of them walked down a steep, dusty path lined with eucalyptus and pepper trees. Just ahead was Kedane Mehret, a small church built upon a sacred spring not far from Addis Ababa, the capital of Ethiopia. They'd been in the country just over a day, gathering supplies and preparing for the bone-jarring ride to Axum, far up in the northern mountains. It was Tyler's first visit to a developing country, and he was surprised at the choking exhaust fumes, the flies, the number of beggars, and the toilet facilities that did not include such luxuries as a bowl, a seat . . . or toilet paper.

He was also surprised at the importance of religion here. Everywhere he looked, there was something to remind him — people bowing three times when passing churches; elaborate crucifixion jewelry; even the swimming pool at their hotel was formed into the shape of a giant cross. Before them, at the bottom of the hill, lay the church. Beside it a small blue building with white latticework doors. Here the sick and "demon possessed" came to shower and be healed. Nearby, one of several priests wrapped in white robes was rubbing a large crucifix up and down the bony back of a kneeling man, as another person, most likely a relative, poured icy water from the spring over his head. The air was hot and dusty, nearly choking Tyler with the smell of eucalyptus. And although the red-dirt plaza had a definite feel of peace and tranquillity, he couldn't help noticing the presence of more than one policeman.

Daniel cleared his throat slightly, indicating that he was about to enter their conversation. "Nayra, as we said before, isn't the pivotal difference between our two faiths how we view Jesus Christ?"

Tyler threw him a look. Although he had major issues with his father, one thing he could say about the man was that he was cool. He never tried pushing his religion down anybody's throat. Of course Tyler knew he looked down his pious, holier-than-thou nose at anybody who disagreed with him, especially those of different faiths, like Nayra. But he also knew the guy was far too "civil" to argue unless asked. Still, here, surrounded by a hundred pilgrims milling about, all waiting for their turn to be "healed," it must have seemed like a natural enough place for him to enter their discussion.

"Actually," Nayra corrected, "your belief and my belief regarding Jesus are quite similar."

"Really?" Daniel asked.

"Certainly. Like you, we also believe in his virgin birth and that he lived a sinless life and healed and raised people from the dead."

"You believe all that?" Tyler asked from behind the camera.

She nodded. "In reality we attribute more miracles to his life than you do."

"Like what?"

"Like Jesus speaking to his mother when he was still in the cradle, like his creating living birds out of clay."

"No kidding?" Daniel asked.

"We also believe that one day he will return from heaven to defeat the Antichrist."

"Sounds like you got it all covered," Tyler said.

"We believe so."

"Except . . . ," Doc interjected, "you don't believe Jesus was God the Son."

Without missing a beat Nayra countered, "Just as you Jews don't."

Doc nodded, looking about the crowd and quoting, "'Behold, the LORD your God is one God.'"

"And the crucifixion?" Daniel asked. "Don't we have different views of the crucifixion?"

"Yes," Nayra nodded, "that is another point of disagreement. Allah would not torture and kill his prophet. Instead at the last moment he selected another to take his place."

"On the cross?" Tyler asked.

"Yes. The crowd was made to believe Jesus was on the cross, but in reality he had already ascended to heaven to be with God."

Tyler shrugged. "Interesting technicality."

"No," Daniel shook his head. "I think it's more than a technicality. Christ's death on the cross is central to the Christian belief. In fact, according to Jesus himself and Old Testament prophecies, that death was the main reason he came to earth."

Nayra frowned. "With the purpose being . . ."

"To pay for our sins. It's his blood that cleans us of our wrongdoings so we can stand before a perfect and holy God. If you ask me, that's a pretty significant difference."

"Yes, it is," Nayra agreed. "We take responsibility for living pure and holy lives. You, on the other hand, believe you may sin all you wish without ever having to — "

Tyler didn't see the woman coming until she shrieked and threw herself on the ground in front of them. He leaped back and zoomed out to capture her writhing and twisting as she screamed in torment. She tore at her clothes, her face, her eyes, as the top half of her robes twisted off. Her ebony skin coated itself in the pink dust of the plaza. Immediately a crowd gathered. She threw back her head and cracked it hard on the packed earth. Her eyes widened at the pain. She slammed it into the ground again. Then again. Each time more violently than the last. A woman in the crowd began a loud, trilling chant: "La-la-la-la-la-la-la . . ." Others joined in. Suddenly an old priest appeared and dropped to his knees. Holding an ornate crucifix in his hand, he shouted commands while careful to stay out of harm's way. But he was not careful enough. Like lightning, the woman reached up and grabbed his yellow cotton sleeve. He let out a cry as she clutched it. He continued screaming, trying to get free, but her grip was like iron.

Two officers pushed their way through the crowd and arrived. They shouted at the woman, but she did not respond as she continued writhing, clutching the terrified man's sleeve, and slamming her head on the ground. The younger of the two officers bent down, trying to break her hold, but her nails slashed deeply across his face, immediately drawing blood. He let out a cry and grabbed his cheek as his partner produced a baton and struck her. She barely noticed. He struck here again, then again. Blood flew and splattered. But it did not come from the clubbing. It gushed from the back of her skull as she continued slamming her head on the ground.

"Stop it!"

Tyler glanced from the camera to see Doc moving into the fray. She blocked the officer with the club. "Stop it!" she yelled.

"Helen, what are you—" Daniel's voice was lost in the commotion.

"Stop it! Leave her alone!" She managed to shove the other officer away, then dropped to her knees.

"Helen..."

She forced herself into the flailing arms and legs until the woman released the priest. The old man scampered away as the woman began to strike Doc, blow after blow, arms, fists, legs. Doc grabbed one arm, then the other. She pulled, lifting the body, dragging the head off the ground. The woman continued to twist and kick but she could no longer bang her head. Doc pulled the woman closer, locking herself into a type of embrace, her hands and shirt smearing with blood. "It's okay ...," she whispered fiercely. "You're all right ... you're okay ..."

The woman relaxed slightly, which the officers saw as an opportunity to move in. They grabbed Doc and the woman and began pulling them apart.

"What are you doing?" Doc shouted. "Get away!"

The woman panicked and resumed screaming, her arms and legs flying. More kicks and punches landed. Batons reappeared and came down hard.

"Stop it!" Doc shouted at them. "Stop it!"

The woman gnashed her teeth, snapping and biting at anything she could reach.

"Augh!" A chunk of flesh tore from Doc's left shoulder, then was spit from the woman's mouth.

"Helen . . ." Daniel had joined the brawl, dropping to his knees, trying to untangle the women. "Let go — "

"Get away — "

"Helen — "

The fight continued, but with Daniel's help the officers were finally able to start pulling the two apart.

"Leave her alone!" Doc shouted.

At last the two were separated and the officers began dragging the writhing woman away.

Doc lunged for them. "Leave her alone — "

Still on his knees, Daniel caught her, holding her back. "Helen, no!"

"Leave her — "

"Helen!" He yanked her hard. "Let them handle it!"

"But they — ," she tried again.

"What are you doing!" He spun her around and shouted into her face. "What are you doing!"

She looked at him.

"What are you thinking!"

Exhausted, somewhat dazed, she searched his face.

"What are you thinking!"

"They were beating her." She gulped for air. "She needed someone to — "

"They're experienced; they know what they're doing!"

"But — "

"Look at you!" He angrily wiped the blood from her face. "Look at you!"

"I can take care of myself."

"You could have gotten yourself killed!"

"So?"

"'So'?" He was incredulous. "'So'? This isn't just about you! We're a team!" Looking at the bite wound, he unbuttoned his shirt.

She stared, unsure how to respond.

He removed his shirt. "Try thinking of someone else for a change, will you?" He pressed the material to the wound and began

199

cleaning it. "If something happened to you, how could we ever —" He leaned in, peering at the gash. "First Jill and then you. How could I go on if something happened to you? Did you ever think of that? Did you ever for one minute stop and think what I might be feeling . . ." He slowed to a stop, realizing what he was saying. He looked up at Helen, somewhat startled. She stared at him, equally as surprised.

He swallowed, then returned to his cleaning with a certain briskness. "We're supposed to be a team, the four of us."

She said nothing.

He tried again. "Working together. A team."

She remained silent, watching as he finished cleaning the wound.

"Can you stand?"

"Of course," she answered huskily.

He began helping her to her feet. "Ty, can you give us a hand here?"

Tyler lowered the camera and moved in with Nayra to help as Daniel continued giving orders. "We need to get you to a hospital, get that wound cleaned out before infection sets in."

"What about the woman?" Helen asked.

"We'll check on her but we need to get that cleaned out. It may need stitches. Here, hold the shirt against it. Got it? You sure? Good, good . . ."

But no matter what he said, no matter how he tried to cover, the words had been spoken. The words had been spoken and there was nothing he could do to take them back.

✳

Ibrahim el-Magd sat quietly in the dark. It had been more difficult to find his brother-in-law than he had anticipated. Instead of staying with his second wife at their apartment in Cairo, Yussuf Fazil had taken a room on the outskirts of the city not far from Giza. Word had obviously reached him that the car bomb had failed and Ibrahim was now on the hunt.

But Allah was faithful. Yussuf Fazil had been found and justice would be served.

He had waited six hours. Six hours sitting silently in the hot, airless hotel room. He would have opened a window but an open window could be seen from the street. And if a cautious Yussuf spotted it, he would not enter. The desk clerk had recognized Ibrahim immediately, but once inquiries were made as to the health of the man's family and where they lived, it took little else to ensure his silence.

Now Ibrahim simply waited. And thought. He watched as a shaft of moonlight that spilled between the curtains slowly made its way across the worn sheets of the bed. He reached into his galabiya, as he had a dozen times the past several hours, to check upon the dagger. Of course it was there. It was always there. It had been Allah's servant many times. But never with one so close. Never with one so close to Ibrahim's heart. How hard, how terribly hard, this would be. And how he had pleaded for another solution. But there was none. Justice must be served.

He thought again of their childhood, of the pigeons. And of young Yussuf's courage and faith. *"If we do not kill him, he will make his brothers and sisters —"*

The key scraped, then rattled into the lock of the door. Ibrahim froze as the lock clicked and the door opened. The hall's fluorescent light flickered a blue green hue upon the bed. But Ibrahim could not be seen sitting on the chair in the shadows. Yussuf Fazil entered the room and shut the door. Now the shaft of moonlight was all that lit the room. With a heavy sigh he tossed his jacket upon the bed and walked toward the nightstand lamp. He slowed to a stop before reaching it.

Ibrahim ceased breathing. It did no good. Yussuf had already sensed his presence. "So, you have finally found me," he spoke to the darkness.

"It was not difficult."

"For the great Ibrahim el-Magd it would not be. You are alone?"

"Yes."

With a sigh of resignation Yussuf Fazil eased himself onto the bed, less than a yard from Ibrahim's chair. "And so you have come to kill me. To seek your revenge."

Ibrahim took a breath to steady himself and then he answered. "No. I have not come to seek my will, but the will of Allah. You have shown weakness from the start. I should have known you would not have the faith or patience for our task."

"Every day we wait brings us closer to failure."

"And you tell me this by killing my son! By trying to kill me!" The sudden intensity surprised Ibrahim. He took another breath, reminding himself that this was not about emotion but justice. *One plus one equals two.*

"I have told you this a thousand times, my brother, but you would not listen. We are ready to strike now. To unleash Allah's wrath now. Yet Sheikh Habib has made you weak, allowing you to become obsessed with these stones. Allowing you to believe that you can actually hear the voice of —"

"Silence!" Ibrahim was on his feet. "I will not listen to lies! Satan has filled your mouth!"

Yussuf paused, then answered quietly, "And you will silence him by killing me."

Ibrahim was grateful that darkness veiled the emotions on his face. He opened his mouth to speak but could find no words. Love, hate, duty — all raged and churned inside him. How he hated this man. How he loved him. And how he hated the duty he must now perform.

"And what of Allah's silence?" Yussuf asked. "Why has he not yet spoken to you, my brother? Why, after so great a time, do the stones still elude your possession?"

"You tell me." Ibrahim struggled to keep his voice even. "Perhaps you have also polluted the thinking of those who search for them. Such as your daughter with the American pastor."

"No, I have not," Yussuf said sadly. "Nor do I understand why the pastor is making such progress. In but a few weeks he has retrieved not only three of the stones but the Urim and Thummim as well."

Ibrahim could not believe his ears. "He has found the Urim and Thummim?"

"Nayra is certain of it."

Ibrahim's mind spun. "Why would a Christian, an American, be allowed such a privilege? You lie," he said, seething.

"No, my brother, I tell the truth. And for that I am afraid. Is this not but another distraction of Satan, another manner of placing doubt in your heart?"

Ibrahim's anger grew. "Or to assist her father's plan, is your daughter merely spreading more lies?"

"Nayra knows nothing of my actions."

"Perhaps she does, perhaps she does not. When we are through here, I shall pay her a visit to see."

"This does not concern Nayra."

The fear in Yussuf's voice gave Ibrahim little pleasure.

Rising from the bed, Yussuf repeated, "You should not involve my daughter."

"Nor should you have involved my son!"

"That was a mistake!"

Silence filled the room. Ibrahim closed his eyes as his heart filled with even more sorrow. Until that moment there was still the faintest hope that Yussuf had not been responsible for the air strike. He had known it was true, but hope against hope, love against love, he had prayed that he was wrong.

He was not.

"I begged Sarah not to bring him," Yussuf was saying. "I pleaded with your family to stay home."

Ibrahim felt himself growing cold and focused. "So it *was* you ..."

Yussuf took a step closer. The shaft of moonlight cut across his face. "Ibrahim, please ..."

"The car bombing I understand." Ibrahim's voice trembled but it didn't matter, not now. "But my own family. Muhammad, my only son ..."

"It was a mistake. Intended only to push you into action. I swear by all that is holy, it was a mistake."

Tears filled Ibrahim's eyes. Tears of betrayal, of love, and of pain. Oh, the impossible pain. Ibrahim silently pulled the dagger from his robe as Yussuf continued speaking. "Forgive me, my brother ... forgive me ..." Yussuf was crying now, too. His tears glistened in the moonlight. "Please ..." He spread open his arms, a plea for Ibrahim to embrace him. "I am so sorry ... Please, forgive me."

Ibrahim's heart flooded with passion. It choked him, making it impossible to breathe. His brother's arms continued stretching toward him. Oh, the pain, the impossible pain.

"Can we not take care of it until it gets well? Can we not give it—"

"Ibrahim ..."

"But he is our favorite."

If it was between them, he could find a way to forgive.

Yussuf remained standing, crying. "My friend ..."

But it was not between them. It was between Satan and Allah. *"If we do not kill him, he will make his brothers and sisters sick."* Satan and Allah.

"... please ..."

He must be faithful. Regardless of the cost, he must be strong.

"... my brother ..."

Ibrahim reached out to receive the embrace. With fierce passion he threw his arms around his friend. They hugged one another tightly. And still holding him, unable to breathe from the emotion, Ibrahim el-Magd silently slipped the dagger's blade between his brother's ribs.

Yussuf let out a startled gasp but did not cry out. Ibrahim removed the blade, then thrust it again. Tears streamed down his face as he removed it and thrust it a third and final time.

Gasping and no longer able to stand, Yussuf slumped into his arms. Ibrahim carefully eased him onto the bed, feeling the warm blood spilling over his hands, watching as it soaked the sheet in the moonlight, slowly spreading out its wet blackness.

When Yussuf finally spoke, his words were faint and raspy. "My brother ..."

Ibrahim lowered his head to hear.

"Promise me ..." Another agonizing gasp, the words only a whisper now. "Do not harm Nayra ... Promise me ..."

Ibrahim answered, his voice thick with emotion yet filled with truth. He would not send this man he loved to hell believing a lie. "I am sorry ...," he whispered. "That is a promise I cannot keep."

For the first time Yussuf Fazil cried out in pain. Ibrahim knew it was not from the wound. After drawing a wheezing, ragged breath, Yussuf repeated, "Promise me ... promise ..."

Leaning his mouth to Yussuf's ears, Ibrahim whispered hoarsely. "I make no covenants with the Devil, my brother. Nor with his children."

A quiet, gut-wrenching moan escaped from his friend's throat.

Slowly Ibrahim rose. He reached for the edge of the sheet to clean his blade, his hands shaking with emotion. In the darkness he heard his friend struggling and gurgling for final breaths. He returned the dagger to his galabiya and walked to the sink to wash.

When he had finished, he turned off the water and solemnly dried his hands on a frayed towel.

He turned and walked to the door. He opened it to the bare, flickering fluorescent light. He turned his head from the glare. Now he easily saw his brother on the bed. His chest no longer heaved. It barely moved. Still, he hoped some life remained, for it was important he hear his final words. "Farewell, my friend," Ibrahim softly spoke. "Until this time you have been good to us. Farewell."

Then Ibrahim el-Magd stepped into the hallway and shut the door.

Overwhelmed and exhausted, there was nothing more he wanted than to return home. But he still had one more stop. With a phone call or two he would find his niece's location. And then he must visit her ... and the pastor. He did not enjoy what he had to do. Already a cold dread knotted his gut. But it must be done. As with all things, he must be faithful.

The warped door rattled as Daniel knocked on the peeling veneer. There was no answer. For the briefest moment he hoped for a reprieve. It had been forty-eight hours since the attack on Helen at Kedane Mehret. This was followed by a trip to the hospital, a detailed conversation with an official of the Ethiopian Orthodox Church to set up a meeting in Axum, some last-minute preparations, and finally the longest automobile ride in human history — not only because of the dusty, carburetor-clogging roads but because of the tension inside the vehicle caused by his absurd comment during the attack. How he could have said something so ludicrous was beyond him. In fact, it took much of the trip just to figure it out and rehearse the right words to explain it. Once he worked them out, all he had to worry about was the timing of those words (as soon as possible) and their audience (as few as possible).

Unfortunately, no opportunity had proved available. Until now ... Now, at 9:56 p.m., in the hallway of this rundown hotel in Axum, just thirty minutes after they'd arrived in town. The time had come for Daniel Lawson to make his explanation, to set the record straight and to clear the decks. Either that or to make a total fool of himself.

He reached for the door and was about to knock again, when it suddenly opened. A wilted Helen appeared. She was barefoot, wearing those skimpy white shorts and a blouse that could stand to be buttoned one more button. In her left hand was a wet washcloth to cool herself, in the other an open can of Diet Coke.

"Hey, Preacher Man," she said, shaking back her hair and nervously running her hand through it. Unfortunately, it was the same hand that held the Diet Coke ... causing the icy drink to spill onto her shoulder and down her blouse. She let out an oath, immediately trying to brush it away. She would have been more successful if the can wasn't still in her hand, which meant dumping more of the icy refreshment down her front. Again she swore as she bent over, set the can on the floor, and continuing brushing.

Daniel forced himself to glance away from her open blouse. When she finally rose, she was red-faced and flustered. "Look, I'm sorry about that," she said.

"It could happen to anybody."

"No, I mean, you know, about my mouth."

"Pardon me?"

"My language. I've been working on it since we first ... uh, well, I've been working on it."

The conversation had barely started and it was already strained. "Oh ... yes, well, that's okay; don't worry about it."

"I mean, I don't usually do that."

"Swear?"

"Spill Coke down my shirt."

"Ah."

Catching herself, she added, "Or swear. I don't do that a lot, either. Well, not much."

"Ah, good." He forced a chuckle. "I mean, that's your choice; I wasn't being judgmental. You can swear all you want. Not that you should, but, well, you know what I mean."

"No. I mean yes, I know what you mean."

"Good." Daniel cleared his throat. "Well, listen, I was just checking on your accommodations."

"Couldn't be better. Hot and cold running sludge, minimal amount of holes in my mosquito netting, and a communal bathroom just two flights up. How 'bout you?"

"Pretty much the same except for the wildlife."

"Cockroaches?" she asked.

"The size of Buicks."

"Ah." There was the slightest pause. Opening the door wider, she asked, "So do you want to come in?"

"No, uh ... I should be getting back."

"Oh, all right."

Another pause.

"So how's the wound?"

She reached up and touched the bandages on her left shoulder. "A little tender. The antibiotics are keeping down the infection — though I swear by the size of those pills, they were intended for a horse."

"We humans can pack a pretty vicious bite."

"Tell me about it."

"Listen, about that ..." He cleared his throat again.

"That?"

"The attack. I want to apologize for anything I might have — "

"No, no, you did the right thing, pulling me away like that. I don't know what I was thinking. I guess it was seeing one woman against all those men that — "

"No, actually I meant about what I said."

"What you said?"

He swallowed. She was not making this easy. "Yes, I want to apologize for what I said ... you know, about needing you and everything."

"Oh, that ..."

"I mean, you're important to this little venture of ours; we couldn't do it without you. But ..." He paused, trying to remember the words he'd so carefully rehearsed.

"But ..."

"But insinuating there was more to our relationship than that ... well, I certainly didn't intend to make you feel uncomfortable."

"Uncomfortable."

"Yes, hinting that there was some sort of romantic interest or something. I certainly didn't want to give the wrong impression."

"Oh, right."

"There isn't of course. I mean, interest."

"No, of course."

"I figured you'd want to know."

"Yes, you're right," she agreed. "It's good to know."

"Good."

"Not that I thought there was any."

"Right."

"But you're right, it is good . . . to know."

"Right."

"Right." She paused. "Thank you."

"You're welcome."

Another pause.

"Is there anything else?"

"Uh, no, just wanted to clear that up."

"It's clear." She smiled.

"Good . . . good."

"Crystal clear."

"Good." He coughed slightly. "So, uh, we'll see you in the morning, then. We have an appointment with the EOC official at nine o'clock sharp."

"Nine o'clock sharp," she repeated, nodding.

"Right. Well, good night, then."

"Good night." Helen started to close the door, but not before kicking over the can of Diet Coke she'd left sitting on the floor. She let out another oath as she stooped to pick it up, then resumed shutting the door, again muttering, "Sorry . . ."

"That's all right," Daniel said. "Good ni—"

The door closed in his face. He hesitated, then turned, surprised at how warm his cheeks felt. But at least he had said it. At least he had cleared the air. He'd feel a lot better now; he was certain of it. Yet even as he headed down the hall toward his room, he realized he did *not* feel better. He did not feel better at all.

✻

It was only 9:20, but the sun was already brutally hot as they threaded their way through the tall, dry grass. The air was thinner at this altitude and full of the roasted-oat smell of grass mixed with the pungent smell of livestock. The four of them followed the hunched-over priest through the dusty field. He used a piece of cane taller than himself to negotiate the rocky terrain. On every side were the broken, crumbling remains of a hundred stone monoliths that had fallen to the ground centuries earlier. Yet not all of them had fallen. A handful still stood, some towering up to ten stories above their heads.

The old man turned to Daniel with a frown. "We are not ignorant savages, Reverend."

"I never meant to imply that you were."

"You imply it when you speak of sending missionaries to assist us in spreading the gospel."

"I simply meant that in the past our church — "

"And we appreciate your 'humanitarian' efforts very much. But please keep in mind that our country became Christian in A.D. 341. That is several hundred years before England became Christian."

"I didn't know that."

"Hm. And over a thousand years before your country was even discovered."

"I'm sorry. I simply meant that — "

"I understand what you meant, Reverend. And though your heart may be right, it is your mind that needs to be educated."

Daniel accepted the rebuke. Not because he was trying to win over the EOC official but because he had been legitimately wrong. He had known nothing of Ethiopia's spiritual heritage, and in his arrogance he just naturally figured he was superior. But why?

He'd barely asked the question before the answer came. It made him wince but he knew it was true. He was superior because he was white and they were black. Because his heritage was European and theirs was African. How odd. He had never thought of himself as having the slightest trace of prejudice. On the contrary, he'd gone out of his way to support inner-city programs, to reach out and help the needy, to —

There it was again . . . *to help the needy*. It was true: he'd always considered the black population as "needy," as people who needed to be "helped," as a people who were . . . inferior. Despite his rhetoric, his sermons, his programs, had he ever once considered them as equals? Equal before God, yes. But equal to himself?

He scowled at the question. He was no bigot. What about Bill White? Hadn't he hired an African American to be his associate pastor at the church? Hadn't one of the main reasons been to reach down to the poor and disadvantaged of the community who —

There it was again . . . *reaching down*. Not reaching out but reaching down.

Okay, but regarding Bill White, the other reason he hired the man was because he had risen from the south side of Chicago and —

Risen? Daniel couldn't believe it. Was there no end to it? How subtle. How insidious. Oh, he loved the black people, all right, but they were always "they" — the inferior, the needy, those whom he could help ... reach down to ... raise up. It was amazing.

But just as amazing was how quickly the deception was being revealed. In less than twenty minutes the old EOC priest had shone light on a lifetime of bigotry. Was it happening again? Was he being shown another blind spot, another area of prejudice? Like Guido and Charlie Rue? Like Helen and Linda Grossman?

The old man continued his lecture. "Our priests are encouraged to spend up to twelve hours a day in worship. And the layperson is to pray seven times a day."

"Seven?" Nayra asked.

"Yes. And 180 days of the year are spent fasting."

"That's half of each year," Tyler said from behind his camera.

"You are correct. And regarding our heritage ... In the fourth and fifth century we were considered to be one of the four great civilizations in the world. There was Persia, China, Rome, and Ethiopia."

"Is that when these were built?" Tyler asked, turning his camera to one of the long segments of broken stone that lay on the ground before them.

"Yes. We know for a fact that the last was erected before A.D. 341."

Shading his eyes from the midmorning sun, Daniel looked up at one of the tallest still standing. It had clear geometric designs carved on each of its four sides.

"And you say they were grave markers?" Helen asked.

"Correct. Tombstones for the kings. And this ..." — he walked over to a large piece of fallen rock, another in a long line of broken stones, and tapped it with his cane — "This is the largest monolith in the world."

"In the world?" Tyler asked.

The priest nodded. "It was 108 feet tall."

"Bigger than the Egyptian obelisks?" Nayra challenged.

"Yes, easily. The largest decorated single stones ever erected are right here. This one, it weighed over seven hundred tons."

Tyler whistled softly. "How did they get them to stand upright?"

"That, my friends, is why you have come to visit."

"With the ark?" Tyler asked. "They raised them with the help of the ark?"

Ignoring the boy's question, the priest turned and leveled his gaze directly at Daniel. "You have the stones?"

"Yes."

"At the hotel?"

"No, the locks on the doors aren't all that trustworthy, and they didn't have a safe."

"You are a wise man. May I see them, please?"

Daniel hesitated, throwing a look to Helen.

The old man spotted it and clicked his tongue. "Come, Reverend, if we are to hold any discussion, we must first be assured that you have what you claim to have."

Helen countered, "As we must be assured that you have what you claim."

The priest looked at her with the slightest disdain. He turned back to Daniel and answered, "You will have your proof. If what you say is true, you will have your proof."

Once again Daniel glanced at Helen. She gave the slightest nod. He looked about the grassy field, making sure no one else was in sight, then motioned to Tyler and Nayra. Taking their cue, all three reached into their pockets to produce the carefully wrapped stones.

"You keep them separate?" the priest asked. "In case you are robbed?"

"No," Daniel answered as he carefully unwrapped the Urim and Thummim from the scarf he'd bought in Nimes. "We keep them separate because of the heat."

"Heat?"

"Yes. When we bring them together, they generate heat."

The priest did not comment but motioned to Helen, Tyler, and Nayra as they finished unwrapping their stones. "You let women and children touch them?"

Helen's look was ice but before she could respond, Daniel explained, "We are a team. We are equals."

The priest scowled, obviously not appreciating the concept.

Daniel placed the scarf upon a knee-high portion of fallen obelisk. Carefully he laid the two granite rocks, the Urim and

Thummim, in the center. He motioned to Tyler, who reached over and laid the Levi Stone upon the scarf, inscription side up. Helen did the same with the Benjamin Stone, as did Nayra with the Naphtali Stone.

The priest said nothing but squatted for a better look. "You did not tell me where you acquired these. Was it from Sudan?"

"Sudan?" Daniel asked.

"Yes, from the one who has been collecting them in Sudan?"

Daniel exchanged looks with the group. "Uh, no. These were, well, they were from different places."

The priest leaned forward, examining Helen's clear green stone. Looking up, he asked, "Benjamin?"

Daniel wasn't sure if he'd read the writing or recognized it by some other means. In either case he nodded. "Yes."

Next the old man leaned over and examined Guido's clear crystal. "Naphtali," he said, this time more of a statement than a question.

"Yes."

He turned to the last stone, the one Jill had acquired in Istanbul. The stone whose tribe in so many ways represented Daniel's own life. "Levi."

"Yes."

"And these . . ." He motioned to the two granite rocks without inscription.

"We believe them to be the Urim and Thummim."

He bent down even closer, careful not to touch them with his hands but observing every detail, every fleck in the red stones.

Daniel glanced up at the others. He was pleased to see Tyler scanning the field, keeping an eye out for any unwelcome visitors.

After a long moment the priest reached toward Guido's stone. Again he did not touch it but let his fingers hover over its surface. He looked up at Daniel, startled. "You are right; it does give heat."

"When it's close to these," Daniel said, motioning to the Urim and Thummim.

The priest nodded and reached over to the Benjamin Stone. Once again he felt the heat. Then he stretched his hand to the Levi Stone. He frowned slightly, bringing his fingers closer. "This one, it gives no heat."

"We know."

He looked up. "Why?"

Daniel shook his head. "I'm not sure."

The priest gave no response but went back to each of the stones, carefully examining them but never touching them. Minutes dragged on. The sun grew oppressive. Tyler began to fidget. Helen blew the bangs out of her eyes. Even Daniel found himself growing impatient. But the man would not be hurried.

Finally he straightened up; then, with the help of his cane, he rose to a standing position. "Thank you," he said.

Daniel nodded.

The man responded with a polite bow of his head. Without looking at the others, he turned and started retracing their steps through the tall, dusty grass.

Daniel glanced at Helen, not understanding.

"'Thank you'?" Tyler called. "We come all the way here, show you these stones, and all we get is a thank-you?"

The man gave no answer as he continued along the uneven ground.

Helen shouted after him, "What about the ark? You said if these were authentic . . . You said we could have a meeting."

"Yes," the man called without looking back.

"When . . . how?"

"I will talk with the guardian of the ark. Together he and I will determine if it is appropriate."

"When will that be?" Daniel asked. "How long must we wait?"

"It will be God's timing."

"Yes, but —"

The old man continued walking, his cane rising up and down as he threaded his way through the grass and fallen stones.

"Excuse me," Daniel shouted. "Excuse me?"

But he neither looked back nor spoke anything more.

chapter eleven

"No," Daniel said.

"What?" Helen couldn't believe her ears.

The elderly EOC priest leaned forward on the staff, which he'd carried even here into the hotel lobby. "I do not understand," he said.

"Tell your guardian of the ark that either Dr. Zimmerman and I go together or we don't go at all."

The priest raised his eyebrows in surprise. "You cannot be serious."

"I am very serious. Those are my conditions."

"But he is the guardian of the ark. Nobody makes conditions to the guardian."

"Then we have no meeting."

"Daniel . . . ," Helen tried again. "This is the chance of a lifetime. You would be the only person in the world other than the guardian to actually see the ark, to know if it's really there."

"Yes," the priest said, nodding. "Listen to your friend."

Daniel turned to her. "We're a team. We've come this far together; I'm not going to let sexual bigotry split us apart now."

Helen's impatience grew. "Daniel, don't be stupi —"

"You say we have bigotry?"

Daniel turned to the man. "What do you call it?"

"We believe that women have their place."

"So do I. Equally, beside men."

The old man looked first at Daniel, then at Helen, then back at Daniel again. "Perhaps you do not realize what an honor this is. Even I, in all my years of service, have not been allowed to see the ark. Not so much as a glimpse. People have died for such an opportunity. Over thousands of years many people have died."

"He's right," Helen insisted. "Please, Daniel, don't be so pigheaded."

"No. We go together or we do not go at all."

Helen sighed in exasperation. As always, she was impressed with the man's honesty and sensitivity ... when she wasn't frustrated out of her mind by them.

The priest shook his head. "The guardian, he will not be pleased. He too wished to see the stones you showed me."

"And we wish to see the ark. But not if it means accepting his sexism."

The official frowned. "And this is the answer you wish me to deliver?"

"Yes, it is."

Once again the priest shook his head. Then without another word he turned and started toward the door. He continued shaking his head, his lips moving silently, either muttering or praying, as he hobbled out of the lobby and into the warm night.

Helen stared after him, not believing what she'd just seen and heard. Then she turned to Daniel. But what could she say? Once again he had left her completely and utterly at a loss for words.

The kiss had nothing to do with desire. For Tyler this was a first ... and a surprise. He simply wanted some way to express his feelings toward her, to share his ... *tenderness* — yes, that was the word. To share the tenderness that he felt toward her, that warmth in his chest that left him staring up at the ceiling until all hours of the night, that made his heart beat a little faster whenever they were together during the day.

Earlier they'd had dinner at a one-star restaurant where they weren't entirely sure what they were eating (and because of Nayra's dietary restrictions, were afraid to ask). There she had laughed until tears came to her eyes as he told of his childhood pranks in America ... like the time he ran the church sound board and left the wireless microphone open while Daniel used the rest room. Or when, from a hidden location, he ran a remote-control model car up and down the aisles during one of his dad's sermons. It took three ushers to finally catch it.

"Why do you ..." — Nayra dabbed the tears from her dark eyes with her scarf — "why do you torment him so? He is a good man."

"Got me." Tyler shrugged. "I guess 'cause he's such an easy target."

"But the way you two fight. Even when no words are spoken, there is such tension. And in your heart I see so much anger inside you."

Tyler shook his head. "I guess it's just ... it's that the man always has to be right."

"I have seen him make mistakes; I have seen him acknowledge them."

"That's what I'm saying — even when he's wrong, he turns it to right."

"And this upsets you?"

"It makes me crazy."

"Why?"

"I don't ... I'm not ..." Emotions welled up before he could stop them. "He's got it all sewed up, that's all."

She looked at him quizzically.

"He's got life all figured out; everything's neat and perfect. And there's no room for anything else."

"I still don't — "

"I can't breathe around him, Nayra. I can't move. It's like he's this giant ... sun. And every time I get near him, I'm dragged into his gravitational pull. And before I know it, I'm just another orbiting planet. I can't get out. I can't break out of his stupid gravitational pull."

"Without bickering and fighting."

Tyler looked down at his plate.

After a moment Nayra continued. "If you could see the pain you cause him. Sometimes his eyes, they are so — "

"You don't think I see it? Every day I see it. Sadness. Disappointment. Oh, he won't say it — he's too good for that — but it's there. It's always there." Tyler felt the back of his throat start to ache. "But I'm me. I'm my own man. I've got my own way of doing things; I've got my own beliefs."

"And what are they, Tyler? What are those beliefs?"

He looked into her eyes, feeling the loneliness wash over him, the abandonment he'd felt every day since his mother died. "I don't know." He fought through his thickening voice. "That's just it. I don't know." He stared down at the table, tears blurring his vision. "I mean, you, Dad, even Doc — you all have something you believe in, some sort of center."

"And you do not."

He gave his eyes a quick swipe. "If I just had something ... something of my own ..." He swallowed. "I mean, this whole quest thing, this whole business of trying to hear God's voice. It's not just because of Mom or because of what she told him. I mean ... it's probably just as much for me as it is for him." Quietly he added, "Maybe more ..."

She did not try to answer and for that he was grateful. How long they sat in the silence of the restaurant, he wasn't sure. But he was sure that no person he had ever met could open him up as quickly and effortlessly as this mysterious young woman from another land.

Later they had walked for nearly two hours. The streets of Axum were no great tourist attraction, but it didn't matter to Tyler. It could have been the surface of the moon, for all he cared. Because he saw nothing but Nayra. Felt nothing but her presence. Heard nothing but her soft voice with its enchanting accent. The stories of her own childhood in a tiny village along the banks of the Nile were endearing in their charm and simplicity. How she loved her parents, both of them, and how she would do anything for their happiness. She was an incredible jewel, and the absolute goodness of who she was made his chest hurt. But it was impossible for him to voice such things.

"Oh, come on," he teased. "You must have done something wrong. You must have been rebellious sometime."

Nayra frowned, seriously trying to remember. Then her face lit up.

"Ah." Tyler chuckled. "I knew it would come to you."

"When I was eleven and we went to Cairo ..." She smiled, obviously embarrassed.

"Go on ..."

"One evening I dressed as a boy so I could follow my father into a coffeehouse and stay near him."

"And . . ."

She shrugged. "That is all."

"That's it? That's the worst thing you've ever done?"

"It was really quite embarrassing. When they found out, I mean."

Tyler had to grin. The thought of a little girl with that much love for her dad made his heart swell. How he wished he had what she had. So much trueness in just one person. So much — well, here was another word he never used — so much . . . *purity.*

But how to express such things? How do you show the depth of such feelings? Not by holding hands, that much was certain. Even the slightest brush of their bodies made her blush and recoil. Yet he had to do something. It wasn't until they arrived at the door of her hotel room that he had a solution. It wasn't calculated or premeditated . . . just a spontaneous kiss, gently, atop her forehead. And though he'd kissed a dozen girls in his life, usually with desire and hunger, this kiss was filled with more meaning than all the other kisses combined.

As he withdrew his lips, she looked up to him, startled but not offended. She searched his eyes. He did not look away or hide what he was feeling. Nor did she. Taking her hand into his, he gently shook it.

"Good night to you, Nayra Fazil," he said.

She broke into a smile and his chest exploded.

"Good night to you, Tyler Lawson. *Allah yukaththir khayraka.*"

He tilted his head. "What does that mean?"

"May Allah increase your well-being."

It was Tyler's turn to smile. "Thank you," he said. "And *Allah yukaththir khayraka* to you too."

She nodded, holding his gaze.

He grinned, then turned and started down the hallway.

"Tyler Lawson?"

He slowed and turned back to her.

"You are a good man and a good friend."

He grinned again. "No. You're the one who is good. But I'm learning . . . From you I am learning."

Her smile broadened. "Good night, my friend."

"Good night." Turning, he headed down the hall toward his room. He wasn't sure how he managed, since his feet never touched the ground, but somehow, some way, he made it into his room.

✳

"*Allah yukaththir khayraka* ... is that how one greets one's enemy?"

Nayra stifled a gasp and whirled around. She spotted him sitting on her bed. Immediately her face lit up. "Uncle?!" she cried.

And with that single word she broke his heart. How he loved this child. Smart, articulate, full of life, and as committed to Allah as any man he knew. She dashed to him, and he barely had time to rise before catching her into his arms. She clung to him as if she were five years old again. He clenched his eyes, fighting back the emotion. How hard this would be. How terribly hard.

As if suddenly remembering she was a woman, she pulled from the embrace and rearranged herself, attempting to hide her embarrassment. "What brings you all the way here?" she asked.

He tried to answer but his voice caught. *Oh, Allah, have mercy. Have mercy. Not the child, not this one too.* He forced a smile, hoping it would somehow mask his dread.

"What is wrong?" she asked, searching his face. "Is something wrong with Mother ... with Father?"

"No, no." He forced the smile into a grin.

She continued studying him. "You are certain?"

"Yes, Little Bird," he lied. "I am certain."

"Then ... what is it?"

"I have come to personally check on your progress."

She looked at him, still dubious. "It is a long way for the great Ibrahim el-Magd to pay a personal visit."

"It is true," he said, chuckling. "Yes, it is. Yet your father tells me you have found the Urim and Thummim."

She nodded, traces of her little-girl enthusiasm returning. "Yes, yes. Plus three additional stones."

"Three stones?" He pretended surprise.

"Yes, yes. Well, actually four."

"Four? Are such things possible?"

"It is a miracle. The blessings from Allah are very great!"

As far as he could tell, she still knew nothing of the Day of Wrath, just as he and Yussuf had agreed. Her only assignment was to inform

219

them of the pastor's progress. "Then why, little one," he asked, "have you not told us so we could secure them for ourselves?"

"Did not Father tell you?"

"Your father said nothing except that the pastor is quite blessed in his search."

"Yes, exactly. We discussed it by phone, and Father felt I should stay as long as possible. If Allah is using the man as our instrument to find the stones, then we should not interfere with his blessing."

"'The wealth of the unrighteous is stored for the righteous.'"

She broke into another grin. "Exactly. Yes, yes."

Ibrahim el-Magd nodded. Was it possible? Had Yussuf told him the truth? Was she completely unaware of his treachery? If so, then perhaps her life could be spared. Perhaps she could—

No! He closed his eyes, refusing to let emotions rule. He had come here to seek truth and, if necessary, to carry out justice. He must not let feelings override obedience.

"It is most unusual," Nayra continued. "When the stones are brought together with the Urim and Thummim . . ."—she talked so fast that she had to catch her breath—"when they are brought together, they generate heat."

"Heat?"

"Yes, yes."

Ibrahim el-Magd frowned. His four stones did not create any such heat.

As if reading his mind, she explained, "From the Urim and Thummim. The pastor believes it is from the Urim and Thummim."

"Where is he now? The pastor."

"He is with officials from the Ethiopian Orthodox Church. He believes they have more of the stones, and he is trying to see them."

"More stones?"

"Yes."

Ibrahim scowled. He too had heard of such rumors, had even sent an envoy to speak with the government officials some thirteen months earlier. They'd had little success. Perhaps Allah was indeed using the efforts of the pastor for their gain. "Do you believe he will succeed?"

"He is a good man. He and his son are men of the Book."

"But will they succeed?"

"I am not certain, Uncle; time will tell."

"Time is something we have nearly exhausted, little one."

"He is making very great progress."

Ibrahim el-Magd looked into his niece's eyes. They sparkled with such enthusiasm, such hope. And as he looked, as he judged her words and her candor, the heaviness in his chest began to lighten. It was indeed possible that she did not know, that she knew nothing of her father's treachery, that she was simply working hard at her assigned task. And if that was true ... He closed his eyes, allowing relief to begin flowing through him.

"Uncle, what is wrong?"

He opened his eyes to see her looking at him with concern. He broke into another smile, this time unforced. "Nothing, Little Bird, nothing at all." Taking both her hands into his, he spoke earnestly. "But you must hurry him on his course."

"I will do my best."

"I know," he said, nodding. "This I know."

"But we have one problem."

He eyed her carefully. "Yes?"

"The woman."

"Woman?"

"I explained her to Father. I am surprised he did not tell you."

"Your father and I are involved in many things. What woman?"

"The pastor has an escort. An archaeologist. A Jew."

Ibrahim frowned.

"She has been helpful in some areas."

"Then Allah will use her efforts for us as well."

Nayra nodded. "Except I do not trust her."

"Of course. She is a Jew."

"It is more than that. She has held back one stone from him."

"Are you certain?"

"Yes, the Simeon Stone. In Palestine the man who gave us the Benjamin Stone had two. But she hid it from the pastor, pretending he gave us only one."

"Then you must expose her."

"I was uncertain. She has been helpful."

"No, you must expose her and do so quickly."

"Yes?"

"Yes." He nodded. "The sooner the better. Expose her and retrieve the stone."

"I understand. And the pastor?"

"Bring him to us. As soon as possible. There are many looking for the stones and we must keep them safe."

Nayra nodded. "But I am uncertain how I can convince him to — "

"That is the son you were speaking to, was it not? *Allah yukaththir khayraka* — was that not his son?"

"Yes . . ."

"Then use him."

"They are good men, Uncle. People of the Book."

"They will be safe." It was his second lie but Allah would understand. "Bring them to us, little one; every second counts. When their task is through, bring them to us quickly."

She looked at him and he held her eyes, watching her struggle as she searched for some other solution.

"Nayra . . ."

She scowled.

"It is important that you obey. Do you understand?"

"Yes, but — "

"They will be safe. I have promised you they will be safe." He held her gaze, convincing her of his sincerity.

Slowly she began to nod. "I understand. I understand, Uncle, and I will obey."

"Good . . . good. As soon as possible. It is for their own safety. If others find them, I cannot protect them. Do you understand?"

"Yes, I understand."

Ibrahim held her look one last moment to confirm her loyalty. *Allah be praised.* He was certain. *Allah be praised!* "Now, little one, I am afraid I must leave."

"But you have just arrived."

"I have much to do. And so do you. And so do you."

"Yes." She embraced him again. This time he returned it with far more enthusiasm. Allah be praised. He did not have to kill her. Nor did he have to kill the pastor and his son. Not yet. Nayra was good. Nayra was competent. She would bring them to him . . . stones and all. He was certain of it. Nayra Fazil was loyal, more loyal than her father had ever been.

✳

"What did he say?" Daniel asked.

Without waiting for translation, the guardian of the ark, a gaunt, middle-aged man in lemon yellow robes, repeated his statement.

The EOC priest leaned on his staff and turned to Daniel and Helen, preparing to translate. He had fetched them from the hotel not twenty minutes earlier. Through the bright moonlight he had led them onto the grounds of St. Mary's Church and to a small, outside sanctuary. It was a modest thirty-by-thirty-foot building made of stone blocks. In the front, at the center, a long piece of red cloth acted as a door to a twelve-foot-high entrance. On either side of the entrance was a curtained window nearly as tall. The entire structure was surrounded by forty feet of unmowed grass and weeds, closed in by a ten-foot-tall iron fence. A broken-stone walkway led from the front gate to the dozen porch steps that led up to the draped entrance. It was here, at the top of the steps, before the billowing curtain, that they stood as the guardian of the ark spoke and the EOC priest translated. "He asks why you will not respect our refusal to allow women upon holy sites?"

Daniel nodded and answered. "Because she is equal before God."

The priest asked, "You are not saying this because she is your wife?"

"That is correct. I am saying this because she is a woman."

The guardian paused a moment to consider the thought. He spoke and the priest translated. "Though people have longed to see the ark for three thousand years, you will deprive yourself of such an honor if she cannot accompany you?"

It took little effort for Daniel to hold his ground. He'd run the scenario in his head a dozen times. He knew what was right and he would not back down. "That is correct."

The guardian looked at him a long moment, carefully evaluating what he heard and saw. Daniel stood firm.

Finally, after careful consideration, the frail man shook his head.

The priest turned to him. "I am sorry, Reverend."

Daniel nodded. He was disappointed, greatly disappointed, but he was not surprised. It was the last test, the final showdown, and he had refused to blink. Unfortunately, neither had the guardian. Daniel cleared his throat. "Tell him I am sorry, too. And thank him for his time." With nothing more to say, he turned and started down the steps.

"Daniel . . ." It was Helen's final attempt to make him see reason. He shook his head. "Let's go."

But he'd only descended five or six steps before the guardian spoke and the priest translated. "You have not been dismissed."

Daniel slowed to a stop and turned back to look up at them.

The guardian spoke again and the priest translated. "Men spend their entire life striving to be good enough to become my successor and enter the ark's presence. They follow every rule, every law, to the finest detail."

Daniel stood, enduring the lecture.

"But you . . . for you the laws are not as important as the people."

Daniel nodded, impressed with the man's insight. "That's certainly one way of seeing it."

The guardian paused, still searching him. Finally he answered. "And that is the way our Lord sees it."

Daniel frowned, not understanding.

The guardian continued as the priest translated. "In the past your service to God has been one of rules. Righteous rules but rules nonetheless."

Daniel shifted uncomfortably. "What do you know of my service to God?"

"I know a great deal about you. And I know of the great loss you have suffered because of such rules."

The hairs on Daniel's neck stood up. Was he talking about Jill? About her death?

"I know of your search for him—and the lives that have been lost in that pursuit."

The chill crept across both shoulders and down his arms. How could he have known? Who could have told him?

"And now . . . now you would sacrifice it all because you refuse to abide by our traditions and rules . . . because you consider people more important than such things."

Daniel swallowed but his mouth was bone dry. Somehow this man knew. He seemed to know everything. When he could trust his voice, he answered. "That is correct."

The slightest trace of a smile crossed the guardian's face. "You have come a long way, my brother . . . and our Lord is pleased."

Daniel's response was husky. "Pardon me?"

The guardian did not answer but spoke again. "Your son, and his friend who is a woman, where are they?"

"Back at the hotel."

"Are they not worthy to join you? Are they not your equals as well?"

"I didn't think … I mean, if you were so hesitant with Dr. Zimmerman, I didn't figure my son or the girl …"

The guardian nodded and spoke. The priest translated. "The Lord knows. You have traveled a long distance, Reverend, though you still have some way to go. Continue your journey and do not stop until all is accomplished."

Daniel waited for more but the man had apparently finished. He stood silently in the doorway, before the billowing red cloth, and said nothing more.

When the silence grew uncomfortable, Helen spoke up. "Does that mean … does that mean you've changed your mind and we can go in?"

Without waiting for translation the guardian shook his head. "No."

"Then what was the purpose of — "

The guardian motioned for her silence. Reluctantly she complied. They continued to stand. Ever so slightly he began to nod. But not to them. It was as if he were agreeing with some conclusion he'd reached long before. After a moment he excused himself and disappeared behind the curtain. Helen, Daniel, and the old priest exchanged questioning looks but said nothing.

At last he reappeared. In his arms he carried a square bundle. It was no more than twelve inches across and about three inches thick. It was wrapped in blue cloth embroidered with golden stars. When he spoke, his voice was a little heavier and a little sadder. The priest translated. "You may not stand before the ark of the covenant, but you may receive this." With great care and reverence the guardian held out the bundle to Daniel, who hesitated a moment, glanced at Helen, then slowly walked back up the steps to receive it. Carefully, lovingly, the guardian placed it into his hands.

"What is it?" Daniel asked quietly.

The guardian answered, his voice still heavy. "I have known for many months you would come."

"How?" Daniel whispered.

The guardian did not answer. "Once you arrived and proved yourself, I was to place this in your care."

"Proved myself?"

The guardian merely looked at him but Daniel already had his answer. He knew exactly what the man was talking about. In quiet reverence he looked down to the bundle in his hands. He had no idea what it was but he knew it was of great value. When he looked up, he saw the sadness in the guardian's eyes. And for some reason it made him sad. Again he spoke. Just above a whisper. "Are you certain you want to do this?"

The guardian nodded. "Yes." His gaze dropped to the bundle. "The Lord has made it clear. It is your time. You are worthy to receive it."

Except for a slight breeze that bowed the curtain, the night was completely still. Daniel stood a moment, unsure what to do.

The guardian spoke one final time, the priest translating. "Go now." His voice was firm, almost resentful. "Your journey is nearly complete. You have only one more land to visit. But beware — this final destination will be the most treacherous of all."

Daniel looked back at him but the man avoided his gaze. Without another word the guardian turned and again stepped behind the red curtain. This time he would not return. Daniel knew it. And so did the priest.

"Come," the priest quietly spoke. "Let us go. Our time is over."

They turned and headed back down the steps, then along the pathway to the iron gate. It creaked as the priest opened it. They passed through and he shut and locked it. They started across the grounds, back to the hotel. But just before they rounded the building, Daniel felt compelled to look over his shoulder one last time. And there, all alone at the top of the stairs, watching after them, stood the guardian. Even from this distance Daniel could feel his sadness. Sadness mixed, no doubt, with the satisfaction of obedience. He knew that mixture of emotions, had felt it a hundred times himself. God's will . . . it was not always easy or even logical, but to obey it was, in time, always satisfying.

And just as the guardian had obeyed, Daniel knew he would obey. "*You have traveled a long distance, Reverend, though you still have some way to go. Continue your journey; do not stop until all is accomplished.*"

✳

"Where's Nayra?" Daniel asked.

"She said to start without her."

"We can wait."

"No, she said it was okay, we can start without —"

"We're a team, Tyler. She's as much a part of what we're doing as everyone else."

"Yeah, right," his son said scornfully.

"What does that mean?"

"She's not part of any team, Dad. She's just some smart, third-world 'fundy' you like having around."

"What?"

"Oh, please," Tyler said with a sigh. "I see it every time you guys talk. She's the poor, misinformed Muslim; you're the enlightened Christian waiting to show her the light."

Daniel frowned. "If we have the light, isn't that what we're supposed to do?"

"I'm talking about your attitude, Dad. That I'm-superior-to-you-'cause-I'm-righter-than-you attitude you always carry around."

"I don't carry around any —"

"Of course you do. I see it all the time."

Daniel bit his tongue. Tyler had done it again, pushed all his buttons. Would the kid ever let up? And although most of Daniel wanted to put the boy in his place, another part wondered if he might somehow have a point. It was twisted and exaggerated, as only Tyler could twist and exaggerate, but was there some truth to what his son was saying? He'd certainly seen it in his attitude toward the others — toward the Guidos and the Helens and the Africans. Was this yet another area he was blind to? Did he also consider himself superior to the Arabs or somehow better than the Muslims? To be right is one thing, but to think you're better because you're right . . .

"Look," Tyler said, softening a little, "she said it was okay, so it's okay. She just has some personal junk to take care of, that's all." Pointing at the table, he added, "So let's get on with it, okay?"

Daniel looked over at Helen, who shrugged, then down to the bundle of blue cloth on the table before them.

"It's okay," Tyler insisted. "She'll join us later."

The conversation had to be continued; Daniel knew that. If this was another issue God was trying to address, he'd better listen. But for now there was the bundle — and everyone's impatience, including his own, to see what it contained. Without further hesitation he took it into his hands. The blue material was made of finely woven linen. He pulled back its top fold, then its second. There were two more layers to go. More slowly he pulled back the third. Now it was possible to see something dark and flat underneath. Another, larger stone? No, this was more flexible. He hesitated.

"Go for it," Tyler said.

Daniel reached out to the fourth and final fold. Ever so gently he pulled it aside. And there before them lay a piece of material nine or ten inches square. Although much of it had rotted, there were enough gold threads woven throughout to hold it together. Attached to each of the four corners was a cord about a foot long braided from the same material. Woven into the front surface of the cloth, evenly spaced, were twelve rectangular sockets of gold. Three rows down and four across. Four of the sockets were filled with stones identical in size and shape to the ones they had recovered. And like the others, each had a different inscription. Their color and composition varied but their size and shape were identical.

Daniel glanced anxiously at Helen. She stared, knuckles pressed to her mouth. "What is it?" he asked.

She shook her head, not ready to speak.

He turned back to the table. Slowly he reached for one of the mounted stones.

"Be careful," she warned.

"Why?"

"What is it, Doc?" Tyler asked.

"I can't be positive but it looks like the *Choshen* ... or at least a facsimile of it."

"The what?" Daniel asked.

"The Choshen. It means 'Speaking Place.'"

"Speaking Place?"

"Yes ...," Helen said. "The breastplate of judgment."

"The high priest's breastplate?" Tyler could barely say the words.

Helen nodded, still staring. "Yes. The Choshen, the Speaking Place."

The name definitely had Daniel's attention. Tyler's too.

"What about these stones?" Tyler asked, pointing at the new ones.

"More of what we have, I imagine." Helen leaned forward to examine them. "They're not the original mounting—looks like they've been glued or soldered in—but I'm betting it's their original position." She moved closer to examine the inscriptions. "What do we have here . . ." She paused, then read, "Asher." She turned to the next and squinted. "Judah." And the next. "Dan." She adjusted herself to better read the last. "And finally . . ."

Daniel spoke the name as she did. "Issachar."

She looked up at him in surprise. "How did you know?"

"They were the tribe known for bearing the burdens of others."

Helen frowned. "Yes, but the name. How did you know it was the—"

Daniel shook his head. In part it was an educated guess, yet deep inside he knew. It was too long to explain, too thin a theory to articulate . . . but in his heart he knew. Just as he had learned from the dreams, had discovered from his meticulous studies of Scripture, he knew that each stone represented a type of person, a group that he had, one way or another, shut out of his heart. It was little wonder, then, that after the lecture by the EOC priest exposing his unknown racism, the four stones representing traits of his African brothers had now surfaced as well: Judah, the overcomers; Asher, the selfless ones; Dan, those leaning toward superstition and the occult; and Issachar, the bearer of burdens. Whether they were true or not, at least in his mind these were the stereotypes, the broad strokes with which he painted the people of this vast continent. Not only the people of this continent but their American cousins as well.

Amazing. What was God doing? What was he trying to say? It was more than coincidence; Daniel knew that. What incredible, remarkable thing was God doing?

"So this is where our stones originally came from?" Tyler asked, motioning toward the breastplate.

"Yes," Helen agreed, "or one like this. As you can see, each stone had a very specific location in Choshen."

"Cool," Tyler said. "So let's put ours in there with the others and see what happens. Maybe with the Urim and Thummim we'll finally kick things into action."

Daniel glanced at Helen, who slowly nodded. "It's worth a try," she said. "As long as we're careful."

Tyler rose and crossed the room to retrieve the Levi Stone, the one Daniel so closely associated with Jill and himself. He also grabbed the Naphtali Stone, which Nayra had given him earlier. Helen followed suit by reaching into her pocket and unwrapping the Benjamin Stone.

"So how do we begin?" Tyler asked. "What order do we put them in?"

Daniel took a deep breath to settle himself, then looked at Helen before venturing his answer. "I imagine they were placed in the order of the twelve tribes, the birth order of Jacob's twelve children."

Helen nodded. "I agree."

"So Reuben and Simeon, they would go in those first two empty positions."

"I see you've been doing some studying."

Daniel nodded. "And Levi ..." He took Tyler's stone and started to set it in the third socket.

"No!" Helen grabbed his arm. He turned to her as she shook her head. "In Hebrew we read right to left, not left to right. The last position on that row would actually be the first."

"Of course," Daniel agreed. He moved the Levi Stone to the third position and held it over the empty socket. Once again he hesitated and looked to both of them for confirmation.

"Do it," Tyler said.

Helen nodded.

Ever so carefully he placed the Levi Stone into the empty gold socket. It fit perfectly. Everyone waited breathlessly. But there was no change. Nothing happened.

"Okay, that's one down," Tyler said, obviously trying to stay calm. "Let's keep going."

The overhead fan slapped the air in uneven rhythms. Other than that, the room was absolutely silent.

Daniel continued. "After Levi came — "

"Judah." Helen pointed to the second row. The stone was already in place.

"Right. Then ... Dan." He indicated the next stone, which was also set in its place. "And next to that is, uh ..." He looked at Helen.

"I'm not sure," she said.

"Hang on." Daniel reached over and grabbed his Bible. "Let's make sure we get this right." He flipped to Exodus, the twenty-eighth chapter, one of the sections he'd been studying for so many days. "And the next one is ... Naphtali."

Tyler nodded and carefully placed Guido's clear crystal into the empty socket at the end of the second row.

They waited and again there was no reaction.

Daniel continued. "Then Gad ..."

"Don't have it," Tyler said.

"Asher."

"Right there," Tyler said, motioning to the multilayered agate already in place.

"And Issachar."

"There."

Daniel looked up. That was it for the first three rows. There was one more to go. "Zebulun—"

"Nope," Tyler said.

"Joseph."

"Nope."

"And the last stone ..." He looked at Helen. "Benjamin."

Taking the transparent green stone, Helen carefully set it into the empty socket, then quickly withdrew her hand.

Again they waited. Again there was no response. Absolutely none. Daniel could feel his disappointment rising, until Tyler spoke up. "Okay, Dad, let's bring them over."

"Them?"

"The Urim and Thummim."

"Oh, right. Of course." In the excitement Daniel had forgotten. He rose to his feet and walked to the closet where he'd hung his jacket. From the pocket he pulled out the two rocks, still wrapped in their silk scarf. He returned to the table and was just about to set them down, when Helen stuck out her hand.

"Hold it!"

He froze.

She pointed to Guido's stone, the clear Naphtali Stone. At its very center was what looked like an electrical arc, no more than an eighth inch across but definitely visible.

"And here." Helen pointed to the light green Benjamin Stone, which was also sparking.

"And here ..." Tyler pointed. "And here and here ... and here ..."

Cautiously they leaned over to examine each of the stones. As far as Daniel saw, every one was glowing — faintly, but glowing nonetheless.

"And here's our heat," Helen said, holding her hand first over one and then another. "They're putting out heat, just as before. Only more."

Tyler double-checked and nodded in agreement. "Every one except for this Levi Stone. It's as cold as ever. All the others are on fire."

"What about those?" Helen asked, motioning to the Urim and Thummim in Daniel's hands. "What are they doing?"

He carefully unwrapped the two granite rocks. As far as he could tell, they gave off no heat whatsoever. He held them up to the light, looking for something, anything. But they remained as lifeless and inert as always ... just like the Levi Stone.

He shook his head. "Nothing."

"Bring them closer," Tyler said.

"But slowly," Helen cautioned. "Nice and slow."

Daniel obeyed, inching the two stones closer and closer to the breastplate. As he did, Tyler and Helen peered at each of the existing stones, watching for any increased activity.

But there was no difference. Even when Daniel laid the two rocks directly beside the breastplate, nothing more happened. Just the arcing glow from each of the stones.

"So what do you think?" Tyler asked. "We need the others, don't we?"

"The other stones?" Daniel asked.

"We have seven now," Helen said.

"No."

The group gave a start and turned to see Nayra standing at the door.

"We have eight," she said.

232

"Nayra" — Tyler rose to his feet — "did you see what happened? The glowing?"

"Yes," she said, slowly moving into the room. There was no missing her intensity.

Daniel spoke next. "You said 'eight.' What do you mean, 'eight'?"

She turned to Helen. "Perhaps you can answer that better than I?"

"I'm sorry?" Helen asked.

"We actually have eight stones, don't we?"

"I'm not sure what you mean," Helen said.

Nayra's response was cool and determined. "I think you are sure." She raised her right hand out to them, then turned it over and slowly opened her palm. In it rested another stone, like the others, only sea green in color.

"Where did you get that?" Helen asked.

"In your room. Your suitcase."

"You went through my stuff?"

"Yes."

"I don't . . ." Daniel looked from Nayra to Helen, then back to Nayra. "I don't understand."

Keeping her eyes fixed on Helen, Nayra asked, "Do you wish to tell him or should I?"

Helen said nothing, holding the girl's gaze.

"Very well, then I shall." Nayra turned to Daniel. "The old man in Ramallah, he did not have one stone. He had two."

"Two?"

"Yes. He told me earlier, before you arrived. He had the Benjamin Stone" — she motioned to it, now sitting in the breastplate — "and he had this one." She indicated the one in her hand.

Daniel turned to Helen, frowning. "Is that . . . is that true?"

She looked at him but said nothing.

He felt anger and confusion beginning to stir. "Is that true?"

Finally she nodded. "Yes." Unable to hold his look, she glanced away.

"Why?"

Again she did not answer.

"*Why?*"

"I . . ." She still could not look at him. "I was asked . . . to keep an eye on you."

"On me? By who?"

No answer.

His anger increased. *"Who?"*

Nayra responded. "I have my ideas." Daniel turned to her, waiting for an explanation. She continued. "Did you not find it odd how easily we were able to leave Palestine? How quickly she was able to secure tickets for all four of us?"

Helen's eyes shot to her. Nayra smiled at the affirmation of guilt.

Daniel missed none of it. Turning back to Helen, he demanded, "Who hired you?"

Still unable to look at him, she only swallowed.

"Who?"

When she gave her answer, it was quiet and flat. "Somebody in the government."

"The *Israeli* government," Nayra clarified. "It was the *Mossad*, wasn't it?"

"The what?" Daniel asked.

"Israeli secret intelligence."

He turned to Helen, incredulous. "Is that true? Was it the Mossad?"

Taking a deep breath, and with no course but to tell the truth, Helen finally nodded. Then she explained. "I've been trying to secure permits for months to start a new dig. The hoops they make you jump through ... the red tape ..." She paused, obviously hoping it would be unnecessary to go on. She was mistaken. Daniel would hear it. He would hear all of it. People had given their lives for these stones. People he respected. People he loved. He would hear everything she had to say and he would hear it now.

She continued. "When they learned of my connection with Dr. Hermann in Chicago ... and said I might lose the site if I didn't cooperate ..." She took another breath. "I've worked with them before, but never on anything major, so ..." Finally she was able to look up to him. "So I said yes."

Still grappling with the revelation, Daniel repeated it. "You're an agent for the Mossad?"

She glanced away, not denying it.

He felt his cheeks starting to burn. "So this was all a lie, then? Your having to stay out of Israel, your wanting to work with us?

Everything ... everything was a lie?" His anger grew hotter. His head throbbed. "Everything about you was a lie!"

When she looked up, her eyes glistened. "Not everything."

But Daniel was in no mood for splitting hairs. He'd been deceived. Lied to from the beginning. No, it was more than that. It was betrayal. He had been betrayed since the beginning and it sent his head spinning. He didn't understand the depth of his emotion. He'd been lied to by others; why did this deception hit him so much harder? He looked down at his hands and saw them shaking. It made him all the more angry.

"What stone is it?" Tyler asked.

"From the Simeon tribe," she answered.

"Were you ever going to give it to us?"

Daniel looked at her, waiting for a response. She paused for a moment, then shook her head. "No."

"And what would happen when we completed our search?" Nayra asked.

Helen did not answer.

Nayra repeated the question. "What would happen when we completed our search?"

Helen's response was barely audible. "They would take the stones from you."

"All of them?"

"Yes."

"Just like that?" Tyler said, his anger also growing.

"Just like that," she repeated.

Tyler ran his hands over his face. "So you were just using us."

She nodded. "At first, yes." She was about to say more, then stopped.

Daniel waited a moment, hoping for something else. Some reason not to say what he had to say. But she did not speak. He wanted to yell at her. He wanted to shout in her face, to shake her silly. But he knew his response had to be as mature as hers. When he thought he had enough control, he spoke. "I think ..." His voice caught and he tried again. "I think you'd better go." He noticed that the trembling in his hands had spread to his voice.

She remained silent.

He repeated himself more firmly. "I said you'd better go."

Still looking down, she nodded but did not move. Finally, slowly, she looked up at him. "When I took the job, I didn't ... I didn't know who you were. I didn't ..." — she cleared her throat — "I didn't think it was possible that I could ... that you ..." She dropped off, looking for help.

He gave her none. Coolly, evenly, he repeated, "You'd better go."

She searched his eyes, looking for some indecision. He made certain she saw none. When it was clear he meant what he had said, she began to nod. "Yes," she answered quietly, "you're right. I'd better go."

Without a word she turned and headed to the door. When she arrived, she opened it. For the briefest moment she paused, as if to turn and say something more, perhaps offer further explanation. But thinking better of it, she stepped into the hallway and slowly, quietly, shut the door behind her.

Daniel reached for a nearby chair to steady himself. He wasn't sure how or why, but as Helen Zimmerman left, she took much of himself with her.

part
five

chapter twelve

"Sudan?" Daniel asked incredulously.

"Sure," Tyler said. "Remember what that priest said? Some guy in Sudan is also collecting these stones?"

Daniel frowned. "I understand that, but . . ." Turning to Nayra, he asked, "And you say you've heard of this man?"

"Yes."

"Why didn't you mention it before?"

"I was not . . . I did not entirely trust Dr. Zimmerman. But now that she has left . . ."

Daniel ran his hands through his wet hair. At three in the afternoon the hotel room was stifling. As often happened, the power had gone off, which meant the overhead fan was off, which meant the air was hot, nearly intolerable. It had been thirty-six hours since Helen departed. No good-byes, no notes. Just departed. And for thirty-six hours they had waited as Daniel prayed, as he searched the Scriptures, as he tried to determine what to do. But as usual, at least for him, the heavens remained silent.

"Dad, it's next door to us, just across the border."

He nodded. "Yes, but aren't they in a civil war or something?"

"You are correct," Nayra agreed. "For years the southern rebels have been trying to overthrow the Muslim government."

"Really?" Tyler asked.

"Well," Daniel said, clearing his throat, "that's not exactly how I've heard it."

"I suppose it depends upon who you believe," Nayra replied. "Upon who is telling the truth."

Daniel nodded. To be frank, his knowledge of foreign affairs was pretty sketchy, but he did remember something else. "Isn't that where women and children are being kidnapped and sent up north to be sold as slaves?"

"I have heard such rumors but I give no credence to them."

"Yes, but — "

"Dad!" Tyler's frustration erupted. "What are you trying to do?"

"I just — "

"Nayra is trying to help us."

"I understand that, but — "

"We have good information that more stones are with some guy in Sudan, right?"

"Right."

"And Nayra says she's also heard of him."

"Yes, but — "

"And Sudan's just next door." Tyler raised his hands. "How much clearer can it be?"

"There's a civil war going on there. It's dangerous."

"In case you haven't noticed, this whole trip has been dangerous. And now we're this close, Dad . . . *this* close."

"Would they even let us into the country?" Daniel asked.

Nayra nodded. "There are many ways."

"She could be our guide, just like Doc was."

"I don't know; I need to think about it some — "

"What's to think?"

"I just don't . . . I don't know, that's all."

"Well, I do. And if it means going there without you, then we'll go without you."

"Ty — "

"No, I'm serious." Looking at Nayra, he rephrased the statement. "*We're* serious."

Daniel took a moment to search his son's face. The boy was serious; there was no doubt about it. And as best as he could tell, so was Nayra. Finally, with a heavy sigh he asked, "Will you at least let me sleep on it?"

"You can sleep all you want." Tyler turned and started for the door. "But our decision is already made."

"Ty . . ."

"I'm not your little boy anymore. I can make my own decisions." He arrived at the door and opened it. "Now, you can come with us if you want or you can stay behind. But either way we're going."

"Tyler—"

"Either way. Just let us know." Turning to Nayra, he asked. "Are you coming?"

"In a moment," she answered softly.

"All right. I'll see you both in the morning." With that he turned and exited into the hallway.

"I am sorry, Pastor," Nayra apologized. "I did not mean to create division."

"It's not your fault."

"Your son, he is a good boy."

"Yes, and . . . though I may not have said it, you bring out the best in him. Thank you for that."

She looked at the ground. The electrical power surged back on, and they both looked up to see the overhead fan start to turn.

"You're certain that this fellow exists," he asked, "the one who claims to have the stones?"

"Yes. I even know of people who have spoken to him."

"And he'd be open to meet us, to share what we've all found?"

"Yes, yes, he would be most interested."

Daniel stood for a moment, thinking. "I still need to sleep on it. And pray."

"Yes, I understand. Pray very hard about this, Pastor. Very hard."

"I will."

Finally she turned and headed toward the door. "Good night."

"Good night, Nayra." He followed her to the doorway. "Oh, and Nayra?"

She turned to him.

"Thanks. For all you've done . . . for both of us. Thank you."

Once again she smiled, though this time he detected the slightest trace of sadness. Turning, she walked into the hallway, then toward her room. Daniel watched her a moment, then slowly, quietly, shut the door. He leaned against it and sighed. He would pray; of course he would pray. But even now he knew, even now he feared, what the answer would be . . .

*

Once again he is wearing the breastplate of the high priest. Once again he is enveloped by the overpowering Light, by a love saturating his every pore. He feels its warmth soaking through his skin, his muscles, his ribs . . . until it enters his heart and strikes the rock-hard substance buried within it. The impact of the Light against the substance and its resistance is so strong that it forces him to his knees. He drops in front of the red pool, the pool with the battered face. As before, he begins to retch. Again and again he coughs and chokes, until the first stone comes up. It is the clear green Benjamin Stone. It spews from his mouth, splashing into the red pool, changing the battered, reflected face into Helen Zimmerman, then to Linda Grossman.

Again he coughs and convulses, this time bringing up the crystal clear Naphtali Stone. It also splashes into the pool, rippling the reflection into that of Guido the gypsy king, then Charlie Rue from church.

Another stone comes up, then another, and another, and another, in rapid succession, each splashing into the pool. He is not surprised to see they are the four stones from Ethiopia. Nor is he surprised to see the reflection change to that of the EOC priest and then to his own black associate pastor, Bill White.

He retches again, and again a stone is expelled. It is the sea green stone of Simeon, the tribe known for its religious zeal. It splashes into the pool, and he watches the reflection ripple and change into the face of . . . at first he does not recognize it. It is the face of another church member back home, the face of Oscar Matar, his congregation's token zealot. He'd nearly forgotten the man, it had been so many lifetimes ago — his bullheadedness, his insistence upon clinging to certain interpretations of Scripture regardless of how narrow-minded and at times wrong they may be. The image lasts only a moment before it too shimmers and shifts, finally turning into the face of . . . Nayra Fazil.

Daniel leans over, catching his breath, staring into her face. What did Tyler say? "I'm talking about your I'm-superior-to-you-'cause-I'm-righter-than-you attitude you always carry around." He moans audibly. It is true, like it or not: he has been clinging to an attitude of superiority. Toward the Oscar Matars of the world.

Toward the Nayra Fazils. Toward any extremist who isn't as right as he is right. How could he have been so arrogant, so prideful?

But he isn't through. Not yet. There is still one more. He can feel it lodged in his chest, in the very center of his heart. He coughs again and again. He retches, he gags, but nothing helps. He gasps for breath, sweat dripping from his face. He has gone this far; he will not stop, not until it is done. "Please, Lord," he cries. "Show me . . ." More coughing. "Show — " And then he convulses so strongly that he fears he will choke to death. But at last it comes up. The final stone fills his mouth, then splashes into the pool. It is translucent red like the liquid. Immediately he recognizes it. From his late-night studies. It is the Reuben Stone. Reuben, the firstborn. Reuben, described by his father, Jacob, as "unstable as water." Reuben, whose face ripples and changes the pool's reflection into one final image. An image he knows as well as his own. The image of his first-born, Tyler Lawson.

Daniel awoke. The sheets clung to him from his sweat. For the most part the dream was more confirmation than surprise. But it was the final image, the one of his son, that he found the most unsettling. He understood his pride and his prejudice toward others . . . but toward his own son? The boy he loved more than his own life? Well, at least that's what he'd always told himself. But this? Was it possible? Did he really harbor the same lack of respect toward him, the same superiority that he had toward the others? Toward his own son? Was it really possible?

"You can come with us if you want or you can stay behind." With a heavy sigh he rolled onto his back. He stared up at the mosquito netting draped above him, its soiled beige pleats glowing white in the moonlight. It reminded him of Tyler's arms, the scars, the last time he'd seen them glowing in the moonlight. *"I just wish I could make him see what he's doing to him. Please, Lord, do whatever is necessary to make him see."*

Daniel closed his eyes. Sudan. The stories he'd heard. The nightmare conditions he'd read of. What was he getting into . . .

✳

For Tyler the flight into the Nuba Mountains from Ethiopia was anything but relaxing. Nayra and Daniel had managed to sweet-talk some relief agency refueling in Addis Ababa into letting them

243

tag along. After all, a short three-hour flight into Sudan would be far kinder to their bodies than a two- or three-day bone-jarring drive. According to Nayra's memory, although Sudan was one-third the size of the United States, it had under a thousand miles of paved highways. Unfortunately, the cargo plane was packed to the gills with seven tons of relief packages, leaving virtually no place to sit — well, except atop the relief packages. Even that wouldn't have been so bad if the pilot hadn't managed to hit every existing air pocket between the two countries.

Fortunately, the conversation with the fellow in charge was interesting — well, at least what Tyler could hear of it over the throb of the prop engines. He instantly liked the guy, Brad Dickson, or Diggers, as he was called. He was just a year or two older than Tyler, and he had absolutely no pretension. What you saw was what you got. He had a wry, cutting humor which Daniel would probably call sarcastic, and absolute zero need to impress anyone with anything. He'd attended Taylor University, a conservative Christian school in Fort Wayne. One evening he was at his graduation ceremony; the next morning he was on a plane heading to Sudan. That had been three years ago. Now he was a seasoned pro with shaggy hair, overgrown goatee, and sandaled feet.

Tyler zoomed in to a close-up of him as he fielded their questions. "Yeah, 1989," he shouted. "That's when things really got ugly."

"Why's that?" Daniel yelled.

"That's when the National Islamic Front took over. When they got serious about trying to convert the country to Islam."

"Why is that such a problem?" Nayra shouted.

"When the entire southern half of the country is African and not Arab . . . you tell me."

Nayra looked at him, then asked, "What of these rumors of slavery?"

He cocked his head toward her. "What about them?"

Daniel explained. "Are boys taken from their homes and shipped north to become slaves?"

Diggers nodded. "Or put into training camps, where they're forced to memorize the Qur'an and convert to Islam."

Nayra frowned. "What about the girls?" she shouted.

"Some of them, as young as ten, are forced to become concubines."

The thought silenced them all for a moment. Finally Tyler called from behind the camera, "So it's all true?"

"Only for the lucky ones."

"What does that mean?"

"You'll see . . ."

"Is it dangerous for you to come in here?" Daniel shouted. "I mean, as part of a Christian organization?"

"The people here are caught between two forces. The government in the north and the more sympathetic Sudan People Liberation Army in the south. Neither is particularly shy about violence and shedding blood."

"So there's really nothing to guarantee your safety?" Daniel asked.

He shook his head.

"Why do you do it?" Tyler shouted.

Diggers turned to him. "What do you mean?"

"I know you want to help people and stuff . . . but to risk your life? I mean, you're a college graduate, for crying out loud. Why this?"

Diggers broke into an uneven grin. "You're kidding, right?"

Tyler shrugged.

"'Whatever you do for the least of these, my brothers, you do for me.'"

"What?"

"You're a preacher's kid; you should know that one."

Tyler shrugged again.

"That's Jesus talking."

Tyler gave a vague nod. "So . . ."

"So they don't come any more 'least' than these people."

The plane lurched more violently than usual and started a steep bank to the left. Seeing the concern cross their faces, Diggers shouted, "Relax." He motioned toward the pilot up front. "Gus has been flying in and out of here for years." He rose to his feet and duck-footed to the round portal in the door. "We'll be landing in about ten minutes," he shouted over his shoulder. "Stay close to me. There should be no government troops where we're going, but you never can tell. Just do what I do and pretend you're part of the team."

Everyone nodded.

"Oh, and Tyler?"

"Yeah?"

He motioned to the video camera. "Be careful where you point that thing. The use of cameras by foreigners is frowned upon."

"Why?"

"You'll see." His answer carried no wit, no smile, just flat sadness. "You'll see."

Ten minutes later the plane's wheels slammed onto an uneven field of grass and dusty red dirt. It was a bumpy ride, full of ruts and chuckholes, but no worse than their last three hours in the air. At the end of the field, Tyler spotted several dozen mud huts with thatched roofs. People were streaming out to greet them. They were dark, ebony skinned, as black as the Ethiopians, but there were differences. Even at a hundred yards he could see their gaunt thinness. Many were simply bones covered in skin, strange stick figures silhouetted in the setting sun. And their clothes ... Although bright in color — oranges, blues, greens — the closer the plane approached, the more clearly he saw that they were more rags than clothes. But strangest of all was their jumping and yelling.

"What are they doing?" Tyler called. "What are they shouting?"

Diggers grinned. "They're not shouting. They're singing."

And he was right. As the plane came to a stop and they dropped open the door (to be hit by a stifling blanket of wet heat), the entire village was gathering at the stairs, singing and dancing. The engines coughed, choked, then mercifully sputtered to a stop — though for several minutes Tyler's body still felt as if it were vibrating.

Daniel crossed to the door and looked out over Diggers' shoulder. "This is quite a welcome," he said.

Nayra joined them. "They don't sound all that desperate to me," she observed.

Diggers said nothing but waved to a man who was working his way through the crowd. Instead of singing, he was shouting — a greeting, as best as Tyler could tell, though it was hard to know if the man was happy or angry, since his mouth was twisted in shiny, black and pink scar tissue that covered most of his face.

Diggers shouted excitedly, "Pastor Tano, Pastor Tano!"

The man broke into what must have been a grin, his joy radiating even through his grotesqueness.

"Who?" Tyler asked.

"He's the town's pastor," Diggers said.

"What happened to his face?"

"The Islamic soldiers stopped by."

"And?"

"And what? He wouldn't convert."

"They burned his face?"

"His body. They soaked him in gasoline, locked him in his church, and tossed a match."

Diggers turned and headed down the steps to greet the man. They met and threw their arms around each other. Tyler watched as they hugged, as the crowd cheered and sang and danced. The emotions were so real, so contagious, that for the first time in a very long time he forgot to turn on his camera.

Nayra joined him. "Quite a celebration," she said.

He nodded. "Guess they figure it's Christmas with all these relief packages."

"I'm not so sure that's their reason."

"What do you mean?"

"Have you looked inside one of those packages?"

He shook his head. "You?"

She nodded. "A tin of biscuits, mosquito netting, and a Bible."

He turned to her in surprise. "That's it? That's all they're getting?"

She nodded and looked out at the celebration. "That's it."

✳

"It's all we could afford this year," Diggers replied, poking at the bonfire. Red embers rose to join a thousand stars blazing in the sky. The village had moved their celebration over to the broken-down cinder block walls of what used to be a schoolhouse. Diggers continued his explanation. "When news is slow, the media reports their suffering and our donations go up. When there are more important stories to cover, like Madonna's latest wedding, we're no longer the flavor of the month and our donations go down. Last year all we gave them were used blankets."

Tyler turned the camera across the fire's rippling heat to the dancing people. "How many villages are there like this?" he asked.

"Here and in southern Sudan? Hundreds ... thousands."

"They seem so grateful," Tyler said, zooming in on the sweating, laughing faces. "Even when they didn't get that much."

Diggers chuckled. "This has nothing to do with what we brought them."

Tyler looked up at him from the viewfinder.

"The happiness you see is because they know they haven't been forgotten. Because brothers and sisters somewhere else in the world have remembered them." He paused, smiling at what he saw. "Look at them, will you? Have you ever seen such joy?"

"They're not the only ones happy," Tyler said.

"What do you mean?"

"You should take a look at yourself. You're like a little kid — all giggling and excited."

Diggers' grin broadened as he looked back at the people. "It doesn't get any better than this, my friend. 'Give and it will be given to you, pressed down, shaken together, and running over.' Another quote from Jesus, in case you forgot."

Tyler smirked at the gibe. "Yup. I hear it every time the church begs for money."

Diggers nodded. "But I don't think the dude was just talking about money. I think he was also talking about life. It's like, the more of my life I pour into these people, the more of life I get back. It's like I can't outgive the guy. I give him more of my life and he just gives me more and more of his."

Tyler looked out across the fire and nodded. More quietly he repeated, "'Whatever you do for the least of these, you do for me.'"

"It's true," Diggers said. "I tell you, sometimes when I look into those faces, I swear, sometimes it's like I'm looking right into God's. A pretty cool gig ... if you don't mind the heat and the flies."

Tyler smiled.

"And you know what's even cooler?" Diggers asked.

"What's that?"

"There's always room for one more."

Tyler turned to him and saw that lopsided grin again. "What?"

"I'm not the only one who lights up around these guys."

Tyler scoffed. "Yeah, right."

"I'm serious. You should have seen your own face when you were giving out those relief packages."

"I think I'll pass," Tyler said, chuckling.

Diggers shrugged. "Whatever. It's just a thought ... in case you ever get tired of playing Steven Spielberg there."

Tyler shook his head and grinned. Diggers couldn't be more wrong. Tyler Lawson: missionary? Not exactly the title he hoped to rule the world by. Still, he had to admit there was a lot of joy here. How strange ... Here in this ugly, godforsaken place, with its flies, its people starving to death, its crushing daytime heat that wasn't much better at night ... here where, according to Diggers, there were sixty-three varieties of mosquitoes (some carrying malaria) ... here where there was more suffering and need than he'd seen in his entire life, there was also more peace and joy. And Diggers was right; it wasn't just the villagers. As Tyler helped pass out the relief packages earlier that evening, as he returned hugs or offered simple smiles, the peace and joy that he himself felt was also amazing. How strange. How very, very strange.

"Check it out," Diggers said. He motioned across the fire.

Tyler looked over to see Nayra laughing and giggling with a ragged little girl of four or five. This was no surprise. Nayra had told him earlier how much she loved working with children. What did surprise him, though, was that the girl's left leg had been sheared off just above the knee.

"What happened to her?"

"Land mine," Diggers said.

"Here?"

"Ever wonder why these people are starving if the land is good enough to grow crops?"

"Now that you mention it, yeah. Why can't they grow more food?"

"Every time the soldiers come by, they plant mines around the usable fields."

Tyler slowly nodded in understanding. "So they're starving them into leaving?"

Diggers looked at him. "No. They're starving them into dying."

Before Tyler could respond, the popping began. At first he thought it was firecrackers ... until the headlights bounced into view ... until Diggers saw the trucks, leaped to his feet, and shouted to the crowd. "Soldiers!" He began waving his arms. "Soldiers! Soldiers!" The festivities came to a stop. He motioned to Pastor Tano, who had also spotted them. "Soldiers! They must have seen the plane!"

Panic swept through the crowd. Pastor Tano raised his hands, trying to calm them, but it did little good. The people began shouting to one another, gathering their children. Some helped the crippled and weaker ones as everyone began to scatter.

Diggers whirled to Tyler. "Where's your dad?"

Tyler searched the crowd. "There! Over there!"

Diggers spotted him and started toward him. "Pastor!"

Tyler grabbed his arm and shouted, "What are you doing?"

"Your dad's a leader; it will be worse for him!" Pointing toward Nayra, he shouted, "You two hide! Stay out of their sight!" Turning back to Tyler's dad, he began to wade through the panicked crowd.

Tyler turned back to see three, maybe four Jeeplike trucks approaching, their headlights bouncing into his eyes. In the back of the vehicles stood dark forms, shouting, yelling, their faces occasionally lit by muzzle flashes. He spun around to the crowd and searched for Nayra. She'd disappeared from sight. He began to push his way through the people. "Nayra!" There! There she was, with the little girl, turning her over to her mother. "Nayra!"

She looked up as he worked his way toward her.

A woman behind him screamed. He turned to see her eight-year-old son fall to the ground, suddenly lifeless — before her own body jerked once, twice, then tumbled, joining his in the dirt. The shouts surrounding him turned to screams.

"Nayra!"

She ran toward him.

He heard a dull, wet thud directly beside him, followed by a groan as a man staggered, then sprawled onto the ground. Tyler threw a look over his shoulder. The trucks were splitting up, circling around, trying to corral them.

"Tyler!" He turned just in time to catch Nayra in his arms.

"Are you okay?" he shouted.

"Yes, yes!"

Red dirt exploded in a rapid line not three yards from them. Desperately he searched for a way out. Behind one of the trucks he spotted an opening. He grabbed her hand. "Come on!"

The trucks closed in, tightening their circle, shooting at those trying to break through the parameter. Off to Tyler's right a young mother with a baby cried out. She tumbled forward, dead before she hit the ground, the screaming infant falling into the dirt but still clinging to his mother.

Nayra slowed.

"Come on!" Tyler shouted.

She released his hand and raced for the child.

"Nayra!"

She reached the child and scooped him up.

"What are you doing?"

She gave no answer but quickly rose to join Tyler. They started off again, this time veering to the left, Tyler doing his best to shield her body from any gunfire.

A fourth truck approached, lagging behind the others. It seemed to come directly at them. Searching for an escape, for any place to hide, he spotted part of the broken-down wall of the schoolhouse. At best it was only three feet high but it would have to do. He turned, managing to avoid the truck's attention, and raced to the wall. They leaped behind it, hitting the ground hard. Nayra was somehow able to protect the baby as Tyler instinctively cradled the camera strapped to his wrist.

The truck roared past and joined the others as they continued to tighten the circle.

"What do we do?" Nayra shouted over the crying baby and the trucks and guns.

Tyler rose to his knees, looking for some escape. There was none. Any direction he chose would put them back into the open, back into the lights of the circling trucks.

The baby cried louder.

One of the vehicles skidded to a stop not thirty feet in front of them. Tyler ducked as its headlights flashed across the wall. Inching his way up, he watched the soldiers leap from the back. One grabbed a passing girl, no more than fifteen, who was trying to escape. She screamed, squirming and kicking, trying to get away. But the soldier only laughed, seeming to enjoy the struggle. Suddenly, as if tired of the game, he punched her in the face. The action barely phased her. It took two more blows to settle her down. Dark blood flowed from her left nostril. Spotting another section of wall, the soldier dragged her toward it, forcing her to sit less than twenty feet from Tyler, Nayra, and the crying baby.

The soldier shouted at the girl over the noise. She did not answer. He shouted again and slapped her.

"What's he saying?" Tyler asked.

At first Nayra would not reply.

The soldier shouted again. This time the girl nodded.

"Nayra, what's he saying?"

"He wants to know if she's an infidel."

"An infidel?"

"A Christian." Nayra turned back to the baby in her arms and tried to quiet it.

The soldier continued to shout, but this time the girl remained silent, no longer answering.

"What's he saying?" Tyler asked. "Nayra, what's he saying?"

"He wants her to deny Christ. He wants her to accept the one true God."

The soldier turned and shouted to a couple of comrades. They headed toward him. One heard the crying baby and started toward it. Tyler and Nayra flattened lower behind the wall as Nayra desperately tried to coax the infant into silence. The first soldier shouted at the second, who grunted, then turned to join the others. Now three of them surrounded the girl, the first continuing to yell and threaten her, the other two laughing and taunting.

"What's he saying now?" Tyler asked.

"More of the same."

Cautiously the two lifted their eyes above the wall just as the first soldier ripped off the girl's top. Filling with rage, Tyler started to rise until Nayra pulled him back down. "What are you doing?" she demanded.

"We can't just sit here."

"There's nothing we can do."

The men continued laughing, making coarse gestures.

Again Tyler started to rise and again Nayra stopped him. "Tyler!"

"I'm not going to sit here and watch some girl get raped."

"They're not going to rape her."

"What?"

One of the soldiers produced a shiny saber. It momentarily gleamed in the headlights.

"They're not going to rape her."

He motioned to his two companions, who grabbed the girl's shoulders and pulled them back. He turned and shouted toward the rest of the village as if they could hear.

"What's he saying?"

Nayra answered, "He said that she will serve as an example."

"An example?"

Nayra hesitated.

"An example of what?"

"Of all who refuse to accept the one true God."

The soldier turned back to the girl and shouted again.

Despite her bleeding face, her nakedness, her uncontrollable trembling, she refused to answer. He shouted again and was met with the same results. Finally, shaking his head over her foolishness, he rested the saber atop one of her breasts. He lifted the blade high into the air, its steel glinting in the light.

Instinctively Tyler turned away. He heard the shriek of pain and looked back to see the soldiers release the girl. She fell into the dust, screaming and writhing. An older woman raced toward her, pushing past the men. They did not stop her as she tried to comfort the girl, as she produced a dirty rag and pressed it against the gaping wound.

Sick with revulsion, Tyler barely noticed the second soldier turning toward them, toward the sound of the crying baby, until Nayra pulled him down out of sight.

"Get the truck," she ordered.

"What?"

"There's no one in the truck; get the truck."

He turned to peer through a crack in the wall. She was right. It stood thirty feet away, empty and idling.

The soldier continued his approach.

"But how — "

"Just do it," she ordered, trying to silence the baby.

The soldier was nearly on top of them, three yards away.

Seeing no other choice, Tyler leaped to his feet. The soldier shouted in surprise. The other two turned.

Tyler started to run. But instead of hearing shouts or gunshots, Tyler heard something entirely different. He heard Nayra yelling. He threw a look over his shoulder to see her rising to her feet. He looked at the soldiers. Now they were really startled. Instead of some starving black African, they saw before them a beautiful Arab princess . . . with a crying baby . . . lecturing them. Loudly. He had no idea what she was saying but suspected it had something to do with their behavior and how they were bringing shame upon all true Muslims.

The scene startled them enough to give Tyler the seconds he needed to reach the truck and leap in. He tossed his camera onto the seat and ground the gears, desperately trying to find first. Nayra stood directly ahead of him in the lights, still holding court, still giving them a piece of her mind.

He heard a shout from behind and turned to see another soldier racing at him. He focused back on the gears, still grinding away, until he finally found first. The man leaped onto the vehicle just as Tyler popped the clutch, lurching forward, throwing the soldier off and onto the ground with a cry.

Everyone turned from Nayra to him. But before they had a chance to fumble for their weapons, Tyler tromped on the gas and steered straight at them. They yelled and leaped out of the way. Tyler cut the truck hard to the right, throwing dirt and sand over them as he headed for Nayra.

"Get in!" he shouted. "Get in! Get in!"

He skidded to a stop and she jumped in, still holding the crying baby. The men staggered to their feet and shouted. Again he stomped on the accelerator, throwing more sand over them, causing the truck to leap ahead, bouncing crazily out of control. A gunshot exploded from behind. Then another. A moment later headlights glared into his mirror. Fighting the wheel for all he was worth, he turned to Nayra and shouted, "Where to?"

She searched the blackness that surrounded them on all sides, then pointed straight ahead. "There!"

It was good enough for him.

chapter thirteen

The truck bounced crazily through the rocky field as Tyler fought the wheel, barely keeping it under control. The engine whined loudly, pathetically, begging to be shifted into some other gear — which one, Tyler hadn't a clue.

"Over there!" Nayra pointed to the right. "There is the road!"

Tyler cranked the wheel just as they hit a ditch, throwing the truck on two wheels, nearly flipping it over before it came back down hard.

"Be careful!" Nayra cried, gripping the baby more tightly.

He glanced in the mirror. The pursuing headlights slid into view, bouncing behind them. He arrived at the road and turned hard to the left, again sending the truck into a skid.

"Tyler!"

He looked back in the mirror. The pursuers were closing in. More shots were fired. For the most part they were wild and off target ... except for the one that struck the rearview mirror, exploding it into a cloud of spraying glass inches from his face.

"Tyler!" Nayra cried, covering the baby's head.

"What am I supposed to do?" he shouted. "Ask them to be more careful?!"

He pushed the accelerator to the floor. The engine screamed even louder as they continued losing ground. He glanced at the gearshift. He'd found first and second, but there was no telling where they'd hidden third. He could take a chance, but what if he shifted back down or into reverse and destroyed the transmission?

Nor could he find the high beams. Even now he was outrunning his lights by a dozen feet. Whatever lurked in the darkness before him would barely be seen before he hit it. Maybe he should slow down. Maybe he should—

Another bullet struck, ricocheting off the back fender. Maybe not.

"What you saw back there," Nayra shouted, "that's not the Islamic way."

"What?"

"That's not what the Qur'an teaches."

Tyler glanced at her.

She shook her head. "It definitely is not."

Another shot zinged off the rear bumper. Since there was no way to outrun these guys, maybe he could outmaneuver them. "Hang on!" he shouted. He cranked the wheel hard to the left. Nayra screamed as they sailed back off the road and bounced into a field of grass and stone. For a moment they were free of their pursuers. For a moment. The truck lights bounced back onto them and once again closed in. More shots were fired. He continued outrunning his headlights, seeing the rocks and ruts only as he flew over them.

He swerved to the right. The truck stayed glued to his tail, closing in. He guessed it was about twenty feet away. He swerved to the left. They would not be put off. Another bullet glanced off the rear fender. Then another, skimming across his door panel. Not only were they getting closer; they were getting better.

He threw a look over his shoulder. He could see their faces now. Shouting, laughing. It was a game. He turned back just in time to spot the gully and ridge, but not in time to avoid it. They roared down and up, shooting high into the air, Nayra screaming, the baby crying. They slammed down onto an outcropping of rock, so hard that he felt something in the steering give way. He no longer had control. The wheel spun lifelessly in his hands as the truck veered one way, then another, depending upon which rock or rut they hit.

"Tyler, look out!"

A giant boulder appeared. He slammed on the brakes. The truck skidded and turned, but not enough to avoid a partial head-on. Metal exploded. The left front crumbled as they flew forward. They hit the dash, not hard enough to be hurt but enough to be stunned.

The soldiers slid beside them. There was no time to recover, let alone run, as the men leaped from their truck, shouting and yelling. They came at them from both sides. Two grabbed Tyler and without bothering to open the door, dragged him up and out. He was jostled and kicked, yelled at and cursed in a language he didn't understand. It was only when they'd thrown him onto the hood of their truck that he recognized one of their words. "American?!"

"Yes," he gasped, searching for the face that spoke, only to be rewarded with two sharp punches to the kidney. The pain took away his breath. It continued, searing, as he tried to breathe. Still, some part of him was able to worry about Nayra. "Where is she!" he shouted. "What have you done with — "

Another blow, this time to the face.

They flipped him onto his stomach and threw his arms behind him while grinding his face into the hot, gritty hood. That's when he caught a glimpse of her. They'd pinned her against the rear fender of his truck. Her scarf was gone and the soldier was tearing at her blouse.

"Nayra!"

"Want to watch?" one of the men holding him growled. "Does American want to watch?"

Tyler tried to move but they held him, yanking both arms up so hard that he thought they'd tear from their sockets.

"Nayra!"

In the garish light and shadows he caught glimpses of her legs, twisting, kicking. Suddenly her assailant cried out and staggered backward, dropping to his knees in agony. The others laughed as another took his place. Tyler could hear Nayra's voice shouting. She wasn't screaming, she wasn't crying, she was shouting. The soldiers slowed their attack. She continued yelling, repeating the same phrase over and over again.

"What?" the man restraining Tyler shouted.

Nayra did not answer but continued shouting until she eventually brought all her assailants to a stop.

"What?" the man holding Tyler repeated. Turning to him, he asked, "Is it true?"

Tyler had no idea what he meant.

The soldier shook him. "Is it true!"

"What?" Tyler gasped. "Is what true?"

"She is niece? Of Ibrahim el-Magd?!" Before Tyler could respond, the man turned to Nayra and shouted something in Arabic.

"*Naam! Naam!*" Nayra shouted back. "Ibrahim el-Magd! Ibrahim el-Magd!"

Tyler's captor barked out orders and the soldiers stopped, immediately releasing her. One even stooped down to hand her the remains of her blouse. She yanked it from him, spitting into his face. The man was about to retaliate, until Tyler's captor shouted at him to stop. Turning back to Tyler, he angrily repeated, "Ibrahim el-Magd — it is true? She is niece of Ibrahim el-Magd?"

✳

"Any word yet?" Diggers asked as Daniel entered their hut. Although the sun had set over an hour ago, the air was still damp and suffocating.

Daniel shook his head. "They found the truck."

"That's it?"

"Yes." Daniel unbuttoned his sweat-soaked shirt. "There was no sign of the kids."

"So they've taken them somewhere?" Diggers tried to rise up on the grass mat but the pain was too great. A bullet from last night's raid was lodged somewhere deep in his gut. They'd managed to stop the bleeding but infection was quickly setting in.

Daniel nodded as he peeled off his shirt. "We just used the plane's radio to contact the State Department, to see if there's any word."

"And?"

"Nothing yet." He did his best to sound matter-of-fact. "They suspect it'll become a hostage situation." He began searching for a dry shirt on the twine they'd stretched across the hut.

"What does that mean?" Diggers asked.

"The U.S. State Department does not negotiate ransom demands, so we'll probably be on our own."

"You're kidding."

"I wish I was." He found the driest shirt and slipped it on. "There is one possibility, though."

"What's that?"

"I've contacted our congressman, who will ask the FBI to ask the State Department to ask the U.S. embassy here to make an official request for FBI negotiators to fly into the country."

Diggers shook his head. "Good ol' American red tape."

Daniel sighed and began to button his shirt. "I suppose so."

"You seem awfully calm about it."

Daniel glanced at him, unsure whether to take that as a compliment or not. "These things take time. Waiting on the official channels takes patience."

"That's all you're going to do? Just wait?"

"What else is there?"

"I don't know, but I tell you, if it were my kid ..." Diggers slowed to a stop.

Daniel turned to him. "What?"

Diggers shook his head.

"No, what?" Daniel persisted. "If it were your kid, what would you do?"

"Well, I sure wouldn't be sitting around waiting on a bunch of officials. I'd be out there doing ... something."

The accusation irritated Daniel. Between the lack of sleep and the pressure, he found it difficult to remain as civil as he liked. "Doing what, Diggers? Racing blindly into the desert? Stirring up trouble? Taking the chance of getting caught or killed?"

"Yes, exactly."

Daniel resumed buttoning his shirt. "Not really the rational approach."

"Who said anything about rational?" Diggers' intensity grew. "If it were me, I'd be getting a little crazy about now. I'd be taking a few risks, busting a few heads ... I mean, if it were my kid."

Daniel felt his face redden. Whether by accident or design, Diggers had hit a nerve. Maybe he was being too pragmatic; maybe he was too prudent. No. He was doing the right thing, the mature thing. Others might run into that desert playing Rambo, but this was the smart way, the correct way. So instead of snapping back at Diggers or becoming defensive, Daniel exercised restraint and did what was necessary to maintain civility. He changed subjects. "How are you feeling?"

"I'll be all right."

Daniel crossed the room and knelt down to feel his forehead. It was on fire.

Seeing his expression, Diggers shrugged. "Nothing a good dose of antibiotics won't kill—soon as Gus gets the plane up and running."

Daniel nodded and glanced away. He'd just talked to the pilot twenty minutes ago. Whoever shot up the plane in last night's raid knew exactly what they were doing. It could not fly out on its own. Parts had to be flown in and that would take time. Probably days.

"I know," Diggers said, reading his mind. "I talked to Gus, too. But God knows what he's doing. I mean, it's not like the dude's going to accidentally let us slip through his fingers, right?"

Daniel glanced up, surprised at the youth's language. *Dude?* Had he heard correctly? Had he just addressed God as *dude?* As in, *Lord Dude, Almighty?* The kid gave no indication that it was unusual and Daniel chose to remain silent. Did he approve? Of course not. To reduce God to street jargon was anything but respectful. Yet he hadn't sensed that Diggers was speaking with disrespect. Instead it was more like he was talking about a friend. *Friend.* It had been a long time since Daniel had thought of God in those terms.

"Maybe we should, like, pray," Diggers said. He held out his hand and fought back a shiver, obviously from his rising temperature.

Daniel nodded. "Sounds like a good idea."

So he took Digger's hand and the two of them began to pray. They prayed for Diggers' health, they prayed for the plane, and most importantly, they prayed for Tyler. It wasn't a long prayer or particularly profound. But as Diggers poured out his heart, friend to friend, buddy to buddy, it was all Daniel could do to hold back the tears. He used to pray like that. He used to believe like that . . . . back before he became a respectable man of God.

"So I'm a prisoner?" Tyler asked.

"Of course not."

"Then I can leave anytime I want?"

"When the time is correct, yes."

"And what time is that? What time is the correct time?"

Ibrahim el-Magd did not answer the youth's question. Instead he methodically ripped his bread into quarters. Pulling back his sleeve, he dipped a piece into the hummus. The boy had been brought in from the desert just a few hours earlier. Nayra had done her job well and was now upstairs resting. They had found no stones on him. He claimed they were all back at the village with his father. A father who, if he loved his son as Ibrahim suspected, would soon be joining them.

Changing the subject, he asked, "Nayra tells me you have an interest in our faith?"

The boy eyed him from across the table, obviously trying to decide which tack to take. His answer was cautious. "I'm impressed by your devotion."

"That is all?"

"And the lack of hypocrisy — well, except for the soldiers. Your boys were anything but impressive."

"They are not my boys; they belong to the government."

"And you're not part of the government?"

"No, not at all." Ibrahim dipped another piece of bread into the hummus. "I am merely a humble servant of Allah, may his name be praised. I am but the sword of his wrath." He paused a moment to quietly chew his bread. "Tell me of this ... hypocrisy."

"Huh?"

"You mentioned hypocrisy."

"Sure. You guys, you at least try to practice your faith. I mean, the stuff Nayra says and does, it's pretty cool, but in America ..." The boy shook his head. "I don't know; there just seems to be a lot of hypocrisy and stuff with my faith."

Ibrahim looked surprised. "Your faith? I was told you did not have a faith."

The boy shifted in his chair. "Well, yeah ... sort of."

"That is why I invited Sheikh Salad Habib to spend time with us." The sheikh, who had been sitting on a pillow against the wall, gave a slight nod. "To better help you understand the logic of Islam. To clear up your ... misconceptions, and to answer your questions."

"The only question I have is when you're going to let me leave."

Ibrahim found the insolence annoying. No youth should be allowed to address his elders with such disrespect. He paused a moment before answering. "That, my young friend, will depend a great deal upon your father, upon when he decides to join us."

"My father? Join us?"

Ibrahim nodded.

The boy gave a scornful laugh. "What, you think he's going to blaze in here and try to rescue me?"

Ibrahim said nothing.

"You think he's going to risk facing all those soldiers, travel all the way across the desert, and risk his life to try and save mine?"

"In time, yes. According to the greatness of his love."

"Yeah, right."

"Pardon me?"

"You'll have yourself a long wait, pal."

Ibrahim el-Magd frowned, not entirely understanding. From the hallway one of his aides appeared and caught his attention. Ibrahim nodded. He had wasted enough time with this boy. The Shura were gathering. He had asked them to wait a fortnight and a fortnight it had been. Now they would begin arriving, one by one, pressing him to keep his word, to begin the Day of Wrath.

"If you will excuse me." Ibrahim rose to his feet and adjusted his robes. "I have many urgent matters to attend to." He glanced at Sheikh Salad Habib, who understood and rose to his feet as well. "I will leave you in Sheikh Habib's most capable hands." With that Ibrahim el-Magd turned to exit the room.

"Hey, wait a minute!" The boy rose. "You can't just keep me here. I'm an American citizen . . ."

Ibrahim continued toward the door.

"What about Nayra? Is she all right? I want to talk to Nayra! Listen, you —"

Ibrahim heard the shuffle of feet as the boy started at him, but he did not bother to turn. He trusted his bodyguards. He heard them dart from the sides of the room to intercept the boy. He heard the youth's struggles and oaths. He winced at the sound of his belly being struck once, twice, many more times. But it must be done. As Ibrahim el-Magd stepped from the room, he knew it was the only way to ensure the boy's education. And he would be educated; make no mistake about it.

*

"That's it?" Helen exclaimed. She pointed at the green rock sitting in an aluminum briefcase on the desk before her. "That's the *real* Levi Stone?"

"That is correct. We had an exact duplicate made from the one in Chicago. We switched it long before the pastor came to Israel. Just in case."

"In case of what?" Helen barely controlled her anger. Not only had she been tricked, but she'd also been made a fool of. Neither particularly put her in a good mood.

Colonel Berkhof, part-time case officer and full-time paper pusher at Mossad headquarters in Tel Aviv, sighed heavily. He leaned back and folded his hands upon a rather large belly. His attitude and the multiple stacks of folders on his desk made it clear he had more important matters to attend to, but Helen had insisted that she and Field Agent Brent Appleton be granted an appointment. So there they were in the smoke-filled office with its worn, coffee-stained carpet, listening to Berkhof give his answer. "In case there were problems, Dr. Zimmerman. Problems such as . . . oh, I don't know, killing an Israeli soldier, suddenly departing Israel, breaking our agreement by — "

"The agreement was that I stay with him for as long as he was in your country."

"Yes, and though permission was granted, your decision to stay with him after he left brings about many more questions."

Helen ignored the inference and returned to her own questions. "So what did you need me for if you already had the original?"

"To keep an eye on him, of course."

"That was it? You just needed a baby-sitter?"

"Yes," Colonel Berkhof said as a secretary entered, setting another half dozen folders on his desk. He was not pleased. "It was important that we know if others tried to contact him in our country."

"And," Brent added from the chair beside her, "to see if he was lucky enough to find any more."

"Which apparently he was," Berkhof said. "Very lucky indeed."

"He worked hard for what he found," Helen said.

"I'm sure he did."

"And now you're going to send someone in and just yank those stones from him, leaving him with nothing?" Helen's disposition was not getting better.

"That is correct."

"Regardless of his risks, his sacrifices — the fact that his own wife died because of them?"

Colonel Berkhof glanced out the dirty third-story window. "The casualties of war, I am afraid."

"War? What war?"

Brent pushed his blond hair out of those gorgeous blue eyes and explained, "We are not the only ones searching for the stones, Helen. Other . . . less responsible governments are also interested."

"Who?"

Brent glanced at Colonel Berkhof, who answered, "I am afraid that is privileged information."

"Why would another government want them?"

"There are multiple reasons, Dr. Zimmerman."

"Such as?"

He took a patient breath, then explained, "There is the slightest possibility that the stones may somehow enable their owners to determine the outcome of a particular conflict before it is waged — that is, if the Scriptures are to be trusted."

"That's a pretty big if," she said.

"Still, it is a possibility."

She frowned. "But . . . I still don't understand . . ."

"Knowing whether one is going to win a particular battle would be an asset to any country — particularly one surrounded by as many enemies as our own. Imagine the safety we would enjoy if we knew which of our enemies we could successfully . . . remove."

Helen's mouth dropped open. "You'd use these stones for war? To decide who you'd declare war upon?"

The men exchanged glances.

"Strictly as a matter of survival," Brent explained. "For self-defense."

"Do you see a problem with that, Doctor?"

The question was loaded. What they were proposing was anything but moral, yet she knew it was important not to show her hand. Not to these guys. She'd never trusted them. Neither, however, did they trust her. She shook her head. "No, I don't see a problem with that. Especially if, as you say, it involves your country's survival."

She could feel the room relax some. "Exactly," Brent said a bit too eagerly. "That is exactly what we think."

Understanding his attempt for peace and realizing she needed to justify her outburst, she added, "It just seems a pity, that's all."

"How is that?" Berkhof asked.

"After all he's had to sacrifice to get them." Neither man responded. She continued. "Maybe ... maybe if I could go back, persuade him to return here with the stones. Explain to him our purposes ..."

"I am afraid that is not possible, Doctor. Since you have left, he has encountered a rather dangerous situation."

"Dangerous?" she asked.

"Yes. Apparently, his son has been kidnapped by the Sudanese."

"Tyler?"

"Yes."

Her anxiety rose. "Where is he? How is he?"

"We do not know."

"Is he alive? Is he hurt?"

"We don't — "

"Surely you know something — "

"Dr. Zimmerman, we — "

"You're an intelligence agency; you ought to — "

"Dr. Zimmerman!" The colonel brought her to a stop. "We know nothing further. In that country, as you may imagine, our intelligence capabilities are somewhat limited."

Helen's mind spun. They were talking about Tyler, for heaven's sake — Daniel's only child! But for the moment control was essential and she strove to regain it. "Yes," she said. "I'm sorry. It's just, we became somewhat close." She felt Brent staring at her and added, "The family and I."

Berkhof nodded. "We understand. From what we've seen, we understand."

Helen let the comment go. For even as he spoke, her thoughts continued to race. She reached over and picked up the Levi Stone from the briefcase, the *real* Levi Stone. A thought was taking shape. She turned the stone over, running her finger across the inscription. It was an absurd idea. She glanced out the dirty window to the Shalom Tower dominating the Tel Aviv skyline. An absurd idea, yes. But Daniel was in serious trouble. Tyler's life was in danger ...

Her thoughts were broken by Colonel Berkhof rising to his feet. Apparently, the meeting was over. He was offering his hand. "So once again, Dr. Zimmerman, please accept our sincere thanks."

She rose and shook it. "Certainly, Colonel, certainly. It was my privilege to serve you." As an afterthought she added, "I was wondering..."

"Yes."

"This Levi Stone ... may I borrow it over the weekend?"

The colonel exchanged looks with Brent.

"I'd like to run a few more tests on it, if you don't mind."

Colonel Berkhof hesitated. "I don't know, Doctor; it is most valuable."

"I'm well aware of its value, Colonel. I've been with seven others exactly like it. I would simply like to run a few more tests, compare its properties with what I've witnessed in the others."

More silence.

"After all, for better or worse, I have become an expert on them." She kept talking. "I'll have it back in your hands first thing Monday morning; I give you my word. Eight o'clock sharp."

The men traded looks.

"And if you need someone to make sure it's safe and secure ... I'm certain Appleton here wouldn't mind keeping an eye on me during that time." She fixed her eyes on Brent, whose face twisted into a knowing grin. "What do you say, Agent Appleton?"

Brent cleared his throat. "I suppose ... that's a possibility. And it is true, sir: she has become an expert. Maybe she can provide us further insight." The colonel stared at the stacks of folders on his desk. Brent continued. "And I am free this weekend to provide security; that is, if it meets with your approval."

"You're willing to stay with her?" the colonel asked.

"Yes sir, I'm willing to make that sacrifice ... if you feel it's necessary."

The colonel returned to his seat, letting out a heavy sigh. "Very well. Just make sure the stone is back here first thing Monday morning."

"Thank you, Colonel," Helen said. "First thing Monday. You have my word on it. Thank you very much."

He gave her a wave and she placed the Levi Stone back in its aluminum briefcase.

"You need help with that?" Brent asked.

"No, I have it." She closed the lid and turned to leave.

Without looking up, the colonel called out, "Just don't charge the room to the agency."

Helen and Brent exchanged grins. "Yes sir," Brent replied.

With that the two exited the office and headed for the elevators. She felt Brent's hand resting on her shoulder, gently guiding her down the hall. But that was okay. It wouldn't be there long.

chapter fourteen

"Yet I hold this against you: You have forsaken your first love."
Daniel looked at the Levi Stone in his hand and closed his eyes.
How had it happened? Fresh out of seminary he'd been so energetic, so on fire. That tiny church they'd first pastored in North
Dakota, that tiny church where on a good Sunday they'd have sixty
people. The size meant no difference. Back then all that mattered
was their love, their zeal, and their hunger for holiness.

Holiness. That's what he'd been called to pursue. *"Be ye holy;
for I am holy."* And he did pursue holiness. With all of his heart.
But somehow that holiness had gradually shifted into legalism. He
saw that now . . . in his demands and silent judgments of strangers,
of his congregation, of his family.

"I wish I could make him see what he's doing to him."

"You don't think God's ever seen bare shoulders before?"

"You think I killed her? You think I'm responsible for her death?"
Daniel closed his eyes. How had it happened?

Yet even now what would he do differently? Holiness. Legalism. What was the difference? Christ had called them to holiness;
he made that crystal clear. Yet at the same time he made it clear how
much he hated religious legalism. In fact, it was that criticism, particularly of the scribes and Pharisees, that led to his murder.

*"You didn't kill her, Dad. Your religion did. Just like it killed
Jesus."*

But how was it possible to pursue holiness without legalism?
How could he urge his congregation, himself, toward holiness
without becoming legalistic? There had to be a difference. But
what?

He looked at the stones and breastplate over on the table. He understood their symbolism now, understood what he'd learned — his pride, his prejudice against his son, against Guido, Helen, Nayra, the people of Africa. But did that mean they were always right? Guido with his impulsiveness and superstitions? Helen with her atheism? Nayra with her false beliefs? Was he simply to ignore their errors and shortcomings? Had God suddenly become a God of situational ethics, with no absolutes? He shook his head. No, he knew better than that. Scripture clearly set forth absolutes. Yet … how do you have absolutes without having … absolutes? How do you pursue holiness without legalism?

He looked again at the Levi Stone in his hand. And this one? Why did all the others respond except this one? The one he'd always associated so closely with himself?

These were the questions roiling in his mind throughout the hot day and long into the sweltering night.

*

"Why did you not tell me sooner?"

"Nayra, Little Bird, I did not know until my return from our visit in Axum."

She looked at him with eyes red from crying. "So I am to find out by calling my mother in Cairo?"

"I had planned to speak with you after you had rested. Your journey was long; I thought you needed rest."

He watched as she lowered her head, staring at the thick Persian rug of his office. Quietly she mumbled, "She said it was murder."

Ibrahim nodded. "That part of Cairo is a most dangerous place. Why he chose to rent a room there instead of going to your mother's, I do not understand."

He could not tell if she believed him. He doubted Yussuf Fazil had discussed their growing rift with his wife, just as he doubted his daughter would now stand so boldly before him if she knew the truth. But he was not certain. So he held out his arms to offer an embrace of sympathy. "Nayra …" If she came, all would be fine. If she did not … He pushed the thought from his mind.

She looked up.

"I am so sorry," he said.

Tears silently fell from her lashes. Angrily she swiped at them.

He remained standing, arms outstretched. Was it possible? Had her father somehow warned her? *Dear Allah, please, no.* And if he had, would she alert the Shura? *No, this must not happen, not until the stones have been retrieved. At all costs this must not happen.*

He raised his arms higher, a final plea. "I am so very sorry . . ."

Her chin began to tremble. She hesitated. At last she stepped toward him. Gratefully he wrapped his arms about her, holding her as she began to sob.

"It is all right . . . It is okay." He continued holding her and consoling her. "Your father was a great man. A mighty man. Allah will reward him greatly."

She nodded, unable to speak, her body shuddering. He felt her anguish against his chest, shared her ache deep in his heart. He closed his own eyes against the emotion. So hard, so hard. Why was Allah's will always so hard?

Tyler tried to escape from his six-by-six-foot room on two separate occasions. The first time he was given a severe lecture, the second time a beating. He actually managed to get some of the latter on videotape, until they spotted the glowing red light of his camera in the corner and confiscated it. Now, except for two bathroom breaks a day (a small cubicle with a hole in the floor) and five minutes of exercise (a brief walk around the compound's roof), he was manacled to his bed. "For your own protection," he was assured. "You have no idea how fierce the desert outside these walls can be."

He had not seen Nayra since the first day, though he had been assured she was still there. And despite the betrayal, he still saw her lovely face and those liquid black eyes during the endlessly long nights of staring at the ceiling. But it wasn't just *her* face. He also saw the faces of the Sudanese villagers — those half-starved, sunken faces of the men, the women, the children. Their desperate needs . . . and their great happiness. The hideous, scarred face of the pastor . . . and his boundless joy. Yet it wasn't just *his* joy; it was also Tyler's. For in those few hours of unloading the relief packages in the unbearable heat, as he offered who he was, through smiles and hugs, to total strangers . . . well, it had been a long time since he'd felt such fulfillment, since he'd felt so alive.

What had Diggers said? *"The more of my life I pour into these people, the more of life I get back."* Life — that's what he had experienced in those few short hours. And as brief as that time had been, he knew he would never forget it.

That had been four days ago. One day and night of traveling across the fiery desert, three days of imprisonment here. Three days with no visitors except Sheikh Salad Habib, the feeble old man with the snow-white beard who stopped by several times a day to check on his studies and to answer any questions. "Studies," as in Tyler was allowed no TV, radio, or written material except for an English translation of the Qur'an. "Answer questions," as in Sheikh Habib was the only one with whom he was allowed to talk. Initially Tyler resisted the strong-arm tactics, but a day of nonstop boredom, punctuated by visits of a man who remained mute on any subject except religion ... well, he eventually began to pick up the book to read ... and he eventually began to ask questions.

He was surprised at his own ignorance. Despite his positive impressions of Nayra, as well as the media blitz for tolerance ever since the attack on the World Trade Center, somewhere in the back of his mind he still suspected that devout Muslims were crazed terrorists. After all, isn't that what he usually saw on the news — screaming mobs of veiled women, bearded men blowing up buildings, children brandishing firearms? But that's not what he read in the Qur'an. Instead the small book of 6,666 verses seemed to be a clear guide on how to live life — precise, step-by-step instructions on how to treat others and how to follow God.

"Exactly," Sheikh Habib had agreed. "It is a guidebook showing us how to live in complete submission to God. In fact, the name Islam means 'submission.'"

Tyler had been impressed. Submission to God. Isn't that exactly what he'd been taught as a Christian all his life? All those rules and regulations, all the hoops his dad had tried to get him to jump through? And, as he had challenged his father and Nayra, was there really that much difference between the two religions?

"In many ways no," Sheikh Habib had said. "But in many ways yes."

"How so?"

"Our religion is one of logic. Unlike your Bible, which is written by many men and is therefore full of much error, the Qur'an was recited to Muhammad, may his name be praised, by a holy angel of God."

"Really?"

"Yes, the angel Gabriel."

Tyler had heard something like this about the Mormons, but didn't know it was true with the Muslims.

"Yes," Sheikh Habib repeated. "And because of this, its logic is pure and undefiled."

"Like how?"

"In our faith, when one does wrong, one must pay. Cause and effect. Like all the other laws of nature. When one jumps off a cliff, one is subjected to the law of gravity and pays the price by falling. When one sins against Allah, one must also pay the price."

"So Allah has no mercy?"

The sheikh shook his head in scorn. "Of course he is merciful. Every breath that I take is because of his mercy. All beauty that surrounds me, all food, all drink, the necessities of life, everything that is, is because of his mercy. The Qur'an speaks of such things many, many times, but it also speaks of the necessity of following his ways. Your faith, on the other hand . . ." — he raised his hands — "it is very illogical."

"I don't understand."

"Your Scriptures, they lay out rigorous laws for one to follow and obey . . . and then, in complete contradiction, they say one no longer has to follow and obey them. You people of the Book, you break ten, twenty, a hundred laws a day, any that you choose, and then you simply say, 'I am forgiven.'"

Tyler had to nod. "I know what you mean; there's a ton of hypocrisy."

The sheikh shook his head again. "It is more than hypocrisy, my young friend. It is, how do you call it . . . schizophrenia. For us the laws are clear, unbreakable. To approach a perfect and holy God, you must be perfect and holy. For you it does not matter. You speak of Allah's unapproachable holiness; then you teach unspeakable blasphemies."

"Blasphemies?"

"Claiming that such holiness would lower itself to our sinful level, that he would die on a cross as a filthy sinner so you can sin." The sheikh's voice grew more impassioned. "This is more than illogic; it is blasphemy. For holy and perfect Allah to become nothing more than the world's refuse for filthy transgressors? It defies the laws of nature. It tramples all that is good and righteous and holy!"

And so the discussions continued several times a day as Tyler gained a deeper understanding of Islam, as he appreciated the purity of its logic. Yet every time he closed his eyes, he saw those Sudanese villagers. He saw their suffering faces radiating incredible faith, immeasurable joy. And he wondered. Where was the logic in that?

✳

It had taken very little cunning for Helen to outmaneuver Brent Appleton ...

Get drunk, as they always did ... pretend she needed more than the usual amount of liquor to loosen up ... order more from room service (vodka was his substance abuse of choice) ... use her additional glasses to drown a potted fern (which would soon be developing cirrhosis of the frond) ... and patiently wait for him to pass out.

It was a piece of cake, no problem at all ... well, except for the pounding headache that dogged her from Tel Aviv to Nairobi, and the breakfast-hurling flight she had chartered from Nairobi to that godforsaken village Brent had mentioned Daniel was stranded in.

Still, all that had been relatively easy compared with her current challenge — convincing Daniel Lawson to head back to civilization, where he'd have better access to diplomatic channels and state-of-the-art communication. She'd arrived not more than twenty minutes ago and now, as they helped carry some wounded relief worker back to the plane, they were already going at it.

"Daniel."

"No."

"But — "

"No. This is the country my son is in, and this is the country where I'm staying until I get him back."

"But it's too dangerous. And primitive. Your chances of helping Tyler are much better if you — "

"No."

"But — "

"No."

Helen blew the hair out of her eyes. She'd never thought it possible to discover somebody more stubborn than herself. But she'd found him.

They approached the plane, which was already surrounded by half the village. The local pastor, a pleasant man with a hideously scarred face, stayed at the relief worker's side, speaking softly to him, cooling his dangerously high fever with a wet rag. They would be taking off in just a few minutes, so Helen tried another tack.

"All right," she said, "if you're staying, I'm staying, too."

"Absolutely not."

"Daniel —"

"What part of no don't you understand?"

"I'm telling you, I can help."

"It's too dangerous for you to stay."

"You're staying."

"He's my son."

"And he's my friend ... and so are you, when you're not so bullheaded and acting so superior."

The accusation brought him to a stop. She wasn't sure why but she quickly used it to her advantage. "Listen, Preacher Man, we're a team. And for those past few weeks we'd been a pretty good one, in case you hadn't noticed."

Apparently he had, because he said nothing.

"And there's no reason why we can't continue working together to help find your son."

They arrived at the plane and opened the door.

"Easy ...," the pilot ordered as they lifted the kid into the aircraft. "Nice and easy." He crawled toward the back and began strapping the boy down.

The scar-faced pastor turned to Helen. "To stay here, as the only whites, it will be very dangerous. And being Christian to boot. That is not good."

"I'm not a Christian," Helen said. "I'm a Jew."

The pastor looked surprised. He turned to Daniel, who nodded, then back to Helen. "I am afraid that makes matters all the worse."

"Why?"

"We're in a Muslim state," Daniel explained. "Sworn to destroy Israel."

"But I'm an American Jew."

The pastor looked even less pleased. "That will do little to help your cause, should you be captured."

"I'll take my chances."

Once again Daniel shook his head. "No, I will not allow it."

Helen struggled to keep her temper in check. "Daniel, listen ... I respect your concern, I really do. In fact, I find it kind of quaint, almost endearing." That was all she could muster before she lost it. "But it's a pain in the rear! Now, I'm staying here and unless you plan on tying *me* down inside the plane, you'd better get used to it." With that she turned to make a dramatic exit back to the village. The exit might have been a bit more dramatic if her blouse had not caught the latch of the door, bringing her up short. She turned and tugged.

"Here, let me get that," he offered.

"I've got it," she insisted.

"I know, but just let me — "

"I said I've — "

The blouse gave a sickening rip and she suddenly felt fresh air against her back.

Great, she thought. *Just great.* She glanced at the village pastor, who traded amused looks with Daniel. She tried again but was still caught. Well, most of the damage was already done; she might as well finish it. With her typical, iron-willed determination, she pulled harder until what remained of the back of the blouse gave way. Without hesitation she turned and stormed toward the village ... as much of its population remained standing and staring.

"Helen ...," Daniel called after her. "Helen!"

But she was not stopping. Instead, trying to salvage whatever dignity she had left, she called over her shoulder. "And don't forget my bags. You'll find the aluminum briefcase particularly interesting."

The whispers and titters followed as she walked away, her face growing hotter by the second, something that she knew had little to do with the unbearable heat.

✳

Once again the ten-inch-square breastplate, the Choshen, was stretched out upon the wooden table in the hut. Seven of the golden sockets were filled with their stones. Daniel had already removed the fake Levi Stone, and now Helen reached into the aluminum briefcase to produce the original. He looked on. The Mossad had known exactly what they were doing. From where he stood, the two stones appeared identical in every way, shape, and form.

Holding the stone in her hand, Helen slowly approached the table. There appeared to be no reaction. She brought it beside the breastplate. Still nothing. She glanced up at Daniel, who gave her a nod of encouragement. Ever so carefully, ever so delicately, she set the stone into the empty socket and stepped back to wait.

Nothing. No glow, no reaction.

But neither Daniel nor Helen was surprised. After all, the Urim and Thummim were not yet present, and they had always acted as the catalyst.

"Okay," Helen said. "Let's bring them in and see what happens."

Daniel crossed to the other side of the hut. He stooped down to his suitcase and retrieved the two granite rocks, which were carefully folded inside the silk scarf. He gently unwrapped them and laid them in the bare palm of his hand.

"You ready?" he asked.

Helen, peering down at the breastplate, nodded. "Ready."

Since the Levi Stone had played such a critical part in his dreams, and since it was the high priest's stone, they hoped its presence would somehow create a greater reaction. Though they were still missing four stones, they hoped this key stone would cause . . . would somehow cause . . . well, that's what they were about to find out.

Daniel started toward the table but had barely taken a step before Helen cried out. "Whoa!"

He stopped.

"We're getting something!" she exclaimed. "They're already starting to glow." She moved closer to the table and motioned to him. "Keep coming. Nice and slow, though."

Daniel carefully inched forward.

"Easy . . . easy . . ."

He cocked his head, trying to see over her shoulder. "What's happening now?"

"Hm?"

"What's happening?"

"More of the same. Just the glow." She held her hands over them. "And heat. They're producing heat like before. Keep coming."

Daniel continued to ease forward. He closed the distance by half, with three more feet to go. Helen repositioned herself and now he could see the glow, too — tiny electrical arcs sparking deep inside the stones. "I see them," he said.

Helen nodded. "It's more intense than before. And the Levi Stone — can you see? — it's glowing now, too." She held her hand over it. "And it's giving off heat. Just like the others. And ... whoa — "

Daniel slowed.

"Do you hear that?"

He strained to listen. "I don't hear any — "

"Shh ..."

He stopped, then held his breath.

"Don't you hear that? It's really high-pitched, like a TV set or computer monitor when it's going bad. Don't you hear that?"

Daniel strained to listen. Yes, there it was, just barely on the edge of his hearing — a high, thin whine.

Helen tilted her ear, carefully listening over each stone. "I can't tell where it's coming from ... it's so high. Move closer."

Daniel took another step. He couldn't be certain if it grew louder or not. Then another. Yes, it was louder, or at least he could hear it better. He leaned forward, straining to listen. Only then did he realize the sound was not coming from the breastplate. It was coming from the two rocks in his hand. "Helen?"

She looked up. He motioned to the Urim and Thummim. "It's coming from these."

She frowned, then joined him. She lowered her ear to the stones in his palm and listened. "Yes," she half whispered, looking up at him, "you're right." Ever so cautiously she reached out to touch the two rocks. But her fingers barely grazed the surface before she yanked them back, startling him.

"What?" he cried.

"Don't you feel that?"

"Feel what?"

She looked at her fingertips, carefully examining them. Then she held them out for him to see. To his astonishment, they were beet red and badly burnt.

"What happened?"

She shook her head and stared at them. Then she slowly looked at him. "Why aren't they burning you?"

He looked at the rocks, shifted them into his other hand. They weren't even warm.

She examined the burns more closely, gingerly touching them. That's when Daniel noticed it. "Look!" he shouted. The glow of the stones remained the same but the breastplate itself had started to react. Not glowing, not really. Instead the golden threads woven throughout seemed to be shimmering.

"Reverend Lawson!" The shout from outside the hut startled both of them. "Reverend Lawson!" They exchanged looks and moved toward the opening.

Outside, the sun had just set, but there was still enough light to recognize Pastor Tano racing toward them. He was accompanied by a young man, an Arab in his twenties. More importantly, there was enough light to see what the young man held in his hand.

Tyler's camera.

"Where did you get that!" Daniel shouted as they arrived.

But the young man was panting too hard to answer.

"I said, where did you get that!"

Again he gave no answer. Instead he held out his other hand and opened it. Inside was yet another stone from Daniel's dream — the Reuben Stone. The stone representing the firstborn. Tyler's stone.

"And you are certain the father will follow?"

Ibrahim el-Magd nodded. "He will come."

"He possesses the remaining stones and the Urim and Thummim?"

"Yes."

Sharif Abdu Massud pushed up his glasses and spoke. "Everything is in place. Our heroes, the suitcases, the canisters. Within just a few hours, when you give the word, the Day of Wrath will commence."

Ibrahim looked about the long table. Most of the Shura had already arrived, and it was clear that he had already lost much of their support. "Brothers, I can appreciate — "

Abdullah Muhammad Fadi spoke up. "Four years of hard work, the risk of our lives, the risk of hundreds of lives. Everything is in place, Ibrahim. The impossible has been achieved."

"And you would risk it all on this father's decision to rescue his son?" Sharif asked.

"Brothers," Ibrahim said, holding out his hands, "I understand your impatience. If you will grant me but another seventy-two hours, I swear by all that is holy, everything will take place just as we have planned."

"All because of one man?" Sharif asked.

"Sharif speaks the truth," Abdullah said. "All of our actions, the entire Day of Wrath, it rests upon this single man?"

"How can we be certain he will even come?" Sharif persisted.

"I have sent him a very personal invitation," Ibrahim answered. "One he cannot resist."

Young Mustafa Muhammad Dahab, Ibrahim's favorite, spoke up. "But are we certain, Ibrahim — with all of the stones in place, are we certain that even then they will speak?"

"He has a point," Abdullah insisted. "Are we not jeopardizing the wrath of Allah for what may simply be the tales of old women?" He turned to Sheikh Habib. "I know what the ancient Scriptures say. But for today" — he motioned to the center of the table, where the pillow with the three stones lay — "what proof do we have that they will still work for us today?"

"Or," Mustafa quietly added, "that they are even authentic?"

Ibrahim el-Magd looked about the table, then up to an aide who stood by the door. He gave a single nod. The young man turned and disappeared into the hallway. A moment later he returned with Nayra Fazil. She looked more worn than when Ibrahim had last seen her, the period of mourning obviously taking its toll. She did not even raise her eyes to meet his.

The Shura grew silent.

As she approached, Ibrahim explained. "The daughter of Yussuf Fazil has seen the additional stones, she has seen the Urim and Thummim, and she has seen the breastplate of judgment." All eyes watched as she approached the table, her bare feet silent against the stone tile. Ibrahim continued. "She has seen what they do. She has seen the beginnings of their work."

Instead of joining his side, Nayra stopped at the opposite end of the table, in deference to her position as a woman. He could see her trembling. Poor child. When he spoke, it was with great tenderness. "Nayra Fazil. Thank you for joining us, even in this, your time of great grief."

She did not respond.

"Your father was a great man, a great friend. We all mourn his passing."

The Shura nodded in silent agreement. She still could not look up.

"But tell these men what you have told me. Tell our brothers of the workings of the stones, of the Urim and Thummim. Tell them what you have witnessed."

Slowly she raised her head. Eyes puffy and swollen, she looked at no one, not even Ibrahim. She started to speak but her voice caught.

"Tell us," Ibrahim softly encouraged. "Tell us what you have learned."

At last her eyes met his. Besides their anguish, they held an emotion he had not anticipated. Hate. Before he could recover, she answered, her voice quivering with rage. "I have learned that you, my uncle ... are the one who murdered my father."

chapter fifteen

"No!" Daniel paced the confines of the small hut. "Dear God!" Like a caged animal, he was unsure where to go, what to do. "That's my son! My God! What are you doing? *What are you doing!*"

"Daniel . . ." Helen moved toward him. "It's not over. We need to — "

"My son!" he shouted at her. *"My son!"*

She nodded, taking his arm to offer solace. He yanked it away, continuing to pace the dirt floor. He stole a glance back at the camera's viewfinder as the playback of the tape continued. Mercifully, the beatings had come to an end. There was no more blur of yellow white canes tearing into his boy's back. No more tortured screams. Instead a man was speaking on the tape. An Arab about his age with a beard. Spotting him, Daniel pushed past Helen to the table and leaned forward, straining to listen.

". . . will be your guide. He is a faithful servant and will bring you safely to us." The man spoke with a thick accent. "But come, Pastor. Come as quickly as possible. How long your son will last, I do not know. Come. Bring what you have and come." The man paused, gave a somber nod to someone just out of the frame, and the screen went blank.

Daniel stared. "That's it?" He turned to the young man who had just brought the camera and delivered the stone. "That's all there is?!"

The young man looked at him, obviously weighing how to respond. Daniel saved him the effort. He grabbed the kid by his robes and pulled him into his face. "Where's my son!" he shouted. "What have you done to my son!"

"Daniel . . ." Helen moved in, forcing her way between them.

"Where's my son!"

"Daniel . . ." With effort she finally managed to break his grip.

The young man staggered backward, shaking off the attack, struggling to regain his machismo.

"*Where is he!*"

"You will come with me."

Daniel roared. "WHERE IS HE!"

Helen reached out and touched his arm. It was enough to remind Daniel he was out of control. He took a breath, closed his eyes, and with restraint repeated, "Where is my boy? Where am I to go?"

"It is a secret location. The location of Ibrahim el-Magd."

"Who?"

"Ibrahim el-Magd?" Helen asked. "The terrorist?"

The boy shook his head. "El-Magd, servant of Allah."

"What?" Daniel's rage bubbled back to the surface. "My son is with some terrorist?" The youth took a half step back, preparing for another outburst. "You know their location? You know where he is?"

"Perhaps I do, perhaps I — "

"Where?" Daniel leaped at him. This time the young man was prepared. He sidestepped the attack and delivered a powerful punch to his side.

"*Daniel!*"

He gasped, slowly dropping to his knees. The boy stood over him, glowering, waiting for more.

"Daniel . . ."

Fighting through the pain, he gasped, "Where is he!" He looked up, held the youth's gaze, and repeated, "Where is my boy?"

"You must come with me," the youth ordered. "Come with me or he will die."

Slowly, deliberately, Daniel rose to his feet. The youth stepped back, ready, but Daniel did not fight. He stood evaluating the boy, evaluating the situation. He noticed the Reuben Stone, still on the table where the youth had set it. The last stone of his dream, of Jill's dream. The stone that choked and gagged and nearly killed him as he struggled to bring it up and out of his own rocky heart. The stone that represented his firstborn, the child he had once loved more than

282

life itself. The child whom — and here it was — the child whom he *still* loved more than his life. He saw that now. It took losing him for Daniel to understand the depth of his love. Tears burned his eyes as he remembered Jill's prayer. *"Please, Lord, speak to him, do whatever is necessary to make him see."* God was faithful. During the past weeks he had done just that — given him eyes to look past the failures, to look beyond unmet expectations, to see a son he loved passionately, regardless of what he was ... regardless of what he was not.

"Daniel ...," Helen spoke softly.

But he did not respond. Instead he looked back at the youth. When he spoke, it was barely audible. "All right ... let's go."

"Daniel ..."

"It is a long journey," the youth said. "A night and a day. You must pack. Bring plenty of water."

"A night and a day?" Daniel asked.

"You must hurry. Every minute counts."

Daniel paused to look about the room. Then he moved into action, gathering his things.

Helen was immediately at his side. "You don't know where he's taking you. You don't know if it's a trap."

He motioned toward the camera. "I know that's my son on that video." He began pulling clothes from the line stretched across the hut.

"You don't know what they'll do to you."

"He's my son, Helen. My ... son."

"Yes, but ..." She took a breath. "You don't even know if he's still alive."

The phrase brought him up short. She bit her lip, obviously hating what she'd said, but having to say it. He reached down and picked up his suitcase. Then he threw open the lid and began dumping in the clothes.

"Daniel, listen to me. This is crazy. Let's contact the officials. Radio the embassy. Let's let them — "

"I've been radioing the embassy every day." He continued packing.

"This is insane. It makes no sense."

"It doesn't have to make sense. That's my kid. How many days am I supposed to wait? How many days am I supposed to be rational and sensible?"

"But—"

"What did Guido say? About the heart and the brain?"

She looked at him.

"'When it comes to matters of the heart, the brain doesn't matter.' Isn't that what he said?"

"But ..."

He turned to her, moisture in his eyes. "He's my son. Do you understand that? My son."

She looked at him a long moment. She was beginning to understand and for that he was pleased. He was not so pleased with her next statement.

"If you're going, then I'm going."

He smiled tightly at the gesture. "Thanks, but it's too—"

"No. I'm going, too."

"Don't be ridicu—"

"What makes you think you're the only one who gets to act from the heart?"

"It's too—"

"If you're going, I'm going."

He watched her as she set her chin. It would do no good to argue; he knew that. She'd already made up her mind. And though much of him was frustrated at her foolish stubbornness and equally concerned for her safety, part of him was very, very grateful.

Twenty-four hours. That's all the time the Shura would give him. Allah be merciful and forgive them. Regardless of whether the stones arrived or not, he had twenty-four hours before the Day of Wrath began.

Ibrahim el-Magd headed down the long hallway of the compound, his sandaled feet scraping the smooth stone tiles. Behind him walked an ever present bodyguard. To his left young Mustafa Muhammad Dahab would act as a trusted witness. To his right was Mary Rahman, the compound's nurse, someone familiar with the medical maladies that plagued women. They were heading to Nayra's room.

Twenty-four hours. All canisters of the agent were in place; all heroes and their briefcases stood by. All they needed was Ibrahim's word. A simple phrase that even the Shura did not know, one that he and the heroes had personally chosen. He would speak that phrase. Within twenty-four hours he would call the first hero and recite it. The Shura gave him little option. Allah be merciful; Allah forgive their impatience.

Not that Ibrahim entirely blamed the Shura. How could he? After Nayra Fazil's dramatic confrontation in the council room, what choice did they have? It was a cold, calculated move, one that he would never have suspected of her. Until he realized the true source ... the American. Of course. The boy had obviously corrupted her. He was certain of it. And this visit would be the proof.

It had been a difficult confrontation. He never enjoyed lying, and he took little comfort in diminishing his niece to tears. But there had been no other way.

"Nayra," he had said after her accusation before the group. "You are still very distraught. This we understand." She had remained standing before the Shura, trembling, glaring at him. "Your mind, it is playing tricks on you. In times of great grief these things can happen."

Her voice had trembled with rage. "My father would have died for you!"

"And I for him."

"*Liar!*"

He had paused, letting the outburst echo against the council walls, allowing it to prove her volatility. Then he answered calmly, compassionately. "No. Your father was absolutely vital in our great and glorious plan. That is why the infidels had him killed."

"*You* killed him," she said, seething.

Ibrahim looked at the Shura as if to shrug, making it clear that she was obviously speaking from female hysteria.

"If you do not believe I know this as truth," she continued, "then ask my father's second wife." She never took her eyes from him. "Ask your sister."

Ibrahim turned back to her. It stabbed his heart to see eyes once so full of love now consumed by such hate. "My sister?" he asked in feigned surprise.

"Yes."

"How would my sister know?"

"Ask her," Nayra hissed.

Ibrahim held her gaze. His sister's betrayal could be solved easily enough. After all, she was family. But this, this sudden fire within his court, had to be extinguished — and quickly. He responded, "There are many things you do not understand, Little Bird. Many peoples and countries who wish to destroy each of us. Your father was no exception. They would do anything to prevent the day of Allah's great and final wrath."

"Ibrahim …" It was a cautionary word, spoken by Abdullah Muhammad Fadi. She must not be told their plans. But Ibrahim knew what he was doing. She had to be distracted. She had to see the overall picture. He knew her. Knew that in such matters she could still be trusted. After all, she had already served them so well.

Just as he anticipated, she took the bait. "Wrath?" she asked.

He nodded. "The great and final day of judgment has arrived. Very shortly Allah's winnowing fork will separate the chaff from the wheat. Apostates and infidels around the world will be destroyed."

She paused a moment and blinked. She looked at the Shura, then back at him. "What are you saying?"

Sheikh Salad Habib spoke from his cushion along the wall. "Millions of nonbelievers will soon be sent to hell."

She looked to Ibrahim for confirmation. He slowly nodded. "And Allah has selected us, Little Bird. This great Shura has been chosen by Allah himself to become his swift and terrible sword." He watched, seeing she had momentarily lost her focus. Good.

When she spoke, her voice was weaker. "Where … where will such a thing take place? How many will die?"

"Hundreds of millions," he answered. "From around the world. America, Europe, Asia …"

She looked at him in astonishment. He was pleased that she was impressed, that she now saw the magnitude of their plan. He nodded to her in affirmation.

She spoke again. "You are … you are not serious."

Again Ibrahim nodded. But instead of watching her astonishment turn to reverent awe, he was surprised to see it twist into fear.

"You are crazy," she half whispered.

"Nayra."

"Madmen." She looked about the room. "You are all mad."

"You are distraught," Ibrahim said. "That is understandable."

"You would kill millions ... hundreds of millions of innocent — "

"Hundreds of millions of nonbelievers," Sheikh Habib corrected. "Infidels."

"And the people of the Book? Who will protect them? Who will prevent them from being destroyed?"

"Allah will judge as he sees fit."

"Allah ... ?" She looked incredulously about the Shura. "This is not the work of Allah. This is the work of man. This is your decision, not Allah's. This is your — "

"Nayra, please ... " Ibrahim started toward her.

She took half a step back. "There are many good people," she said. "They do not have the full truth but they are good."

"Partial truth is the same as partial lie," Sheikh Habib stated.

She turned to him. "I have seen these people. I have lived with them."

"Ah," the sheikh said. "'A little leaven leavens the whole loaf.'"

She turned back to the Shura. "Some are my friends. My *good* friends."

The council exchanged glances. Seeing their expressions, realizing she'd gone too far, she started to back away. "You are deranged ... This is not the will of Allah."

"Nayra," Ibrahim tried to reason, "you are young. You have much to learn in the ways of — "

"He would not do this. This is not the will of Allah!"

Ibrahim's voice grew firm. "He will do this. And very soon. It will be a cleansing such as our world has never seen."

"No ..." She continued backing away.

"Nayra ... Little Bird."

"No ..."

"We have had plans. For many, many years we have — "

"I will not listen."

"Your father has been instrumental in — "

"I will not listen to this!" She turned and started for the door.

"Nayra."

"No!"

An aide moved to block her but Ibrahim motioned to let her pass. She stormed out of the chamber and down the hall.

That had been nearly ninety minutes ago. It had taken that much time to extinguish the fire she had so impetuously started.

The Shura weren't fools. They knew she was a woman, unstable in emotion. But she had raised doubts. Created suspicion. And for that he had to pay the price.

Twenty-four hours. That was their decree. That was all the time they would permit him to seek Allah's will and hear his voice. That was all the time remaining before the Day of Wrath began.

He hoped, he prayed, it would be enough.

Contact with the pastor had been made. Word had been sent that they were on their way. They would arrive in eighteen hours. He had considered sending one of their Russian-made helicopters to swoop into the desert and pluck them up, but the reports of a massive storm approaching made such a flight impossible.

As they headed toward Nayra's room, he thought again of his dream. Of the face. The awesome holiness of Allah. His indignant rage. The vengeance that would soon be poured out. But for now cracks had to be sealed, newly sown weeds of mistrust plucked. He did not entirely blame Nayra. Not only had she lost her father, but it was obvious she had been seduced by the American boy — in her mind and, no doubt, in her body as well. After all, that is what Americans do when they are attracted to the opposite sex. Like animals, they have no control or restraint.

And that is why Mary Rahman walked beside him. With a quick physical examination she could tell. If there was proof Nayra was no longer pure, then he would have adequate explanation to give the Shura for her actions. And with that explanation perhaps he could convince them to extend the deadline.

They would not hold it against her. After all, she was a woman and everyone knew women cannot control their sexual desires. That is why most girls from his village were circumcised before entering womanhood. That is why Yussuf and his wife had terrible fights about this practice concerning Nayra. And because the wife had won out, because Nayra had been excused from the ritual, Ibrahim must now reap the harvest of her parents' indulgence.

But that would soon change. For Nayra's own good. It was not too late to help her regain control of her womanly urges. Regardless of whether she had been soiled or not, Mary Rahman had brought a clean towel and sterilized scalpel, one that would help free Nayra from the burden of such desires.

They arrived at the door and he knocked. "Nayra?"

There was no answer. He knocked again. "Nayra, open the door, please."

Again there was no answer.

After a suitable pause he nodded to the bodyguard, who stepped forward, dropped his shoulder, and slammed hard into the wooden door. Once . . . twice . . . It gave way on the third try.

They stepped inside.

"Nayra . . ."

But she was nowhere to be seen. The small apartment was vacant. Without a word Ibrahim turned and raced back into the hall.

"Ibrahim?" Mustafa Muhammad Dahab called. "Where are you going?"

Ibrahim did not turn back. He did not have time. "The boy's room!" he shouted. "She has gone to help the boy!"

✳

Daniel had spotted it through the passenger window nearly forty minutes ago. The three of them had been traveling in the Land Rover nonstop for fifteen hours, living off bread, cucumbers, pistachios, and water. Earlier the night had offered some relief, at least from the heat. But there was nothing for the bruises, and yes, blisters, from the continual assault of the vehicle against their bodies.

"What is that?" he had shouted, pointing out his window.

Helen leaned past him and looked, searching the desolate terrain.

"Over there." He motioned to the horizon, to what looked like a long black curtain with uneven fingers rising into the sky.

She swore quietly.

"What?" Daniel repeated.

She turned from the window and yelled to the driver, the young man who had brought the video camera and the Reuben Stone. "Sandstorm!" she shouted. "Hasan, there's a sandstorm coming!"

Hasan, who had been fighting the wheel all night and into the morning, yelled, "What? What you say?"

"Sandstorm!" she shouted. She pointed out Daniel's window.

He glanced from the road and scowled at her, not understanding.

"Sandstorm!" she repeated.

Finally the light dawned. "Haboob?" he shouted. "Haboob?"

"Yes, haboob!"

He lowered his head to look out Daniel's window and spotted it. Muttering angrily, he turned back to the road and pressed the accelerator to the floor, squeezing out an additional five, maybe eight miles per hour as they bounced and banged their way across the rocks and sand.

"What's he doing?" Daniel shouted.

Helen leaned past him, looking back out the window. "He's going to try to outrun it."

That had been forty minutes ago. And for forty minutes Daniel had watched the black curtain grow to an immense height, spreading in both directions as far as the eye could see, parallel to their road — well, if you could call it a road. It was simply a line of telephone poles that stretched forever into the rugged, blazing inferno.

"Look!" Helen shouted. She pointed ahead. Not far in the distance, part of the curtain was crossing their path. She turned to the driver and shouted, "Hasan!"

He said nothing but looked straight ahead.

"Hasan, we have to turn back!"

"No!"

"What!"

"No time. Every minute is important." As if proving his point, he drove straight through a large stand of wiry *mokheit* bushes that scraped and scratched the underside of the Rover.

Helen pointed at the black curtain. "We can't go through that!"

"We are nearly there. Just a few hours!"

"Hasan!"

He said nothing, concentrating upon his driving.

"Hasan!"

No response.

"Hasan!"

He had obviously shut her out.

"It's getting close," Daniel shouted. "How long before we hit it?"

Helen shook her head, then turned back to Hasan. "We cannot drive through a haboob; you know that! We cannot survive!"

His resolve seemed to be weakening but he continued forward. As did the storm. Daniel watched as wisps and bursts of sand blew across their path, as he felt the vehicle give an occasional shudder.

"Hasan!" Helen shouted. "We have to turn back now! We can't go through that! Hasan!"

Finally, at long last, the youth gave in. With an oath of his own he slammed on the brakes. Daniel threw his hands against the dash as the truck skidded and eventually bounced to a stop.

"What are you doing?" Daniel shouted.

Hasan did not answer. Leaping from the truck, he raced to the back. He opened it and pulled out an armload of thick wool blankets. "Hurry!" he shouted at them. "Hurry!"

Daniel exchanged glances with Helen and then popped the door. He'd barely pushed it open before the wind yanked it from his hands and slammed it into the side of the truck. Immediately sand bit and stung his face. He took a breath and stepped into the fury. Helen followed, covering her face with her arm.

"What are we doing?" he shouted.

"I'm not sure!" she yelled.

He turned to the black curtain. It was taller and much closer.

Hasan moved to the front of the vehicle. They followed. He opened the hood, shoving it up against the wind. "Come!" he motioned to Daniel. "Come!"

Daniel approached and took the end of the coarse blanket Hasan held out to him. Together they unfolded it. Taking Hasan's lead, he tried to lay it across the engine. It momentarily snapped out of his hands and he had to retrieve it. He tried again, this time diligently tucking the ends of the blanket into any nook or cranny that could be found in and around the motor. When the engine was entirely covered, Hasan reached up and slammed down the hood to finish holding the blanket in place.

Daniel turned back to the storm. The looming black curtain had blotted out the sun.

"Here!" Hasan shoved another blanket at Daniel. Then to Helen.

"What do we do with these?" Daniel yelled.

"Wrap them around us!" Helen shouted as she unfolded hers. "To protect us!"

"No!" Hasan grabbed her arm. "Not yet!"

"But —"

"Come!"

They followed him to the back of the truck. The wind whistled across the metal surfaces. Hasan opened the tailgate and produced two U.S. Army retractable spades. He pushed them at Helen and Daniel, shouting, "Dig! Dig!"

"Dig what?" Helen shouted.

"Hurry! Dig!"

"A place to hide?" Daniel shouted. "He wants us to dig a shelter?"

Helen shrugged. "I don't know!"

"Dig!" Hasan yelled impatiently. "Dig!"

"All right!" Daniel shouted. "All right!"

Hasan turned back to the truck. They wedged their blankets into nearby rocks and started to dig. When he spotted them, Hasan shouted, "No! Farther from truck. Farther, to be safe!"

"In case it blows over?" Daniel yelled.

"Farther from truck! Farther from truck!"

They retrieved their blankets and staggered forward against the wind. It grew darker by the second. Some twenty paces away they stopped and began to dig. The first six inches was easy going, just loose sand and gravel. But below that was hard, packed dirt which took forever to scrape and chip through. The wind made it more difficult, pushing against them, snapping their clothes, making it impossible to keep their eyes open. Hasan remained back at the Land Rover, breaking apart boards that had been laid down as part of its makeshift bed. When he finished, he hauled an armload of broken and split planks to them and dropped it onto the ground.

"Okay, down!" he shouted. "Down!"

"What?" Helen yelled.

"He wants us to get down into the hole!"

"It's not ready! There's not enough room!"

"Down!"

"No!" She jerked her thumb toward the Land Rover. "I'll take my chances in there!"

"No! Too dangerous!"

"Don't tell me no! I'll go where I — "

That was when Hasan produced the small black pistol and pointed it at her.

"You don't frighten me!" she shouted.

"Helen!"

"He's supposed to deliver us safely. He's not going to — "

Hasan fired a round into the air.

"All right! Fine!" she shouted. "You've made your point!"

"Down!" he said, motioning. "Down!"

Together they stepped into the hole, then dropped to their knees. It was no more than eighteen inches deep, less than a yard wide.

Hasan reached for their blankets and handed them to them. They unfolded them, wrapping the scratchy wool around their bodies, pulling it up to their faces.

"Down!" Hasan said, motioning again. "Down!"

Reluctantly they lowered themselves, Daniel lying on his left side, Helen pressing close to his back, their knees drawn up together. They were still settling in when Hasan began covering them with the planks. Daniel flattened lower as he watched the dimming light being replaced with wide strips of blackness. He did not really consider himself claustrophobic, but this — this took all of his concentration not to panic.

Once the boards were in place, he heard Hasan digging into the lose dirt, then piling it atop the wood above them. *Scrape . . . rumble, rumble, rumble. Scrape . . . rumble, rumble, rumble.* They were literally being buried alive.

"Helen?" he called.

"I'm all right." Her lips were not six inches from his ear. "I'm all right."

Scrape . . . rumble, rumble, rumble. Scrape . . . rumble, rumble, rumble.

The grave grew darker as the slits between the boards filled. Some dirt sifted through the cracks. Most remained in place. Struggling to hold back his panic, Daniel practiced what he'd learned with Guido in the cave.

Breathe . . . easy . . . easy . . . exhale . . .

He readjusted himself, creating an air pocket in the scratchy material around his mouth.

Breathe . . . easy . . . easy . . .

Eventually the digging stopped.

"Okay?" Hasan shouted, his voice faint in the roaring wind.

"Okay!" Daniel and Helen yelled.

The roar continued to grow, thundering like an approaching train.

Easy . . . easy . . . exhale . . .

He felt movement against his back. Helen's hand was reaching around his waist. He took it and held on. Despite the heat and wind, it felt cold and clammy.

Dear God, he prayed. *Help us. Protect us. Help me see my boy again. Let me see my son . . .*

✳

Tyler readjusted his turban, the final piece of wardrobe he'd changed into as they hid inside the janitor's closet. In the dim light he turned to Nayra and asked, "So how do I look?"

She pulled an anxious face from the crack in the doorway to look at him. For the briefest moment her eyes sparkled in amusement.

He grinned back. It felt good to smile. He hadn't done it in days. Despite the tension and the need to hurry, he couldn't help joking, "Just like Peter O'Toole in *Lawrence of Arabia*?"

She frowned. "Who?"

"Peter O — never mind." He adjusted the long robe, or tried to, until Nayra came to his assistance and began redraping it over his shoulders.

"It is not a bathrobe," she scolded. "It must be worn with dignity and — "

"Ouch," he winced as she tugged the material over the welts on his back.

"I am sorry."

He shrugged. "This sure seems like a lot of stuff to wear in the heat."

She continued to work. "It keeps away the sun and the flies."

He watched as those deep dark eyes with their long lashes evaluated every detail. Even now her beauty made his throat ache. "I still don't understand why you're doing this," he said. "First you trick me into coming here — "

The dark eyes flashed with anger. "I did not trick you. I simply did not tell you everything." Softening slightly, she added, "I would never lie to you, Tyler Lawson. Never."

He held her gaze a moment, pleased with what he heard . . . but not with what he saw. She'd been through a lot since they'd been separated. He could see it in her eyes, the corners of her mouth. She looked older, more weary. But it was more than that. It was as if part of her innocence had been stolen. The freshness, the candidness that was once such a part of her, had started to harden and cloud.

"Won't you get busted for helping me get away?" he asked.

"'Busted'?"

"You know, punished."

"I will be killed."

"Nayra!"

She continued her work. "My uncle, the Shura, they are great men, but they are making a very grave mistake."

"How so? I've been talking with Sheikh Habib; he makes a lot of sense."

"He is a mighty man of religion. Like my uncle. Like the Shura. But I am afraid it is not enough."

"It isn't?"

She pulled on the robe, adjusting his sleeve. "What did you once say? It is religion that killed Christ?"

"Yeah, something like that."

"I am afraid it is religion that is about to do something equally as evil." She put the final touches on the robe. "There." She stepped back to examine him.

"Cool?" he asked, striking his best Bedouin pose.

She broke into another smile. "Yes, Tyler Lawson, very cool." Then, frowning, she added, "Your skin, it is too pale to be Arab. You must only be seen from a distance." She turned back to the door and opened it a crack. It creaked quietly.

"Where can we go?" he asked. "Where can we—"

She quickly shut the door and motioned for silence. Voices approached. Men's voices. They grew louder, passed, and began to fade. A moment later Nayra reopened the door, first a crack, then wider. "Come," she whispered. "Come."

He followed her into the hallway. Together they stole down the corridor as quickly as possible. They approached the corner and slowed. Voices could be heard on the other side. Cautiously Nayra peeked around the wall, then pulled back. "Wait here," she whispered. "We must wait here until—"

More voices. This time from behind. They spun around to see three men enter the hallway at the opposite end and begin to approach.

"What do we do?" Tyler whispered.

"I don't know." Nayra moved away from the wall and straightened herself to avoid suspicion. Tyler did the same, keeping his back toward the approaching men while pretending to be in conversation with her. For a moment he thought it might work. For a moment.

"Nayra Fazil?" one of the men called.

Tyler froze.

Nayra did little better.

"Nayra?"

Finally she answered. But even in Arabic, Tyler could tell her response was stiff and nervous.

The men continued their approach. More words were spoken. Nayra nodded and answered. They were twenty feet away and rapidly closing in. Fifteen feet. They continued to speak. Ten feet. Suddenly—

A voice screamed so loud that it made Tyler jump. But it wasn't a scream; it was a song, half singing, half wailing, and it came from the outside loudspeaker.

Allah u Akabar.

Allah u Akabar.

The Adhan, the call to prayer. Tyler had heard it hundreds of times in Israel, in Ethiopia, and certainly here. He'd always found it grating and irritating (especially the one at five in the morning), but right now it was the most beautiful sound he'd ever heard.

The men stopped and exchanged another set of words with Nayra. She nodded. They wished her well, then turned and retraced their steps, exiting the way they'd come.

"They going to pray?" Tyler whispered.

"Shh . . ." She waited until they were out of earshot before she answered. "Yes. Everyone is going to prayers." She peaked around the corner, then reached out and took his hand. "Come. They are gone. We have only minutes. We must hurry."

"Where?" Tyler asked. "Where can we go?"

"The village, it is very close. Hurry . . ."

chapter sixteen

Daniel's joy swelled as he felt Jill sleeping beside him, her arms wrapped around him from behind. How long he'd missed this, hungered for it. They were back together in bed. Everything was safe and cozy; everything was as it had been before ... before ... He felt the moist, scratchy fibers of the wool blanket against his face, the jagged pebbles digging into the side of his skull. And the sand. All around him the hot, prickly sand.

He wasn't in bed. And it wasn't Jill pressed against his back. The thirty-plus hours of no sleep had taken their toll. He'd dozed off. As his mind cleared, it filled with anger, then with guilt over his mistake. How dare he. This was not Jill. It was another woman! He lay a moment, listening to the silence, hearing only his breathing. And hers.

When he trusted his voice, he called out, "Helen?" He sounded dry and raspy. "You okay?" He felt her stirring. "Helen?"

"Yes," she answered hoarsely. Apparently, she'd been asleep as well.

"It's over," he said, coughing slightly. "I think it's over."

She moved some, then quickly withdrew her arm from him.

He raised a hand to the plank just a couple inches from his face and pushed. Sand filtered in, getting into his eyes, his throat, forcing him to cough some more. He pushed harder. The plank still did not move, though more sand poured in, piling against his cheek, his nose, his mouth. It rapidly built up and panic set in. He was going to suffocate! After all this he was going to drown in four inches of sand! The adrenaline surged. He pushed harder, this time with both hands. He shoved and punched at the wood, fighting for his life, until — "Auuugh!" — a board suddenly flew up. More sand poured in as he pushed against the next plank. It came easier. Then the next, and the next.

He struggled to sit up, shoving away more boards. Helen was beside him, doing the same, until they freed themselves, until they were both sitting up in the grave. A moment passed as he drank in the hot, fresh air, as the sunlight struck his face.

Then he pushed aside the last remaining boards and rose from the sandy pit. He reached down and helped Helen out. He wiped the sand off his face and spit it from his mouth. It felt good to move, to feel the air. And to breathe. Looking around, he saw an entirely different landscape than he'd seen earlier. It reminded him of winter mornings in Illinois after a heavy snowfall. There were no sharp edges. Everything was covered in a thick, creamy cushion of sand. There were no longer rocks or ruts or craters. All the land as far as he could see was sandy velvet. He turned toward the Land Rover. Mounds of the softness had piled against the wheels and upon the hood. Pockets clung against the mirror, the windows, the fenders.

Daniel cupped his hands and shouted, "Hasan?"

There was no answer. Only the silence.

"Hasan?"

"Where could he be?" Helen asked.

He shook his head. Together they started for the truck. "Hasan?"

As they approached, he saw that one of the wooden planks had broken through the windshield. It now stuck out like a listing gun turret. Amid the smoothness that piled around the hole, jagged edges of glass reflected the afternoon sun. "Hasan ..."

When they arrived, Daniel brushed the sand from the passenger door handle and pulled. It opened with a gritty creak followed by a foot of sand that hissed from the seat and floorboard to his feet. And there, across the cab, slumped against the opposite door, sat Hasan. His face was coated in a fine layer of sand ... except around the forehead, where it was much thicker, where it stuck to the blood surrounding the other end of the plank that had crushed his skull.

Helen stifled a gasp.

Daniel forced himself to enter the vehicle and slide across the sandy seat. Tentatively he reached out to the neck to feel for a pulse. He felt no movement. He reached to the mouth for breath. Again he felt nothing. Nothing except the caked sand on his fingers, now moist with Hasan's blood. Daniel felt his face growing wet, then cold. He scooted back to the door, barely making it outside before dropping to his knees and vomiting. He heaved once, twice, and after a pause, a third time onto the white, pristine sand. When would it end? All this death? All this destruction?

Helen knelt beside him. He felt her hand on his back, gently rubbing it in comfort. No words were spoken. No words were necessary. He wiped his mouth and a moment later, with her help, rose to his feet. Together they looked out across the desert. It was flat and smooth and endless ... broken only by the line of telephone poles, pitched at odd angles, stretching forever.

"How far — " Daniel coughed and tried again. "How far did he say we had?"

"Several more hours." She squinted into the distance. "We'll never make it. Not by foot."

Daniel nodded and turned back to the Land Rover. It was their only hope.

"You think it will still run?" she asked.

"I don't know." He headed for the hood and she followed. When he arrived, he groped under the hot metal for the release latch. He found it and gave a tug. After the second or third try the hood popped open. It groaned and grated as he pushed it up to reveal the blanket inside. It was full of pockets of sand. He moved to one side and Helen to the other as they worked the blanket loose, carefully pulling out the edges and corners. When it was free, they slowly raised it from the engine, doing their best not to spill any of the sand until they were over the ground. Then they simply dropped it.

Hasan knew the desert. He'd done everything he could to ensure their safety. And as they closed the hood and walked to the driver's side, where they would remove his body and bury it, Daniel silently prayed for God's mercy upon the man's soul. And just as importantly, that his efforts would not be in vain.

"You promised me twenty-four hours," Ibrahim el-Magd said.

"And you promised that our heroes would be safe," argued Abdullah Muhammad Fadi.

"When did you hear of the arrest?" Ibrahim asked.

"We received the call from St. Petersburg twenty minutes ago."

"From whom?"

"Does it matter?"

"Yes, it matters. To base our entire timing upon a single phone call. To jeopardize all that we have worked and planned so hard —"

"No, Ibrahim." Abdullah's interruption brought silence to the Shura gathered about the table. "You are the one who has jeopardized our plans. By insisting we wait, you are the one who has endangered the operation." Abdullah turned to the other members of the council. "Once Russian intelligence discovers the plans of our St. Petersburg hero —"

"And they will," Sharif Abdu Massud said. "The Russians are experienced in methods of interrogation."

Abdullah continued. "Then word of the operation will quickly flow through all intelligence communities, and all of our planning and preparation will have been in vain."

"We must strike now," Sharif Abdu Massud concluded, "while the other six heroes are still in place."

Ibrahim raised his hands in protest. "But is there any confirmation of this arrest, or are we merely —"

"Ibrahim . . ."

"All I am asking for is verification. We cannot —"

"Ibrahim, this must stop!" A palpable tension filled the chamber. Abdullah continued. "This fixation of yours, of finding these stones, of hearing the voice of Allah — we must bring it to its conclusion now. We must act and we must act swift —"

"No!" Ibrahim's voice cut sharply and clearly. He paused, letting the silence fill the room, pleased to see his anger still held power. "You have not seen what I have seen!"

No one had the courage to respond. Not even Abdullah. It was young Mustafa who finally asked quietly, "Then tell us, Ibrahim, what have you seen? Please, tell us of this vision you speak of."

Ibrahim stole a look to Sheikh Salad Habib, who closed his eyes. After a moment the old man nodded. The time had come.

Ibrahim el-Magd took a breath and began. "I have seen the face of Allah. Three times in a vision of the night." He watched as the council looked at one another. He knew some would think it blasphemy, but the time had come. "Yes," he nodded, his voice just above a whisper. "His face. It is an awesome face, terrifying. The face of a warrior, filled with rage, consumed with unspeakable wrath and power. It is a face covered with the splattered blood of his enemies, a face covered with the blood of infidels." Gathering his robes, he rose from the end of the long table. "As I have said countless times before, to unleash such wrath, to be the agents of such terrible fury ... it is not something we do lightly."

"Ibrahim," Abdullah interjected. "No one here has ever underestimated the seriousness of our — "

"Three times!" The chamber rang with his voice. "Three times I have seen his awesome fury! Three times I have quaked in his presence, my heart pounding in terror." Slowly he moved around the table. "Do you still not understand? To unleash such rage, to pour out the wrath of Allah ... we must be absolutely certain. Our timing, our means, must be in the absolute center of his will."

"Yes, but how is it certain these stones will — "

"It is certain," Sheikh Habib interrupted from the side wall. "The Scriptures are clear. The possessor of the stones will hear the voice of Allah."

"Not only that ..." — Ibrahim slowed to a stop and looked over the group — "the one who possesses the stones will know the outcome of every battle before it is fought. He will know at all times which battles will bring victory and which must be avoided."

"Are such things true?" young Mustafa asked.

Sheikh Salad Habib nodded. "It is in the Scriptures; they are true."

"So to have them ...," Mustafa thought out loud, "to have them will be beneficial both now and in the future."

Ibrahim nodded. "Yes ... Should those who survive, should they refuse to bow their knee and attempt to retaliate — "

Mustafa quietly finished the thought, "We would know how to deal with each of them."

Once again silence stole over the group. Ibrahim carefully studied the faces. Not only were these men devoted to Allah, but they were keenly pragmatic. If they did not appreciate the awesome responsibility of his wrath, they would at least appreciate the need for self-preservation.

"And the stones will arrive ...," Abdullah asked.

"Within hours." Ibrahim saw no need to speak of Nayra and the boy, nor of their disappearance. It made little difference now.

The bait had been set and the father had taken it. He was on his way.

The chamber returned to its silence. An aide to Mustafa quietly entered and stooped to whisper a message. As he did, Ibrahim continued to study the group. He had regained control. For how long he wasn't certain, but at least for the moment he —

"Ibrahim . . ." Mustafa looked up apologetically. "I am afraid I have more bad news."

The members of the Shura turned to him.

"I have been informed that we have now lost contact with the hero of Munich."

"Lost contact?"

"He can no longer be reached."

"He has been arrested?" Ibrahim asked.

"I do not know."

"And so it begins." Abdullah rose wearily to his feet. "Do we need any more proof that our plan is unraveling? Do we need any more evidence that we must act immediately?"

"Abdullah is right," Sharif agreed. "Before our very eyes the plan is evaporating."

"Yes, Ibrahim," Abdullah insisted. "We must trust the guidance Allah has already provided. We must act now and we must act swiftly."

Other members of the Shura nodded and spoke in agreement.

"Yes, now."

"We must strike now . . ."

Ibrahim looked on. His sadness grew heavy. He had lost. He knew that now. Nothing he could do would bring them back. But he was not angry. Only grieved. Grieved over their impatience and over their fear. Once again he looked to Sheikh Salad Habib. The man's eyes remained closed. He gave no council. Ibrahim was on his own.

"We must start the operation," Abdullah insisted. "We must place the call now."

"Yes," Sharif insisted, "before we lose any more heroes. We must start the operation now."

One final time Ibrahim looked about the Shura. If he were to refuse them, they would turn on him. Over the years he had grown to know each of these men. He knew how to lead and cajole and

302

intimidate. And he knew when he could go no further. Allah forgive him, he had done his best. Allah have mercy.

Slowly, sadly, he nodded.

"Let us make the call," Abdullah repeated. "Let us prepare our hearts and make the call!"

"Allah be praised!" another cried.

"Yes!" Sharif shouted. "The great and glorious Day of his Wrath has arrived!"

Ibrahim looked on. He had tried and he had failed. Allah be merciful. Allah forgive him. Allah forgive them all.

By the time prayers were completed, Tyler and Nayra had made it out of the compound and were well on their way toward the village. The dirt road was firm with a thin layer of red dust on either side. Except for two boys on camels, there was no other traffic. Still, just to be safe, Nayra had veiled herself and insisted that Tyler walk in front of her as her husband. "And keep your face turned away from any passersby, just in case."

Tyler obeyed. It wasn't until they were about to enter the village that they ran into a problem. He was a semi-toothed old man in a rickety, horse-drawn cart. Approaching Tyler from behind, he called out a greeting. Tyler raised his hand in response but was careful not to look in his direction.

The old man pulled beside him and spoke again.

Suspecting that he was being offered a ride, Tyler kept his face turned away, gave a grunt, and continued walking. But it wasn't enough to satisfy the chatty old-timer. He ordered his horse to a stop, no doubt expecting Tyler to stop as well.

But Tyler kept on walking.

Again he shouted and again Tyler waved.

Still chattering, he clicked his horse forward and pulled beside Tyler a second time. That was when Nayra moved in to assist. As she approached, she called out something through her veil.

The old man turned to her and replied in concern.

She spoke for several moments. Then, turning so only Tyler could hear, she whispered, "Drop to the ground."

"What?"

303

"Drop to the ground and start screaming." She turned back to the man and continued talking. Glancing again to Tyler, she repeated the command. "Drop!"

Tyler wasn't crazy about getting his handsome new wardrobe dirty, but he thought he understood. So, kneeling carefully to the ground, he gave a halfhearted shout.

"Louder," she whispered. "And roll."

He called out a little louder. But acting had never been his strong suit, especially when he wasn't sure of his motivation. So once again Nayra offered her assistance. Spinning around, she hissed, "Roll!" while at the same time kicking him hard in the groin.

Now he yelled. And now he rolled.

The old man's eyes widened. Apparently, he had seen enough. He called to his horse and quickly pulled away. Not, however, without several wary looks over his shoulder.

Immediately Nayra stooped down to Tyler. "Are you all right?" she asked.

"Are you crazy?" Tyler groaned when he could finally breathe.

"I am sorry, but for a crazy person you were not very believable."

"That's what you told him?" Tyler asked, rising to his knees. "That I was crazy?"

"Yes."

"Do you think it worked?"

Nayra shook her head. "No. But I believe he thinks that for a man to let his wife do such a thing to him, something must be wrong in his head. May I help you up?"

He offered his arm and she helped him to his feet, where he stayed bent over another minute or so, catching his breath. When he finally rose and looked, the old man had disappeared into the village.

Nayra helped dust him off and straighten his robe. "Come," she finally urged, "we must go." Tyler nodded and started off, Nayra following behind.

Minutes later they entered the village. It was a moderate settlement of thirty, perhaps forty buildings, all covered in plaster and painted in various shades of whitewash. Near the center was a large structure with multiple pillars and a single wall. Here a large group of boys were congregated. Tyler guessed that it was a school. He also suspected that this was the town's market day, as the street they'd entered was lined with crude lean-tos made of sticks and twigs lashed together. Men and women stooped or sat underneath tattered cloth roofs, selling daggers, camel whips, leather slippers, swords, scabbards, tunics, soap, spices, carpets, woven baskets, and red plastic gas containers. There was also gaunt livestock as well as poultry in cages made of the same tied sticks and twigs.

Tyler picked up his pace, walking briskly forward as if on an important errand, while doing his best to keep his face hidden. From time to time a merchant would call out. He wasn't sure if they were talking to him, but he ignored them just the same. During one of his glances back to Nayra he saw her slowing to talk with a boy, eleven or twelve years old. He wore a ragged tunic and in his hands he held a flat wooden slate used for writing. More noticeably, his feet were shackled. Only four or five links of chain separated the black iron cuffs around each ankle. This forced the boy to shuffle more than walk as he slowly made his way through the dust of the street.

Tyler pretended to examine something on his robe as he stopped and waited for Nayra and the boy. When they caught up, he asked Nayra, "What's going on?"

Glancing about to make sure they weren't overheard, she answered, "He has to circle the town with his feet chained."

"Why?"

"Until he memorizes the Qur'an." Nayra turned to the boy to ask something. He responded and she turned back to Tyler. "He says he is Christian, from the south."

"Was he kidnapped?"

Not waiting for a translation, the boy nodded.

"Ask him about his family."

She leaned down and spoke to the child. As they conversed, Tyler glanced over at the school. They were directly across from it now. Dozens of boys stood around a water trough, laughing and splashing as they washed their tablets in the milky brown water. The conversation between the two finally ended, and Nayra rose as the boy shuffled off to join his friends. Because she held a veil across her face, Tyler could only see her eyes. But that was enough to tell him something was wrong.

"Are you all right?"

At first she did not respond.

"Nayra ... what's wrong?"

Taking a breath, she turned to watch the child as she numbly reported the facts. "His village was attacked by the Islamic Brotherhood. Their houses were burned, all of their cattle killed."

Tyler turned toward the boy as he joined his buddies. They all seemed to be having a good time.

Nayra continued. "His father, all the men who refused to convert to Islam, were forced to lie down in the road. And in front of their wives and children they were driven over by a truck — back and forth, several times, until ..." She dropped off, unable to continue.

Tyler reached his hand out to her. He knew the public display of affection was forbidden but he didn't care. Apparently, neither did she. She took it and stepped closer. He saw tears filling her eyes as she forced herself to continue. "His mother was burned alive, and he and his nine-year-old sister were forced to march thirty days by foot through the desert to this village."

Tyler looked back at the school as the students splashed and washed their slates. "Where is she?" he asked. "His sister? All I see are boys."

At first she did not answer.

"Nayra?"

"His sister was sold as a concubine." She swallowed. "When he memorizes the Qur'an, he will be sold as a slave to a family in Khartoum." She said nothing more. She didn't have to.

Together they stood and watched as the boys dropped to their knees in front of the trough and began drinking the very water in which they'd washed their slates. Without being asked, Nayra gave the explanation. "They'd written portions of the Qur'an on the slates. By drinking the water, they've been told that they will more quickly memorize its words."

Tyler looked back at her. The story had taken much from her and he wanted to hold her, to somehow absorb her pain. Nearby an approaching truck blew its horn at pedestrians who strayed in its way. Some yelled back; most simply ignored it. The vehicle continued rattling forward until it suddenly slammed on its brakes, barely missing a small herd of goats. More impatient honking. Several of the men from the market yelled, some with obscene arm and hand gestures, but the driver appeared oblivious as his engine revved, as he ground more than his fair share of gears, as the truck finally lurched forward. When it lumbered by, Tyler glanced up to the passenger window. Only then did he catch a glimpse of the white woman yelling at the driver, her auburn hair sparkling in the sunlight.

Tyler froze. Was it possible? The truck continued down the road. Grabbing Nayra's hand, he started after it. "Doc! . . . Doc!"

The vehicle continued forward, swerving hard to miss a stack of caged chickens and its owner. More oaths were shouted, more gestures made.

"Doc!" Tyler continued running.

"What are you doing!" Nayra demanded.

The Land Rover skidded to a stop, this time to avoid a withered cow chewing its cud in the middle of the road. The horn blasted. The animal turned and stared dully.

"Doc! Doc!"

The passenger finally heard and looked out over her shoulder. It *was* her!

"Tyler?!" She turned to the driver and shouted something. Fumbling with the door, she leaped out. "Tyler!" She raced to him and they fell into an embrace, which eventually included Nayra as well.

"What are you doing here?" Tyler cried. "What—"

"Tyler!" He looked up to see his dad running to him from the truck.

He pulled from Helen and rushed to the man. "Dad!" They met halfway, throwing their arms around each other. He could not remember the last time he'd hugged his father, but now he clung to him fiercely, hoping never to let go. He felt his eyes sting with moisture. The men separated just enough for Tyler to see his father's own wet eyes before falling into another embrace.

"I thought," Daniel said, choking, "I thought I'd never see you again. I thought . . . I thought . . ." The man could not continue. He remained in Tyler's arms, beginning to sob.

"It's okay, Dad," Tyler croaked. "I'm all right. I'm all right. It's . . ." His throat tightened, making it impossible to speak. How long they stood holding one another he did not know. It didn't matter. A handful of merchants gathered at the spectacle but it didn't matter. None of it mattered. Not now. How many years had he wanted this? Just this. "I'm sorry ..." He choked. "I'm so sorry ..." But Tyler wasn't talking about being lost; he was talking about everything. "I'm so—" His father hugged him tighter, making it clear that words were no longer necessary. And Tyler understood. For the first time in a long time, they both understood.

"Tyler ..." Nayra was standing beside them, her voice gentle but insistent. "We have visitors."

He looked up to see another Land Rover approaching, this one from the direction of the compound.

"Oh man," Tyler groaned. "Now what?"

"Who are they?" Daniel asked as they separated and wiped their eyes.

"You don't want to know," Tyler said. He glanced around, looking for some means of escape.

Nayra did the same. "Where do we go?"

"The truck," Daniel said. He moved toward it, motioning for the others to follow. "Come on, get in."

"What ..."

"Come on!" He motioned them forward.

"You're going to try to outrun them?" Tyler asked.

"Unless you have a better idea."

Tyler didn't. He followed them and was the last to crawl inside as Daniel revved the engine and ground the gears.

"You know how to drive this thing?" Tyler shouted.

"No sweat!" Daniel yelled, continuing to rev and grind without moving an inch. "I know this thing like the back of my—"

The vehicle lurched forward. The cow had moved but unfortunately not far enough. Daniel swerved hard to the left to avoid it. Not a bad move, except for the half dozen merchant stalls he took out in the process.

"Sorry!" he shouted out the window.

Nobody was injured, at least from what Tyler could see through the dust and shaking fists trailing after them.

"I thought you said you knew how to—"

"I do!" Daniel turned and shouted to him. "I do!"

"Look out!" Doc cried.

He turned back just in time to see them smashing through the water trough next to the school. The kids had gone. The water hadn't. It splashed onto the broken windshield, turning the thick dust into thicker streaks of mud.

"Dad!"

Poking his head out the window to see, he shouted, "I've got it covered!"

As best as Tyler could tell, they were swerving inside the school's courtyard, barely missing the dozen scattered pillars. The wooden tables and benches were not so lucky. They crunched and exploded under the truck's wheels.

"Daniel!" Doc shouted.

But Daniel was too busy weaving through the slalom course to respond. At last they made it to the other side, popping out onto the adjacent street. Daniel took a hard left, gunned it, and they shot down the dirt road, which was still impossible to see because of the mud-coated windshield.

"Daniel!"

"It's okay," he yelled, leaning out his window. "I've got it, I've got it."

Tyler stole a glance at Nayra, who sat beside him. She clung to the seat, her skin nearly as white as his.

Thanks to the shortcut through the school, they'd eluded their pursuers. For the moment.

"Up ahead!" Doc shouted. "Pull between those buildings and hide."

Daniel nodded and threw the truck into a skid. He took a hard left into what looked like a narrow alley. He squeezed between the buildings, then jolted to a sudden stop, throwing everyone forward.

"Hop out and let me take over!" Helen shouted.

"What!"

"I'll decoy them. Hop out!"

"But . . . that's crazy . . ."

She was scooting against Daniel, trying to force him out the door. "They'll think you're still in here and follow me. That'll give you time to find another way out."

"And when they catch you?" Daniel argued.

"They want you guys, not me."

"I know, but—"

She leaned past him and opened the door. "Get out, get out!"

"What happens if they catch you?"

"That's a big if!"

"Helen . . ."

"Get out! They'll be here any second."

Daniel hesitated. But Tyler saw the logic and opened his door to step outside. He reached in to help Nayra.

"Get out!" Helen continued shouting at his father. "Will you get out of here!"

Not at all pleased, but seeing no other way, Daniel let out a heavy sigh and stepped down from the vehicle. His foot had barely touched the ground before Doc slid behind the wheel. He had to quickly withdraw the other foot as she slammed the door.

He leaned in the window. "Be careful, there's some — "

"Tyler," she interrupted, reaching behind the seat to produce an aluminum briefcase. She brought it to the front and slid it across to him. "Take this."

He nodded and grabbed it.

Daniel tried again. "There's some slippage between second and third, so be careful when — " She suddenly turned and kissed him squarely and lingeringly upon the lips.

At last they separated and before he could recover, she dropped the vehicle into reverse. "For luck!" she cried as she stomped on the accelerator.

The three leaped away as the Land Rover spun backward into the street. It slid to a stop, ground a few gears, then accelerated, fishtailing as it took off. Helen laid on the horn just in case her pursuers had lost track of her. The truck barely disappeared before they heard the other approach. They flattened themselves against the alley wall as the other Land Rover raced by.

The briefest moment of silence followed before Daniel asked, "Now what?"

"Now we find another vehicle," Tyler said as he grabbed Nayra's hand and they started toward the street.

Daniel followed. "But where?"

"There are several more at the compound," Nayra said as they approached the corner. "But first we must change your clothes."

Daniel nodded.

"I saw lots of clothes at the market," Tyler said.

Nayra agreed. "They should be the clothes of a woman."

"Of a woman?" Daniel exclaimed.

"Yes, with a very thick veil."

Tyler threw him a mischievous grin. "Don't worry, Dad. With a veil and one of those big tent dresses, you'll look just like all the other old ladies." Nayra gave him a look, which he tried to ignore as they rounded the corner. "We buy you some clothes, get you changed, steal ourselves a truck, and — " He stopped, coming face-to-face with two young men and their raised AK 47s.

Everyone froze. Tyler searched for a way out, for someplace to run. The men did not speak but shoved the barrels closer. Apparently, escape was not an option.

chapter seventeen

The time had come. Ibrahim sat with the Shura in the council chamber, waiting for the call from the hero of New York. Careful never to use a satellite or cellular phone, lest the use of satellites and microwaves reveal their location, they had put in the predetermined call to their contact in Rome, who in turn paged the hero of New York, who in turn was to call them directly on a hard line for confirmation before he began. That had been thirty-five minutes ago. Now they waited. Some prayed, some paced. Others simply sat about the table, deep in thought.

This would be the only communication. Once the hero had confirmation from them, he would proceed to the specified location, and exactly thirty minutes after the sun set over New York, he would detonate himself and enter paradise. This would give maximum time for the smallpox virus to spread before the morning sun rose and began breaking it down with its ultraviolet light. Three hours after the New York detonation, the hero of Los Angeles would follow suit. And so it would continue across the Pacific with Tokyo, Hong Kong, hopefully Munich, and concluding in London. In twenty hours the Day of Wrath would be complete. Over the following few weeks it would be up to Allah to determine which of those exposed from the blast and the disease would die.

Ibrahim el-Magd sat on the pillows beside Sheikh Salad Habib. Like the rest of the Shura, he was lost in thought. So many years. So many sacrifices ... little Muhammad, Yussuf, Dalal, the heroes themselves. Such cost. Such a heavy burden to bear. There was no glory in this task. Just death, sacrifice ... and always, always, the obedience.

The phone on the table rang, jarring him from his thoughts. Slowly, measurably, Ibrahim rose. It rang a second time. All eyes were upon him. He gave the slightest nod to Abdullah Muhammad Fadi. The man acknowledged and walked toward the phone. In the middle of the third ring, he lifted the receiver and brought it to his ear. "Hello?" He frowned. Again he spoke. "Hello?"

The Shura exchanged glances.

Abdullah covered his other ear and shouted. "Hello? You must speak up!" He paused again, scowling, trying to hear. "I am sorry. Call back. You must call back. Can you hear me? You must call back. If you can hear me, you must immediately call back." He lowered the receiver and slowly placed it on its cradle. Looking first to Ibrahim and then to the rest of the group, he explained, "The connection, it was very bad. Much static. He will try again, immediately."

The Shura stirred.

"Patience, my brothers," Sharif Abdu Massud assured them. "Very soon now. We need only patience."

A young aide appeared in the doorway of the chamber and waited for permission to enter.

"Yes?" Ibrahim asked.

He stepped into the room and spoke. "The pastor. He has arrived."

"Now?"

"Yes. With his son and your niece."

"Bring them in. Bring them here immediately."

"Ibrahim ...," Abdullah warned.

"This is what we have been waiting for. Allah's timing is perfect." Turning to the group, Ibrahim motioned toward the phone. "The poor connection, it is our sign. We are to wait to hear from Allah. Now, after so long, he is about to speak!"

"Ibrahim ..."

"Finally we will hear his voice!"

The men about the table glanced at one another, unsure how to respond.

Pressing the point, Ibrahim turned to the aide. "I have asked you to bring them in. Why do you hesitate? Bring them at once."

The aide stole a glance at the table. No one would look at him. He nodded and quickly exited.

Daniel entered the council room with Tyler and Nayra. The man approaching them appeared to be about his age. He had a full beard and mustache. Like the villagers, he wore long white robes and had a white turban wrapped about his head. "Welcome, Pastor," he said, extending his hand. "My name is Ibrahim el-Magd."

Daniel stretched out his hand, allowing it to be shook.

"Thank you for coming."

"I didn't know I had a choice."

The man smiled. "We all have choices. Your son, he thought you would decide not to. But as a father, I knew better."

Daniel threw a look to Tyler. Had his son really thought he wouldn't come, that he cared so little?

"I am pleased ..." — the man motioned toward the others who sat about the long table — "we are all pleased that you have decided to join us." He indicated the empty chairs near the center. "Sit. Please, sit. You have had a long journey."

"I think I would rather stand."

The man took a moment to size up Daniel, then shrugged. "As you wish."

Glancing about the room, Daniel saw that it was nearly thirty feet long and about half that wide. Six white pillars rose to a high ceiling with multiple arches that blended into one another. Two fans hung over the ten-foot-long table. Against the side wall an older, white-bearded man sat on cushions. And at the far end of the table sat a small burgundy pillow that —

Daniel caught his breath. For resting upon the pillow were the three remaining stones.

Ibrahim chuckled warmly. "I see you are not unfamiliar with my collection."

"May I ... come closer?"

The man gave a gracious gesture. "Please ..."

Daniel slowly approached. They appeared identical in shape and size to the other nine. He knew their names now, from the hours of study. There was the white and brown onyx of Joseph. Beside it the yellow jacinth of Gad. And last was the yellow citrine of Zebulun. He arrived and stooped down to take a closer look.

"I see you too appreciate their value." The close proximity of Ibrahim's voice startled him. He had moved beside him. "So much history here. Such sacred history."

Daniel nodded and quietly added, "It's more than that."

"Yes, it is," Ibrahim agreed. "There is the price. The terrible price we have both paid."

Daniel rose from the stones to look into the man's eyes. He could see a type of understanding there. A kinship. Here was a man who was also aware of the cost of the stones, of the death, of the destruction they brought.

Ibrahim continued. "We have both paid a tremendous price, have we not? We understand more than most the great expense, the heavy weight of obedience."

Daniel slowly nodded. Their outlook and experience seemed identical.

The man continued. "We are different from the others. We understand the heavy burden of holiness. We understand the need to pursue it at any cost."

Daniel tried to swallow but his mouth had turned strangely dry. It was as if he were listening to himself speak. Amazing. Unnerving. A terrorist and a Bible-believing Christian with similar views? Was such a thing possible?

Ibrahim reached down to the pillow and gently touched each stone as he spoke. "As men of God, we would sacrifice *all* for his holiness. We hunger to do his will, do we not? To know his commands. And you and I, we will follow them at any cost."

Daniel felt an eerie chill creep across his shoulders. It was true; these words could just have easily been his own ... Except ... except ...

"Holiness. Purity. You and I, we have given up all we are to pursue such things ... to hear his voice, to follow his commands."

No ... there was a difference. This was how the old Daniel talked, the one who insisted his wife's shoulders be covered, who refused Linda Grossman, who frowned upon Charlie Rue ... who secretly despised his son's failures. The last thought surprised him but he pressed on, working through it. This was the old Daniel Lawson talking. The one with the lists and rules of what God expected. But the one who had forgotten ... in the process, the one who had forgotten who God was.

"Yet I hold this against you: You have forsaken your first love."
Daniel closed his eyes as Ibrahim continued.

"You and I, we live only to serve and do his will."

"I think you love serving God . . . But I don't think you really love him, not anymore."

Yes, there was a difference. He saw that now. On the surface it was subtle, indistinguishable, but underneath it was profound. For in Daniel's heart over the past weeks it had become as different as night from day.

"Soon you and I, we shall hear his voice. And soon we above all men will know his perfect will and obey it."

Like this man, the old Daniel had been pursuing God's rules but not his presence. He had been seeking God's will but not God's heart. His voice, not his face.

Suddenly, as he had with each of the other stones, Daniel felt a compassion rising up for this, the last of the owners. Once again misjudgments and preconceptions began melting away. Once again his head and his heart filled with understanding. And love. Love for a man who was, like he himself had been, so completely devoted and yet so wrong.

Noticing his expression, Ibrahim asked, "Are you not well? Is something the matter?"

Daniel looked down and discreetly pressed the moisture from his eyes. When he looked up, he smiled gently.

"Please . . ." Ibrahim was obviously intrigued. "Tell me, what is on your mind?"

A peace settled upon Daniel. A peace he'd experienced several times during his life, but one he had not felt in a very long time.

Again Ibrahim asked, "Please . . ."

Daniel cleared his throat. "You keep speaking of our similarities."

"Yes, exactly. Our pursuit of righteousness and holiness."

Daniel gently shook his head. "I am afraid you are mistaken."

"What do you mean?"

"You pursue knowing God's righteousness. I no longer do that."

Ibrahim frowned.

Daniel explained. "Now I pursue knowing God."

The frown deepened. "Knowing Allah? Such things are not possible. Allah is infinite. You may know his ways, but you, a mere man, may never come to know him."

Again Daniel shook his head. "No, that's not true. I am no longer pursuing God's holiness. Instead I am pursuing his presence."

The man's mouth closed. He clenched his jaws, then released them. "You are wrong. You do not say what you mean."

Daniel's answer was gentle but firm. "Yes, I do. And that is the great difference between our faiths. I pursue God and he fills me with his presence. You pursue his laws and are filled with his law."

The man's eyes narrowed. "This is blasphemy. God cannot dwell in man."

Calmly holding his ground, Daniel answered, "Oh, but he did. You certainly know of Christ's claims to deity. "

"The Infinite cannot become finite."

"He did it once, my friend. And as I seek him, he does it again ... not in Christ but inside me. Daily. Changing me. Making me like him. Not by his rules ... but by his presence."

Ibrahim's face reddened as Daniel continued. "I'd forgotten that truth. For a very long time I'd forgotten. But I am finding it again. And it is changing me. Your faith is based upon rules. Mine is based upon friendship."

The man said nothing. The muscles in his jaw tightened and released, tightened and released, as he obviously strove for control.

"Ibrahim ..." One of the men at the table rose to his feet. He motioned toward the phone. "We have so little time."

Ibrahim hesitated.

"Please ..."

Reluctantly he pulled himself from the discussion. It was obvious he had more to say but it would have to wait. Changing gears, he turned back to Daniel and asked, "You have the other stones?"

"Yes."

"And the Reuben Stone?"

"The stone of the firstborn?" Daniel asked.

"Yes."

Daniel nodded. "Yes." Glancing at Tyler, he added, "It is my most precious."

"Where are they?"

Turning to the guard who had escorted them in, Daniel said, "They are in the briefcase he is holding."

Tension eased in Ibrahim's face. He motioned to the guard and called something in Arabic. The young man nodded and approached with the briefcase. As he came forward, Daniel stepped back from the pillow. Ever since the reaction in the hut, he had been careful to keep the other stones separate from the Urim and Thummim. While the other nine stones remained safely confined inside the briefcase, he held the Urim and Thummim on his own person, carefully wrapped in his pocket.

"What are you doing?" Ibrahim asked. "Why do you move away?"

"We've seen their past reaction."

"Reaction?"

"Yes. They generate much heat and light. And now to bring all twelve together . . ."

Ibrahim frowned.

Tyler spoke up. "Haven't you heard what happened at Avignon, at the Palace of the Popes?"

Ibrahim glanced at him impatiently. "Of course." Turning back to Daniel, he asked, "Are such things possible?"

By now Daniel had distanced himself some eight feet from the table. Instead of answering, he simply nodded to the three stones on the pillow beside Ibrahim. Each had begun to emit a faint glow. Seeing them, the man could not hide his surprise. Cautiously he bent to them for a closer inspection. Others about the table exchanged uneasy glances.

Suddenly the guard yelped. The entire room gave a start as the youth dropped the briefcase to the floor. It clattered noisily onto the stone tile as he bent over and grabbed his hand, wincing in pain.

Ibrahim shouted something and the boy responded, still holding his hand. Again Ibrahim gave an order. Ever so slowly the guard rose and opened his hand. Red and black oozing flesh covered the inside of his palm and the pads of his fingers where he had gripped the handle.

Two or three of the men at the table rose to their feet.

Obviously striving to maintain his composure, Ibrahim gave another order to the young man. The youth looked at him, his eyes wide, his face already damp with perspiration. Again Ibrahim spoke. But instead of answering, the guard stared down at the briefcase, then at his burned hand. Slowly, cautiously, he began backing away. Ibrahim repeated the order but the youth did not respond. Instead he turned and quickly moved toward the door. Ibrahim shouted after him but—

"Listen!" Tyler interrupted. "Do you hear that?"

It was the same faint, high-pitched whine Daniel had heard back in the hut. Only this time it was coming from his pocket.

Eyes darted from the briefcase to Daniel and back to the briefcase. More members of the council rose to their feet. A few started to murmur. One or two glanced toward the open doorway.

Carefully Daniel reached into his pocket for the Urim and Thummim. As before, he felt no heat, no vibration. There was only the sound. Keeping his hand on them, he took an experimental step toward the table. And then another. The whine grew louder; the stones on the pillow glowed more brightly.

"What is that sound?" Ibrahim demanded. "What are you doing?"

Daniel said nothing but took another step, with the same results. And another. The whine became piercing. Several of the men pressed their fingers to their ears. Some found this as their excuse to exit the room. Even the old man on the pillows had risen to his feet.

Again Ibrahim shouted. "What are you doing?"

Daniel remained silent but pulled the two rocks out of his pocket. Carefully he unwrapped them from their silk scarf. Although the sound was louder, they felt as cool and inert as always.

"What are they?" Ibrahim shouted over the whine.

Tyler called out, "The Urim and Thummim."

Daniel stood four feet away and continued to slowly move forward. The stones on the pillow continued to glow even more brightly.

"Stop!" Ibrahim ordered. "You will stop at once!"

But Daniel was in no mood for stopping. He had come this far, waited this long; he was not about to stop now. The remaining men of the council had risen to their feet and were easing toward the door. The old man from the pillows would soon follow. Daniel glanced at Tyler, who, although frightened, obviously intended to hold his ground. The same went for Nayra, who had reached for Tyler's hand.

Daniel continued forward until he arrived at the table. The whine was unbearable. The clearer stones on the pillow glowed like a welder's torch, so bright that they were impossible to look at. He

319

glanced back at the Urim and Thummim in his hand. As he did, an idea began to form. Slowly, cautiously, he reached his free hand toward the stones on the pillow.

"Dad . . . ," Tyler cautioned.

Daniel nodded. He understood the danger but continued to stretch his hand toward them. As expected, he felt heat, but not nearly as much as in the past. Brighter light, less heat? It made no sense. He continued reaching until his fingers touched the closest stone, the white and brown Joseph Stone. It was warm but not hot. He looked at the group, puzzled, then moved his hand to the next stone. It was the same. And to the next. Each of them was warm but none of them hot.

Intrigued, Ibrahim cautiously approached the table. He did the same. Reaching out, he too felt the heat from the stones. He stretched farther until the tips of his fingers finally touched the Joseph Stone . . . and he let out a cry and grabbed his hand.

Daniel saw traces of smoke rising from the man's flesh, followed by the acrid smell of burned skin. He moved to help, encouraging Ibrahim to open his hand. Finally Ibrahim complied. He uncurled his fingers to reveal their charred and oozing tips.

Looks were exchanged. No one understood. Yet somewhere in the back of his mind Daniel had a vague suspicion. When he'd handled the stones or worn the breastplate in his dreams, he'd never been burned or injured in any way. On the contrary, the heat they'd given off had always felt warm and comforting. He turned to look at the briefcase on the floor.

Following his gaze, Tyler called out another warning. "Dad . . ."

But Daniel paid no attention. He started toward it. As he approached, the whine grew even louder, turning to a shrieking, piercing scream. Yet he would not stop. He arrived at the case on the floor, then slowly stooped down to it. Still holding the Urim and Thummim in his left hand, he reached out his other to the handle. It radiated a slight heat but nothing alarming. He gingerly touched the handle and pulled back. Nothing. No burning. No pain. Unlike the guard, he experienced no negative reaction. He reached for the handle and touched it again. Again there was nothing. He turned to Tyler, who gave a faint, encouraging nod. Looking back to the briefcase, he reached out, wrapped his hand about the grip, and finally picked it up.

He rose and started toward the group. Except for Tyler, the others backed away. Understanding their fear, he slowed to a stop, then turned to the table. He crossed to it and carefully laid the briefcase upon it. He unsnapped one latch, then the other. The whine increased slightly as he raised the lid.

The first thing he saw was the fiery yellow glow of the breastplate. Every one of the golden threads woven into it was alive with light ... as were each of the stones resting in their golden sockets.

Once again Daniel looked up, seeking encouragement from his son. And once again Tyler nodded.

Tentatively he reached out to the breastplate. He did not expect his flesh to burn, but neither was he prepared for what happened. As soon as his fingers made contact ... the whine stopped. The glow of the breastplate and all its stones ceased. It was as if he had somehow grounded it. As if he had completed a type of circuit. He withdrew his hand and the whine and glow returned. He brought it back and they stopped. He turned and looked at the three stones on the pillow. They too had stopped glowing.

"What is happening?" Ibrahim whispered. "What are you doing?"

Daniel shook his head. He wasn't certain. Still keeping the Urim and Thummim in his left hand, he pulled the breastplate from the case. All nine stones remained firmly in their sockets. The braided tie cords dangled from each of the four corners. He turned again toward the stones on the pillow. Taking a breath, he started for them.

"Dad ..." It was Tyler again. "Are you sure you want to do this?"

Daniel turned and looked into his son's eyes. He had never been more sure of anything in his life. This is what Jill spoke about, what they'd dreamed of; in many ways this is why she'd given up her life. As Tyler studied him, he seemed to understand. Slowly, almost imperceptibly, he began to nod. He understood. They both understood.

Daniel arrived at the end of the table. Carefully he laid the breastplate upon it. He smoothed out the material while checking the three empty sockets. Each contained enough malleable gold to hold its stone in place.

He reached for the remaining three stones on the pillow, but in doing so, removed his hands from the breastplate. Immediately the

Urim and Thummim began to whine; immediately the stones began to glow. He quickly replaced his hand and they stopped. He was still a part of the circuit. He freed his left hand by setting the Urim and Thummim on the table. The reaction was identical. He picked them back up and it stopped. How odd. As long as he continued to touch both the Urim and Thummim and the breastplate, everything was fine. But by releasing one or the other, he set off the reaction.

He scowled, perplexed. How was he to maintain contact with the breastplate, hold the Urim and Thummim, and pick up the three remaining stones all at the same time? There were various solutions but immediately he knew which one to pursue.

As if reading his mind, Ibrahim spoke. "You must put it on. You must wear the breastplate."

Daniel nodded. By wearing it, his body would be in constant contact and his hands would be free to hold the stones. It was an obvious solution. But just as obvious was the fact that it wasn't entirely his idea. Or Ibrahim's. Like everything else, it was also from his dream. From Jill's dream. From each and every time he had worn the breastplate.

He looked down at it resting on the table, and for the first time he began to experience fear. He had to force himself to continue. He picked up the breastplate. The four tie cords dangled as he brought it up and pressed it to his chest. Even through the thick material he could feel his heart pounding. He took the upper two cords and tried to tie them behind his neck. But with the stones in his hand he was having some problems. Tyler moved in to help.

"Tyler, don't," he warned. "You saw what happened to the others."

The boy nodded but he was obviously as determined as his father. Taking a breath for his own courage, he carefully reached out and touched the cords. To Daniel's relief there was no reaction. As long as the breastplate was grounded, it was apparently safe. Without a word Tyler tied the first two cords around Daniel's neck. Then he took the other two and tied them about his lower back. When he had finished, he took a step back and waited.

Daniel looked down at his chest, at the nine stones pressed into their gold sockets. He turned to the pillow and the other three stones. His heart hammered in his ears; he was breathing faster. But this was why he'd come. This was why he was here. Still keeping the Urim and Thummim in his left hand, Daniel reached toward the pillow and picked up the first stone — the stone of Joseph, the tribe whose founder was noted for his tenacious faith. From his studies Daniel knew its position. With trembling fingers he brought it to his chest. Carefully he pressed it into the middle socket of the last row. The soft gold held it in place. He paused a moment, waiting. There was no response.

Two stones to go.

It grew more difficult to catch his breath but he continued. He reached for the fiery yellow stone of Gad, the tribe famous for its fierce fighting. He fumbled with it slightly, nearly dropping it. He took a moment to regain his composure. When he was certain he had control, he slowly brought the stone to the breastplate. He pressed it into the empty socket, above and to the right of the Joseph Stone.

There was still no reaction.

Eleven stones were in place. One more remained. The citrine stone from the tribe of Zebulun. The last stone, representing Ibrahim el-Magd and those like him. The tribe of unwavering allegiance, of obedience at any cost. He stared at it resting upon the pillow, beautiful in its yellow translucence. He looked up at his son. Then at Nayra. And finally Ibrahim. Each watched, frightened and transfixed. He looked back to the stone. His fear was giving way to something deeper. Something colder. Dread. Deep and dark. For a moment he forgot to breathe. He had to literally force the air into his lungs.

Then at last he reached for it.

*

"Hurry! Run! They're almost here! Hurry! Hurry! Go! Go!" Helen stole a look to the second Land Rover as it skidded to a stop behind hers. She'd already thrown open both doors to her own vehicle and stood next to the raised hood. Now she was cupping her hands and shouting to a scraggy stand of brush and trees fifty yards to her left. "Keep going! Run! Hide! They're coming! Hurry! Hurry!"

Two men piled out of the Land Rover, shouting to each other in Arabic. One veered off toward the trees, firing a warning burst from his automatic rifle. The other, the driver, headed toward her. She'd given them a good chase that would have continued if she hadn't run out of gas. And now, though she couldn't handle both of them, she was pretty certain she could handle one. She shouted to her imaginary friends one last time, "Hurry! Run! Run!" then turned to the young man approaching her.

He yelled something at her in Arabic.

She shrugged, giving her best smile, and motioned toward the open hood. She hoped he'd simmer down from the chase and realize he needed to return to the compound not only with his captives but with both Land Rovers as well.

He arrived, still yelling.

"I think it's broken," she said, pointing at the engine.

More yelling.

"Yes, yes." She nodded, stepping to the vehicle and peering under the hood. "Broken."

He turned to check on his friend's progress.

"See." Helen pointed, redirecting his attention. "In here. In here."

With an oath he turned back to look where she was pointing.

"It's this scatzamaratz thingie. See?" She pointed at the distributor cap that she'd managed to disconnect just before they arrived. "I think it's all discombooberated." He moved in for a closer look. "Shouldn't it be hooked up to this thingamajiggy here?"

Spotting the lose connection, he gave a grunt and leaned under the hood. He obviously saw it was a simple fix. It would have been simpler if Helen had not reached up to the hood and slammed it down onto his head. Hard.

The man yelled.

In response Helen quickly raised the hood and repeated the process even harder. He yelled again but seemed far less energetic about the prospect. The third time was the charm. He collapsed into the engine, out cold. She lifted the hood and pulled him from the engine, careful not to let his pretty face scrape over the grill. Then she dropped him onto the ground like a sack of potatoes.

A burst of gunfire snapped her attention back to the trees. The second kid was racing toward her. Apparently, he'd realized the ruse. He was fifty yards from the truck and closing fast. She spun around and dashed behind her own vehicle toward theirs. The kid fired off another burst of gunfire, this time not into the air. A rapid series of plinks and plunks hit her truck, forcing her to duck as she ran. She arrived at their Land Rover and threw open the driver's door. The kid had closed his distance to her by half.

She leaped behind the wheel, grateful to see the key in the ignition. A line of sparks flew off the hood as more shots were fired. She turned the key and the truck roared to life. She dropped it into gear and hit the accelerator. Dirt and rocks flew. For the briefest second she was unsure which way to go — to the Christian village and the eventual repair of the plane ... or back to the compound to help Preacher Man and Video Boy. Muttering at her foolishness, she cranked the wheel hard to the left. If she hurried, she could be back at the compound within an hour.

chapter eighteen

He barely places the Zebulun Stone into its socket before the room begins to shift and waver. It quickly darkens. He turns to the others but they simply look at him, noticing nothing. A wall of mud, rock, and clay shimmers around him, superimposing over their faces, over the entire room, until only the wall itself can be seen. He appears to be in some sort of pit. It is impossibly cold. Numbing. He shivers violently and can see his breath. He looks up. High above him is the Light from his dreams. Accompanying it is the rolling, rumbling thunder. Despite the intimidating sound, he recalls the Light's warmth, the acceptance, the overwhelming compassion that filled him during its embrace. That's what he needs now, what he yearns for, what he must have to survive. He must reach the Light. He must climb from the pit and enter its love.

He searches the wet, glistening walls, looking for a ladder, for steps, for any way out. There is none. He must make his own way. He starts toward the nearest wall and stumbles, his legs impossibly heavy. He looks down and discovers they are once again made of stone. As before, his entire body has become stone. Stone inscribed with thousands of Scriptures.

"No..." His cry reverberates against the walls. Has he traveled this far only to begin again? He does not know. But there is still the Light. There is still his need to reach it, to feel its embrace.

Concentrating, using all his effort, he reaches down and lifts one leg, pulling it forward and dropping it. He reaches to the other leg and does the same. Slowly he makes his way to the wall, one exhausting step after another. But he will not stop until he arrives.

Once there, he pauses to catch his breath. Raising his stony arms, he touches the wall. It is wet and slick, impossibly smooth. There are no footholds, nothing to grab on to. He looks back up to the Light. It will draw no closer. He must reach it on his own.

Groaning with effort, he lifts his right foot, then slams it hard into the wall, digging a step out of the soft clay and mud. He reaches up and jams a rocky hand into the mud above him, hoping it will somehow hold. It does. So far, so good. He raises himself up until both holds suddenly give way and he tumbles back to the ground.

But he will not quit. He struggles to his feet and tries again. He fails again. The walls are too soft, his body too heavy. Filled with desperation, he raises his head and cries to the Light. "Help me! Please ... help!"

There is no answer. Just the rolling, brooding thunder.

He tries again, grabbing the wall with his hands and jamming his foot hard into its side. And this time as he puts weight upon it, it holds. At last he's found a foothold. But it isn't a foothold. For when he looks down, he sees it is a human shoulder. A female shoulder covered in a sweater ... Jill's sweater. There is no head, no torso, just her shoulder and sweater protruding from the clay. Realizing it cannot possibly be real, that it must be some sort of symbol, he looks back up to the Light. His desperation grows. He puts more of his weight onto the shoulder. It continues to hold. At last he pushes off. He hears his wife's muffled groan. It is a haunting sound but he does not look down; he must continue up.

His foot finds another hold and he digs into it. He hears a cry of pain and looks down to discover he is standing upon the head of a woman — Linda Grossman from church. She continues to cry out from his immense weight but he is making progress. He must continue. If this is the only way to reach the Light, then he must continue. He struggles for yet another step and finds it. This time he hears a chilling scream. He looks down to see that he is standing directly upon the upturned face of Charlie Rue, the sound engineer. He quickly removes his foot and scrambles up faster, slipping and sliding until he finds yet another hold. It begins shrieking. "Get off, get off, get off!" Immediately he recognizes the voice and looks down to see ... Tyler! But it is not his son's shoulder or head or even his face. No. Instead he is standing upon the raw, opened arteries of his son's forearms.

Crying out in surprise, he loses his balance and falls, tumbling back to the damp, hard floor. He moans with pain, physical and emotional. He raises up to look at the wall. The footholds are gone. Now there are only the wet, slippery walls of the pit.

But the wetness isn't water. It can't be. Not in this freezing cold. He glances to his hands and discovers they are wet, but not with water. They are wet with blood. From the wall. More astonishingly, he notices that wherever the blood has touched, he is no longer stone. The tips of his fingers, the palms of his hands, they have become flesh — soft, supple flesh. It is the blood from his dreams, from the pool! He looks to his feet. They are also wet. They have also become flesh.

He struggles to stand. Lifting his head toward the Light, he again shouts, "Help me! Please . . . help me!"

He hears the trickling of water and looks at the walls. But it is not water; it is more blood. It streams down the walls into the pit, faster and faster, all around him, on every side. Faster and harder. Splashing, growing to a roar. It covers the floor, quickly rising to his ankles, then to his knees, turning everything of him it touches into flesh. It rises to his thighs, then his waist. The turbulence is so strong that it finally knocks him off his feet, but he is able to keep his face above the liquid. The pit continues to fill deeper and deeper until he must start swimming. He struggles with all his might to keep his heavy stone head above the surface. He succeeds, but only for a few seconds. The weight is too great. The current pulls him under. And once submerged, his head too becomes flesh.

He tumbles and turns, losing track of the surface. But he must find it to breathe. He takes a guess and swims forward until he slams hard into a wall. More spinning and tumbling. His lungs begin to burn. Panic rises. He can no longer hold his breath. He must breathe. He sets off again and crashes into another wall, or the same wall, he cannot tell. He must breathe. Now. His lungs are on fire. Even if it means breathing in the liquid, he must breathe. Something! Anything! He must extinguish the fire. Now! He opens his mouth. There is no other way. Now! He must breathe! Now!

He gives in. He inhales the liquid. But to his surprise he does not choke. He does not even cough. Instead he breathes in the liquid as naturally as if it were air. And as it enters his body, his stony insides are also turned to flesh . . . his mouth, his throat, his lungs. The sensation is warm and pleasant. Eventually he stops thrashing and begins to rise . . . effortlessly, naturally. Soon he bobs to the surface to discover he is floating at the top of the pit and in full presence of the Light. The all-loving, all-powerful Light.

He swims to the shore and climbs out. The Light is much closer now. Just a few yards away. He stands before it, eagerly stretching out his arms like a child. The Light approaches. It grows brighter and brighter until finally, at last, at long last, it envelopes him. It wraps its all-consuming love and warmth around him. As in his dream, he feels the love soaking into his pores, saturating his flesh, his mind, working its way into the depths of his soul. But this is no dream. It is a thousand times more vivid. And this time there is no retching and coughing up of stones. They too have been saturated and dissolved by the blood.

At last his journey is over. Daniel knows that now. At last he is free. Freer than he has ever been in his life. Free to absorb the Light's presence, its love, its complete acceptance. Yet he feels something more than acceptance. He feels the Light's . . . joy. His eyes brim with moisture. Somehow, as insignificant as he, Daniel Lawson, is, he is able to give the Light joy — not through anything he's done, just by his presence. Unbelievable. Unthinkable. He, a mere man, giving the Creator of the universe joy.

The tears spill onto his cheeks. He closes his eyes, barely able to contain the emotion. At last, after all these months, after all these years, he hears the voice. The voice he has been seeking, searching for with all of his heart, praying for with all of his soul. They are two words. As powerful as thunder. As tender as a newborn's breath. Two words. They roar in every fiber of his consciousness, resonate through his mind and body. Yet they are softer than a whisper. Two words:

"My friend."

The phrase takes his breath away. Weakens his knees. He collapses to the ground as tears give themselves to weeping. Unashamed, gut-wrenching sobs. He cannot stop. There is so much love here, so much adoration. Daniel's adoration of the Light. But far more overpowering . . . the Light's adoration of Daniel.

And so he lays upon the ground, sobbing, his heart bursting with joy, when he feels a presence. The Light has solidified and stands *above him. He wants to open his eyes but is afraid; he cannot endure any more love. A hand tenderly touches his shoulder. And with that touch strength flows into his body until he knows he is able to stand. Slowly, unsteadily, he rises to his feet. Yet he still will not look up. He cannot look. With eyes lowered, he sees a pair of feet, glowing brilliantly, carved from the light of the sun, from a thousand suns. Perfect in every aspect ... except for the holes.*

The image brings a new flood of tears. Slowly he crumbles back to the ground, kneeling at the feet, weeping over them, his tears washing their beauty.

The presence kneels to join him. But Daniel still cannot look into the face. Again the voice speaks. Just as soft, just as commanding.

"I no longer call you servant ...
Instead I have called you friend."

Daniel gasps, unable to breathe, still unable to look up. For as much as he loves him, as much as he is loved, he cannot look into the face. At last a perfect hand—perfect except for the hole—reaches out and holds his chin. Daniel closes his eyes. Tenderly, firmly, the hand raises Daniel's head. The time has come. He must see the face. Slowly, trembling, he opens his eyes. The brilliance causes him to wince but he forces himself to look. And there at last, kneeling before him, eyes also filled with tears of compassion, is the face of ... Jill.

Daniel blinks in confusion ... and suddenly the face transforms into that of Linda Grossman. He tries refocusing his eyes. Now it becomes the face of Charlie Rue. Then it ripples into the face of Bill White, then the grinning Guido. It changes again. Now he is staring at the priest at Axum, now the pastor in Sudan, now Diggers, now the various villagers, until finally ...

Daniel sucks in his breath. For now the face he is looking into is that of his own son, Tyler Lawson.

Daniel closes his eyes, trying to comprehend. When he reopens them, he sees an entirely different face. The one from his dreams. The one reflected in the pool—beaten, covered in blood, swollen beyond recognition. But only for a moment, before it transforms into another. Into one he knows very, very well. It is now the face of himself, Daniel Lawson. No, now it is the beaten face, covered in blood. No, now it is Daniel's face. Now the beaten face. Back and forth the image shifts — his face, the beaten face, his face, the beaten face — faster and faster until they blur, until for the briefest instant they become one and the same. And in that instant the face speaks a final time.

"Father . . . I have given them the glory that you gave me,
that they may be one as we are one:
I in them and you in me."

And with that revelation, that impossible truth, Daniel collapses to the ground, losing consciousness. But even as the sounds and images slip away, he knows he has not seen the entire face . . . for who could see such glory and live? No, he has only seen the tiniest reflection of that glory, the glory God has chosen to share with his friend.

✳

Tyler's father crumpled to the floor, unconscious. "Dad?!"

Without giving a second thought, Tyler raced to him and unfastened the cords of the breastplate. He quickly pulled it from his father's chest and dropped it to the floor. As soon as contact was broken, the Urim and Thummim emitted their loud whine. Tyler reached down and pried them out of the man's clutched fist. He tossed them onto the floor near the breastplate and turned back to his father. Nayra had already joined him on the floor, picking up his head and holding it, pushing back his hair.

"Dad . . . ," he cried. "Dad, can you hear me?"

The man's eyes shifted under their lids. They fluttered a moment, then finally opened. It took a moment for him to focus, to recognize Tyler, but when he did, he broke into a weak smile. He tried to speak but didn't have the strength.

"Take it easy," Tyler urged. "Not now. Tell us later, not now."

"I do not understand." Ibrahim stood several feet away, shouting over the whine.

Tyler looked up. "Understand what?"

"How you can handle them." He motioned toward the breastplate and stones. "How you and your father can handle them but we cannot."

Tyler glanced at the breastplate. Until then he'd given it no thought. But it was true: he was able to handle it just as safely as could his father. He looked down at his fingers. There were no burns, no welts or marks of any kind.

"They are different," Nayra replied.

"Different?" Ibrahim asked. "How?"

"I do not understand, but from our discussions, from what I've seen . . ." She tried to find the words but could not. She shook her head and looked back to Tyler's dad. "What did he say? Ours is a religion of law. Theirs is one of . . . friendship?"

Ibrahim looked at her incredulously. "You believe such blasphemy?"

"I do not . . . I do not know what I believe anymore."

In measured tones Ibrahim recited, "One plus one equals two. There are no shortcuts to holiness. This man" — he motioned to Daniel — "perhaps he is pure enough. He is a sincere, dedicated man of the Book. But this boy . . ." — he scowled at Tyler — "I see no devotion in him, no commitment."

"That is not true," Nayra answered. "You do not see his heart."

"And you do?"

For the briefest moment Nayra glanced away. Then, returning his gaze, she replied, "Yes. I do."

"One plus one equals two. That is the logic of Allah. One cannot approach his absolute purity without obeying his absolute commands. One jumps from a cliff, one is killed. One breaks his law, one dies. One plus one equals two."

"So Allah has no mercy?" Tyler asked.

"Allah is full of mercy. But one cannot stand in his holy presence as a sinner. One plus one. This is logic. This is truth."

In no mood for a theological debate, Tyler turned back to his father.

But not Nayra. "What of love?" she asked.

"Allah has great love."

"But love, it is not always logical. This man, coming all the way here, risking his life to save his son, this is not logic. But it is love."

"That is different."

"How?"

There was a moment's silence, broken only by the whine of the Urim and Thummim.

"You are a child," Ibrahim said scornfully. "You do not yet understand."

"Perhaps. And if that is your answer, perhaps I do not wish to."

Ibrahim's eyes flashed in a rage. He looked from Nayra to Tyler and finally to Daniel. Without a word he rose and moved toward the breastplate.

"Uncle . . . what are you doing?"

He said nothing.

"Uncle, you know what will happen if your skin touches it."

"It will not touch my skin." He looked down at Tyler. "You will handle it. You will place this over my robes. You will attach it."

"You're crazy."

With blinding speed he reached down and seized Tyler's wrist.

"Uncle!" Nayra cried.

His grip was iron, causing Tyler to wince in pain. "You will obey me. You will place it over my robes so it does not touch my flesh. You will attach it, or you will suffer the consequences."

Tyler looked at the man. He was deadly serious. He turned to Nayra, who watched in fear, and then to his father, who urgently shook his head, trying to speak.

"Now!" Ibrahim crushed his wrist harder. "You will put the breastplate upon me and you will do so now!"

Grimacing in pain, Tyler cried out. "All right, all right! Take it easy, man. Take it easy."

Satisfied, Ibrahim released his grip.

Tyler rubbed his wrist and reached for the breastplate. "Have it your way; what do I care?" He threw another glance to Daniel, who still shook his head, trying to speak. But it was obvious to Tyler that neither of them had much say in the matter. If the guy wanted to put it on, let him put it on. If he wanted to turn into a crispy critter, let him fry.

Suddenly the phone on the table rang.

Ibrahim shot a look to it and froze. It rang a second time. Turning back to Tyler, he ordered, "Hurry! Place it upon me at once!"

Tyler scooped up the Urim and Thummim, then carefully picked up the breastplate. As before, the piercing whine immediately ceased.

The phone rang a third time.

"Quickly!"

Tyler held out the breastplate for Ibrahim to slip on. The man hesitated the briefest moment, then with determined resolve stepped forward to receive it.

Tyler pressed it against the front of his robes. There was no reaction.

The phone rang a fourth time.

"Quickly!"

Tyler could hear his father trying to speak, saw him shaking his head. But it made no difference. This guy obviously wanted to have his way. He took the top two ties and fastened them around Ibrahim's neck. He took the bottom two and fastened them around his waist.

Still no reaction.

Ibrahim turned to face him, momentarily breaking contact with the Urim and Thummim, which Tyler held in his hand. They began to whine until Tyler reached out and again touched the breastplate. Everything fell silent. The slightest trace of a smile spread across Ibrahim's face. It may have been from fear, or anticipation of victory; Tyler couldn't tell. In any case Ibrahim held out his hand for the Urim and Thummim.

The phone rang a fifth time.

Tyler raised the stones and hesitated, giving Ibrahim one final chance. The man nodded. Tyler shrugged and dropped them into Ibrahim's hand while at the same time releasing contact with the breastplate. The man blinked but gave no other response.

"Uncle?" Nayra asked. "Uncle, are you all right?"

He remained mute, staring straight ahead.

"Uncle ..."

He continued standing and staring. But, as had been the case with his dad, Tyler suspected something far more dramatic was happening inside.

Even though the pit is icy cold, Ibrahim pauses to wipe his sweat-covered face. He gasps for breath, straining, utilizing every muscle to climb the impossibly steep wall up to the Light — the roaring, thundering, perfect Light. He does not understand why his body is made of rock, but he is grateful that it makes him insensitive to pain. Nor does he understand why he is covered with the writings of the Qur'an, but he is grateful for the honor. Step by excruciating step he scales the wall. It is an effort of gut-wrenching commitment,

requiring all his strength, all his concentration. Yet he has no other course; it is the only way to the Light.

Still, Allah be praised, he has not been forsaken. Miraculously, as he shoves his feet into the soft clay, footholds appear. Symbols of the trials he has faced on this journey, of the tests he has endured and has passed. He looks down and discovers his foot resting upon Samson, the dead pigeon from his childhood. It gives him little pleasure, but by putting his full weight upon it, he is able to raise his other foot. It lands upon the severed hand of the young man from the Farm. It grieves him but he presses upon it and pushes off again. Next he is standing upon the head of Dalal, the temptress who gave up her life in the car explosion. He hears her anguished cry over the roar of the Light. He hesitates at her pain, can barely continue. But he must. He is so close. Oh, the torment, the burden . . . the unbearable burden. But he must continue; he has no choice. Now he stands upon the hunched shoulders of Sarah, his wife, as she was when she was stooped down, weeping over their son. He hears her groan as his rock foot grinds into her flesh. The anguish is so unbearable that he himself cries out. But he must push forward. He is so close. So close and there is no other choice.

Nearly spent, his body numb with exhaustion, he pauses to catch his breath and looks up to the Light. He thinks of calling to it, of pleading for help, but he knows better. He is the one who is in the pit and he is the one who must climb out. Despite the inner torment and outward exhaustion he forces himself upward.

One by one he steps upon the heads of the heroes. The boys he personally selected and trained. The ones waiting to die. They scream under his crushing weight, but he continues upward, step after agonizing step. He is so close, he is nearly there.

He sees the lifeless body of his son emerging from the wall, facing upward. He hesitates, unable to continue. Yet he has come so far, the Light is so close, he cannot give up. Raising his leg, he looks down with remorse upon his boy, then sets his foot squarely upon his fragile chest. He both hears and feels his son's ribs cracking under his immense weight. He screams with the boy in mutual agony, but there is no other way.

He is almost there. One last step. He knows who it is before he takes it. He tries not to look but cannot help himself. It is the upturned face of Yussuf Fazil. It is twisting, contorting in pain. Its

335

lips move. Ibrahim can barely discern the words over the Light's roar.

"Help me, Brother ... help me ..."

Ibrahim closes his eyes against the tears. They stream down his face, mixing with his sweat. He swallows back a sob.

"Forgive me ..." *Tears fill Yussuf's own eyes.* "Forgive ..."

One more step. One more step to go.

"But he's our favorite."

"My brother ... "

"If we do not kill him, he will make his brothers and sisters sick."

Oh, why is this so difficult? Why is the cost of holiness so impossible?

"My friend ... please forgive ..."

He swallows back another sob. But he is nearly there. Unlike all others, Ibrahim el-Magd has sacrificed everything to reach the Light. And he is nearly there. One step to go. Finally, with steeled resolve he raises his foot of stone and, crying out in tortured agony, sets it squarely upon the man's face. He hears the cartilage of the nose break as he pushes off. He hears the chilling scream until ...

He pulls himself up over the edge and onto the surface. He lays there on his rock belly, panting for breath. He has made it. Through sheer will and raw determination he has arrived. Where he is, he is not certain; he can only see the Light. How long he lays there, he does not know. But as his strength returns, he understands the time has come. Now at last he will behold the face of Allah.

With difficulty he rolls onto his back. The Light glares so intensely that he must shield his eyes. It hovers above him, roaring, thundering. But it is more than the Light that thunders. He feels it in his body as well. Throughout his stone body there is an intense vibration, a shaking. It is frightening but this is why he has come. With the greatest effort he struggles to his feet. Finally, at long last, he raises his eyes to face the Light.

It slowly approaches. He wants to run, to bolt, but forces himself to remain. Despite the terror he will see his God. The roar fills his ears; the shaking grows so fierce that he can barely stand. His rock body is so hard, so inflexible, that he watches in astonishment as cracks start to run across his arms, his chest, his legs. Small pieces begin to crumble and break off. He cries out in pain and terror, but there is nothing he can do as the Light approaches.

The shaking grows more fierce. Larger pieces break off, falling to the ground. "What is happening!" he screams. "What are you doing?"

The Light gives no answer. It is nearly upon him.

Unable to move, paralyzed with fear, Ibrahim el-Magd can only watch in horror as the Light begins to encompass him. Its purity is hotter than fire. His stone body begins to glow; the searing heat spreads in every direction. He tries to escape, to turn and run, but he only falls to the ground.

And still the Light wraps itself about him, embracing him, caressing him . . . igniting him.

"Why?" he screams. "I am your servant! I am your servant!"

There is no answer. Now he is entirely enveloped. Completely embraced. Every surface of his stone body glows. Everything is molten rock. The pain is excruciating. Unbearable.

"Why?" he shrieks. "Look at what I have done for you! Look at what I have done!"

The Light soaks deeper into him, igniting more of him with its torturous glow, its absolute purity.

"Look at what I have done!"

And then he hears It. All-powerful, all-tender.

"Look at what you are."

He turns to his hands, his arms, his entire body. Everything glows brilliantly, as brilliantly as did the twelve stones. Brilliantly but not clearly. Because every square inch is filled with imperfection — dark flecks of impurity that refuse to glow. This is the source of the pain. Not the Light, not the molten, glowing stone . . . but the impurities. For as he watches, they ignite, hundreds at a time, flaring up and burning, and with their fire the unspeakable pain.

He watches, horrified, as the Light continues to soak into him, attempting to share its brilliance, its glory — the same glory as that of the stones. But all the flecks, all the impurities, make it impossible.

The pain is too intense. He cannot remain in the Light's presence. He must escape its purity. Desperately he looks for some escape, for someplace to flee. The Light is everywhere . . . everywhere but in the pit. The very pit he has crawled out of. Seeing its safety, he starts toward it, crawling on his stomach, dragging himself toward its edge. If he can just reach it, if he can crawl back into

337

it and get away ... Deeper and deeper the Light soaks into him, igniting more and more of his body — the pain excruciating.

Finally he arrives at the edge of the pit. He is surprised to see that it is now filled with liquid. Red liquid. Even more surprising is the reflected face. The face of his dreams. The face of Allah covered in the blood of his enemies. But no, no ... this is not the face of Allah. It cannot be. The blood is not from his enemies. It is from the cuts and welts across Allah's own face. They are from Allah's own wounds. No, Allah would not have wounds. Allah is majesty. Allah is holiness. This blood should be from the wounds of his enemies, not from himself, not —

And then he sees it. For the first time. Atop the head is a crown of thorns.

He recognizes the image and recoils. "No! This is not possible! This cannot be!"

The words strike the liquid, causing the reflection to waver. Seeing their power, the power of his will, he shouts again. "No! I do not believe this! I refuse this! I will not accept this!"

Once again the reflection wavers ...

"I refuse this!"

... until it breaks up and disappears altogether. Not because the image is gone but because the pool of blood is gone. The pit is suddenly empty again. He rejoices. Now he can reenter it. Now he can hide and be safe from the Light's purity. He pulls his molten body the remaining inches to the edge of the pit. With relief he looks into the darkness — the blessed, safe darkness. He pushes one last time. His weight does the rest, dragging him over the edge and into the hole. He begins falling, tumbling head over heels, away from the Light. Faster and faster he falls, grateful for the growing darkness. Deeper and deeper he falls, away from the Light, into the darkness, into a pit that seems to have no end ...

"Uncle!"

She started for him but Tyler held her back. "Nayra, no!"

She struggled to get free. "Uncle ..."

But Tyler would not release her. And for good reason. The man was twisting and writhing on the floor. His arms and legs flailed and kicked, his eyes bulged in unknown terror as he gnashed his teeth like a crazed animal.

"Remove it!" Nayra cried. "We must remove it from him!"

By now Daniel was strong enough to stagger to his feet and lean against the table, but he did not have enough energy to help. He watched as Tyler tried to get through Ibrahim's kicking and convulsing. But the man was too wild, too dangerous. Through the movement Daniel saw wisps of smoke from the breastplate. It had burned through Ibrahim's robes. Not only through the robes but now it seemed to be sinking into his body. It was as if his chest had turned molten and the breastplate was sinking into it.

"Uncle!"

As it had a dozen times before, Ibrahim's fist, the one holding the Urim and Thummim, slammed into the stone tile. This time, however, the impact finally loosened his grip and they flew from his hand, rolling across the floor. With the contact broken, their piercing whine returned. And the breastplate began to glow. But not just the breastplate.

"Look!" Nayra shouted.

To Daniel's astonishment the glow began to spread — past the breastplate, across Ibrahim's chest, into his shoulders and arms, down his stomach and into his legs. Soon everything but his face was glowing. Glowing with the same light as that of the stones. But that was only the beginning.

From his body the light spread to the floor, causing the stone tiles to heat until they too began to glow. Although it spread in all directions, much of the glow seemed attracted to the Urim and Thummim, which lay a dozen feet away.

Daniel was unsure what would happen next, but if his dreams and the accounts of Avignon were correct, he knew they had to escape. "We have to — " He coughed and tried again. "We have to go!" Tyler and Nayra turned to him. "We have to leave. Now!"

They looked back at the Urim and Thummim. The glow had reached the rocks and was surrounding them. But unlike the floor, the two rocks remained as dark and inert as ever. Except for the whine they were completely unaffected. Well, not exactly. Even from where Daniel stood, he could see them starting to vibrate.

Tyler stepped closer to investigate.

Daniel shouted over the whine. "Tyler!"

The stones shook harder, as if coming alive.

"Do you feel that?" Nayra shouted.

Daniel did. For it wasn't just the two stones that were shaking; it was the entire floor. And not just the floor. He looked at the ceiling. Cracks forked their way across its surface. Dust and plaster began to fall. He turned to Tyler. "Earthquake! We've got to get out!"

But the boy continued to stare at the Urim and Thummim.

"Tyler!" The shaking grew worse. "Remember the Palace of the Popes? Remember Mount Sinai!"

Tyler looked at his father and nodded, then turned to Ibrahim and the breastplate. Daniel followed his gaze. Ibrahim was glowing white-hot, brighter than fire. The breastplate had disappeared into his chest, impossible to see for the light blazing from it. Daniel turned back to Tyler and the Urim and Thummim. The glow surrounding the rocks was rapidly expanding across the tiles, spreading in all directions, spreading toward his son. But it wasn't just the glow. Like Ibrahim, the tiles too seemed to be liquefying, the Urim and Thummim sinking into them.

"Get back!" Daniel shouted. The shaking grew more violent, creating a roar that started to fill the room. "We've got to get out of here!"

A huge chunk of plaster gave way from the ceiling. It crashed to the floor, throwing dust up in all directions.

"Now!" Daniel shouted.

Tyler turned back to Ibrahim.

"*Now!*"

The pillar beside him creaked.

"Daniel!"

Over the roar he heard another voice. At first he thought it was Jill, until he spun around and saw Helen standing in the distant doorway. The pillar groaned louder. More plaster fell. He looked up just as it started falling, bringing much of the ceiling down with it, directly onto —

"Tyler!"

The boy didn't have a chance. It hit him hard, slamming him into the ground.

"*Tyler!*"

Another pillar gave way. Plaster and debris poured everywhere. The lights went out, but it made no difference to Daniel as he staggered through the choking dust and blackness toward his son. "Tyler!" The floor started rolling as more of the building fell. "Ty — " He stumbled, then lost his balance and smashed headfirst into a jagged piece of concrete. He may have lost consciousness; he wasn't sure. But even before his mind cleared, he was on his hands and knees, crawling. "Tyler!" He could feel warm liquid trickling through his hair but it didn't matter.

"Daniel!" Helen shouted over the roar.

"Tyler!" He thought he heard an answer. He shouted again, choking, barely able to breathe from the dust.

"Here ..." A faint voice to his right coughed. He turned to the pile of rubble and in the dimness saw movement.

"Tyler!" Daniel coughed and gagged, breathing more dust than air. He dug and shoved and pushed his way through the concrete and plaster. "Are you ..." — more coughing — "okay?" There was no answer. "Tyler!"

"Yeah ...," came the weak reply.

At last he saw his son's eyes, the only thing not coated in dust. He dug harder and faster through the fallen debris — lifting, pushing.

"My leg!" Tyler cried.

Daniel froze.

"I think ..." — more coughing, his voice racked with pain — "it's broken."

Plaster and concrete continued to fall as Daniel scurried down to the leg. The left pant leg was crushed and soaked with blood.

"Daniel ...," Helen continued to shout into the room.

"We have to get out of here!" Daniel yelled to him.

Tyler nodded and coughed. "What about Nayra?" He turned and cried into the darkness. "Nayra!"

"Right here," she gasped as she crawled through the rubble.

"Daniel ... Tyler?" Helen shouted.

"We're here!" Daniel yelled, coughing. "Over here ..."

More of the ceiling collapsed, throwing up even greater dust as the ground pitched and rolled.

"Follow my voice!" Helen shouted. "I'm at the door." Another pillar started to tip. "Hurry! The whole place is coming down!"

It crashed with a deafening roar.

Daniel and Nayra lifted and pushed the remaining concrete off Tyler's leg, then tried to help him stand, but the leg held no weight.

"Put your arm around me!" Daniel shouted.

Together Nayra and Daniel lifted him to his feet as all three fought to keep their balance on the rolling floor.

"Hurry!" Helen shouted. "Hurry!"

They staggered forward, coughing and choking in the dark, stumbling over the rubble. Twice they had to climb over waist-high debris, hoisting Tyler up, then easing him down on the other side.

"Over here!" Helen cried. "Here!" At last they spotted her, wading toward them, a silhouette against the doorway lit from the hall's windows. "Come on, come on!"

They staggered toward her and arrived, nearly falling until she helped catch Tyler's weight. Together they made their way through the door and out into the hall. Conditions there were not much better.

"This way!" Helen shouted. "I've got the truck! Come on!"

The floor heaved and fell in waves, exploding tile, shattering windows, bringing down slabs of wall. They could hear panicked screams as other shadows stumbled past them.

"Here!" Helen coughed. "Over here!"

They followed her to the shell of a window. She climbed up, kicking out the remaining shards of glass before crawling through. They hoisted up Tyler. Nayra followed. Daniel was the last to exit, tumbling from the opening and into the broken glass and debris of the courtyard. Nayra was already helping Tyler stand. Daniel moved to his other side, and together they supported him as they followed Helen across the rolling ground.

All around them men, women, children ran and shouted, screaming in terror. Daniel threw a look back at the building. The setting sun gave it a golden glow as a giant cloud of dust slowly rose. To his amazement, just as with the breastplate, just as with the Urim and Thummim, the entire structure seemed to be sinking . . . as if the ground supporting it were turning to liquid.

"Over there!" Helen pointed to the Land Rover near the iron gates.

Tyler could no longer help as they half carried, half dragged him across the ground. They passed a group of preschoolers huddled in a terrified knot around a fallen adult, most likely their teacher. Nayra saw them and hesitated.

"Let's go!" Helen yelled. "Let's go! Let's go!"

They continued forward until they arrived at the truck, the ground shaking, roaring like a freight train. Daniel could see that Tyler was conscious but didn't know for how much longer. Together they lifted him into the backseat. Daniel raced around to join him on the other side. "Hang in there, buddy!" he shouted. "Hang on!"

Helen had already climbed behind the wheel and was firing up the truck. But Nayra remained standing at Tyler's open door, not moving.

"Come on!" Daniel shouted. "Get in! Nayra, what are you doing?"

She turned back to the frightened preschoolers. The ground lurched, throwing her against the side of the truck. "Get in!" Daniel shouted. "We've got to go!"

She looked at him, then back at the children.

"Nayra . . ."

She began to shake her head.

"Nayra!"

"No," she shouted. "I must stay."

"What!"

She turned to him. "They need my help. I must stay here. For now I must stay."

"No . . . ," Tyler gasped from the seat.

She looked at him. "They need my help; I must stay."

"Then we'll all stay," Daniel said as he started climbing from the truck. "We'll all stay until — "

"No!" Nayra shook her head. "You must leave; it is not safe for you. And you" — she looked down to Tyler — "you must see a doctor at once."

"No," Tyler cried hoarsely.

Nayra bent closer. "We will meet again, my love."

Tyler tried to speak but was drowned out by a series of explosions ripping the air. Daniel looked up to see multiple fireballs rolling out of the building. The children screamed, huddling closer together, dropping to their knees in terror. When he turned back to Tyler, he saw his son clinging to Nayra's wrist. "Too dangerous . . . ," he croaked. "You . . . could die!"

Her answer was gentle but firm. "And if I do? Would I not simply be loving as you say Allah loves?"

The phrase stunned him. She smiled at his surprise. "When his Son came from heaven and died for us ... would I not simply be following his ways?"

Tyler stared, trying to digest what he'd just heard. "You ..." — he took a ragged breath — "you believe?"

She smiled softly, then bent down to kiss his forehead. Another series of explosions shook the air. She reached to her wrist and gently removed his hand. Raising it to her face, she kissed it. *"Allah Issalmak,"* she said. "God keep you safe."

Tears rolled down Tyler's cheeks. Nayra reached out and tenderly touched their wetness, her own eyes brimming with moisture. He clenched his eyes shut, fighting for control. When he reopened them, he seemed a little better, as if he understood. Slowly he began to nod. And through a voice so thick he could barely speak, he quietly repeated, *"Allah Issalmak ..."*

Gunfire drew their attention. Three men were running toward them. They shouted and brandished weapons, no doubt seeing the Land Rover as a means of escape.

"Go!" Nayra shouted to Helen. She stepped back and slammed the passenger door. "Go!"

Helen dropped the Land Rover into gear and they leaped forward, wheels spinning.

"Nayra..." Tyler turned back, looking for her, wincing in pain. Daniel tried to stop him from twisting, but the boy would have none of it. "Nayra!" He turned with his son and watched as the girl started to disappear into the smoke and dust. Feeling a burning in his own eyes and a choking in his own throat, Daniel raised his hand to her. For a moment she returned the wave until it was interrupted by the angry, shouting men. He caught the briefest glimpse of her shouting back until everything was swallowed by the dust.

"Nayra!" Tyler cried. *"Nayra ..."*

Daniel reached over and wrapped his arms around him, holding him like a child. His son buried his face into his chest, and he thought his own heart was going to burst.

Up ahead someone was trying to close the gates, but it made little difference to Helen. She accelerated, and the self-appointed guard leaped out of the way with a scream.

Even outside the compound Daniel could see the ground shaking. In a few moments they would pull aside and get a tourniquet on Tyler's leg, but right now it was important that they get as far away as possible. He turned and looked back over his shoulder. The buildings continued to crumble, sending smoke and flames roiling into the air. Then there was the surrounding sand. Like Ibrahim's chest, like the floor tile, it had started to glow ... and ripple. In the setting sun it almost appeared to be turning to liquid ... molten and glowing. The entire compound seemed to be sinking into it ... deeper and deeper, as if it were being swallowed alive. Perhaps it was some sort of mirage, a trick of the sun.

Perhaps. But Daniel had his doubts.

*

They continued driving east on the only road leading from the compound. Once they'd passed through the village and were a safe distance away, they stopped and tied off Tyler's leg just below the knee. The rest of it was crushed and broken in more than one place. Whether they saved it or not would depend upon Helen's driving and navigational skills. She said that if she pushed hard, they would hit the capital city of Khartoum and a hospital by dawn. He had offered to drive but she'd refused, insisting that he stay in the backseat with his son. She was right of course. And so now, in the darkness, he sat with Tyler, sometimes gazing out the window, sometimes quietly watching Helen silhouetted against the reflection of their headlights. What a remarkable person this woman was — smart, sensitive, determined, and full of compassion. Yes indeed, very, very remarkable.

But it wasn't just Helen. He looked back to his son. The youth sat with his head turned away, either sleeping or staring out into the desert night. He too was remarkable. Honest, forthright, and with greater courage than he had ever imagined. Why had he never seen this before? And in his own son? He wasn't sure but he saw it now. For the first time in a very long time he saw his immeasurable value. He saw it of Tyler; he also saw it of Helen, Nayra ... Truth be told, he saw it of nearly every person he'd met on this journey — persons he'd met, come to respect, and yes, even love.

Love. It was exactly as Jill had promised him. Exactly as God had promised her.

Amid the vehicle's jarring bounces and its droning roar, Pastor Daniel Lawson closed his eyes. There was much to think over and contemplate. But it was still there, clearly in his mind. The face. The face, agonizing in its unbearable sacrifice, its overwhelming love. Love for him . . . and love for others. He'd caught the briefest glimpse of that love. He had seen it in the vision, yes, but he had also seen it in the people, the reflection of God's love for them within their faces. He had seen it and he would not be the same. He knew that now. He would never be the same.

epilogue

Dr. Helen Zimmerman was late by nearly two hours. When the kid at Avis rentals had given her directions from the Bismarck airport, he'd failed to mention the thirty-mile detour around construction on Highway 94. Then there was the additional time lost trying to find a parking place anywhere near the church. She blew the hair out of her eyes as she finally pulled into a spot three blocks away. Interesting. According to her research, Jud, North Dakota, had a population of eighty-nine people, yet there were more cars than that parked along the various roads surrounding the church.

She locked the doors of the Buick Le Sabre, stepped outside, and headed for the church, her beige, calfskin pumps crunching and popping gravel along the dirt road. There was no other sound — no traffic, no planes, just the gravel . . . and the faintest pounding of her heart. She took a breath to relax. Closing her eyes, she breathed in the rich, moist greenness — the summer corn, the wheat, the miles of pastures. What a difference from Israel.

She pulled at her snug white skirt and adjusted her matching silk blouse. She knew she was a bit overdressed for these parts, but she was willing to risk it — just as long as she took his breath away that first moment he saw her. Why, she wasn't certain, though she suspected it had something to do with her inability to get him out of her mind these last eighteen months. After the Mossad grillings and the CIA debriefings it had been eighteen months since they'd seen each other. A year and a half and he was still there. Not that she hadn't tried to forget him. Granted, she had written two or three letters, but she'd always found the strength to throw them away before they were sent. And it's true, she'd started twice that many e-mails, but each time she'd had the good sense to hit the delete key before it was too late. Yet to her irritation he still remained, somewhere there in her mind. So when the recent request came from the Israeli government, what better person to deliver it than herself?

She rounded the block and saw the church. It was anything but impressive. A "pole barn," she believed it was called. White aluminum walls with a minimum of windows and a low-pitched blue roof. In the front, two pairs of matching blue doors had been propped open. Through these drifted strains of some of the worst music Helen had ever heard. And the closer she approached, the worse it got — guitar, drums, some sort of keyboard . . . and a singer. The musicians were fine. It was the soloist who made the hairs on her neck rise. A thin, elderly voice that continually struggled to find the right note, not to mention the right key.

Helen approached the building and nodded to those milling around outside. Most were young mothers with toddlers and babies; one or two nursed with a towel thrown over their front. They smiled politely enough, but as she passed she could feel their eyes staring. She gave a discreet tug at her skirt and stepped through the doors.

Inside was a small lobby with more people — men in suits, Dockers, blue jeans; women in dresses, some in pants. As she headed for what must have been the sanctuary doors, an older fellow with a string tie opened one for her. She thanked him and stepped inside.

The music was much louder and no better. There on the stage, fifty feet away, stood the culprit, arms raised, eyes closed — some wiry blue-hair singing her heart out. Strangely enough, the congregation seemed oblivious to the damage she was inflicting upon the music. Instead many smiled and nodded. Some even had their eyes closed, pretending to enjoy it as much as the old woman.

Thankfully, mercifully, she was on the last chorus and it soon came to an end. To Helen's surprise the entire congregation broke into applause. Applause? In a church? For that? The old woman grinned back to the crowd, absolutely beaming. She raised her hand toward heaven, making it clear she was giving God all the credit. As if he wanted it. The applause continued as she was joined by a tall, athletic man in khakis and a polo shirt. He kissed her lightly on the cheek, and it was only when he turned to face the audience that Helen knew for sure it was Daniel Lawson. He still looked good. A bit grayer around the edges, maybe a pound or two heavier, but other than that, the last year and a half had been good to him. Very good. Once again Helen tugged at her skirt.

"Thank you, Irene," he shouted over the applause. "That was lovely, just lovely."

Irene beamed even more brightly.

At last the clapping faded. Daniel raised his hand over the room. The congregation settled and lowered their heads as he began to pray. "And now may the Lord bless you and protect you. May he continue to make you whole and complete, lacking in nothing, men and women of God whose hearts follow hard after him. In Christ's name we pray. Amen."

The congregation repeated, "Amen," and came to life.

"Hug a few necks," he shouted over the commotion, "and we'll see you Wednesday night."

As people began turning to leave, the band struck up a reprise of the song. Thankfully, the old woman felt no need to join them. Instead she allowed Daniel to help her off the stage and down to exuberant family and friends. Daniel smiled and laughed with them, occasionally hugging someone, occasionally being hugged.

Helen looked on from the back. The man was definitely in his element. She decided to wait there until the crowd thinned. That's when he would finally look up ... and that's when he'd see her.

Unfortunately, the crowd did not thin. At least not quickly. Instead she had to stand there looking spontaneously lovely for nearly twenty minutes. What was wrong with these people? Didn't they have lives? But gradually, one by one, group after group began to file past her, heading for the door. Eventually only a few pocketfuls were left. Finally Daniel, who had been kneeling to speak with a little boy, rose to his feet.

She stopped breathing, waiting for him to turn and see her.

And when he did, he froze. Stunned. It was perfect. Just as she'd planned.

She smiled demurely.

Finally, breaking into a grin, he shouted, "Helen!" He started toward her. Conversation in the building slowed to a stop. People turned to look. But he took little notice. He arrived, throwing his arms around her in an enthusiastic embrace. "Helen!" he repeated. It was more than she'd hoped for, at least here. And if the people hadn't gotten an eyeful of her before ... well, now they really had something to talk about.

"How are you?" he asked, finally separating. "Why didn't you let me know you were coming?"

She coughed, surprised at how tight her throat had become. "Daniel" — she cleared her voice — "it's good to see you."

"Look at you," he said, stepping back. "You look incredible!"

"Uh ..." — throwing a nervous look at the others, she straightened her blouse — "thanks." She grinned stupidly.

"I mean it; you really do."

She nodded, feeling her face grow hot. He was doing it again. After all this time. Making her feel like some awkward, self-conscious junior higher. How dare he!

Keeping one arm about her, he turned toward the front. "Jimmy, will you lock up for me this afternoon?"

"Will do, Pastor," a voice echoed from somewhere backstage.

He turned back to her. "How long are you staying?" Before she could answer, he asked, "You haven't had lunch, have you?"

"Uh ..." She coughed again, her mouth unusually dry. She shook her head.

"Great. I'm starved."

She grinned again. That stupid grin. How dare he.

"There's only one restaurant in town, but they make a great pot roast. If you're interested?"

With concentrated effort she regained control. First over the grin, then over the rest of her body. Soon she felt herself returning to the self-assured professional that she was. "That would be fine, Daniel."

"Great."

They turned toward the doors and started walking. It felt good to be back in control again. It would have felt better if her foot had not caught the outside leg of an errant folding chair ... and if she hadn't tripped and lost her balance, falling into the next row of chairs ... and if she hadn't dragged those chairs down with her to the floor.

"Helen?" He was immediately at her side. "Are you all right?"

She nodded, doing her best to untangle herself from the chairs while trying to rise ladylike to her feet (no small task with such a short skirt). Of course by now everyone in the building was wondering about the pastor's new friend and what hospital she'd escaped from. But it wasn't everyone in the building that irritated her. Only him.

"Are you sure?" he asked, trying to help.

"Yes, I'm sure," she said as she finally made it to her feet. Gathering herself together, she turned and headed for the door, Daniel following right behind. She arrived and pulled on the handle.

"Uh, Helen . . ."

She pulled harder, giving it a yank, but it wouldn't budge.

"Helen . . ."

"What?"

He reached past her and gently pushed it open. "They swing out."

Blowing the hair out of her eyes, she muttered, "I knew that," then started through the lobby. He joined her side and together they stepped through the other doors and out into the warm summer sun.

"Watch your step here." He pointed to the uneven pavement.

"I've got it, thanks."

"No, I mean this here, it's kind of — "

"I said I've got it." She blew the hair out of her eyes and continued forward.

"Uh, Helen . . ."

She slowed and turned to him in exasperation.

"The restaurant, it's, uh . . ." — he motioned in the opposite direction — "it's this way."

✳

"So you turned chicken and ran away from big churches."

Daniel gave Helen a look, then broke into a grin. He'd forgotten how much he missed her candor. He shook his head and answered, "I saw — we *all* saw — what awful damage religion can do . . . religion without relationship." She seemed to agree and he continued. "I didn't want to create another machine, that's all."

"So you traveled out here in the hinterlands to pastor some tiny church — "

"Eighty people when I started."

"—and now it's turning into the same institution you had before."

Daniel nodded and took another forkful of mashed potatoes and gravy. "We're growing by about twenty people a week."

"So you're right back where you started—well, except for your choice of musical talent." She smiled wryly.

He forgot how much he missed that too. "She was pretty bad, wasn't she?" He grinned.

"Not if you're deaf."

He laughed. "But you see, that's the difference."

She looked at him, waiting for more.

"The other church, my last one, it became like this monster, this religious machine that used people, that made them conform and fit into its box."

"And this one?"

"This is just the opposite. At least so far."

"What do you mean?"

He set down his fork and explained, his excitement rising. "Instead of some machine that people are expected to serve, we've flipped it around. We're trying to make it something that serves the people."

Helen frowned, still not understanding.

"Take Mrs. Nelson, today's soloist. All her life she's wanted to sing to the Lord. And now, from time to time, we let her."

"But she's terrible."

"Of course she is, but what difference does it make?"

"I'd say it makes a difference to the poor congregation."

He shook his head. "You saw their faces; they love it. They love it because they know she loves it." He leaned forward. "Do you see the difference? It's service. I'm no longer interested in creating the perfect machine with the perfect programs to serve my dreams. Now I'm interested in finding out what the people's dreams are and how I can help them achieve them. It's so simple but so incredibly different. The church is serving the people to accomplish their goals, instead of the other way around."

"Can't that get a little frightening?" Helen asked.

"It's terrifying. Every second. But it keeps me alive. It forces me to keep turning to God instead of my programs. Because the programs, the rules and regulations, the religion ... let's face it — it's a thousand times safer to follow those than a relationship."

Helen cocked her head at him. "So we're back to that again ... relationship."

He grinned. "Always. I'd just forgotten."

She glanced out the window and slowly nodded. He was glad. It was important she understand. He wasn't sure why ... except that they had been through so much together and had become such good friends. In fact, to this day he often found himself thinking of her, wondering what she was doing, how she was doing.

"What about Video Boy?" she asked, changing the subject. "I got an e-mail from Tyler a while back saying he was thinking of returning to Sudan."

Daniel nodded. "He left about seven months ago."

"Looking for Nayra?"

"Yes."

"And?"

"There's not the slightest sign of the compound or even the village beside it."

"Nothing at all?"

Daniel shook his head.

"And the reason? Officially, I mean?"

"Seems it was built upon some giant fault line, one that was completely unknown until our little visit."

Helen nodded. "I thought it might be something like that." Then she added, "It must have been pretty rough on him."

Daniel quietly agreed. "Yeah ..."

"He's still over there, still looking?"

"I got a letter from him three weeks ago. Seems he's traded in his video camera and is doing full-time relief work with the people in southern Sudan."

"Really?"

He nodded. "Pretty exhausting, the way he paints it — working with the people twenty-four/seven. But he says he's never been happier."

"You're serious?"

Daniel grinned and nodded. "Pretty amazing, huh? He also claims that he's never been closer to God."

Helen quietly shook her head.

Spotting her empty ice water, Daniel motioned to the passing waitress, who paused to refill it. Unwilling to let the silence grow too long, he cleared his throat. "So ... what about you?"

"Me?" she asked.

"How have you been?"

"Couldn't be better." She took another drink. "You'll be happy to know that I've started attending synagogue."

"You?"

She shrugged, careful not to look at him. "I've found there's a certain ... I don't know ... comfort in the Scriptures."

"I thought you didn't believe in them."

"I don't ... well, not all of them. But after what you and I saw, what we experienced, I'd be a fool to completely discount them."

She gave him a glance and caught him smiling. "What?" she asked.

He shook his head.

"What?"

"Nothing," he said, glancing down, not entirely successful at hiding his grin.

Obviously choosing to ignore him, she continued. "I'm also up to my neck in the Jerusalem dig, the one I'd started when you first came over."

"No kidding."

She nodded. "Had a few fires to put out after our little adventure, but now ... now I've got the largest support staff I've ever had. You should see them; my team is incredible. And for the first time we almost have enough money. It's wonderful. So I'm doing great, too."

"Good."

She continued to nod. "Yup, just great."

"Good ... good."

Once again silence crept over the conversation. He watched as she pushed a group of peas about her plate. "So ..." He coughed slightly. "What, uh, what brings you all the way out here?"

"Other than visiting an old friend?" she asked.

"I'm flattered, but North Dakota is a bit out of the way."

She nodded. "Did you know it's the least visited state in the union?"

He grinned. "So I've heard."

She focused back on the peas.

He tried again. "What's up, Helen?"

"I'm that easy to read?"

He smiled. "We've put in a few miles together."

She nodded. Then without looking up, she said, "The Mossad contacted me last week."

"Still playing secret agent?" he asked, returning to his own meal.

She shook her head. "Not anymore. Well, except . . ." She glanced about the café and lowered her voice slightly. "It appears that some nut, a real fruitcake . . . well, he claims he's found the Garden of Eden."

Daniel almost choked. "What?"

"Well, not the whole Garden, but parts of it. Including remnants of some sort of tree or something whose fruit supposedly alters DNA to increase our longevity."

Daniel's mind whirred. "Longevity?"

"Some sort of fountain of youth . . . or in this case, tree."

"The Tree of Life?" he asked incredulously. "Are you talking about the Tree of Life?"

"Yeah, something like that."

"And you believe it?"

"Of course not," she scoffed. "But since we were pretty successful in tracking down that last set of artifacts — "

"Which we completely lost to the desert."

She nodded. "Which we completely lost to the desert . . . " She returned to her food. "In any case, he and his 'remnants' are now missing, and they wanted to know if we'd be willing to team up and help find him."

"The two of us?"

"That's what they asked."

"But . . . I've got my church."

"Exactly. And I've got my dig. It would be absurd to leave them."

"You're right. Absolutely."

"Especially over something like that."

Daniel nodded and they continued eating. A moment later he shook his head and chuckled. "The Tree of Life. What some people dream up."

Helen nodded. "Completely absurd."

"Of course it is."

More silence. Helen reached for her glass of water and took another drink. "I mean, you believe it's just an allegory, right?"

"What's that?"

"The Tree of Life ..."

"Not necessarily."

She coughed over her drink. "What? Tell me you're not serious?"

He shrugged. "Sure, why not?"

She gave him a look, then resumed drinking. "Unbelievable."

He ignored the barb. "But for someone to claim they've actually found it ..." He shook his head and returned to eating. "Well now, that *is* absurd."

She nodded. "On that we both agree."

"Yes," he said, nodding.

And so the two sat together in the growing silence, their forks occasionally scraping their plates, their minds racing — each knowing what the other was thinking, and each wondering who would be the first to voice it.

"Absurd," she quietly mused.

"Yes." He chuckled again. "Completely absurd ..."

chapter one

It had started again. The voice. Five hours earlier in Wal-Mart.

He'd been doing his usual stalking up and down the aisles, this time for laundry detergent. Why was it every month they were determined to move at least one item to a new location? Over the years, since Jacqueline left, he felt he'd become quite the veteran shopper — reading labels, clipping coupons, even watching as the cashier rang up each purchase on the register. But this moving of products, especially to the least likely places, always frustrated him. He was reaching the peak of just such a frustration when he heard the child crying one row over.

"Daddy! Daddy, where are you?"

The fear in her voice brought him to a stop. It was the same panic, the same desperation that had haunted him for weeks.

"Daddy, come get me!"

The tone was so similar to another that David forgot the laundry detergent. He hesitated, then pushed his cart to the end of the aisle. He slowed as he rounded the corner and peered up the next row. A little blonde, about kindergarten age, sat alone in a cart. She was bundled in a bright red coat, pink tights, and shiny black shoes. Tears streamed down her face as she cried.

"Daddy, please don't leave me!"

He scowled, glancing around. There was no one near. What parent would leave a child like this? Had the father no sense of responsibility? He pushed his cart up the aisle toward her. "Sweetie, are you all right?"

She turned, eyeing him, then took a brave, trembling breath.

He continued to approach. "It'll be okay, darling. I'm sure your —"

Suddenly her face brightened as she looked past him. "Daddy!"

He turned to see a concerned young man in a green fleece jacket and worn jeans stride up the aisle toward them. In his hands he held a new push broom, grasped tightly enough to assure David he would not hesitate to use it if necessary. David forced a reassuring grin. The young man sized him up and said nothing as he brushed by and joined his daughter.

"Oh, Daddy." The little girl sobbed as she stretched out her arms.

"I was just around the corner." Laughing, he scooped her out of the cart. "Did you think I forgot you?" She nodded and he hugged her. Then, pushing aside her damp hair, he kissed her cheek. "You know I wouldn't do that." Again she nodded, but continued to whimper — an obvious attempt to make him pay penance.

David thought of stopping and turning his cart around, but that would be clumsy and awkward, only adding fuel to the parent's suspicion. So he continued up the aisle. As he passed, he felt he should say something to the young father, something instructive, something to remind him what a precious responsibility he held in his arms. He said nothing.

But the voice remained. A whisper in the back of his mind. It remained through the wooden conversation between Grams, Luke, and himself over dinner. It remained through the forced laughter as Grams recounted some scene from one of her daytime soaps. It even remained as David got on his son about the poor progress reports they'd received in the mail from school.

And now, several hours later, as David Kauffman stood alone in the dark, silent living room, the whisper grew louder, becoming more familiar. The one that always filled his head and swelled his heart to breaking.

"Daddy, I'll be good! I promise . . . please . . . please!"

He reached for the back of the overstuffed chair to steady himself. He had not bothered to turn on a light. Across the room on the mantle, he heard the clock ticking. Outside, a faint stirring of wind chimes. He caught the shadowy movement of the cat — her cat — scurrying past and up the stairs to safety. David hated this room. Tried his best to avoid it. The memories were too painful —

as bad as the upstairs bathroom, its lock still broken from when he'd busted through it to find her opening her veins...

The first time.

"*Daddy*..."

David closed his eyes against the memories, but he could still hear feet scuffing the carpet, attendants' muffled grunts as they grabbed her flailing arms, pinning them to her side. And, of course, her frantic pleas.

"*I'll do better, I promise! Please, don't make me go!*"

Images flickered in his head as if under a strobe light. Flying hair, twisting body, kicking feet, the appearance of a pearl-white syringe... Emily's eyes widening in panic.

"*Daddy, no!*"

"*To help you relax,*" the attendant had said.

"*Don't let them take me...*" She no longer sounded sixteen. She was four, five. So helpless. "*Daddy...*"

He leaned against the chair, his throat tightening.

"*Daddy...*"

That was the deepest cut. The word. *Daddy*. Protector. Defender. *Daddy.* The one who always made things right. That was the word that had gripped him in Wal-Mart. The word that sucked breath out of him every time he heard it, that drew tears to his eyes before he could stop them. Even in front of Luke.

He tried his best not to cry when he was with his son. The boy had been through so much already. What he needed now was stability, and David was the only one who could provide it. If his twelve-year-old saw tears it would spell weakness, and weakness meant things were still out of control. No. Now more than ever, Luke needed to know things were returning to normal, that there was someone he could depend upon.

But David was by himself now. Alone. Luke was upstairs sleeping (or more likely on the Internet) while Grams snored quietly just down the hall.

Emily's voice returned, softer, thicker. The drug taking effect. "*Daddy...*"

"*Just a few weeks, honey,*" he had promised. "*You'll get better and then you can come home.*"

He remembered her eyes. Those startling, violet-blue eyes. Eyes so astonishing that people assumed she wore colored contacts.

Eyes glassing over from the drug. Eyes once so full of anger and confusion and accusation and . . . and — this is what always did him in — eyes that had been so full of trust at that moment.

He had held her look. Then slowly, with the intimacy of a father to his daughter, he gave a little nod, his silent assurance.

And she believed him.

She still sobbed, tears still ran down her cheeks, but she no longer fought. In that single act, that quiet nod, her daddy told her everything would be all right. And she trusted him. She *trusted* him!

David leaned forward onto the back of the chair, tears falling. He remembered the front door opening — bright sunlight pouring in, flaunting its cheeriness.

"I'll be right behind you," he had promised. *"Grams and I will be in the car right behind you."*

She could no longer wipe her nose. She could only nod and mumble, *"Okay."*

The last word she ever spoke in the house. *Okay, I believe you. Okay, I'm depending upon you. Okay . . . I trust you.*

David lowered his head against the chair. He was trembling again, trying to breathe. The house was asleep and he was alone. "Where are you, baby girl?" His hoarse whisper cut through the silence. "Just tell me. Let me know so I can help."

The screen door groaned. He looked up and quickly wiped his face. This was no memory. The boy was here. He'd called half an hour ago, asking if he could come over. David straightened himself, listening. There was a tentative knock. He took a breath and ordered his legs to move. Somehow they obeyed. He reached out to the cold door. He took another breath, wiped his face, and pulled the door open.

The boy wore a gray sweatshirt with the word *Panthers* and red paw prints across his chest. He was tall and lanky, around six feet, with curly brown, unkempt hair. Long, dark lashes highlighted even darker eyes. His chin was strong and his nose slightly large, almost classical. David blinked. In many ways he was looking at a younger version of himself, back when he was in high school.

He forced a smile. "Rory?"

"Cory," the boy corrected. His voice was clogged. He coughed slightly and plumes of uneven breath came from his mouth.

"Well" — David opened the door wider, as if to an old friend — "come in."

The kid swallowed. "No thanks, I gotta" — he shifted — "I gotta be going."

David's heart both sank and eased. Though he wanted this confrontation more than anything, he also feared it. This was the famous Cory. Cory, the sensitive. Cory, the "You'll really like him, Dad, he's just like you." Cory, the boy Emily couldn't stop talking about the last few times he'd visited her at the hospital.

And now this same Cory had come to meet the parent. A bit ironic. Maybe even macabre. But, better late than never.

With long, delicate fingers the boy produced a cloth-covered notebook. "This is what I was telling you about." He cleared his throat again. "I know she'd want you to have it."

David took it into his hands, but he barely looked down. Instead, he was drinking in every detail of the boy, every nuance — those dark eyes, the frail shoulders under the too-big sweatshirt, his nervous, painful energy. He'd just been released from the hospital the day before yesterday. And, if possible, this meeting seemed even harder on him than David.

"She left it in my room the night she, uh …" He lowered his head, examining the porch.

David nodded, watching. He looked at the notebook. It was six inches long, four inches wide, and nearly an inch thick. The cover was pale pink with a white iris on the front. It felt like silk. He stared at it a long moment.

The boy shifted.

Coming to — more on autopilot than anything else — David repeated, "You sure you don't want to come in?"

"No" — the boy cleared his throat again — "no, thanks." He motioned over his shoulder to a van that was idling. "I've got people waiting."

"Oh … right." Hiding his neediness, David forced a shrug. "Well, maybe we can have coffee together or something sometime … if you want."

Cory glanced up to him. "I'd like that." His eyes faltered then dropped back down. Speaking softer now, and still to his shoes, he added, "She was pretty amazing. I mean I never met anyone like her. Never." He took a breath, then looked up.

David saw the sheen in the boy's eyes, felt his own starting to burn. "Yeah." He struggled for another smile.

Cory glanced away, studying the porch light above them — "So... uh..." — then over to a window.

David came to his rescue. "I'll give you a call next week, how does that sound?"

Cory gave the slightest nod.

David watched, waiting.

The boy took a deep breath and blew it out, as if he'd completed an impossible mission. He nodded more broadly and turned to start down the walk. David watched, absorbing everything he saw.

Halfway to the street, Cory paused and turned. "I just, uh..." He cleared his throat. "It just doesn't, you know, seem right."

David swallowed, then nodded.

"I mean, she was getting so strong... so healthy. She was really happy, Mr. Kauffman. The happiest I'd seen her."

David wanted to respond, but he no longer trusted his voice.

Cory shook his head. "It just doesn't... things just don't seem right." With that he turned and headed toward the van.

David remained at the door. Moisture blurred his vision as he watched Cory arrive at the vehicle, open the door, and climb into the passenger's side. A moment passed before the van slowly pulled away. The boy never looked up.

It wasn't until the vehicle disappeared around the corner that David glanced back to the journal in his hands. He was trembling again. The meeting had taken a lot out of him. And it was still taking, because he knew exactly what he held.

Emily's journal. Her final thoughts and hopes and dreams — and nightmares.

He turned and reentered the house. He eased the door shut behind him. But he could go no farther. He leaned against the closed door and lifted the notebook to his face with both hands. He inhaled deeply, hoping for some fragrance, some lingering trace of his daughter. There was nothing. Only the faint odor of smoke and antiseptic. He brought the cover to his lips and kissed it. This was all he had left. All that remained.

"Where are you, baby girl? Where are you?"

✳

"You never get married?!" Nubee cried.

"It is possible."

"But, must be somebody . . ." He hesitated looking for the right word.

"Somebody what?" Gita asked.

"Somebody blind enough to think you look beautif — OW!"

Gita gave her little brother a playful smack upside the head. Well, most of it was playful. It made no difference that he was thirty-two and so physically disabled that he could not look after himself, and that she was pushing his wheelchair on the walk past other residents. There were some things she just wouldn't cut him slack on.

"Help me!" he cried to Rosa, a passing staff member. "Help me! Help me!"

"You picking on your sister again, Nubee?"

"She beating me! Cruelty to animals, cruelty to animals!"

Rosa smiled. "How's it going, Dr. Patekar?"

"Very well. And you?"

"Still breathing."

Gita smiled. "That is a good sign."

"At least around this place." The plump Hispanic woman chuckled as she started up the ramp toward the building.

Gita continued along the walk with her brother. She lifted her face and closed her eyes to feel the warmth of the winter sun flickering through the bare mulberry branches. In her faster-than-the-speed-of-light world, these few hours a week spent with her little brother always brought a certain peace. Many saw her visits as compassion for her only living relative, but the truth was she needed them more than he did.

Gita had flown Nubee over from their home in Nepal as soon as she'd settled in. That was part of her agreement with the Orbolitz Group. She would work for them and commit her sizeable experience to their new Life After Life program. All they had to do was offer reasonable pay and pull a string or two to bring her little brother to the States so she could look after him. To her surprise, not only did they agree, but they made certain Nubee was admitted to one of the finest nursing homes in Southern California. They also insisted on picking up the tab for his room and board. It was a gracious offer, but typical of Norman H. Orbolitz. Granted, he was an eccentric recluse, a billionaire who owned one of the world's largest communication empires. It was also true that he was a master at playing hardball with any and all competitors. But he was known equally well for his generosity and philanthropic outreaches. That fact as much as any other convinced Gita to move halfway around the world and join his organization.

As a thanatologist, someone who studies death and dying, Gita had made a name for herself by exposing one of Great Britain's most famous psychics as a fraud. It wasn't intentional, just the outcome of her unwavering, dogged research. But it had created a stir that caught the attention of the Orbolitz people. In a matter of months they'd convinced her to leave her position at Tribhuvan University in Nepal and join their Life After Life program in the States.

Unfortunately, her focus quickly became something more along the lines of Hoax after Life. Apparently the Orbolitz Group — more precisely Gita's department head, Dr. Richard Griffin — wasn't as interested in her research as in her ability to expose false psychics, particularly those who exploited the grief-stricken with promises of contacting their deceased loved ones. It wasn't exactly the program she'd signed up for, but she had always seen the importance of truth, the need to separate fact from fiction. And, like it or not, she was getting quite good at it. No surprise there. Dr. Gita Patekar enjoyed success at everything she put her mind to.

Well, almost everything . . .

"So, nobody in all world think you pretty?" Nubee was doing his best to get another rise out of her.

"I am afraid you are correct." She sighed, playing along. Unfortunately, the opposite was true, and she knew it. For better or worse, she'd been attractive all of her life. And not just to the Asian community. Her petite frame, high cheekbones, coal black eyes, and well-endowed figure made her fresh meat in any male shark tank — even at the church singles' group. Then there was the problem of her intellect. It was supposed to be one of her better features, but she found herself having to use it mostly as a weapon of self-defense.

Last night's fiasco with Geoffrey Boltten was the perfect example. Was there some unspoken law that said after the third date men were entitled to have sex with women? Was that the new definition of lifelong commitment? Because, just like clockwork, after a romantic dinner and enjoying Mozart's *Magic Flute* at the Civic Arts Plaza, Dr. Boltten — respected surgeon and churchgoer — felt he was entitled to make his move.

Gita had barely let him inside her townhouse — supposedly to use the bathroom — when he grabbed her shoulders. Always the understanding type, she stepped back and tried to diffuse the awkward situation with an obvious scientific explanation.

"It is okay, I understand. It is simply your phenylethylamine. Do not worry. Some was bound to have been released during our time together this evening."

"Oh, Gita," he gasped, pulling her to him. "I can't stop thinking of you." It was on old line, an even older move.

She shrugged him off and tried pivoting away. "With the rise of your PEA levels, you knew this would happen. You also know that further touching will increase both of our dehydroepiansdrosterone levels which will lead to a rise in oxytocin." She was being as kind and forthright as possible.

"Oh, baby . . ." He grabbed the back of her head, pulling it toward his, forcing his mouth over hers.

Coming up for air, she tried one last time. "And now we must contend with testosterone and vasopressin. Doctor, you know you are merely reacting to chemicals being released within your — "

"No more talking." He yanked her toward him. "No more talking." That was when Gita realized the time for talking had indeed come to an end. All it took was one quick knee raise followed by a sharp blow to his larynx and the good doctor was on the floor, writhing, unsure what part of his anatomy to be holding in pain.

She looked down at him and sighed wearily. No doubt here was yet another man who would never call her again.

Nubee continued his teasing, pulling her back from the memory. "Not to worry. We find somebody. Somebody blind . . . maybe deaf too."

She smiled weakly, because it wasn't just the culture's sexual promiscuity that she struggled against. There was something else. Something deep inside of her. And the books she'd read, the counselor she'd been seeing, they all pointed to the same cause. They insisted it stemmed from the nightmare childhood that she and her brother had lived while on the streets of Katmandu.

"These things can take a long, long time to heal," her counselor had said. "Someone who has endured your level of abuse may take years, even decades, to fully recover."

Gita hated that thought. She fought against it with every fiber of who she was. But deep inside she knew it was true. Deep inside she knew that loving another, that sharing her heart and soul with a man would be difficult. No, *difficult* wasn't the word. For her, there was another. And it was one that frequently brought tears to her eyes when she slept alone at night. It crippled and hobbled her heart as much now as when she was that eleven-year-old-girl sleeping with men for food, for rupees, for anything to keep her and her brother alive. Because, as much as she wanted to give herself to another, as much as she begged God to free and heal her, Dr. Gita Patekar feared that when it came to love, she would now and forever be . . . *unable*.

"You make me listen to Bible, now?"

She barely heard her brother.

"Gitty?"

They had arrived at their favorite bench, the one between two eucalyptus trees. Coming to, she answered, "Yes, it is time to make you listen to Bible again. What part do you wish to hear today?"

"More Revelations."

"Again?" She reached down and locked the wheels of his chair. She pulled the wool blanket up around his chest. "Are we not always reading Revelation?"

"I like the angels. I like the monsters."

"Of course," she sighed, "then we shall read Revelation." She sat on the wooden bench across from him and produced a small New Testament from her pocket. And there, in the warmth and cold of the winter light, she opened the book and began to read.

✳

"I'm hearing something now," the boy said. "Kind of a low hum, like a machine."

"Yes," Dr. Richard Griffin agreed, "that's fairly normal. Just try to relax." He caught a reflection of himself in the stainless steel tray on the table next to the bed. Who could believe he was fifty? Early forties would be his best guess, as long as he held in his stomach and paid close attention to how he combed and sprayed his thinning hair.

He glanced at the digital readout over the subject's bed. It cast a blue-green glow upon the white tiles of the cubicle. They were coming up to the seven minute mark. Seven minutes since he'd injected the kid with 3 mg of dimethyltryptamine, an hallucinogenic better known as DMT.

"Do you see any movement?" He peered at the boy. "Any type of . . . beings?"

"No."

"Be patient, they'll show up," Griffin assured him. "And when they do, stay calm, don't panic."

Seventeen-year-old Jason Morris nodded. He licked his lips in nervous anticipation and no doubt a little fear.

Dr. Griffin had picked him up as a volunteer from their "off-campus" site near Hollywood Boulevard. Kids, mostly runaways and street ilk, came to the place in droves looking to sell themselves as volunteers for various medical experiments. Experiments that weren't always legal, but that were absolutely necessary if the Human Longevity Division of the Orbolitz Group was to stay on the cutting edge of its research. For the most part, the procedures were harmless and everyone benefited — the kids got their money for drugs, important data was secured without jumping through bureaucratic hoops, local authorities were provided enough financial incentive to look the other way — and on those rare occasions when Griffin needed to cross divisions and secure a subject for his Life After Life program, they were there for the taking. It was win/win for everyone involved.

"There, I see something."

"The creatures?" Dr. Griffin asked. "Do you see the creatures?"

Jason's acne-ravaged face twitched under the black eye-shades.

"Jason?"

"Yeah . . ."

"Do you see them?"

"Yes . . ."

"How many?"

"Just one."

Earlier, the boy had assured Dr. Griffin that he was a frequent user of psychedelics — LSD, ketamine, MDMA — he said he'd tried them all. Griffin had his doubts, but it really didn't matter. Although DMT was classified as an hallucinogenic, its devotees more commonly referred to it as the *spirit molecule.* It was a rare chemical that they insisted opened them up to a strange, mystical world, often populated by gargoyles and troll-like creatures. Creatures identical to several of the near death experiences — NDEs — Griffin had recorded. If that was the case, if the same creatures that appeared in NDEs also appeared while using the drug, then it was important he add at least one of the drug experiences to his database.

"There's another," the boy said.

"That's two?" Dr. Griffin asked.

"No, three . . . four, five." Jason's voice grew shaky. "They're everywhere!"

Griffin tried to soothe him. "Just relax. That's not unusual. Let them approach. It'll be okay." He threw a look over to Wendell Nordstrom, a wiry technician with red hair and a stringy goatee. Nordstrom stood on the other side of a portable console, watching the boy's readouts — heart rate, blood pressure, EEG . . . and one very peculiar video monitor off to his left.

Jason's face twitched again. He scowled, then lifted his eyebrows, raising a wire and fabric skullcap. The cap contained paper-thin electrodes strategically placed throughout it. These picked up the electrical firings from a handful of neural synapses within his brain. Firings that were amplified, sorted, and eventually fed into PNEUMA, the project's giant, fifteen teraflops supercomputer.

Initially the skullcap was a cumbersome helmet that recorded tens of thousands of impulses. But gradually, thanks to the research of scientists such as Frances Crick of double helix fame, a small set of neurons leading from the back of the cortex to the front were isolated. To some, these few neurons were the elusive location of human consciousness — a small group of cells connected in such a way that they made us different from animals by making us self-conscious.

To others, it wasn't the cells or even their connections that mattered. Instead, it was what resided *within* those cells. Something the more religious and superstitious might call . . . the soul.

In either case, this drug, this DMT, seemed to stimulate those same neurons, particularly in the frontal lobe where so many near death experiences are registered. And if those very same neurons were being fired by the drug, then their experiences had to be entered into the system.

"I can't . . ." Jason scowled. "They're trying to talk, but I can't . . . I can't hear what they're saying."

"Relax. Let them have their way."

Jason's face twitched again, and he gave the slightest nod. A thin veneer of sweat appeared across his forehead and above his upper lip.

Griffin looked at the clock. They were almost at the eight-minute mark.

Wendell's voice came from behind the console. "We're getting images."

Dr. Griffin nodded. This was the pivotal point of the experiment. For nearly four years they'd been studying the brain functions of the dying. They recorded those last few moments as the subject approached death, followed by the six to twelve minutes as the brain slowly shut down from the outside in. Theirs was an extensive, nationwide program involving over eighty hospitals and nearly two hundred hospice organizations. Each case was handled with care and sensitivity, as the terminally ill and their relatives were seldom in the mood to participate in experiments. Yet in the name of science — and with the added incentive of $2,500 per subject (thanks to the very deep pockets of Norman E. Orbolitz) — nearly 1,300 patients had agreed to wear the small, unobtrusive skull cap to record the last electrical firings of their brains as they died.

"Jason, can you hear them yet? Can you tell me what they're saying?"

The kid rolled his head. "I can't . . ." His face twitched. "I can't make it out. But they're everywhere."

Dr. Griffin glanced at the empty syringe in the stainless steel tray. They'd given him 3 mg. The experts claimed that was more than enough to "interact" with the creatures. But if this was all the further they could go, after investing all their time and energy, then the experiment was essentially a failure. Griffin did not have time for failures.

He glanced to the vial beside the syringe. It contained another 6 mg. "Are they coming any closer?"

Jason shook his head.

"You must be holding them back. Relax, there's nothing to fear. Give in to the drug. Let them have their way."

Jason scowled. It was obvious he was trying but still failing.

Griffin looked back to the vial on the table. He knew the answer to their problem, but hesitated. Not for ethical reasons. As far as he was concerned, ethics were manmade restraints created by timid moralists. This was science. More important, this was *his* science. Besides, Jason was homeless — street flotsam and jetsam that would never be missed. No, it wasn't ethics or even the fear of being caught that gave Griffin pause. It was simply the bother of having to go back to the Boulevard and begin the screening process all over again.

But the kid gave him little choice.

Dr. Griffin reached for the vial and syringe. He drew out another 3 mg, hesitated, then continued until the entire 6 mg was in the syringe.

"Dr. Griffin?"

Griffin didn't know if his assistant was calling out a word of caution or if he'd seen something of interest on the monitor. It didn't matter. The decision was made. He inserted the needle into the boy's right arm and emptied the syringe.

"Okay, Jason, I've increased the dosage. Now I want you to — "

"Inside . . ." the youth whispered. "They want . . . inside."

"Inside? Inside what?"

Jason gave no answer. His face twitched again, then again. He began to roll his head. Harder. Faster. His entire body began to flinch, then squirm.

Griffin reached for the leather restraint on the bed rail and buckled down the boy's right arm. "Jason . . . Jason, can you hear me?" He crossed to the other side and repeated the process. Then to each of the ankles. "Jason? You said they wanted inside. Inside of what?"

Faint crescents of sweat appeared under the arms of the kid's hospital gown. The sheen on his face beaded into drops.

"Jason?"

His head continued to roll. Faint whimperings escaped from his throat.

"Jason? Jason can you hear me?"

He opened his mouth and panted in uneven gasps. The whimpering grew louder.

Wendell called from the console, "Dr. Griffin, you need to see this."

Suddenly the boy's body contracted. His arms and legs yanked at the restraints. His head flew back, then rolled faster and faster. His whimperings grew to choking cries.

"Dr. Griffin!"

The doctor scurried to join Wendell behind the console. Readouts showed the boy's pulse at 148; his blood pressure was skyrocketing. But it was the TV monitor to the left that grabbed Griffin's attention. The images were crude, like an eighties' video game — the result of raw data being translated by a portable, in-lab computer. They would become much more refined when fed into PNEUMA and prepared for the Virtual Reality lab. But for now there was no missing Jason's form, or at least how he perceived his form. He was floating in a dazzling star field. Closing in on him from all sides were the gargoyle-like creatures — some with amphibian faces, others more reptilian — all with sharp, protruding teeth and long claws. Several had already leaped on top of the boy's chest. More followed.

No wonder he was writhing.

"Jason?" Griffin called. "Jason, can you hear me?"

But Jason did not answer. His chest heaved then went into a series of convulsions.

"Pulse 185!" There was no missing the fear in Wendell's voice.

The boy screamed — then swallowed it into gagging coughs and gasps.

"*Jason!*"

"200!"

Griffin spun back to the monitor and stared. Two of the creatures had pried open the boy's jaw with their claws. Even more astonishing were the creatures on his chest. One after another raced toward his head and leaped into the air. As they hovered over his face they suddenly dissolved into a black, vaporous cloud that rushed into the boy's mouth and shot down his throat. Creature after creature followed. Black cloud after black cloud. Leaping and entering with such frightening speed that they became a thick, continuous stream of blackness.

Jason tried to scream but could not. Only choke and gag.

"Jason! Jason!!"

An alarm sounded.

"He's in V-fib!"

371

"Get the medical team here!"

Wendell nodded and hit the intercom as Griffin raced to the bed. "Jason! Jason, close your mouth!"

But the boy's mouth was locked open as he continued gasping, choking.

Griffin ripped aside the boy's hospital gown, yanking off a handful of the sensors taped to his chest, ready to begin CPR if needed.

The alarm continued.

The boy gagged as Wendell called for the medical team again.

But even as his assistant's voice echoed through the complex, Dr. Griffin changed his mind. Slowly and quite deliberately, he stepped back from the bed. It was better to do nothing. He knew that. And if the kid was lucky, the medical team would arrive too late to help. Granted, there would be some inconvenience in disposing the body, but it was best for the boy. Griffin had seen these creatures before in the Virtual Reality chambers. He had seen what they did to a select handful of dying. The mental agony those patients endured, the impossible anguish they suffered ... it was a horror worse than any pain of physical death.

It was a horror that the kid should not have to take back with him into the land of the living.

Things are finally falling into place. Bryan actually came up to my locker and started talking, which seriously is such a great emotional high. I feel like I could just run around twirling and jumping in the bright shinning sun. I want to embrace life and give back so much. I know he's working up the courage to ask me to the dance. Kind of a spastic thought, but this gives me a great outfit to plan. I was thinking about like an off-white or purple dress. I have always liked purple, it has such an amazing regal feel to it when it is mixed in a sort of burgundy fashion. Seriously, I think that the hot guy in my math class might get jealous of Bryan and what if Mr. Hot asks me to dance at the dance!! How incredibly stellar would that be!!! I just want to bask in this moment of pure happiness and imagine two great guys fighting over my com-

pany. "Oh, I am sorry, were you talking about dancing with me?" Here is where the band breaks out into a slow, romantic tune and we gaze lovingly into each other's feverish eyes. His enchanting mocha browns settle deep into my dazzling violet blues. He softly joins in, singing to me and my entire heart just melts. Ha-ha. I am so psyched!! I want to glide and sway here forever.

David lifted his glasses onto his forehead and rubbed his eyes. He'd been at Starbucks since the place opened three hours ago, sitting at the window counter, reading her journal. Of course he'd read it earlier, had been up all night, devouring its two hundred plus pages. But like a man too starved to taste food, he'd gobbled down sentence after sentence, entire paragraphs without fully comprehending. And he wanted to comprehend, he wanted to savor every moment of his daughter's last few months. So, here he was, a mile from the house at his favorite writing hangout near the corner of Topanga and Ventura Boulevard, nursing his third cappuccino, trying to stay focused.

He might have had more success if it wasn't for the street preacher. The black, barrel-chested old-timer sporting the latest fashion from the Salvation Army stood just outside the window, as he often did, giving no one within earshot a break.

"You, brother!" His voice reverberated against the glass as he dogged a passing shopper. "Yes, I'm talking to you! Have you found the Lord? Have your sins been washed in the blood of the Lamb? Repent! Repent, or when you die you will burn in the fires of hell that have no end!"

David watched with quiet distaste. The two of them had been coming to this shop for months, each plying their trades—the preacher searching for lost sinners out on the sidewalk, David inside, struggling with his next novel on the laptop. Normally, the old-timer's rantings didn't bother him much—just another layer of coffee shop and street noise. But today, with no sleep and spent emotions, the self-righteous railings grew more and more irritating.

David sighed, pulled down his glasses, and turned the page to the next entry.

I feel nothing. I just want to lay here in my warm, safe bed. Living has so entirely drained my blood of substance to the

*point that my parched veins are screaming for any form of
liquid to fill them. My blood has been sucked out venomously
by that stupid leach that I so often refer to as Kaylee. What
a hypocritical jerk if I ever saw one. Honestly, I consider
Kaylee my best friend in the entire world. Why would she
not consider me the same . . . is Amanda such a great friend
considering she ditched you, Kaylee? I seriously stuck
through everything with you! Just because I didn't know you
as long as Amanda doesn't mean we can't be better friends
than you and her. It's stupid, I know. All I do is wallow in
this mental slush, swimming in the sewage hour after hour,
holding my breath, unable to come up for air.*

Talk about emotional whiplash — one page exhilaration, the next
devastation. But apparently roller-coaster emotions came with the
territory of female adolescence.

He remembered one of their very first counseling sessions, the
ones they started not long after his wife left. Emily was burrowed
into the corner of the sofa, feet drawn up, playing with her hair.
"It's just that he's, like, always shouting all the time."

He recalled his jaw going slack. "What? Honey, I never shout."

"Yeah, right." She smirked. "Like yesterday when I didn't
empty the cat box?"

David turned to the woman counselor, lifting his palms. "It had
been nearly two weeks. I merely made it clear that — "

"By shouting," Emily interrupted.

"I don't shout."

"Yes, you do."

"No, I don't."

"You're doing it now."

"Disagreeing with someone is not the same as — "

"Told you."

"Told me what?"

"You're shouting."

"I am not."

"Yes you are."

"Emily!"

Turning to the counselor, she simply shrugged. "See?"

David smiled at the memory. At the tender age of fourteen his
daughter was already playing him like a fiddle. He recalled during

that same session he asked the counselor, "Does *everything* in the house have to be ruled by emotion? Surely, truth and logic must count for something."

Once again the therapist broke into a gentle chuckle. Apparently, he had lots to learn.

But the laughter didn't last long. The frenetic, topsy-turvy world of emotions eventually led to bouts of depression, which only seemed to grow darker and deeper until finally —

"Repent! 'I am the way, the truth and the life. No man comes to the Father but by me!' Turn to him! Turn to the Lord before it's too late! Turn or burn!"

David squinted at the journal, trying to stay focused. But the lunchtime crowd filtered in, opening the door more and more frequently, allowing the preacher's rantings to intrude more and more loudly.

"Time is short. You don't know what tomorrow will bring! Turn to him and flee the torments of hell, where the worm does not die nor the fire is quenched!"

David shifted on his stool, trying to concentrate on the words before him. Emily loved to write. Sometimes the rambling stream-of-consciousness that he saw before him now, sometimes short stories, sometimes poetry. She cherished words. No surprise there. As the child of an author, she was always surrounded by stacks of books and magazines. Her favorite reading haunt? The tub ... which occasionally made for some careful maneuverings in the bathroom.

"I just want to find the toilet in the middle of the night without breaking a toe," he complained once over breakfast.

She nodded with the obvious solution. "Maybe you should drink less liquids before bedtime."

Again David smiled. It was true, when it came to books and writing he gave her plenty of leeway. Particularly with her mother gone. For Emily, reading was a way of affirming her emotions, of discovering what other women thought and felt. And her writing, no matter how emotional or over the top, was her way of exploring her own thoughts and feelings. So often she'd enter his garage office unannounced and plop down on the worn sofa behind his desk to write. And write and write and write.

He treasured those times together — back when she was open and sunny, back before the shadows of the disease had begun hiding her from him. For years she read to him from that sofa, those incredible eyes looking up, so eager for praise. And he gave it, abundantly. He never criticized, sensing that any negative comment would crush her already over-sensitive heart. Instead, he would find poets she loved and encourage her to copy their work in longhand. That was how writers in the old days learned. It forced them to slow down and study each phrase, sip each word, and — most important — begin to understand the workings of the craft.

She practiced this advice religiously. Snips and fragments of great authors filled her journals. She was particularly fond of the poets. Emily Dickinson — her namesake — was her favorite. He flipped through the pages of the journal until he spotted one of the great writer's poems.

> *Some, too fragile for winter winds,*
> *The thoughtful grave encloses, —*
> *Tenderly tucking them in from frost*
> *Before their feet are cold.*
>
> *Never the treasures in her nest*
> *The cautious grave exposes,*
> *Building where schoolboy dare not look*
> *And sportsman is not bold.*
>
> *This covert have all the children*
> *Early aged, and often cold, —*
> *Sparrows unnoticed by the Father:*
> *Lambs for whom time had not a fold.*

He tried to swallow the tightness in his throat. The tears were coming again. How could someone so young, so full of life, become so lonely and full of death? He was reading toward the beginning of the diary, before her hospitalization. During those black, nightmare times when she would not get out of bed, when her grades plummeted, when the two of them continually fought, shouting oaths and threats that he'd give anything to take back now. Those awful times when he had to physically force her to take the medication. Those beggings, those pleadings, those —

"Excuse me, brother?"

With a start David looked up. Through the moisture in his eyes he saw the preacher.

"This seat taken?"

David glanced to the stool beside him, then around the shop for an alternate choice. There was none. The place was packed. Exhausted, emotional, and with an overdose of caffeine, he replied, "Go ahead." He cleared his throat. "Just spare me the hellfire."

Unfazed, the man gave a crooked-tooth grin. "Some folks would say it's a pretty important topic."

David fought to hold back his anger. What right did this person have to talk to him about hell? He had no idea what he'd been living these past nine weeks. The sorrow, the hopelessness, the absolute . . . finality. But instead of making a scene, he exercised all of his self-control and quietly seethed. "And what makes you an expert?"

The preacher pulled out the stool and eased himself onto the seat with a quiet groan. "I guess 'cause I've been there."

"We all have. Some of us more than others."

"Maybe." The man brought a latte up to his thick lips and slurped the foam. "But I'm talkin' the real deal."

David glanced away, angry he'd allowed himself to be pulled into the conversation. But the old-timer wasn't finished. Not quite.

"You know what I'm talkin' 'bout. The real hell." His eyes peered over the cup at David. "That place you're so afraid your daughter is."

The Bloodstone Chronicles
A Journey of Faith

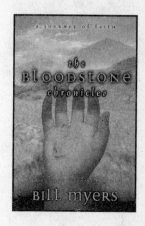

Bill Myers

Through the mysterious Bloodstone, which symbolizes God's great love for mankind, three children are whisked into strange and wondrous worlds. Soon they are visiting places like the Sea of Mirrors, where they are nearly crushed by the weight of their sins; or the Menagerie, whose prisoners are doomed to live in pure selfishness; or Biiq, where one doubting child is allowed to experience the same deep and unfathomable love that Jesus Christ has for us.

With the help of intriguing characters like Aristophenix—the world's worst poet, Listro Q—a tall, purple dude with dyslectic speech, and Weaver—who weaves God's plans into each of our Life Tapestries, the children learn the powers and secrets of living as citizens in the Kingdom of God.

Hardcover: 0-310-24684-9

Pick up a copy today at your favorite bookstore!

ZONDERVAN™

GRAND RAPIDS, MICHIGAN 49530 USA

WWW.ZONDERVAN.COM

Blood of Heaven
Bill Myers

Mass Market: 0-310-25110-9

Softcover: 0-310-20119-5

Threshold
Bill Myers

Mass Market: 0-310-25111-7

Softcover: 0-310-20120-9

Fire of Heaven
Bill Myers

Mass Market: 0-310-25113-3

Softcover: 0-310-21738-5

Abridged Audio Pages® Cassette: 0-310-23002-0

Eli
Bill Myers

Mass Market: 0-310-25114-1

Softcover: 0-310-21803-9

Abridged Audio Pages® Cassette: 0-310-23622-3

Palm Reader: 0-310-24754-3

When everything seems lost, God's love has a way of turning life around.

When the Last Leaf Falls
A Novella

Bill Myers

This retelling of O. Henry's classic short story, *The Last Leaf,* begins with an adolescent girl, Ally, who is deathly ill and angry at God. Her grief stricken father, a pastor on the verge of losing his faith, narrates the story as it unfolds.

Ally's grandpa lives with the family and has become Ally's best friend. He is an artist who has attempted—but never been able—to capture in a painting the essences of God's love. One day, in stubborn despair, Ally declares that she will die when the last leaf falls from the tree outside her bedroom window. Her doctor fears that her negative attitude will hinder her recovery and her words will become a self-fulfilling prophecy.

This stirring story of anger and love, of doubt and hope, speaks about the pain of living in this world, and the reality of the Other world that is not easily seen but can be deeply felt. Talented storyteller Bill Myers enhances and updates a storyline from one of the masters and brings to light the awesome power of love and sacrifice.

Hardcover: 0-310-23091-8

ZONDERVAN™

GRAND RAPIDS, MICHIGAN 49530 USA

WWW.ZONDERVAN.COM

We want to hear from you. Please send your comments about this book to us in care of zreview@zondervan.com. Thank you.

GRAND RAPIDS, MICHIGAN 49530 USA

WWW.ZONDERVAN.COM